PENGUIN BOOKS

The Girlfriend Act

T0322226

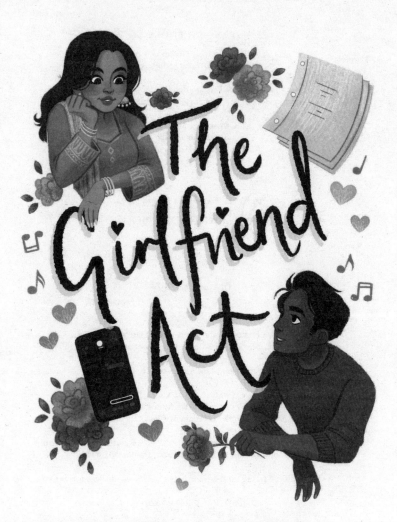

The Girlfriend Act

SAFA AHMED

PENGUIN BOOKS

PENGUIN BOOKS

UK | USA | Canada | Ireland | Australia
India | New Zealand | South Africa

Penguin Books is part of the Penguin Random House group of companies
whose addresses can be found at global.penguinrandomhouse.com.

www.penguin.co.uk
www.puffin.co.uk
www.ladybird.co.uk

First published 2024

001

Set in 10.5/15.5pt Sabon LT Pro
Typeset by Jouve (UK), Milton Keynes
Printed and bound in Great Britain by Clays Ltd, Elcograf S.p.A.

The authorized representative in the EEA is Penguin Random House Ireland,
Morrison Chambers, 32 Nassau Street, Dublin D02 YH68

A CIP catalogue record for this book is available from the British Library

ISBN: 978–0–241–67520–5

All correspondence to:
Penguin Books
Penguin Random House Children's
One Embassy Gardens, 8 Viaduct Gardens, London SW11 7BW

MIX
Paper | Supporting
responsible forestry
FSC® C018179
www.fsc.org

Penguin Random House is committed to a
sustainable future for our business, our readers
and our planet. This book is made from Forest
Stewardship Council® certified paper.

To Mama and Daddy,
for teaching me the meaning of unconditional love.

And to every fanfiction reader out there
who dreamed of falling in love with their celebrity crush,
this story is for you.

Author's Note

Dear reader,

I decided to write this book after I backed out from auditioning for my university's theatre society. I got all the way to audition day, practised my lines, and ended up walking away because I felt I was not brave enough to step out of my comfort zone. It's a regret I've always held on to. So, when I started to write this book, I decided to imagine what would've happened if the main character didn't walk away from an opportunity that could change her life. From that spark of an idea, Farah Sheikh and her rollercoaster of a story appeared in my head.

Now, before you dive into *The Girlfriend Act*, I feel it's important that you know that, while this story is at its heart a romance, it does deal with themes of a sensitive nature. This book has discussions about racism, colourism, depictions of microaggressions and, more blatantly, there is the use of a racial slur.

Along with these content warnings, I would like readers to keep in mind that while Farah and Zayan are Pakistani Muslims, they are by no means 'perfect Muslims'. Ultimately I want my fellow South Asian readers to feel that we are worthy of the swoony romances. We deserve to have our stories explored in literature, and we're allowed to have happy endings in our books.

So, by the end of *The Girlfriend Act*, I hope that you, my dearest reader, decide to stay for that audition, speak up at that meeting, grasp every opportunity life throws your way, and most of all, always dream wildly.

Happy reading!

Safa

Chapter One

I fell in love at eighteen.

Not with a person, but with a feeling. *This* feeling. The buzz of nerves climbing down my spine, the jumble of excited butterfly wings fluttering in the depths of my stomach, the warmth of a blush on my cheeks.

I only ever feel this way right before I'm about to step on stage.

Six months ago, on the night of my eighteenth birthday, after I'd just wrapped up the final show for my high-school drama club's performance of *The Comedy of Errors*, I realized why I loved acting.

It was because, every night, I became someone else.

I wasn't Farah Sheikh: I was Lady Macbeth, I was Luciana, I was Hermione. I was everyone else but myself. For a few fragile hours, I could step into someone else's life and pretend it was my own.

Now, three months later, after moving to London for my first year of university, I stand in the wings, sinking into that feeling once again. My script has been rolled up and stuffed into my bag – I don't need to reread it that much, considering I'm not trying out for the main part. Not by choice, of course. If I had it my way, I'd be reading for Juliet. But this production has a very strict requirement – every actor must have at least a year's worth of experience in either an American or British production.

And while I've been on stage throughout my academic career, it doesn't count because I grew up in Karachi, Pakistan. So, instead of the lead role, I'm trying out for a minor one. But I don't mind. No respected actress makes it big without some struggle (unless there's nepotism involved), and humble roots make the greatest stories on talk shows, right?

I remind myself of this as another actress finishes off her monologue. She *is* auditioning for Juliet, and she's good. Really good.

I consider peeking round the corner, to catch a glimpse of the director and producer of the play, but I stop myself – I don't want to add fear and nerves to the excitement I've got rioting through me. Instead, I will myself to focus on other things. Like what I'm going to watch to relax tonight. I remember there's a new TV series starring Zayan Amin that I still need to dive into. He's my favourite Pakistani actor, and this is supposed to be his big move after seventeen years on a family sitcom. I'll stuff my face with the correct ratio of salty to sweet popcorn, while telling my flatmates about the audition and everything else.

A solid plan.

'Next!'

I jolt out of my thoughts, walk to the 'X'-marked spot on the stage and face the two people who hold my fate in their hands. My own university has a mediocre, underfunded theatre society. The London School of Dramatic and Creative Arts Theatre Society (a mouthful, I know), on the other hand, are nationally recognized, treated with respect by industry professionals and often featured in the news for producing the first plays of many budding actors.

That's why getting even a minor role would mean everything to me.

'Name? Age?' the director, a white man with longish-black hair and blue eyes, demands. There's a roughness to his tone, like he's prone to shouting.

'Farah Sheikh. Eighteen years old. And I'll be auditioning for the role of Balthasar,' I reply evenly, making sure my voice doesn't shake and a smile remains on my face.

I lean forward to hand him my profile, which has all this information on it, along with my contact details for a callback. The director glances at it, the corners of his mouth pinching with something I can't identify. Then he looks up again, his crystal-clear gaze focused on me in a way that makes my skin prickle.

One shot. I've got one shot to get this right.

'Whenever you're ready, Farah,' says the producer, a woman with a long, blonde plait and freckled face. 'I'll read the lines for the opposing role.'

I breathe in deeply, letting that feeling wash over me. If I had to describe what it's like to play a role, I'd say it's like shedding your skin and stepping into someone else's. Your feelings aren't your own, your words aren't either, but they feel like they are. The character's pain is your pain; the character's life is your life.

I've only got five lines, but I've practised them a million different ways – different tones and pitches – and when I say them now, I feel like Balthasar.

Three lines in and I'm bursting with Montague pride. I can see myself performing on opening night; I can feel the audience's stares.

Four lines in, and I'm positively feeding off the daydream.

Five lines in, and –

'I'm going to have to cut you off there,' the director interrupts.

'Henry,' the producer admonishes quietly.

'I'm sorry, Lisa, but we're wasting time here. We've only got two months to get everything ready, and we're throwing time away by auditioning people who we know are unsuitable for this role.'

Unsuitable?

Henry turns away from Lisa and focuses on me, his gaze hard and inscrutable. My stomach tightens in anticipation of the feedback that will be slung my way. I'm ready to hear what my acting lacks, and what I can fix for next time.

'Sorry, uh – Farah, was it? The direction of our programme . . . We're attempting to go back to the historic roots of Shakespeare. We want *real* authenticity, and that requires a cast that – well, that looks more *classically* British.'

I feel a smile twitching at the corner of my mouth, because this has to be a joke. Right? Surely someone is going to come out with cameras and tell me I'm a part of a social experiment or something.

But they're not laughing, and for several long, painful moments, nothing happens. This nightmare is reality.

I should demand more, advocate for myself, but no words pass my lips. Lisa just watches me uncomfortably, Henry rifles through the papers in front of him, unconcerned, and as I walk off the stage in silence, that buzzy, in-love feeling I had wilts away.

Chapter Two

When I jam my key into the lock and step into the flat, I'm still lost in my thoughts. It's not until the door shuts quietly behind me that I finally return to reality.

The numbness disappears, and every physical feeling that was muted before erupts in my body. The disgust makes my stomach clench, the panic makes my hands shake, but the embarrassment is the most overwhelming.

Somewhere in the background, I can hear my flatmates talking, but I really just want to be alone right now.

My flatmates are my two best friends, Amal and Maha; they're from Karachi, Pakistan as well. We went to the same A-level school – Rocate High – and after we all got into universities in London, we moved in together at the start of the academic year. They're like sisters to me, friends that I can't imagine living without. I didn't tell them about the audition – only because, foolishly, I'd wanted it to be a surprise if I got the role. But I can't face them. Not right now.

So, instead, I quietly slip off my shoes and make my way to my bedroom. I close the door ever so gently, hoping that the click of my lock is masked by their conversation.

When I'm sure no one has heard me coming in, I flop directly on to my bed. My head beats like a dull drum, matching the word still pulsing through my mind.

Unsuitable. Unsuitable.

My chest aches with a pain so harsh and deep that I'm sure my heart must be broken. Irrevocably torn apart. That feeling I had while being on stage, right before Henry interrupted me, is so far away now. The phantom whisper of it remains, but it's out of reach.

More classically British.

What does that even mean? Sure, I didn't have the Union Jack painted on my face, but Henry and Lisa had my profile in their hands. They had to know I was *British* Pakistani. And if they didn't have my profile, if I'd just been some anonymous, random actress stumbling into the theatre to audition, they'd never have guessed that I was actually brown. Not based on what I looked like.

I spent eighteen years in Pakistan, hearing comments – sometimes whispered, sometimes casually mentioned – about how cool it was that I had a foreign passport, how enviable it was that my skin was the perfect shade of brown that could almost be considered a tanned sort of white, especially if I stayed out of the sun. The remarks were always said with such reverence, such pride. No one ever considered my dual nationality to be a failing.

So why did Henry say it? Why? Was it even a real critique, or was there something –?

The sound of my phone ringing breaks me out of the cycle of unanswerable questions. I scramble to pick it up, but when I see the caller ID, my stomach clenches with anxiety.

My mother.

Usually, phone calls with my mother are an experience. They tend to begin with her regaling me with tales about back home – which fellow aunty slighted her during a committee lunch, which friend's daughter just got married – but this time, Ammi starts with a question.

'How was the audition, Paari?'

Paari. Fairy. An affectionate nickname Nani and Nana gave me when they gifted me a Tinker Bell costume from the Disney store on Oxford Street . I was in the thick of my fairy phase – I loved *Barbie: Fairytopia* and I read every Rainbow Magic book that existed. Every night, I imagined my wings were yet to sprout and that when they did, I'd fly to the stars and pluck one out of the sky. I'd hold it in my hands and steal all its magic.

My nana was watching me prance around the living room, turning teapots into frogs and waving around a palm-tree leaf for a wand, when he coined the nickname. If I think back hard enough, I can hear his rough laugh, and the gentle way he said, *Look, there's a fairy in this room, brighter and happier than the sun.*

After that, I was Paari. The bright spot of the family. Never sad. Always smiling. Made of magic.

'It was . . .' I struggle to find the right words. 'I didn't get it. I didn't get the role.'

'Oh, Paari,' Ammi replies, her voice sounding so anguished it makes my heart ache. 'Do you want to talk about it?'

I'm lucky my parents are so supportive. They didn't discourage me from wanting to be an actress – they always told me I could achieve whatever I wanted if I tried hard enough. All they ever asked was that I graduate with a degree – any degree – alongside that dream. They asked about every audition, came to every show, sat right in the front row. I just know that my failing this audition is a disappointment for them as well.

'It's fine,' I say, my tone sounding wooden even to my own ears. 'I just want to sleep it off.'

Ammi makes a noise of understanding, and I can hear my father's voice rumbling in the background. Nope. I can't do it. I will quite literally have a breakdown if my father, with all the excitement in his usually gruff voice, asks me how the audition went.

'I'm going to go now, Ammi,' I say quickly. 'Give Abu all my love, OK?'

'OK, but remember –'

'Be safe, don't talk to strangers and always buy the carton of milk right at the back of the shelf because it has a longer expiry date,' I finish for her.

'I love you, Paari.'

My throat swells again at the sound of the all-too-familiar affection in her tone. 'I love you too.'

I drop my phone to my bed once she hangs up, my body a swirl of too many emotions. I feel like I'm going to burst, like my skin and bones are not enough to hold me together any more.

For one flighty moment, I consider telling Amal and Maha everything, if for nothing more than to relieve the pressure building inside me. But I can't bring myself to open the door and call for them.

I log on to Twitter instead, switching to the public account that I use under a pseudonym – the one I keep hidden from all my friends and family because it's nice to tweet out into the void knowing that there's no one reading it who knows the real me, no one I need to face the next day. I draft the tweet quickly, not thinking about the words, running on the fumes of my fraying emotions.

@ConstantlyVictimizedBySociety: Just had the worst audition of my life. I'm not even sure what I'm supposed to do with the LSDCATS feedback!!

It's not a mini poem, but it sums up how awful today was. I post it without a second thought and lie in bed a little longer, before deciding it's better to sleep instead of staying up. Everything will feel a little less harsh in the morning.

I'm in the middle of nurturing my internal melancholy by listening to Lewis Capaldi while doing my night-time skincare routine (even if the world is crashing around me, I'll never go to sleep without doing this) when my phone buzzes. I lean over to look at the message, expecting it to be one of my flatmates, or maybe my mother sending me an article about the rise in London crime rates so she can really hammer in that advice about being safe.

But it's not Amal or Maha or my mother. It's a Twitter notification.

Anushka Menon has added you to a private group.

I abandon my routine to slide my thumb over the notification and open the app. There's only one message in the group.

> Everyone!! I found another one!!

Anushka Menon

My eyebrows lift, and I'm already typing out my questions about who this is and why I've been added to the group.

I'm about to hit 'send' when another message chimes in.

> I wish I could say it's a pleasure to meet you this way, but it really isn't. Anyway, I'm sure you have questions.

David Song

> But before you send them, let me just say, no matter what happens, no matter where you're from and what you face, you're always welcome in THE TRAGEDIES.

Anushka Menon

Chapter Three

> I'm sorry, who are you guys?
>
> @ConstantlyVictimizedBySociety

I instantly regret starting with an apology. I've been trying hard to stop doing that – unnecessarily apologizing for things when I haven't done anything wrong. But I can't unsend the message now.

The Tragedies.

That does sound a little cult-like. I quickly check to see how many members are in the chat.

Five.

OK, an exclusive cult.

> Right, so, we're The Tragedies.
>
> Anushka Menon

> You already said that, genius.
>
> David Song

> Stop interrupting me.

Anushka Menon

> Say intelligent things and I won't feel the need to interrupt.

David Song

From the way they're interacting, I'm guessing they've known one another for a while now. I'm about to repeat my question when another message chimes in.

> I will pay you BOTH to shut up. Please.

Ben Stone

> The Tragedies are a group formed by Anushka for people who've been rejected by LSDCATS. We all auditioned for different roles, and we were given stupid reasons for being rejected.

Ben Stone

I put my phone down, taking a second to absorb this information. I consider seeking out Amal or Maha, but something roots me to my bed. I've been told my whole life that you don't talk to strangers online, but with these few sentences, Ben Stone has tied a thread round my finger and linked me to this group.

I think we've scared her away.

Anushka Menon

Not 'we'. You.

David Song

I promise we're not serial killers.

Anushka Menon

I can feel her relief all the way from here.

David Song

You're one comment away from me breaking into your flat and leaving spiders on your pillow.

Anushka Menon

Where would you even get spiders from??

David Song

Is it really breaking in if you have each other's keys?

Ben Stone

ANYWAY, back to our new member! Any chance we can get your name? Your account doesn't seem to have one. Only your pronouns, and that you're a British Pakistani aspiring actress.

Anushka Menon

> Unless you are called
> **@ConstantlyVictimizedBySociety**.
> Which is totally valid. I, too, feel
> victimized by society.
>
> David Song

My fingers hover over the keyboard and my teeth press into my lower lip. The whole point of my secret Twitter account was that I could stay hidden away from prying eyes. I try something else instead.

> So, you've all been rejected by the
> LSDCATS?
>
> @ConstantlyVictimizedBySociety

> She speaks! No name. I like a
> mystery.
>
> David Song

> Yes, we've all been rejected by the
> LSDCATS. But before I get into
> my story, let me introduce myself.
> Hi, I'm Ben 🐌. I'm a first-year
> chemical engineering student,
> and I was rejected by the
> LSDCATS when I auditioned for
> the role of Benvolio. I was told I
> 'didn't fit the "aesthetic" of the
> play'. Which obviously meant they
> thought a young Black-British man
> couldn't play Benvolio, which is
> ridiculous.
>
> Ben Stone

My jaw drops while reading Ben's introduction, and my fingers hover in mid-air, unsure of what to type. I know racism exists – of course I do. But this – this is so blatant. So unapologetically prejudiced that the only rational emotion for me to feel is an immediate and sudden anger.

> Seriously, have none of them ever heard of David Oyelowo??
>
> David Song

> Exactly, D. EXACTLY. All right, enough about me, though – Anushka?
>
> Ben Stone

> I like these little intros we're giving. Hi, I'm Anushka. I'm a first-year law student (can you hear my parents cheering in the background?), and I was rejected by the LSDCATS when I came forward to volunteer as a director. I was told that I lacked the skill (all lies btw, I have directed three student-led plays this year) and that my 'background' means I wouldn't have the right vision for the play.
>
> Anushka Menon

That burning feeling intensifies – it grows from my stomach, and my hands are shaking so hard, I'm not sure I could type out a reply even if I wanted to.

OK, I'm next. Hi, I'm David. Like spider-girl, I'm also a first-year law student. I came here from Korea to study, and I like to write plays on the side. I asked to join the LSDCATS' writing team as they adapted Romeo and Juliet this year and was told that my perspective, 'while fresh, was too nuanced'.

David Song

Which are all basically ways for the LSDCATS to say that your race meant that you couldn't work on a play written by a white man.

Ben Stone

Exactly.

David Song

David's also the old man of the group.

Anushka Menon

I'M A YEAR OLDER THAN YOU.

David Song

I feel a laugh bubble past my lips as I start drafting my message about the LSDCATS audition, then another message chimes in, forcing me to pause.

Ignore them, **@Constantly VictimizedBySociety**. This group chat isn't usually for their bickering.

Ben Stone

He's not wrong. We usually just complain about our latest racial trauma.

David Song

Yes!! Like how I had to deal with this drunk dude on the bus late last night who was shouting every slur he could come up with.

Anushka Menon

Or like how my classmates for my criminal law module for 'some' reason decided to slow down their speech when talking to me. Even though to get *into* this university you need to be able to speak and write English?? Like, I get it?? No need to dumb yourself down even more, Brian. Not for my sake, please.

David Song

Oof. I had to have a rousing discussion with this girl who kept telling me she had a lot of Black friends, so she understood the Black experience.

Ben Stone

Ahh, the constant struggles.

Anushka Menon

My thumbs hover over the keyboard, unsure and nervous.

The Tragedies' encounters with the LSDCATS are harsh, awful and completely terrible. If I recount what Henry said to me, The Tragedies will probably be horrified. Until they realize who I am. My profile picture for this account is a photo of the back of my head – not my face. The Tragedies don't know what I look like, but if they find out, they'll know I don't look obviously Pakistani. And then they won't be horrified by Henry's response; they'll be *baffled*.

That's when they'll come to the same conclusion that I'm starting to arrive at: the LSDCATS didn't reject me because of my Pakistani heritage, or because of my appearance. They rejected me because I just wasn't good enough.

Horror crystallizes in my veins in response to that singular thought. I wish I could *unthink* it. But I can't. I also can't leave this chat in silence. So I type out a reply that says nothing at all, ignoring the growing balloon in my chest.

Now that I'm sure you guys aren't serial killers, hi! I'm Farah. I'm a first-year history student looking to start my acting career, and I got rejected by LSDCATS today when I auditioned for Balthasar.

Farah Sheikh

> Farah!! What a pretty name!!

Anushka Menon

A hint of a blush tinges my cheeks at the compliment, and I'm relieved they don't question my experience. The panic recedes, even as that thought of being *not good enough* sediments itself in the back of my mind. I'll never know the truth. Not without asking Henry, and that'll never happen.

> Thanks!! It means 'happiness'.
> Totally not a weighty name.

Farah Sheikh

> Wow. I don't think Ben means
> anything.

Ben Stone

> Ben and Jerry's.

David Song

> I . . . I don't think that's why my
> parents named me Ben.

Ben Stone

> Excuse David's dry humour. It's
> past his bedtime.

Anushka Menon

> A YEAR, ANUSHKA. TWELVE
> MONTHS.

David Song

Another laugh bubbles out of me, and I quiet myself when I hear someone's door creaking open. It's probably Amal, stress-baking. I should text Owais – Maha's cousin and a friend of ours who moved from Karachi to London. He always wants to be kept in the loop if Amal appears particularly anxious or worried.

I shoot him a text before sliding back to The Tragedies' chat.

> Not to be a stalker, but I saw there's another person in the group . . .?

Farah Sheikh

> Oh, that's Nur Hadi. You're not gonna get any messages from her until tomorrow morning.

David Song

> I think she's at some freshers' party. Living the life, really.

Anushka Menon

> To summarize her story, Nur wears a hijab and was pretty much shunned from the LSDCATS casting before she'd even arrived.

David Song

I jolt forward, my body overheating with that sudden rage again. I'm not a naturally angry person – I'm the cool-headed one among my friends. But hearing these blatant experiences of racism is stoking a fire inside me.

> That's so messed up. I'm so angry right now.

Farah Sheikh

My words are inconsequential. I don't know what metaphors and purple prose I'm supposed to use to explain how I'm feeling.

> And that's 100% valid to feel!! TBH, I'm sure the LSDCATS have been getting away with this kind of casting for ages. No one has ever got angry enough to stop them. But that's why we have The Tragedies!!

Anushka Menon

> Our group is open to anyone who's trying to survive this industry, any creative who needs a safe space. Doesn't matter what your skin tone is, or where you're from, or how new you are to all of this. Everyone needs a shoulder to lean on.

Ben Stone

I'm piecing together the puzzle in my mind with new understanding. This isn't a cult. This is a place to vent. *This* is what I was looking for. I was screaming into the Twitter void before, not expecting to be heard. Now I have been.

I can't tell The Tragedies the truth of what happened in my audition. I don't want them to think I was trying to equate my experience with theirs when I wrote my tweet. But I can be their friend. I can let them rant, scream, vent all they want. I can make them feel less alone. Just like Ben said – I can be a shoulder to lean on.

So, for the next hour, our conversation flows from the LSDCATS to our classes to setting up a meet-up soon.

> I've got a lecture at ten, so I gotta hit the pillow. Talk to you guys tomorrow?

Ben Stone

I like that. Knowing they talk every day. Knowing they want to talk to one another again. I take a leap and chime in first.

> Sure!

Farah Sheikh

> Yeah, I'll update you guys on how David attempts to kiss up to our seminar leader because he thinks she's hot.

Anushka Menon

> And I'll let you guys know how Anushka stares at our fifty-year-old professor like he's Ryan Gosling.

David Song

> **I WAS STARING INTENTLY AT THE PRESENTATION.**
>
> Anushka Menon

> **EXPLAIN WHY YOU WERE DROOLING THEN?**
>
> David Song

> **LIAR.**
>
> Anushka Menon

> **GOODNIGHT. STOP BLOWING UP MY PHONE WITH YOUR JEALOUSY.**
>
> Ben Stone

A series of meek goodnight messages follow, along with my own. When I finally close my phone, I find a smile etched on my face. The clock says it's 1.00 a.m., which means an hour of texting back and forth. I try to hold on to this happy, lightweight feeling as I turn in for bed.

But my mind has snagged on one thing. Anushka's words.

I'm sure the LSDCATS have been getting away with this kind of casting for ages.

I turn over to lie on my back, staring at the ceiling. Exhaustion tugs at my eyelids, but my thoughts are unrelenting. I can't sleep. Not when there's this unresolved feeling running through me like a live wire.

I'm sure the LSDCATS have been getting away with this kind of casting for ages.

It's not a good idea.

Not under any circumstances.

But I throw off my covers and open my laptop. I choose my old Tumblr account. After three password tries, I've logged in.

I stare at the blank page for a moment. I'm not a writer. Amal is the writer in my friend group. She has a way of turning words into stories, capturing the reader's attention with a poetic line or snappy piece of dialogue. I've fallen in love with her fantasy pieces, her epic tales and retellings of long-lost princes and wickedly smart witches.

Good thing I'm not writing a fairy tale.

I'm typing without any thought. With every sentence, that rage from before is expelled on to the screen. With every harsh word, my anger burns coaxingly. Warming me up. Comforting me.

When I finish, I think about sharing the piece with the rest of The Tragedies. My gaze finally slides to the clock on my bedside table. A glowing red 3.00 a.m. light shines back at me.

They'll be asleep by now.

I consider deleting it. Writing out the LSDCATS' transgressions was cathartic, and maybe that's enough.

Deep down, I know it's not enough.

It's not fair that The Tragedies must talk in a quiet group about what they've faced. We – they – deserve better. Maybe they're afraid to talk about this, knowing how harsh the backlash can be for them. But I have nothing to lose. Not when no one knows who I am online. No one knows who any of us are if we remain anonymous.

With that final thought, I press 'post' and send the piece off into the Tumblr abyss.

And only then, once my anger settles, do I – smug and relieved – let myself fall straight to sleep.

By @ConstantlyVictimizedBySociety
Published: 20 September 2021

THE UNVEILING OF THE LSDCATS

When you're standing on a stage, auditioning for a role, you are also baring a part of your soul. You stand there, vulnerable, in front of a panel of judges who hold your future in their hands. There's an assumed respect there – you for them, and them for you. Simple.

Not for the LSDCATS.

The London School of Dramatic and Creative Arts Theatre Society has an *interesting* auditioning process. They have been harsh, cruel and critical, but not in the way one expects.

They've rejected people for:
   A) Being too dark-skinned for a traditionally white role.
   B) Being too foreign to direct a classically white play.
   C) Wearing a hijab.
   D) Being of a different race and therefore being presumed unable to understand classic literature.

These are just four reasons why the LSDCATS have turned students away from their plays, but they plainly show how terribly prejudiced they are.

And if you're wondering how I know this, it's because I got added into a group yesterday called The Tragedies. All the participants of this group were students rejected by the LSDCATS because of their skin tone and nothing else. It was a group made to look out for one another, but, more than anything, it exposed the LSDCATS for their deep-rooted prejudice.

Theatre was made to entertain spectators, to paint stories with actions and music, to fill an auditorium with imagination. It was not made to breed hatred, to continue fostering this unequivocal racism.

To put it plainly, this is a warning from us to every aspiring actor or actress out there. Stay away from the LSDCATS. Protect your heart. Your mental health. Don't subject yourself to their practices, which are rooted in hate and racism.

The LSDCATS are pretending to champion the theatrical arts, only to ultimately narrow it, restrict it and take it away from people of colour.

But I'm here to tell you that we're not going to let them.

Chapter Four

Before we graduated, my A-level psychology teacher gave every single one of her students the same piece of advice: never decide something when you're feeling the extremes of a negative *or* positive emotion. Never make a choice when you're drowning in sadness or soaring with happiness or burning with anger.

Why?

Because once you move away from that feeling, everything will seem different, and the choice you once made will feel ill-fitting.

Last night, I not only went against her advice, but I also found a new condition to add.

Don't make life-changing decisions at 3.00 a.m.

When I jolted awake at lunchtime to the sound of my don't-forget-to-submit-your-assignment alarm, realizing I'd overslept and missed my 8.00 a.m. and 10.00 a.m. lectures, I didn't expect to see over a hundred notifications lighting up my phone. More than that, I didn't expect to see that I had gained over 5,000 followers on Twitter. It turns out my old Tumblr account is still linked to my pseudonymous Twitter account. As soon as I'd submitted that essay-post raging against the LSDCATS, the link to it had been automatically shared on my Twitter account too. And while I was dead to the world, my post was being read again, and again, and again.

Every time I refresh my screen, the numbers go up. With each like, my stomach twists; with each retweet, my pulse jumps.

'Oh my God.' I breathe out, my heart hammering in my throat. 'Oh my God! What did I do?'

Is that a like from Simone Ashley? A retweet from Mindy Kaling? A fire-emoji comment from Laiba Siddiqi?

Laiba Siddiqi. Zayan Amin's ex-girlfriend. Another favourite celebrity of mine. Right under her comment is a reply from the LSDCATS, the sight of it making my chest tighten.

@TheLSDCATS: We welcome ALL those who wish to audition.

The replies to that are painfully harsh.

@LeenasDreams: @TheLSDCATS Are you guys serious? That's not what the post is saying in the slightest. The way you've been casting actors and actresses is biased, prejudiced and inherently WHITE. Are you going to own up to that?

I probably would've remained in bed, staring at my phone screen, shell-shocked, had someone not knocked on my door.

'Y-yes?' I croak out, my voice still rough with sleep.

'It's me,' Amal says through the door. 'You've missed your morning classes and I need to know if you're still alive.'

'I-I'm fine!' I reply, quickly and unconvincingly. I can practically see the sceptical look painted on Amal's face outside my door. So, for good measure, I throw in an excuse. 'I stayed up late last night and ended up in a YouTube wormhole about penguins. I guess I overslept, but I'll be out in a minute.'

I pause, waiting to see if she'll buy it. When Amal laughs, I feel my tense shoulders relax just a little.

'Of course you did,' Amal replies, her tone amused now. 'All right, well, I've got online lectures today, so I'm in the living room.'

When the sound of Amal's retreating footsteps begins to fade, I look at my phone again – it's still going wild with notifications. So many people are showering the post with support. I scroll through and notice that some of the responses are repeatedly asking, 'Who are you?'

That's when it hits me: no one knows I wrote the post. They only know that someone with the social media handle @ConstantlyVictimizedBySociety wrote it. Not me, Farah Sheikh.

But The Tragedies *can* be found. Internet detectives, who should probably be hired by the FBI, and potential trolls will have no problem working out who The Tragedies are – especially if any of them ever tweeted out about their auditions, like I did, from their personal accounts.

I acted on total impulse last night and I didn't stop to think about what would happen to Ben, David, Anushka and even Nur – who I have yet to meet.

Guilt gnaws at me as I run through all my options. I could delete the tweet before The Tragedies see it, but that feels deceptive – I'm already in the wrong for writing out their stories in the post; I can't hide the truth from them as well. But the longer I leave the tweet and the post up, the more traction it'll get. It's inevitable that they're going to see the post and realize it's their stories that I'm talking about.

In the end, there's only one right choice: I have to tell them myself and ask them what they'd like me to do: delete it, keep it up, or erase my entire digital footprint – if that's even possible.

While trying to work out the right wording for my message to The Tragedies, I decide to delete my Twitter and Tumblr apps to give me and my phone a break from the notifications. I write and rewrite the message in my Notes app while doing my daily post-shower skincare routine, which lacks its usual calming effect. I then slip on whatever is clean from my closet – yellow kameez, dark-blue jeans and a matching banana-yellow dupatta, which I drape round my throat and shoulders as if getting dressed will give me the confidence needed to deal with today.

When I'm finally done with my routine, I re-download Twitter and go straight to the group chat. I paste in the message, all the words I've been poring over for the last twenty minutes, and stare at it.

All I have to do is click 'send' and wait. Wait for The

Tragedies to explode in anger. Wait for them to kick me out of the group. Wait for them to give me exactly what I deserve.

'Breakfast first,' I say to myself, feeling slightly winded. I know I'm avoiding the inevitable, but I *like* The Tragedies. I only got a taste of their friendship, and I'm not ready to lose it just yet. I'm especially not ready to lose it on an empty stomach.

When I finally leave my room, I find Amal sitting on the flower-print sofa in our living room with a bowl of what looks like chocolate-fudge ice cream in her hands.

'We're doing ice cream for lunch?' I ask, and Amal whips her head round to look at me.

'I've got three assignments due in two weeks,' she retorts, 'and everyone knows ice cream makes life's problems easier.'

'Sage advice,' I say, walking straight to the kitchen. I'm going to pick something quick to eat, like cereal, and then send the message. 'Does Owais approve of this method of stress relief?'

'Nope,' Amal replies, dangling her spoon in front of her like it's a wand. 'He makes me do responsible and healthy things, like talk about my worries.'

I smile and pour the cereal, remembering the time Amal wouldn't talk about anything that made her anxious – especially not to Owais, her academic-rival-turned-something-more. But now they're each other's rock.

'Are you going somewhere?' Amal asks, her eyes narrowed on my outfit.

'No,' I say, holding the bowl of cereal between my palms. 'I'm going back into my room in a minute, actually.'

'Huh,' Amal says, her lips curling into a smile. My stomach clenches.

Oh no. She knows. She knows I wrote the Tumblr post. All rational thought flees my body. I'm going to have to tell her about my audition. I'm going to have to tell her that the LSDCATS don't think I'm good enough for the stage, and the humiliation is going to burn my insides alive.

'I was thinking you'd be more interested in Zayan Amin than studying,' Amal adds.

'What?' I blurt out, completely confused now.

'You know his new TV series?'

'Yeah?' I reply, my interest slightly piqued.

'Turns out, Zayan's big post-*Fairbanks* debut hasn't done so well,' she says, a lilt in her voice. 'The reviews came in, and I've never seen a show get cancelled that fast. The studio issued a statement about it.'

'But why?' I ask, attention fully captured now.

'Honestly, I think he's really messed up. Listen to this review.' Amal clears her throat and begins reading from her phone. "Zayan Amin, commonly known as 'Zay', has failed the desi community by playing the lead in a new comedy show where his character is the butt of coded tropes such as 'brown people smell like curry' and 'every brown kid hates their parents'. I had high hopes for Zay. *The Fairbanks* was one of my favourite sitcoms growing up, and watching him progress from the plucky toddler to the dashing young main character was a delight for viewers. But now it's clear he's just another social climber who will insult his roots for success."

'Oof, that *is* bad,' I agree, swallowing a mouthful of cereal. 'And surprising. I don't get why he'd take a role like that. Surely someone must have told him it would be a bad move?'

Amal makes a noise of agreement. 'I'm pretty sure he's going to be marked by this series forever, and we may not be seeing him in anything new for a while. It's sad. I really liked him. He seemed genuinely talented.'

What's the criteria to be considered genuinely talented, though? To be good enough?

That's what I want to ask, but silence fills the space between us instead. Amal's brow quirks, and I'm scrambling to think of something to say when my phone buzzes.

> Hey. We need to meet up. Are you free right now? David, Ben, Nur and I are at the Covent Garden Grind.
>
> Anushka Menon

My eyes shut briefly, as if not looking at the message means it won't exist any more. But nope – when I open my eyes again, Anushka's message is still there. It happened. The Tragedies found out before I could tell them, all because I was too afraid to tell them myself.

They're probably furious at me. Rightfully so. I've betrayed their trust by sharing *their* stories without their consent. But now I need to woman up and face the consequences. I need to take whatever they throw my way, apologize to their faces and step straight out of their lives before causing any more damage.

'Hey,' Amal says, interrupting my thoughts. 'You OK?'

I look up at my best friend's concerned frown. I want to tell her everything. To sit here and lay it all bare. But then I'd have to explain it all, starting from the beginning.

With The Tragedies last night, it had been easy. We were all on the same page, all brought together by the same experience. We understood the gravity of an audition, how badly rejection stung no matter how many times we'd faced it. There was no need to explain anything because we all understood one another. Amal and Maha get me, of course they do, but they're not in the thick of it. They're not aspiring actors, trying to get a foot in the door. With The Tragedies, I'd felt a sense of belonging.

But now I've gone and messed it all up.

'I'm fine,' I reply to Amal, standing up abruptly as a wave of despair hits me. 'I just ... I got an email from my professor. Turns out the lecture was more important than I thought. So I gotta go deal with that.'

Amal looks like she doesn't believe me. Not even a little bit. But she doesn't push, and I love her for that.

'I'll see you for dinner?' she asks, her voice just a tad bit suspicious.

'Yes! We'll do Thai tonight,' I say in a rush, as I practically race out of the door.

Once I'm in the hallway, I type out my reply to The Tragedies.

> Yes, of course. I'll be there ASAP.

Farah Sheikh

♥

Despite my grandparents living in the UK, and my mother growing up here, my family didn't visit London often. Most times, my nani and nana came to Karachi, and my parents preferred warm, beachy locations for holidays. So arriving in London three weeks ago was something of a culture shock for me.

Karachi is all cars, rickshaws and overfilled vehicles, but London is regulated buses, trains and walking. So much walking. No one warns you about that. Which means you end up wearing shoes with flimsy soles, and then you're stuck with a burning, aching pain in your legs until you work out that you need to up your fitness and get better footwear.

But, despite hating all the walking, I think there's something particularly lovely about strolling through Covent Garden. The cobblestoned streets, the quaint shops, the theatres, the Apple Market with its handmade jewellery and other trinkets – I love all of it. Usually, I would spend hours here, but right now I'm weaving past people, calves burning, as I make my way to the Covent Garden Grind.

As I'm about to step into the cafe, I realize two things: my back feels damp with sweat, and The Tragedies are still strangers to me. This meeting could be potentially dangerous; maybe I should've just told my friends the truth and asked them to come along with me, or at least tell them where I was going.

I'm still standing in the doorway, mentally going through a scenario where The Tragedies turn out to be murderers, when I feel someone tap my shoulder. I whirl round with more flair than needed, almost tripping over my own feet.

'Farah?' I take a moment to respond because, wow, this girl is pretty – dark-brown skin, black hair that's been twisted into a knot on top of her head, light-brown doe-eyes, and a small gold nose-ring. Standing in front of her, I become acutely aware of our differences – my wider hips, my lighter skin, my curlier hair – and yet, I still feel like I know her.

'Anushka?' I ask, and the girl's face splits into a wide smile.

'Yes!' Her tone doesn't betray any anger, but my hand tightens round the strap of my cross-body satchel anyway, as I steel myself in readiness.

Maybe you can fix this. Just talk to them openly. Ask for their forgiveness. Be honest. You've got this.

I hold on to this resolve like it's a life jacket keeping me afloat.

Anushka's eyes flick down to my hand, and her smile teeters at the edges before coming back in full force. 'Why don't we go inside? The rest of the group are already here.'

She turns on her heel, leaving me no choice but to follow her. As soon I step into the cafe, I'm hit with the scent of coffee, and the first thing my eyes land on is a pink neon sign on the wall that reads WE CAN BE HEROES JUST FOR ONE DAY.

I try to internalize the positive vibes of the sign as I follow Anushka to the table that's closest to the cafe door, but as we get nearer to the group my heart beats faster, and fear takes root in my chest. When we finally reach the table occupied by three others, Anushka slides into the booth effortlessly.

Leaving one seat for me. Right at the head of the table.

'Hi,' I offer, my voice sounding weak to my own ears.

'Hey, you want to sit down?' the girl closest to me asks. She's wearing a powder-purple hijab and holographic purple highlighter that accentuates her cheekbones so beautifully.

Nur Hadi.

I pull back the chair and tentatively sit down. I twist my satchel round to rest on my lap, relieved to have something to hold on to. Maybe I can use it as cover against the inevitable insults about to be thrown in my direction. There's a beat of awkward silence before Anushka breaks it by taking the lead.

'So, I'll just introduce everyone to you really quick,' she begins. My gaze follows her pointed finger to the lanky boy with a soft, round face and silky brown hair that sweeps over his forehead, sitting on her right. 'This is David, and I know he looks like he's really young, but from the way he acts, we know he's actually ancient –'

'Only twelve months older than her,' David interrupts with an eye-roll. 'Nice to meet you, Farah. The guy beside me is Ben.'

My gaze slides to Ben, taking in his closely cropped curly hair, his dark skin, his warm brown eyes and the kind smile he's throwing my way. He even leans over to shake my hand. 'Seconding D; it's really nice to meet you, Farah.'

'And I'm Nur,' Nur says as soon as Ben lets go of my hand. 'We didn't get to virtually meet last night, but I read your post this morning.'

At the mention of the post, my stomach cramps harder. I was right; they knew it was me from the very beginning. And I need to own up to my mistake *now*.

I straighten my spine and breathe in deeply. 'It's really nice to meet you all, and I want to start by apologizing. What I did was wrong on so many levels. I should never have written your stories without asking for your consent, but I promise I kept it as vague as possible. I made sure not to mention any of your names, or details about who you guys are. Or your university names. I referred to us – you – as The Tragedies the entire time. Still, I should have asked you first, and I have no excuse for what I did. I was angry, so angry. Like, if I was a cartoon, steam would've been coming out of my ears. But it was a mistake –'

'A mistake?' Anushka interrupts.

It takes me a second to realize she looks amused. In fact, they all look deeply entertained.

'None of us here think what you did last night was a mistake,' Ben adds gently. 'I actually thought it was pretty awesome that you were able to voice what we couldn't.'

Unexpectedly, a sudden bitterness sweeps through me. I only wrote The Tragedies' stories – not my own. Their encounters felt weightier, and my rage was more for them than myself. But here Ben is, praising me for being so vocal, when I can't really verbalize how *I* felt about my LSDCATS experience.

That's not their burden to deal with, so I let a small smile curve my lips. 'Still, I'm sorry. I should've asked you guys.'

'OK, yeah, you should've asked us,' David says bluntly. 'In principle, we should've been asked. But we don't mind. So, you've apologized, and we accept.'

I'm not sure what I'm supposed to say back, but thankfully Anushka picks up where David stopped.

'So, you're probably wondering why we invited you here today, and I think this is going to really clarify things,' she says, handing me her phone.

The screen shows my tweet and a reply to it from an account that didn't exist last night, called @TheTragedies.

@TheTragedies: WE ARE EXTREMELY EXCITED AND HUMBLED BY YOUR SUPPORT. IT'S WITH THIS KNOWLEDGE THAT THE TRAGEDIES ARE THRILLED TO ANNOUNCE THAT WE ARE FORMING OUR OWN STUDENT-LED PLAY. FOLLOW FOR MORE DETAILS SOON.

'Woah,' I mumble, falling back into my seat.

'You didn't see this?' David asks curiously.

I shake my head. 'I deleted Twitter and Tumblr off my phone because of all the notifications. But this is you guys?'

'*Us*. All of us,' Nur corrects, and a kernel of warmth takes root in my heart.

I came here expecting to be, quite frankly, verbally massacred by a group of strangers, and to attempt to put a balm over a wound I'd created. I didn't expect this. A spool of anticipation suddenly tightens in me as I envision a new future, one that may lead to me standing on a stage once again. I know I don't really belong in The Tragedies – not yet, at least. They've known one another longer; they probably trust each other more. But a part of me so desperately wants to be included. It's the same part that was so anxious about fixing my relationship with them before coming here.

When they say 'us', I want to believe it includes me too.

'So, what's the plan?' I ask, unable to hold back the questions I have swirling in my mind. A student-led play celebrating marginalized voices sounds like an amazing idea, but it also feels a little too good to be true. 'We form our own play – who's going to be the director? The writer?'

David raises his hand eagerly. 'I'm going to be the writer – I'll adapt whatever text we want to do for the stage.'

Anushka leans into his shoulder. 'I'm going to be the director.' She points to Nur, who smiles shyly. 'Nur is our resident fashion student, so she'll do the costumes.'

I glance again at the girl, mentally acknowledging that her outfit looks ten times more put together than anything I could have thought of. She should definitely design an entire play's worth of costumes.

'What about you?' I ask Ben.

Ben grins, all teeth, all mirth. 'I'm going to be like you. An actor. On the stage.'

'Really,' Nur adds, her voice coated in excitement, 'we've got this all thought out. Everyone will get the role they were once ignored for – this time on our terms.'

I'm still struggling to understand. All of this feels surreal. 'What about the LSDCATS? Do you think we're going to rival them?'

'Yes, and I don't anticipate it being much of a fight,' Ben replies. 'Aside from that one reply, which has now been deleted, the LSDCATS' socials have been deathly quiet ever since your tweet blew up.'

I hate that I have to be the one who voices all these concerns, but if I'm going back on stage, I want it – need it – to be a sure thing. Not a chance, but an understood fact. 'OK, so they've got a little bad press right now. But the LSDCATS are huge. They're going to recover from this. Conversations on Twitter about social issues have an expiration date, and that's tied to the attention span of the world. And when it does die down, and the LSDCATS return, then our play won't have much of a standing. It's no longer going to be a rivalry so much as an annihilation.'

David passes me his phone this time. 'We had the same thoughts. Until The Tragedies' account got this message today.'

> Hello! This is Lacey Parker from Parker's Artists' Agency. I'm Zayan Amin's agent, and I am reaching out on his behalf to show early interest in The Tragedies' production. Mr Amin believes strongly in supporting marginalized voices, and I'd love to set up a meeting with the writer of the post and Mr Amin, if you're interested.

Parker's Artists' Agency

I'm pretty sure my jaw must be on the floor. Or at least hanging a little. Waking up to all the retweets and support was already surreal, but this? Celebrity involvement? That's on a whole other level.

Anushka can't contain her excitement as she speaks. 'I checked out her account, and it's legit. We spoke on the phone, and she wanted to set up a really relaxed, quick get-to-know-you kind of meeting. I made it clear that we didn't have any concrete plans yet, but that we were eager to start as soon as possible.'

'OK,' I say cautiously. 'When's the meeting?'

'Today.'

'What?!' I ask incredulously. 'We're meeting Zayan Amin today?'

'No,' David says. 'You're meeting Zayan Amin today.'

'Me?' I squeak. 'Why me?'

'Well, Lacey said she wanted to meet with the writer of the post. Which is you,' Nur says slowly.

'OK, but – but I mean . . . guys . . .' I splutter uselessly.

They stare back at me patiently, waiting for me to put into words what my problem is. I love the idea of helping The Tragedies form their own play, and I have enough anger to want to rival the LSDCATS, but this sudden responsibility feels heavy. It's one thing to disappoint myself, but it's a whole other thing to let a group of other people down. Again.

'What if I say something stupid? I'm not a professional,' I finally say, nervousness making me babble. 'I mean, I want to be. More than anything. And I suppose an aspiring actress who wants to make it big should be able to talk to industry people, but –'

'Look –' Anushka reaches out and grabs my hand with hers, stilling my swirling worries – 'it's just one meeting. We're not agreeing to anything – even the play. It's not set in stone.'

'Plus you owe us,' David adds, and Anushka throws him a glare. 'What? She's the one who came in apologizing.'

He's not wrong. I do still owe them, and I know I'd regret not going to this meeting. I'd stay up all night, replaying the fact that I walked away. Tormenting myself with half-baked futures, the *could've beens* of my life. Ignoring this opportunity would be like turning my back on my ambitions, and even if I've got dewdrops of doubt dripping through my thoughts from yesterday's audition, I'm not ready to give up yet.

'OK, I'll do it. When's the meeting?'

'Looks like . . . right now,' Ben says, while looking out the window.

I'm about to ask what he means when the door to the coffee shop swings open. My chair is closest, and I narrowly miss being hit. I turn to give the individual an affronted look, but shock stops me.

The soft gasp from Nur, the abrupt noise from David, the excited shake of Anushka's hand on my own, and even Ben's foot kicking my chair – they all blend into the background. My focus is entirely on him.

The guy who almost smacked me in the face with the coffee-shop door.

Zayan Amin.

Chapter Five

There are sixteen oranges sitting in the wire basket behind the counter. One of them is particularly round. A perfect sphere. I know this because I've been staring obsessively at it for the last two minutes while Zayan Amin stands in line, waiting to give his order. The brim of his baseball cap is tipped down as he stares at his phone, shielding his face from me, but that doesn't stop my gaze darting over him.

He's a lot taller in person, and less bulky – there's a languid grace in his stance, like he knows exactly how much space he takes up in this world and doesn't mind it. It's hard to remember him as the little boy with chubby cheeks and witty one-liners from *The Fairbanks*; the guy standing in line is clearly not a little boy any more.

I turn my gaze back to the oranges, a blush making my cheeks hot. If I'd known this was going to happen, I would probably have mentioned my celebrity crush to The Tragedies before I agreed to the meeting.

When he first walked in, The Tragedies all but shoved me out of my chair, my insistent glare doing little to deter their excited smiles. I was running on autopilot once I left my seat, but halfway there, I finally realized *who* I was walking towards.

Zayan Amin.

Oh. My. God.

Terrible TV show aside, this guy was my celebrity crush. Embarrassingly, he was the guy I'd dream up fake romantic scenarios about in my head during maths class to make the time go by faster.

Once that thought really sedimented in my mind, I took a sharp right and went towards the counter instead, pretending I needed more napkins. That was when my obsessive orange-watching began.

The girl behind the counter has begun to look at me strangely. I'm running out of excuses to stand here. I can feel The Tragedies looking my way, their gazes weighty and desperate. I let loose a shuddering breath as I try to fight the festering nervousness that's begun to infect every part of my being.

You can do this, Farah. Do it for The Tragedies. Do it for yourself. Do it for the stage.

The stage. I close my eyes briefly and, right in the centre of my chest, I remember that feeling – it's faint, like wisps of smoke. I want to be there again. I want to stand in front of an audience again. I want to hear thunderous applause, so loud, so sonorous that it vibrates through me.

But are you good enough?

The question has stubbornly rooted itself in my heart. I want the answer to it. I could get one, if I was on stage again. If I had another chance to prove myself. That way, I'd know that the audition with LSDCATS was a one-off. I'd know that my dream of being an actress, a *real* actress, wasn't just that – a dream and nothing more.

I open my eyes, determination taking away the glimmer of worry, but when I look over my shoulder, I see that the guy who holds the key to my lifelong aspiration is nowhere to be found. Panic hits me, and my gaze swings around wildly until I realize that he's at the front of the line.

Right beside me.

I think I may have forgotten how to breathe altogether. My head refuses to turn and let me look directly at him, so I stare straight ahead and focus on his voice instead.

'Hi, I'm good. How are you?'

Oh. My heart wasn't prepared for that. Even while saying some generic, polite statement to a barista, Zayan's voice sounds extremely pleasant. Like melted butter on top of pancakes.

I miss what the barista says next because my heart is being slingshot from my chest to my throat. I consider shifting closer to him, but my feet remain cemented to the ground.

'What types of tea do you guys serve?' I hear him ask.

'Oh! We have a lovely chai tea if you'd like that?'

I wince at the reply. Chai *is* tea. Just like how naan is bread. To call it 'chai tea' is to essentially say 'tea tea'. Maybe this eager barista thought he was giving some clever suggestion because Zayan Amin is clearly brown, but saying the wrong name probably won't have endeared him.

I'm proven right when Zayan replies.

'Right,' he mutters uneasily. 'Uh, just one cup of tea, please. With sugar and milk.'

For some ridiculous reason I find myself excited to know that, just like me, he takes sugar in his tea. I internally facepalm – I sound like thirteen-year-old Farah again, mooning over Zayan Amin's latest movie. Thirteen-year-old Farah definitely couldn't have conducted a professional meeting with him. I'm not sure eighteen-year-old Farah can either, but she doesn't have much of a choice.

Zayan moves away towards a vacant table on the other side of the cafe. He's balancing a tray with a massive blue cup and a sugar pot that looks like a sugar cube on it; he has his phone pressed between his cheek and ear.

People around him in the cafe have started to notice who he is.

I can almost hear their thoughts as they do a double take: *Is that Zayan Amin? Is that Hari Fairbanks? No. No. It can't be. But, wait – he was shooting a TV series in London. But is it really him?*

I follow Zayan, trailing behind in what I hope isn't a creepy way. As he slides into his chair, I realize he's not going to sit facing my direction. He's got his back to me – his dark-green long-sleeved shirt stretches over his muscular shoulders as he answers a phone call. My throat dries up. I wish I'd ordered a cup of tea too.

I take a couple of seconds to collect myself.

You can do this. He's just a boy. You've talked to boys before.

Yes, but not ones this cute!

I force myself to tamp down my internal monologue, giving a quick look back at the gang; Anushka gives a thumbs up, David nods encouragingly and Ben is grinning so widely it must hurt. Nur is the only one who looks as nervous as I feel.

Don't let them down. Don't let them down.

I turn back and move closer to Zayan, so I'm now within earshot of his conversation.

'Listen, Pierre, I can't do this play,' he's saying.

Every part of me screeches to a halt – my mind, my steps, the flutter that was pulsing in me before.

What did he just say?

His voice turns a little harsher with his growing frustration. 'I don't want to be on stage. I hate being on stage – I want to be in front of a camera, OK? Lacey knows this, and she's still making me do this meeting.' He pauses to listen, stirring his tea in short, frustrated swirls. 'Look, I don't *care* if Laiba supports this play. Her opinion is no longer my concern. I don't want to be doing some kid-run play after spending years doing award-nominated TV and movies.'

A kid-run play. Like we're children putting on some pantomime.

His voice pitches lower and I strain to hear more. 'Sorry, Pierre, give me one second. I think there's a fan waiting for an autograph.'

I'm not prepared for his expression as he turns to me – not for his full smile, or his slightly pointed nose, or his deceptively soft brown eyes – and a sledgehammer of disbelief whacks me straight in the head. How can he change his attitude *that* quickly? 'Hi, would you like an autograph?'

There's a slow-motion moment where I hear, very clearly, my grandmother's voice in my head.

Anger is the feeling of the shaytan. Let it go. Drink a glass of water to cool your head.

Sadly, there's no glass of water near me, but even if there was a whole river meandering through this cafe, it wouldn't be enough to calm me down.

'We don't need anything from you,' I snap, and his head cocks to the side. Briefly, I think he kind of looks like a confused puppy. Still, not cute enough for me to ignore what he said. 'And we definitely don't want your half-baked involvement in our "kid-run" play. So you can go back to your life in front of the camera, making TV shows that get cancelled after less than half a season.'

The recognition is slow to come, but when he realizes who I must be, he closes his eyes slowly and sighs deeply. If he makes any attempt to be placating, I'm not sure I won't swing at him. I turn on my heel and stalk straight past The Tragedies, then out of the cafe. I hear their questions as background noise – faded, like a tinny buzzing – and in the depths of my anger I remind myself to message them once I've finally calmed down.

He hates being on stage?

I can't believe I was trying to stop myself from drooling over him, when he just easily discarded something I love – no, something I need. Like how Tinker Bell needs her pixie dust – that's the depth of my desire to be on stage. And people like Zayan Amin get full VIP access to my dreams, while I stand outside the stage door, begging to be let in.

Outside the cafe, I'm enveloped by the cool London air. There are far more people filling the cobblestoned streets of Covent Garden than when I first arrived. They force me to stop for a second, disorientation puzzling my senses as my anger slows to a low thump. As I ready myself to join the crowd and find my way back home, I hear a shout.

'Wait!'

I stop, glancing over my shoulder to see Zayan weaving past people to get to me. I don't know why I don't keep moving – maybe a part of me thought it'd be worse if people saw him chasing me, or maybe thirteen-year-old me just isn't ready to let the fantasy go. Either way, I wait for him.

He reaches me, and his words come out in a rush. 'I am so sorry. You weren't meant to hear that. I've been having a bad day, and I –' The rest of his spiel is lost on me because my anger returns at full force. His voice. That tone. It's the exact same one he used when he thought I wanted his autograph, the same voice I've heard him use in interviews. A disingenuous, polite, perfectly pitched voice made to soothe, made to allure, made to persuade you to like him. So different to how he sounded on the phone.

'Don't,' I interrupt, incredulity colouring my tone. 'I can see past this facade you've built –' my hands wave dramatically – 'and I'm not impressed. Like I said, The Tragedies don't need you.'

His mask slips, and a curl of satisfaction settles in my chest. His jaw works as he chooses his next words, his eyes steelier than before – which for some reason sends a thrill down my spine. 'Look, we got off on the wrong foot. I really didn't –'

'And I really don't care.' At my second interruption, a look of annoyance slides over his polite expression, and I notice a hint of his tongue kissing the top row of his teeth in frustration. 'Let me say it a little slower for you: The. Tragedies. Do. Not. Need. You.'

This time I'm ready to leave. I've got my shoulders pinned back, no nerves curdling in my stomach, anger hardening my stance. In my peripheral vision, I see him reach out, likely so that he can keep me locked in a conversation I don't want to continue.

As soon as I take one step forward, I'm jerked back by the fabric tightening round my neck. I make an awful, garbled noise, and then feel two large palms on my elbows, steadying me. I suck in a sharp breath, twisting violently out of Zayan's hold. My gaze flicks down to see the end of my yellow dupatta has got twisted into his Rolex.

Any other time, I'd have laughed about how audaciously Bollywood this whole scene is; all we'd need is some romantic background music and we'd be straight out of a Shah Rukh Khan film. But right now? The sight of the yellow thread woven into the platinum strap of his watch makes my blood boil. I reach to pull his wrist forward and disentangle myself. I use my nails to pick at the knot, hoping to snap it so I can be free.

'Seriously, I'm trying to apologize here.' Zayan keeps his wrist limp while I work, offering zero help, taking this as his golden opportunity to speak to me. 'Would you please listen? I need –'

The word 'need' makes my head snap upwards once more. His brown eyes widen as he takes in my anger. 'Whatever you're about to say isn't the truth. You can stand here and try to feed me some sob story about how you love acting on stage, and how The Tragedies' cause means so much to you, and how I misunderstood the conversation. Maybe you think you'll flash those dimples, and I'll ask, "What do *you* need?" But I won't. Not after the way you so casually insulted what I love. Do you know how many people would kill to be on stage? And you just sat there, throwing away an opportunity all because it wasn't Hollywood enough for you. Frankly, that's enough for me to know that I will never, ever help out a guy like you.'

With those final words, I pull roughly away, letting a soft ripping noise of fabric slice through his silence. I don't spare Zayan Amin a second glance as I finally walk off, the frayed yellow strands of my dupatta quivering in the wind.

Chapter Six

Though I don't consider myself to be a petty person, I will admit that reading negative reviews about Zayan's latest TV series, while preparing my chai for the night, brings out a vicious sort of delight from within me.

If I was being entirely objective, I'd say some of these reviews are unfairly harsh, lamenting Zayan as the worst actor of our generation, ignoring the years of cinema he's been a part of. He was the Hollywood favourite for so long – beyond being part of *The Fairbanks,* he was also a child actor in a dozen or so movies. Everyone wanted him on screen; everyone was excited to see what he'd do next.

But some of these reviews are asking the right questions: how did Zayan Amin get roped into doing a drama series that had no plot, no real substance and storylines that were heavily stereotyped – from the brown kid hating his religion to the brown girl taking her hijab off for the white boy? His once-loyal fanbase is now calling him a sell-out of his culture. He couldn't have thought this was a good idea – was he blackmailed into it? Forced by his team?

Sources are saying he was desperately trying to get out of his contract before the show was cancelled. If I didn't know exactly what Zayan Amin was like – an egotistical jerk – I would've been torn, as a fan. Do you support him? Cancel him? Wait for the truth to come out?

I set my phone down on the countertop, pushing those unanswerable questions away. I should take a break from my reading to do something productive. I'm alone in the flat – both Maha and Amal are out – so there should be no distractions, but still, I'm in no mood to get started on my university assignments.

Which means turning to the donation link instead.

After my disastrous meeting with Zayan two days ago, I ended up on a late-night Zoom call with The Tragedies, where we discussed how we were going to produce the play. I'd told them everything that happened with Zayan, and we mutually agreed we didn't need a big-shot celebrity for our plan. We could fund this play on our own, through donations. And once we got the money, we could focus on holding auditions, getting a script and broadening the teams for sets and costumes.

But looking at the GoFundMe page I set up, my hope deflates like a balloon.

Here's the thing about going viral: you've got to sustain the hype. A meme becomes popular because it's reshared a million times, and it never truly fades because it's used again and again in texts and replies. An unknown actor or

actress becomes huge when their movie, play or TV show
gains interest and when they maintain that interest by
moving on to the next big project. No stopping.

But, two days later, The Tragedies are falling out of the
limelight. This is the sour side of going viral. The
conversation is already shifting. I switch to the email
account we set up for The Tragedies, scroll down and see
the emails we got yesterday from various news outlets –
Buzzfeed, HuffPost and more. They're all asking for
interviews, and I make a mental note to discuss these
requests with the group.

As if summoned by my thoughts, a message cuts through
my scrolling.

Anushka
Check your Twitter feed
RIGHT NOW, Farah.

What happened??

Anushka
NOW.

Anushka's urgency causes a tight coil of nerves in my
stomach. It takes me a second to log into Twitter, but once
I'm in, I'm faced with a photo of me and Zayan.

Whoever took the photo captured the moment when I was
attempting to disentangle myself from the strap of Zayan's

watch. Except it doesn't look like that. It looks a lot more . . . intimate. It looks like we're seconds away from hugging, our heads bent close, and there's a flush on my cheeks that I'm sure is getting misconstrued as a blush. I scroll through the comments, alarm growing with everything I read.

@FallingForLove: OH MY GOSH!! I AM DYING!! LOOK AT HOW CUTE THEY ARE!!
@DesperatelySad: The next Kajol and Shah Rukh Khan!
@ZayanAminLovesMe: I prefer Laiba, but this is still a cute photo.
@CatTheVampire: I found her! It's **@FarahSheikh**

Oh no, no, no. They've found me. Not that I could've stayed hidden. That tweet has more retweets and likes than the one I posted about The Tragedies. Nausea climbs up my throat when I realize Amal and Maha are going to see this too; they're going to kill me for not telling them.

I read on. My heart is beating so hard I'm sure my neighbours can hear it through the walls.

@TheJudge24: This is literally so disgusting. This girl is doing a disservice to Pakistan with her inappropriate antics.
@DannyMohib: Seriously?? What is wrong with girls these days?? Posing with boys on the street? SOMEONE CONTACT HER PARENTS.
@ZoyaKhan: Dude, is she even desi??? She looks like a tanned white girl. BROWN-FISHING!!

Dread lines my stomach, just as my frustration wakes. There's not one negative comment directed towards Zayan.

Everyone's either harping on about how wonderfully adorable we look, screaming 'OTP, OTP, OTP', or calling me every awful name under the sun.

My fingers fly as I type out my own tweet, setting the story straight. I'm not dating Zayan Amin. I was ripping my dupatta free. I have zero interest in him.

I'm in the middle of deciding how many exclamations I should add when there's a knock at the front door. Irritation cuts through my stress, and while I'm still staring down at my phone, another knock rings out. My eyes shut in frustration, and I drop my phone on to the counter with a clatter.

Expecting it to be one of my flatmates who's left their keys at home, I swing the door open without bothering to check the peephole, deciding it's best to deal with my friends' disbelief and wrath straight on.

But it's not them. And it's not The Tragedies.

Zayan Amin stands in my doorway.

He's no longer wearing a baseball cap – his wavy dark-brown hair is free to curl in a very rakish, princely manner. He's also dressed differently; he's now wearing a soft-looking mint-green sweater with the sleeves pushed up, showcasing his tanned forearms, and a pair of worn-in blue jeans.

We stare at one another in complete silence. His hands hang awkwardly by his sides before he stuffs them into his pockets, an almost bashful smile gracing his lips.

'So,' he says, all buttery and smooth. 'Any chance you'll let me in?'

♥

'How did you find my address?' I ask, hands gripping the door frame. I'm thirty seconds away from slamming the door in Zayan's handsome face.

His mouth lifts with a slight, secretive curve. 'Where there's a will, there's a way.' At my silence, his grin dims. He clears his throat uncomfortably, and a more serious note enters his voice. 'My agent – the one who reached out to you, Lacey Parker – knows how to find people. I'm not really sure how she found you, but she did.'

What does that even mean? Did she stalk me or something?

He must see the alarm written plainly on my face because he hurries on. 'I'll make sure she doesn't give your address to anyone else.'

'Why would you ask for my address?' I say, outraged.

His stance turns defensive, his shoulders hunching upwards. 'I tried contacting you all day. I messaged you on Twitter, Instagram – I even went as far as to send you a message on Facebook messenger, but you didn't reply. So I had to take extreme measures.'

I close the door halfway, so my head is hidden from his line of vision, and I look down at my phone. Amid a hundred notifications, I find him.

ZayanAmin wants to send you a message.

I open the door again. 'All right – still doesn't mean you should go full Liam Neeson on me.'

'You're right,' he concedes, but from the restrained look

61

in his eyes, I think he wouldn't mind arguing his point. His voice turns sugar-sweet, placating, like it did back in the cafe. Once again, I'm impressed by the quick way he can revert to a new tone. 'I'm really sorry about that. I shouldn't have invaded your privacy. Speaking of, I do really need to discuss something with you. And I don't mind doing it in your hallway, it's just . . . I think this is about to become a three-person conversation.'

'Huh?' I reply eloquently. Zayan points to his right discreetly, and as I step out of my doorway to look I catch the back of my neighbour's head just as her door shuts. I sigh resignedly. I swear I live in the nosiest block of flats. 'Fine. You can come in.'

I don't wait for Zayan's response as I make my way back into the flat, but I hear his footsteps following me. He closes the door, and I'm about to tell him that he needs to take his shoes off, but he's automatically doing it anyway.

After toeing off his expensive trainers, he stands awkwardly in my hallway – looking less like a celebrity, and more like your average eighteen-year-old boy. I glance at his feet to see that he's wearing socks with tiny samosas on them.

His gaze follows mine, and his grin widens. He rocks on his heels, unashamed, confidence rolling off him in waves. 'They're a gift. From a friend.'

I battle to withhold my smile. *Zayan Amin wears socks with samosas on them. Who'd have thought?*

I decide the kitchen is the best place to converse – I get to pretend that he's interrupted me cooking and should feel bad for doing so. I move towards the stove first, keeping my back to Zayan, making sure my chai has brewed and not bubbled over.

'Oh, you're making chai. You wouldn't have an extra cup, would you?'

I whip round to see he's made himself comfortable on one of the chairs that was previously tucked under the kitchen island. His elbows rest on the wooden top, hands laced in front of him. He doesn't look out of place at all. It's like he's taken scissors to my life, created a Zayan-shaped hole in it and stitched himself seamlessly into the gap.

'Uh, sure,' I say uneasily. 'Sugar? Milk?'

'Both, please.'

If we were back home, my mother would have a whole spread out right now. Guests coming over for tea means much more than just chai; it's fried jalebis, spring rolls, samosas or an array of dishes to have with the chai. The need to make my guest comfortable is second nature to me. I attempt to quiet that part of myself, but my mother's voice ringing in my head – *don't be badtameez* – wins. 'I have some cake rusks too, and I think my flatmate has some experimental dessert she was trying to make in the fridge. A chocolate mousse type thing?'

'Cake rusk?' A note of nostalgia enters his voice – so quiet that I'm forced to glance at him over my shoulder. That brief glimpse of warmth is quickly replaced with a blank, pleasant smile. He didn't want me seeing that. 'I haven't had that in a while. Sure, yeah. I would love one.'

I pour the chai into two cups and take out a cake rusk for me and another for Zayan. I turn back to face him, quieting the nervous beating of my heart with a deep breath, and slide the chai and cake rusk towards him. Silence fills the room, uncomfortable and painfully loud.

I swallow a bite, savouring the subtly sweet flavour for a second, before plunging into the conversation head first. 'So, what was it you wanted? If it's to apologize again –'

'I'm not here to apologize,' he interrupts, his eyes finally looking up to meet mine. 'I'm not sorry. Well, I'm not entirely sorry.'

'You're not?' I reply with derision.

He uses his cake rusk to gesture, still cool and collected. 'To be fair, you weren't supposed to hear that conversation.'

'I wasn't eavesdropping, if that's what you're trying to imply. I was there for a meeting. With you.'

'And I didn't want to be at that meeting,' he replies honestly. 'I'm not sorry for venting about my situation on a private phone call, but I am sorry for insulting The Tragedies, and your cause. Truly, what you guys are doing is important, and I shouldn't have tried to debase that just because I'm unhappy with how my life is going. It was petty, and wrong, and probably a little bit envious of me.'

I notice he doesn't mention what he said about hating being on stage, and I don't say anything about it either. I'm not sure I'll be able to sound rational as I try to explain how much his distaste for it bugs me.

I'm also not sure I trust him with my feelings.

Instead, I search for sincerity in what he has said, and in the way he holds my stare, unafraid of what I might find reflected in his irises. I can't tell if he's only showing me what he thinks I want to see, or if it's genuine – I mean, he's an actor, after all. But I nod anyway, because the quicker I agree, the sooner he'll leave my flat and I can clear up everything that's happening online.

'So, if you've not come to apologize then why are you here?' I ask, more curious than I care to admit. 'Is it because of the photo?'

The words leave my mouth with little thought, and only when I remember how intimate those pictures looked does my body flush. My eyes drop to his hands, curved round his cup – long fingers, large palms, soft-looking brown skin.

I tear my gaze away, praying he didn't catch me making heart-eyes at his hands. But he's smirking, like he knows exactly what I was thinking.

'Have you forgotten how to speak?' I ask quickly.

'No, I'm just a little stunned by the memory of that photo,' he says, making everything sound like it's been drenched in molten chocolate. My insides start to warm involuntarily, because – come on – my celebrity crush is sitting in my kitchen, looking at me like there are secrets only we know. How can I *not* lose it just a smidge?

'I'm also just thinking over how I'm supposed to say this,' Zayan continues, pulling at my attention once more.

'Say what?'

His fingertip circles the brim of his cup, eyes locking with my own, a breath making his chest expand as he gets the words out in one go. 'I think we could help one another – by going on a date.'

I digest what he's said quickly, and there's no filter in my mind to prevent me laughing. It bursts out of me loudly. Zayan waits for my hysterics to subside with an amused look on his face, taking periodic sips of his tea.

'Funny,' I say. 'Really, tell me, why are you here?'

He drains the last of his chai before responding. 'You have a nice laugh,' he replies unexpectedly, and a wave of pleasure washes over me. If he keeps complimenting me, I'm going to melt into a puddle. 'And I already told you why I'm here. I think I should take you out on a date.' The horror must be exceedingly plain on my face, because he becomes disgruntled. 'To clarify, it will be our first *fake* date, to begin our fake relationship.'

'Are you sure you're all right?' I ask, when I realize he's being serious. 'You're not drunk or high or something, are you?'

'No, I'm completely sober. I don't drink anyway. You should probably know that if we're going to be together,' he replies, with not one ounce of shame. As if he hasn't just stepped into my flat, drunk my chai and made an outrageous request.

My jaw drops at his confidence. 'We're not together.'

'Not yet,' he amends, all businesslike. 'We have some stuff to go over first. Firstly, what are you comfortable with?'

'As in . . .?'

'Physical things. Like –'

'No.' I cut him off before he can finish.

Zayan nods, like he's filing away this information for later. 'Not an issue.'

'Yes, an issue. We're not in a relationship.'

'But we should be,' he argues. 'Let me explain.'

'Please,' I say with a wave of my hand.

'You saw the response we got to that photo from the other day, right? It was huge. I haven't had this much positive publicity since *The Fairbanks*. The public loves you –'

'Uh, no. They don't. Didn't you see the hate?' I interrupt, thinking of the comments people posted about my looks, my outfit, my skin. They hurt unexpectedly, despite being written by random people I'll probably never meet.

He shakes his head dismissively, leaning in, his tone all analytical and calculating. 'Those are just trolls. *Most* of them love you, and they love seeing us together. I'm thinking we should capitalize on it.'

The bulb of the kitchen light throws a golden hue over his expression, illuminating the curve of his cheekbones, the brown of his eyes, the sharpness of his jaw. I swallow nervously as he leans forward, but he doesn't notice, too lost in his speech.

'Look, if I'm being honest, I need you. You're aware of how badly I've been doing since my TV show got cancelled and *The Fairbanks* ended.'

I wince, remembering my harsh words at the cafe. 'I'm –'

'No need to apologize. It was a terrible series. I shouldn't have agreed to do it, but I did. You may not believe me, but I tried to leave, but I was tied up in a contract for at least six episodes. Either way, a bad TV series followed by my girlfriend breaking up with me pretty much shoved me to the bottom of the social-status ladder. And the mistakes I've made mean more because of who I am.'

I falter, confused. 'Who are you?'

He sighs, rubbing his eyes with the palms of his hands. 'I'm Zayan Amin. I'm the child actor who got adopted by Hollywood. Who starred in everyone's favourite wholesome family TV show, who got chosen to do Oscar-nominated movies because of said TV show. But more importantly, no matter how many accolades I pick up, I'm still Pakistani. I'm still brown. And that means I'm not allowed to fail like a white actor is. I won't be forgiven as easily. People already believe I get roles because there's such a call for *diversity* nowadays.'

His words are dripping in weary frustration. I want to ask him why he took the role. Was he trying to ignore his culture? Erase it? The words to probe him with are on the tip of my tongue, but I don't say them. It doesn't feel like my place to ask such things, and it has nothing to do with his offer.

'I'm not sure I'm the right girl,' I reply tentatively. My brain is screaming, *Don't trust him.* There's no way to know how genuine Zayan's vulnerability is – whether this is another side of him or an act he's using to convince me. 'Seriously, I'm not some big influencer or something. My swift rise to popularity is already dwindling.'

Zayan nods quickly. 'It is. But I know how to stop it. Plus, there are benefits for you if you agree to this.'

He leaves that hanging in the air, waiting for me to take the bait. I sit back in my chair, hands gripping my cup tightly. This is some major Shakespearean-level ridiculousness. I can't believe I'm even entertaining his idea, but I can't help the intrigue I feel. I glance at Zayan; he's waiting, watching me with imperceptible eyes. We face one another like we're negotiating a business deal.

'What do I get in return?' I ask, giving in to my curiosity. I tell myself it's best for me to know all the details before saying no.

'Whatever you want,' he replies, the vulnerability from before dissolving so quickly I'm half convinced it was never real. But I can't tell. Not really. 'I was thinking I'd go ahead with the deal Lacey set up. Me being a part of your play. It would mean you guys would get great publicity, I'd fund the entire thing and you'd definitely stick it to the LSDOGS, or whatever they're called.'

'CATS,' I correct. 'LSDCATS.'

My mind conjures up the donation link, and the snail's pace at which donations are coming in. I want to do the play with The Tragedies, I want to help them ruin the LSDCATS, but I know we don't have the same prestige as them. And I want to be on stage again so badly. If we pull it off, I can prove to myself and the LSDCATS that I am a good actress. That I belong in their world. And if I can do that, then my dream of making acting my career won't be so unrealistic.

The want is like a desperate ache in my chest, leaving me hollowed out. There are only dregs left at the bottom of my teacup now, and no matter how hard I stare at them there's no fortune to be read from the black specks.

When I look up, I find Zayan staring at me, his eyes flinty and determined. 'I know it seems unthinkable, but you're golden, Farah,' Zayan says, and my heart throbs in my chest. This doesn't sound like the other compliments; there's no teasing tone lurking in the words. Just sheer honesty that makes my entire body blush. 'You're a social grenade waiting to explode into the world. I need you. I'm one public blunder away from losing it all – my career, my status, everything.' His eyes shut briefly, and I finally see the desperation lining his expression. I see a boy sitting at my table, asking for help. He lets out a shaky breath, as if showing me how he's really feeling has terrified him. 'Please, Farah.'

I swallow roughly, thinking over my choices.

What option gives you the better chance of getting on stage? Which road leads you under the spotlight once again?

I know it's Zayan's. He has better insight into all of this – the publicity, the popularity – and he has the money. Although I'm terrified of going through with it, my fear quiets when I think of The Tragedies.

They deserve to have their dreams come true.

The thought of letting them down pierces that terror, shoves it back down and fills my bones with determination.

'OK, say I agree to this – what do The Tragedies and I personally get?'

'What do you want?' Zayan asks, a little doubt coming into his expression. 'Within reason, I can probably get it for you.'

I pause, a little hesitant, before letting some of my desires spill into the space between us. 'I want to be a professional actress. More than anything in the world. And from what you've told me, that's not going to be an easy ride for someone like me. I don't want to give a director – or a casting agent, a writer, anyone – an excuse to reject me.' I inhale sharply, choosing my next words carefully. 'I want you to teach me everything you know about acting – on film and on stage. I want your knowledge. Train me. Make me better than I am.'

Make me good enough, a quiet voice whispers in my head, but I don't say that to Zayan.

'I can do that,' he replies softly, and I fear that his tone is pitiful, but it doesn't sound exactly like that. The softness of it bothers me, nettles me, and I add one more stipulation to the agreement.

'I also want an in. Casting agents, talent agents, directors – I want them there on opening night. For The Tragedies too – we want the chance to start our own careers.'

I'm not really sure if The Tragedies want to make their talents into careers or if they're simply hobbies, but they deserve to get a foot in the door. Especially if people like the LSDCATS are going to be standing in the way.

Zayan mulls this over, an impressed look glimmering in his eyes. I try not to preen under it. 'OK, I'll set up a meeting with Lacey, me and you tomorrow?' he finally says.

I nod, nerves buzzing at the thought of sitting in front of his agent. A question blinks in my mind. 'How are you so sure people are going to be interested in our relationship?'

A roguish smile curls Zayan's lips, and he leans closer, like he's going to tell me the secrets of the world. 'Well, who wouldn't want to see two good-looking people together?'

I roll my eyes. This boy and his words. If we go through with this, I'm probably never going to have a normal heart rate again.

'That's not a good reason.'

He shrugs. 'People love to see happiness. Maybe it's because they don't have it in their own lives, maybe it's because they get to live vicariously through someone else's joy, but everyone loves a power couple. That's going to be us.'

His determination is so naked and honest it's unnerving. He's like a walking masterclass in how to utilize your emotions when you need to, and despite the gnawing worry that's telling me all of this is going to end terribly, I am excited to learn from him.

'If that's all, I'll take my leave,' he says formally, while rising from his seat.

I walk him to the door, watching as he slips his shoes back on. Before going, he looks around quickly, eyes dropping to one of the many notepads Maha has scattered around the flat – this one is on the table by the door. He bends down, using the pen beside it to scribble something.

'Here's my number. Text me and I'll send you the location of Lacey's office.'

I hold the paper between my fingers, my gaze tracing over the numbers.

I'm holding Zayan Amin's phone number. I wonder how much people would pay for it. Hundreds? Thousands? Millions?

'That's for *you* only,' Zayan stresses, reading the awed look in my eyes perfectly.

'I promise not to share it,' I offer. 'Unless you mess me over with all of this. In which case I will send this out to anyone and everyone who wants it.'

He smiles, before that pleasant mask slips back into place. Our fake relationship probably won't thrive under scrutiny if he refuses to smile at me genuinely, but I'm sure he knows that. Or at least I hope he does.

We continue to face one another, unsure of what to say, and the awkwardness begins to scratch against my skin. Finally, I snap and fill up the silence.

'Should we have a contract drawn up?' I ask, and he takes a moment to mull it over.

I'm not sure why the thought of signing on a dotted line about all of this is making me anxious. Maybe because it's such a cold concept. I know this relationship isn't real, but a contract sucks the life out of every humane part of it. It's one thing to have a written agreement to hire him for the play; it's another thing entirely to employ one another as companions.

'I'd prefer it if we didn't. I can have one drawn up for the casting agents and the reassurances you've asked for. But I'd like to keep the truth about our relationship completely under wraps. Only you and I should know about it. Aside from my publicity team.'

Relief initially floods my system at his response, and then horror takes over.

'My friends –' I panic, thinking of Amal and Maha – 'I'm awful at lying to them.'

Zayan's eyebrows rise ever so slightly. 'Remind me again . . . you're an actress, right?'

I roll my eyes. 'Aspiring. And you don't need to be a good liar to be a good actress, OK? But back to my main point – I can't tell my friends?'

Zayan's gaze turns hard. 'No. You don't really know someone until you get rich and famous. People change a lot faster when you've got coins lining your pockets. And we don't want anything leaking to the press.'

'My friends aren't like that!' I protest. His mouth twists, like he wants to say something but doesn't know how to. 'Fine, I won't tell them.' I gesture between the two of us. 'But I'm not sure they're going to like this.'

'But I'm a *catch*,' Zayan replies with more exaggeration than necessary. I barely hold back a scoff.

Though I don't want my friends to worry, I need this counterfeit relationship. It's my chance to be on stage, and I can't risk losing that opportunity again. *It'll be fine*. I'll figure out something to tell Amal and Maha.

'So, we agree?' I say, slightly dumbfounded. Everything with Zayan up till now has felt like a push and pull. To be on the same page about something . . . well, it feels nice.

He gives me a firm nod and sticks out his hand. 'We should shake on it. Make it official.'

I look down at it, instantly reminded of a line from *Romeo and Juliet*.

And palm to palm is holy palmers' kiss.

I press our palms together, my lines meeting his, and our fate is sealed.

Chapter Seven

Maha holds up her phone with the picture of Zayan and me on it, like it's Exhibit A in her case against me. Beside her, Amal and Owais – Maha's cousin, my friend, Amal's *someone more*, who also came from Rocate High – are curled next to each other, knees touching, arms brushing, always connected.

When they all returned to the flat, after Zayan left, they didn't say anything. They simply went to the couch, sat down and made me sit opposite them, and then Maha showed me that photo.

They all wait patiently, while I avoid making direct eye contact. In the silence, I steal a look at Amal and Owais.

My friendship with Amal grew slowly over time; her trust issues made it hard, but we found one another last year. Out of all of them, she looks the most concerned. Her brown eyes are glinting with questions, but she holds them back and waits for me to speak. Beside her, Owais is watching me with equal calculation and concern. It's hard to imagine that they hated each other only a year ago – that they were rivals, back at Rocate High, who were forced to work together for a debate competition that changed their lives. Especially since they now fit together perfectly, like puzzle pieces. They both watch me with intense stares that scream, *YOU CAN TELL US THE TRUTH.*

I hate lying to them, but I have to. I force myself to remember *why* I'm doing this. *For the stage. For The Tragedies. To prove ourselves.*

'So,' I start, finally looking up from my hands, 'as you can see, I met Zayan Amin.'

The admission tastes bitter against the roof of my mouth.

'How?' Maha asks, shock written plainly across her face. 'Where did you even find him?'

I swallow tightly, avoiding Amal's eyes. 'You know The Tragedies?'

'Those students who are forming their own play?' Owais asks.

I nod. 'Well, I'm sort of involved in it.'

'Involved?' Maha's tone turns curious.

'I wrote the Tumblr post,' I admit, attempting to stay as close to the truth as possible. 'I wrote it after meeting with some of the other members of The Tragedies at an audition. I was outraged by what the LSDCATS had done, and then the post went viral, and Zayan's agent reached out to meet. She was hoping to get Zayan involved in the play, which he is now. We really hit it off, but nothing is official yet.'

I choose not to tell my friends the detail of my own failed audition; I'm embarrassed at the thought of them knowing I wasn't good enough, worried that they'd tell me I overreacted.

'Farah, what are you going to tell your parents?' Maha asks, leaning closer to me.

'If they ask, I'll tell them Zayan's just a friend. They know I'm not planning on finding anyone unless it's a forever type of thing,' I say, hoping my nervous energy translates as giddiness rather than guilt.

'You're in a situationship with Zayan Amin,' Maha breathes out, excitement replacing her anger. 'I can't believe you didn't tell us all this before!'

I shrug, still avoiding Amal's eyes. 'I was going to, but it all happened really fast. Honestly.'

Liar. Liar. Liar.

'Whatever. What's he like?' Owais asks eagerly. 'Is he just like Hari Fairbanks?'

My ripped yellow dupatta flashes in my mind.

'He's, uh . . . well . . . Our first meeting was – eventful.'

Maha's brow rises in question, and another lie slips past my lips. 'I spilled coffee on him, and he sort of freaked out. He's also overconfident. Well, I suppose you could say he's self-assured. And blunt. He's also a little judgemental. He seems kind of untouchable. Maybe that's because he's a celebrity. I'm not really sure.'

My best friends look at me in confusion, and I rush to say something positive about Zayan. I think of that teasing tone of his, and that determination he showed when he sat at our kitchen table – that unwillingness to let his dreams die.

'But he knows what he wants, and he's willing to fight for it,' I finish.

Owais' handsome face splits with an exaggerated, gooey grin. 'And he wants you.'

I laugh weakly. 'It's really early stages.'

Maha snorts loudly. 'It doesn't look like early stages. I can see it in his eyes in the photo, Farah. He's half in love with you already.'

Then he really is a brilliant actor.

'I'm not sure about that,' I say uncertainly.

'I want every detail about how you guys met. From start to finish,' Maha says, and my heart thrums with an anxious beat.

By the time I'm done weaving my romantic tale, my throat is warm, and I've almost made myself believe it happened.

'We've got to meet him, Farah,' Maha says in the end, reaching over to squeeze my hand.

'Sure,' I reply. 'Once we define what we are. Right now, it's all very new.'

Owais grins, looking at Amal with warm eyes. 'The honeymoon phase is the best.'

She shoots a smile his way, before looking at me again – analytical as always.

'Yeah,' I laugh, knowing Zayan and I are nowhere near a honeymoon. 'Anyway. Now that you're all done giving me the third degree, can we eat? I'm starving.'

That triggers everyone to move. Maha goes to her room to change, Owais makes a beeline to the bathroom and I find my way to the kitchen, ready to see what takeaway Amal has brought home. After all that acting, I've worked up an appetite. I'm delighted to see the familiar paper bags of our local Chinese restaurant, and it's while I'm rummaging through them to find my order that Amal taps my shoulder.

I turn, a warm box of kung pao chicken held between my hands. Amal's arms are crossed over her chest; a contemplative look colours her pretty face. My hands clench round the box.

Don't ask me a question. Don't ask me a question. I'll tell you everything if you do.

'I hope you know what you're doing, Farah,' Amal says, her voice soft. 'Giving your heart to a boy is never easy. You have to learn to share things that you never imagined giving to anyone else. Just . . . promise me you'll protect yourself.'

My initial response is to laugh out loud. If Amal knew the truth, there's no way she'd be giving me this piece of advice; it's so entirely unnecessary. Still, her concern warms me, and I grip her hand in my own before agreeing with her.

'I promise.'

Chapter Eight

The conference room at Parker's Artists' Agency looks like something from a movie or TV show – with windows that showcase The Shard, interior design all minimalistic and grey, and a man standing at the end of a particularly long oval table.

He looks up from his papers. 'Pierre Lyon, Zayan's publicist. Your temporary publicist.' He introduces himself, his French accent heavy. His hair is streaked with silver, he wears one ring on his pinkie and his black suit is cut sharply over his lean frame. As he steps towards me, looking me up and down, I resist the urge to clutch my satchel – that has my notebook, lip balm and a chocolate bar inside – to my chest like a defensive shield.

'I'm Fa—'

'I know who you are,' he says, cutting me off, his critical eye trained on my face. 'You're pretty. That helps.'

'I think that's subjective –' I begin, but he continues.

'Good height – there's a small difference between you

and Zayan. That will photograph well. But we need to work on your facial expressions; you betray too many emotions. Then again, most of you actors have little control over your feelings.'

'Excuse me –' I say, beyond offended now.

'Interrupting is rude,' Pierre says hypocritically. I gape at him, but he ignores me. 'When you're being interviewed in the future, never interrupt. If it looks like the interviewer is interrupting you, that is better. You look like you have been faulted, not like you are the one dishing out the rudeness. Be patient. Wait. Listen. Then speak.'

I flounder, entirely baffled and still offended by everything that's come out of this man's mouth.

'Pierre –' a new voice emerges from behind me, and I whip round to see who it is – 'let the poor girl sit, at least.' A woman steps forward for me to shake her hand. 'Hi. Lacey Parker.'

She's a short woman, with a face full of soft features. The urge to trust her is almost instantaneous, but I rein it in. These people work for Zayan, not me.

Zayan, I realize, is standing behind Lacey like a statue, hands tucked into the pockets of his grey plaid pants and shoulders pulled back, so the material of his fitted dark-blue sweater stretches across his chest. His hair looks wind-whipped in a way that can only be styled, with a wayward strand falling over his forehead. His eyes don't meet mine, not fully at least.

The silence between the four of us lasts only a second

before Lacey smiles brightly and grandly announces, 'Well, Farah, allow us to introduce you to media training.'

♥

'So, let me get this straight,' I say. 'You don't want us to tell people we're dating.'

'No,' Pierre says, with more patience than I thought he had. 'We want people to be speculating, reporters to be investigating. I want people asking "are they dating or not?"'

'Why can't we just say we are?'

'Think of your favourite romcom,' Pierre replies, leaning forward so his elbows sit on the glass table.

Multiple films pop into my mind. *You've Got Mail*, *How to Lose a Guy in 10 Days*, *13 Going on 30*, *10 Things I Hate About You* – the classics.

'Now think of the male and female leads,' Pierre says. 'Their chemistry leaps off the big screen and bleeds into real life. The public wants them to be together. Badly. So that couple may be seen together for six months or so until the movie releases. They'll be holding hands walking down the street. But they won't say anything. They won't confirm anything. Their popularity stems from news outlets speculating about their relationship. Once they make their relationship official, the popularity morphs. It's a new kind of interest that comes from power couples and engagements – but the initial intrigue came from the chase. The fans, the public, the entertainment sites, all of them chased that relationship, created rumours, fed into the hype that surrounded them. We need to build that hype. It will prove to directors and casting agents that we have a strong grip on Zayan's public image. That's what we need from you both. We need you to create a media storm and sustain it.'

'So you want things like group dates, being spotted out together,' I reply, piecing the plan together in my head. 'The Tragedies would be useful for that. It would help the play, and you.'

Pierre nods in satisfaction. 'Exactly. It will be easy – you two can be photographed together in rehearsals, picking up lunch for the cast and crew, at parties together. All while building support for your play.'

'What about the LSDCATS?' I ask, remembering their first reply to my post. That hadn't gone over well online, but it showed that the LSDCATS saw us as rivals – people worthy enough for a response, for an attempt at damage control.

Lacey, who is sitting at the head of the conference table, makes a dismissive sound. 'They've gone into total silence after that terrible first tweet. They're likely going to stay that way until this blows over.'

'But it won't blow over,' I point out. 'Surely Zayan getting involved in our play will be another hit against them?'

'Exactly,' Lacey replies. 'And we're going to capitalize on the announcement of Zayan in your play. Really get some positivity thrown your way, in the face of the negativity surrounding the LSDCATS.'

I voice my worries, needing the reassurance. 'But what if, by doing this, we provoke the LSDCATS into retaliating? What if they do something bigger?'

'Bigger than an Oscar-nominated, Emmy Award-winning celebrity in the lead role?' Lacey asks, a smirk touching her lips. 'Once they know Zayan is involved, they will back down. Your play will wholeheartedly overshadow theirs, and they'll be busy fixing their image.'

I nod, despite the knot in my stomach. Throughout this back-and-forth, Zayan has said nothing, but when I flick my gaze to him, to see if he agrees, his is laser-focused on me.

'And when should we announce Zayan's involvement in the play?' I ask, turning back to Lacey, who glances between the two of us. 'Before this relationship begins, I need assurances of my own. The start of all this needs to coincide with The Tragedies' play announcement. If you're right about the power of speculation, that will be even better for the play. So, I agree, no relationship confirmations yet. Just being photographed together.'

Lacey has an impressed look glinting in her eyes. 'You sure know how to pick them, Zayan.'

Two emotions war within me: pride at being acknowledged with respect, and a hint of irritation at who I think she's referring to. The infamous ex-girlfriend: Laiba Siddiqi. I suppose it's something I have to get used to – the constant comparisons to the girl I don't know.

'That seems fine. A good plan,' Lacey finally says, and then she takes her leave. 'I apologize for having to duck out early, but I need to get to another meeting.'

Pierre claps his hands loudly, catching our attention. 'Now, let's focus on what you need to be wearing. Farah, you need bright-coloured clothes. Zayan is naturally in darker colours; that goes with the image we've crafted of a serious actor. But you need to be this new, exciting thing in his life.'

I ignore being referred to as a 'thing' and focus on the instruction instead. 'I don't want to look like a clown.'

'You won't,' Pierre assures me. 'Now, on to the photographs. Lacey will have paparazzi stationed in strategic places when you both are out together. They will take the shots and then leave. You two need to ensure you look your best. No arguments. Smiling is a must. Laughter is good. Farah, laugh for me.'

I feel my brows lift. 'Pardon?'

'Do it,' Pierre instructs. 'I need to see how you look when you're laughing.'

'This is ridiculous,' I snap. I know I should be used to acting on the spot, but this is starting to feel uncomfortable, like I'm being tested on something I wasn't even given time to prepare for.

'If you look ugly when you laugh, then this is a problem,' Pierre replies impatiently.

'I *don't*,' I argue, before turning to Zayan. 'This can't be normal.'

Zayan pins me with a sharp look, irritation loud in his voice. 'This isn't a joke, Farah.'

'I know that, because if it was a joke I'd be genuinely laughing,' I quip back, equally annoyed.

His self-control seems to be thinning, because he leans forward to say his next words. 'Are you taking this seriously? Or not? We have a lot riding on this, on getting this right, on convincing the public that we're in love. If you can't do it, say it now and save me the trouble. I need someone dependable.'

He holds my gaze with his. Hard. Harsh. A little wild. My heart thuds against my ribs, angry and overwhelmed by how much I've had to take on. But I force myself to stiffen my spine, to raise my chin and appear unaffected.

'I can do it,' I reply, my tone even despite my internal trembling. I turn to Pierre, press on a smile and fake a laugh.

Pierre's gaze swings between us before he responds. 'That's good. You look good. Let's move on to mannerisms together . . .'

I let Pierre's instructions wash over me, taking notes as he talks. I don't look at Zayan, fearing that if I do, I'll launch myself over the table and slap him. He's rude. He's broody. He's the antithesis of who I thought he was going to be.

I wish my dupatta had choked him instead.

For the next hour, Pierre relays more instructions on posture, on what to like on social media, on what to say, on what not to say, even on how to hold Zayan's hand – laced fingers, palm to palm. How to angle myself in front of a camera, how to pretend to look shy, how to look bold. My notebook is filled with ink and my wrist is aching from all I've written.

I'm grateful when Lacey pops her head in, hoping that she's come to set us free, but she only calls for Zayan. I slump in my chair, desperate for some way to get out of the room for a few moments.

'I need to use the bathroom,' I announce, just as Pierre takes a large lungful of breath between stretches of monologuing on how to sit with my legs crossed in front of the camera, so I give off a demure, ladylike look.

He waves me off, irritated to be interrupted. 'Go, but be back quickly. It's down the hall and to the left. Don't talk to anyone – I haven't trained you on what to say yet.'

I nod quickly and make my escape. The hallway is lined with doors, all grey with silver handles. I turn the corner, but come to a halt when I see Zayan leaning against the wall, Lacey standing in front of him, and I duck back behind the corner, hoping they haven't seen me. I wait for a couple of breaths, my ears straining to hear if they're walking into another room. But instead of footsteps, soft-spoken words fill the quiet.

'It was another rejection,' Lacey says, with such kindness even my heart aches a little.

'Which movie?' Zayan asks, voice devoid of emotion.

'The historical-fantasy one.'

The moan from Zayan is startling. I lean forward to sneak a peek, catching the way he tips his head back on the wall and presses his palms to his eyelids. Lacey makes an abrupt movement to try and place her hand on his arm but thinks better of it.

He wanted this role. Badly.

'They said that they loved your ability, but they're worried that the negative press surrounding you would bleed into the movie. The fans are still upset with you. They think you're selling out your culture. There's just too much negativity for a studio to risk hiring you. Still, that photo with Farah helped. They didn't say it explicitly, but it's clear: if you're able to change the public's perception of you after that TV series, you'll get more roles. You need this relationship to work, Zayan. A new love story trumps a bad TV series *and* a bad break-up.'

I look at Zayan and feel so keenly what he's feeling. The sharp edge of rejection is still fresh in my own mind – the dull thud of pain in your lungs, the mental games: *what could I have done differently?*

I knew the press was bad for Zayan, but I didn't know it was *this* bad. From a fan's perspective, you see that many actors bounce back from such blunders eventually. But here, being on the inside, it's clear how easy it is to be buried in the graveyard of failed careers.

Lacey leaves Zayan alone to contemplate all of this, turning on her heel and walking down another corridor. I should go too, but instead of briskly walking by and pretending I've heard nothing, I stop beside him. He drops his palms from his eyes, unable to hide his disbelief at me standing there.

I press my back to the wall opposite him. 'How many nos?'

He says nothing for a long moment. He doesn't have to share any of this with me. It's not part of the agreement. 'Seven, as of today.'

'Always the same reasoning?'

'Always.'

We lapse into silence. Seven movies. Seven rejections. Seven chances at a rebound taken away.

'I'm sorry,' I offer, 'for not realizing how serious this all was. I promise, I'm in this. A hundred per cent.'

Zayan swallows roughly. 'I know you are. And I'm sorry for being so harsh with you. I just – I can't take any more chances. I don't have any more chances. You're it. If this doesn't work, I'm not sure what else I can do.'

'We've got this, Zayan,' I reply determinedly. 'We're going to convince the public that we're in love and give them something else to focus on.'

A smile curves his lips. 'I like your confidence. It's an unfairly attractive quality.'

A blush colours my cheeks; my heart jumps in my chest. Half of me hopes I get used to ignoring his compliments, but the other half loves this feeling. This rush of excitement and pleasure.

His gaze travels over the warmth of my face, and, just like a flame being snuffed out, his expression shutters. His eyes meet mine, all the softness from before gone. All the vulnerability tucked into a box and stored away.

'I'm not looking for an actual relationship. Or any relationship for that matter,' Zayan says, his tone blunt. 'There is nothing more important to me than my career right now.'

My defences shoot up, along with my arms, which fold over my chest. Any warmth I'd felt before has turned cold. 'And what should I do with that information?'

'I just want to be absolutely clear. My actions towards you are always going to be calculated.' His tone is light, but his words are like arrows piercing my skin. 'Every touch, everything I say, everything I do with you will be part of our arrangement. This is a mutually beneficial relationship – you need me, and I need you. Let's not allow anything to complicate it.'

Embarrassment curdles in the pit of my stomach – I don't want Zayan to think I'm so soft-minded that I'll allow things like thinking he's good-looking or blushing at his flirting to disrupt everything. He's made it abundantly clear that he's unwilling to envision a long-term relationship. Which is fine for me, because when I'm ready for that, I'll be striving to find someone who will promise forever. Not a five-minute relationship that'll end in heartbreak.

Zayan Amin is clearly not that guy. But the arrogance and presumptuousness that *I'm* the one who's going to mess this plan up by developing real feelings is beyond offensive.

I hold his stare harshly, mouth pressed into a sharp line. 'I assure you, I have no misconceptions of what this is.'

'Good.'

'Good.'

And with that, we return to Pierre's torturous training.

Chapter Nine

The next day, I sit beside Zayan at a picnic table under the September sun, waiting for The Tragedies to show up. I have my textbook out, a bright-pink highlighter poised to underline another important paragraph – with the play taking up the majority of my headspace, it's vital for me to capture moments like this now, so I'm not drowning in work later.

'Are your friends usually this late?' Zayan asks, his tone naked with annoyance.

I roll my eyes, still irritated by the sight of him. Every time he so much as *glances* at me, I think of what he said at media training yesterday, and it makes me want to claw at him. 'I told them 2.15. It's 2.10. Maybe you should learn how to tell the time.'

He huffs, leaning his elbows on the table and dropping his head to hang. Before he can say anything, we're interrupted by a tentative voice.

'H-hi, are you Hari Fairbanks?' A little girl, maybe ten

years old, gently taps Zayan's elbow. His head snaps up, and she startles away before recognition makes her face light up with a smile.

'Hi,' Zayan says, and I almost do a double take at how soft his voice sounds. I crane my neck to get a good look at the smile curving his lips and the way he bends lower to talk to the girl at her own level. 'I most definitely am.'

Her eyes round with awe. 'I love you! You're my favourite person on *The Fairbanks*. I watch you every single night before bed.'

Zayan's smile is so wide, so genuine, that my heart does a little flip at the sight of it. How many people have wished – imagined, daydreamed – to have that smile shot their way?

'Well, it's an honour to be a favourite of yours,' Zayan says, all the seriousness in the world injected into his voice. 'Would you like an autograph?'

The little girl nods so hard I'm sure her head is going to fall off. She produces a slightly crumpled piece of paper, and it's only then that I notice her mother standing behind her. Zayan keeps his attention on his fan, signing his name, asking for hers, and making idle small talk. He even recites his catchphrase from *The Fairbanks*.

Where has this Zayan been for the last few days?

'Thank you so much,' the mother gushes after snapping at least ten photos. 'You're so lovely for entertaining us.'

Zayan shrugs humbly. 'I wouldn't be where I am without fans like your daughter. It's my pleasure.'

Truth rings from his words, so plain and honest, that

even the mother looks moved. Eventually, they start to leave, but not before the mother's gaze falls to me. I fidget awkwardly under the questioning look she directs my way. Zayan slides back on to the bench beside me, waving at the little girl, who keeps looking at him over her shoulder.

'That was nice of you,' I say, once we're alone again.

'Were you expecting me to be a jerk to my fans?'

I laugh, and his offended expression intensifies. 'I'm not sure what to expect of you. You're a constant surprise.'

I don't say it pleasantly, and he knows it. But if he feels guilty about how we ended things at the meeting, it doesn't show on his face.

'In all honesty, I thought you might find it annoying to be accosted by fans all the time,' I continue.

Zayan shakes his head, evidently displeased with my thought process. 'Hari fans are usually little kids, and they rarely want to sell my autograph unless they've got overbearing parents. Children aren't malicious like that.'

'Tell that to my seven-year-old cousins,' I quip back. 'They're mini-demons trapped in human bodies.'

'They're children,' he replies stubbornly. 'And children love Hari. I'll always be Hari to them.'

My ears perk up, and I almost feel like I'm mishearing that note of bitterness in his voice. That twinge of resignation. Maybe a combination of both.

But before I can form any sort of question about it, Zayan's expression turns neutral again.

'I think it's important to be kind to my fans. They got me to where I am today. They hold my future in their hands.'

'So do I,' I say, because it's true, and I want him to remember it.

His mouth – unwillingly, I imagine – lifts halfway to a smile.

♥

Anushka, David, Ben and Nur squish together on the other side of the picnic table, staring at Zayan and me like we've come from another planet.

'Thank you for agreeing to meet me,' Zayan begins, the perfect image of politeness once more. 'I know there was some *confusion* around our first meeting, but I'm Zayan Amin, and you've spoken to my agent about me starring in your play.' He leans closer to me, our elbows brushing. 'But before we get into all of that, I thought it'd be best to let you guys know that Farah and I are getting to know one another on a more personal level.'

Anushka's jaw drops, Nur's eyes go as wide as saucers, Ben's mouth twists, but David stares at us, unblinking.

'You're lying,' he says. 'You two aren't in a relationship.'

Zayan falters, clearly unprepared for such a plain, simple dismissal. 'Well, we aren't in a relationship yet. But we are getting to know one another in that capacity.'

'No,' David replies slowly. 'You aren't.'

'And why not?' Zayan finally asks, a note of exasperation rising in his voice.

David, with more flourish than necessary, pulls his phone out of his pocket. I can tell what's coming, and a full-blown grin threatens to explode the restraint I'm using to keep my face straight.

When Zayan and I were making our way to the table before The Tragedies showed up, he spent at least five minutes explaining how he wanted to take the lead on this first meeting. Maybe I was still feeling slightly petty about the meeting with Pierre, because I didn't let Zayan know that there was no way he could convince my friends about our alleged relationship. Instead, I agreed to let him try, simply because I *knew* it would be entertaining.

And I was right.

'Because Farah doesn't even like you,' David replies, eyeing Zayan in a way that says he doesn't like him either. He holds up a hand when Zayan begins to ready himself for an argument, and the pure, affronted look that paints itself on Zayan's face is hilarious. 'I know she doesn't,' David continues. 'I'm not paraphrasing here. Two days ago, after the whole cafe debacle, Farah's exact message on our group chat reads, "*Zayan Amin's ego is so large I'm surprised he was able to fit into the cafe in the first place.*"'

Zayan turns to look at me, while David carries on.

'She goes on to say, "*He thinks he's so hot, all because he did* The Fairbanks *and a couple of good movies. He's not that great. He's no Leonardo DiCaprio, but I bet he thinks he is. That conceited jerk.*"'

I bite on both sides of my cheek to stop myself from laughing as Zayan's eyebrow lifts.

'And, finally, an all-time favourite. "*Let me tell you guys *now, if I ever see Zayan Amin again, I will choke him with my dupatta and laugh."* '

A giggle finally escapes my lips when Zayan silently mouths, *Choke me?*

'See?' David says, with a satisfied tinge to his voice. 'Farah hates your guts.'

'Really?' Zayan hisses to me. 'I'm not conceited. It's called having confidence in my abilities.'

When I shrug back, he sighs and assesses the situation. His gaze roves over The Tragedies, who watch him back with equal calculation, before his eyes meet mine again. Except, this time, there's no outrage widening his pupils. Instead, an unspoken question sits between us.

Can I really trust them?

I know that there are some secrets I simply won't share with The Tragedies (or anyone) – what happened with the LSDCATS flashes in my mind, but I bury that deep at the back of my memories. But I trust them enough for this.

I lean into Zayan, and he mimics me, so our heads are bent close together. I ignore the fact that I can see the faint imprint of his dimple in his cheek and focus on convincing him. The Tragedies watch us, each with varying looks of bemusement painted on their faces.

'I trust them,' I whisper, and his eyes narrow. 'Seriously, I trust them. And you've got to trust me for this to work, OK?'

He takes a moment; his eyes watch me with such intensity that I want to look away. But I don't. I let him see that I'm serious about this. That I need him to treat me like an equal in this partnership, and value my opinions as well.

'Fine,' he whispers back. 'But we're not telling any other friends, OK? The fewer people who know, the better. So, it's these guys and no one else. Agreed?'

I grin, happy to have won this round. 'Agreed.'

'You know we can hear you, right?' Ben cuts in, brows raised.

Zayan pulls away from our little bubble, turning back to face The Tragedies. 'Fine, we're not in a relationship.'

'Knew it,' David replies, a smug smile pushing at the corners of his mouth.

'But,' Zayan continues, ignoring David's triumph, 'we are in the middle of a business agreement.'

'What?' Ben asks suspiciously. He turns his attention to me, worry lacing his words. 'He hasn't forced you to do anything, has he?'

Ben's concern warms me inside and out, but it makes Zayan scoff in outrage. 'Believe me, I don't think anyone can force Farah to do anything,' he shoots back, and I grin. 'In exchange for my participation in your play, Farah has agreed to simulate a relationship with me for the public.'

'Why should we trust you to follow through?' Anushka asks, scarily perceptive. 'What do you have to gain from all of this?'

Zayan looks slightly uncomfortable, clearly weighing up how much he's willing to share. 'As you are likely all aware, I'm coming off a particularly bad TV series.'

'A racist TV series,' Nur corrects.

Zayan winces, before agreeing plainly. 'Racist TV series.'

His reaction settles something in me – a part of me had

wondered if he had internalized this racism and was OK with the show, but from the sheer pain in his expression it's clear he didn't agree with its content either.

It still begs the question, *why do it in the first place?*

'The backlash from that has been severely damaging to my career,' Zayan continues. 'Bad enough that I'm not getting booked because of the negative press. My agent and publicist believe a new love in my life will engage the public more positively, fix my reputation and divert attention from my mistakes. Hence Farah.'

'So it's a publicity stunt?' Nur asks.

Zayan nods. 'Essentially, yes. We'll fake-date, and in return, I'll star in your play, alongside Farah.'

'But, of course, I'll audition for the lead role –' I interject, not wanting The Tragedies to think I'm getting something I don't deserve, but Zayan cuts me off.

'You have to be my co-star,' he says stubbornly. 'It'll look like our relationship came out of nowhere if you don't.'

I shoot The Tragedies a pained look, even though my heart is thundering in my chest. The lead! That is my dream.

'Look,' Zayan continues, 'I'll fund your play. I'll help you not only rival the LSDCATS but beat them too. All in exchange for Farah being the lead and in a fake relationship with me.'

'And what if we don't agree to this plan? Do we even need you? The LSDCATS have been dead silent lately – maybe we don't need you to boost our play at all,' Anushka says, and heat burns my cheeks.

I thought The Tragedies would be all for this – they were the ones who pushed for the first meeting with Zayan. But I should've consulted them, at some point, about the fake dating. It's not exactly betrayal that's passing over The Tragedies' expressions, but it's something uncomfortable. I hate that I've put it there, that they think I haven't thought of them.

'The LSDCATS have learned their lesson after getting attacked on social media. They are going to stay silent as long as it suits them,' Zayan explains patiently. 'It's not a rivalry to them; they're just waiting for the dust to settle before re-emerging. If you seriously want to end their reign of power and influence, you need to capitalize on your popularity, build intrigue around your play. I can do that. I am a walking story for the press. A story that you need.'

I see The Tragedies thawing, but I also see their worry about the LSDCATS still coming out on top. To hammer away their final doubts about the plan, I rush in with my own assurances.

'If you're worried about the legitimacy of all of this, I've got a contract drawn up about the play, which you can all look over before signing today. And this is beneficial for both sides. Aside from beating the LSDCATS, we'll also have directors, talent agents, casting agents there on opening night. That way, we have an opportunity to make any of our ambitions come true. And –' I take in a sharp breath – 'if you don't want me to be the lead because there's too much conflict of interest, then it's fine. We'll work something out.'

'All right,' David cuts in. 'Assuming the contract checks out, I'm all for this plan. And Farah, as much as it kills me to agree with him, Zayan is right. If we really want to use this publicity to boost the play, you need to be the lead alongside him.'

I wait, with bated breath, for the rest of the group to agree. Slowly, one by one, each of them gives their assent, and the knot of worry loosens in my chest.

'We should really get started with the play,' Anushka adds, a serious look on her face.

'I agree,' Nur chimes in. 'First things first: we need a stage. The LSDCATS are going to be hosting *Romeo and Juliet* in their own theatre, but that's because their theatre is amazing. It's got velvet seats.'

'Don't worry about the stage,' Zayan steps in, all confident and self-assured. 'I'll get you guys a theatre.'

'How?' Ben asks.

Zayan shrugs. 'I'll cash in a favour.'

There's a moment of tension. I see it in all of them. David's narrowed eyes, Nur's uncomfortable smile, Ben's straight face and Anushka drumming her fingers on the table. This is our plan. Our fight. Not Zayan's. Trusting him with something as important as the stage we stand on is a leap, but it's one each of us is going to have to take. My nails dig crescent moons into my palms as I try to get a grip on my flailing feelings.

We need to use Zayan, the same way he's using us. There's no point in this relationship if we don't.

'Good,' I cut in briskly, swallowing my worry and trying

to appear as confident as Zayan sounds. 'Now that that's sorted, we need a script. David?'

I wait for one of them to fight back against my sudden control over the conversation, but David simply nods after a moment of tense silence.

'I can have a script ready in a week.'

'That's brilliant,' I reply, launching into an explanation. 'Once we have the script, Zayan and I will start hinting at our relationship and his involvement in the play. It will drum up support for both things.'

'It'll also fit the timeline,' Zayan adds.

'When will this relationship end, by the way?' Ben asks, amused. 'How long will our play be?'

'The same as the LSDCATS, with the same opening night – the first of December. Almost two months from now. We'll break up right after,' I say. 'David, do you have any ideas for which play we'll do?'

Zayan interrupts. 'Surely it's got to be *Romeo and Juliet*, like the LSDCATS?'

'That's what I thought,' Ben replies. My face crinkles with annoyance, the urge for an eye-roll itching my eyelids. 'But from the way Farah's looking, I think not.'

'We're not trying to *be* the LSDCATS, we're trying to rival them, compete with them,' I attempt to explain. 'We need to stray away from the usual.'

'I understand where you're coming from – you want to support marginalized voices – but you've got to be realistic too,' Zayan argues. 'There's a reason people flock to the theatre to watch stagings of Shakespeare's plays.

They're well known, well respected and have universal themes.'

'They're only universally understood because plays from other cultures have been ignored,' I shoot back, irritation lining my words.

Zayan turns his body to face me fully. 'But no one is going to show up to see a play with a story they've never heard of, produced by someone they haven't heard of.'

'Good thing we have you, then,' I reply acidly. 'You're our publicity ticket. If your name isn't going to get people in the seats, then really, why are you here?'

His jaw clenches, his mouth snapping shut. We stand off against one another, his arms folded over his chest – my eyes *do not* linger on the curves of his biceps – as my hands form into half fists.

'Yeah, so you wanted us to believe that you two are in a relationship?' David breaks in, amused.

Zayan's attention turns to David, but before he can open his mouth and say something possibly insulting, I step in.

I soften my tone but keep a firmness there too. I can concede to keeping our relationship a secret, I'll go through the media training, but I refuse to let this play be seen as a copy of the LSDCATS. 'Choosing a play that showcases marginalized voices is a good reflection on you – fighting against racism, when you did a TV series that perpetrated it. You need to convince your fans you're not still selling out your culture. Won't participating in a play that celebrates it be a perfect way to do that?'

The fight loosens in Zayan. 'Fine. What do you have in mind?'

'Well, what do you guys think this play needs?' I ask The Tragedies directly, my tone shining with an apology for not involving them before. I want *their* opinions, their thoughts. This is for all of us.

'We need something that matches *Romeo and Juliet*,' Anushka says.

'Something tragic,' Nur adds.

'Something romantic,' Ben says.

'Something that's going to make people laugh,' David offers.

Zayan nods. 'And we need something that's going to resonate with the people watching it. You need a story that's simple enough to do in two months, but with enough depth to leave people moved.'

I nod, moderately cushioned by his well-meaning suggestion. I reach for my Kindle; I've got loads of plays on it, original texts that I like to flick through and practise lines from. There's a whole collection of stories I've kept from different parts of Pakistan – tales I began to study when I wanted to read more literature from my own country, rather than just the stories the school curriculum forced me to learn. My eyes land on a love story, fraught with forbidden intentions, tangled with jealousy and poisoned hearts.

'I've got it,' I announce, while turning my Kindle screen to face the group. 'How about the story of *Heer Ranjha*?'

@TheTragedies: We are so excited to share that we are beginning auditions for our play. All you need to do is submit a tape of yourself performing whatever piece of dialogue you like – this is open internationally too. In the meantime, guess in the comments which play we're putting on!

Chapter Ten

ONE WEEK LATER

'You like it?' Zayan asks, voice dripping with smugness.

'Like' is such an inconsequential word for what I'm feeling right now.

The stage I'm standing on is massive; I feel small and large all at the same time. I look up at the ceiling to see it's painted with stars and moons – they're illuminated by the glorious hanging chandelier that makes golden light shine over the theatre. The smooth dark-brown wooden floor is sturdy but worn, like it's been walked upon by a thousand different stories.

I inhale deeply, and the faint scent of dust coupled with cleaning polish invades my senses. I stare at the empty forest-green velvet seats, a feeling of pure excitement coursing through my veins. In two months, these seats will be full of eager people, here to watch *our* play. And among them will be casting agents, directors, talent scouts – people who could take my dream of being an actress and make it a reality.

'It's amazing,' I whisper, dropping my gaze back to Zayan, both of us facing one another now.

'It's more than amazing, child; this theatre is magic.'

I startle violently at the unexpected voice behind me, crashing right into Zayan – my face smacks into his chest. He steadies me with his hands on my forearms, a rumble of laughter vibrating from his chest against the skin of my cheek. I immediately step out of his hold to give myself some space to breathe, my cheeks burning. I turn on my heel to face the person behind me.

The voice turns out to belong to a man; he's short, his back slightly curved with age, his hair a brilliant shock of white, his skin weathered and tanned. He wears lime-green overalls, with a gold pin on his breast pocket that reads MARVIN.

'Uh, hello,' I say, my cheeks still feeling warm and my heart running a mile a minute in my chest.

'Who are you?' Marvin demands, and I realize now that he has an Irish accent. 'Who are *both* of you?' His shrewd gaze narrows on Zayan.

'Zayan Amin.' Zayan introduces himself with practised formality, sticking his hand out for the man to shake. Marvin looks at it with all the suspicion of a true-crime detective until Zayan lets his hand fall. 'We're going to be hosting her play here.'

Zayan jerks his thumb towards me, and I try not to flounder under Marvin's intense stare.

'Today?' Marvin demands. 'The theatre is not ready for a play for today.'

'No, no,' I hurry to correct him. 'In two months. But we will be using the Limelight Theatre for rehearsals – and today we're using it for a photo shoot.'

'Photo shoot?' Marvin throws another question my way. 'What for?'

Zayan's about to step in, but my mouth is running at full speed.

'Well, The Tragedies – that's what our group is called – need promo material. We haven't announced what play we're doing or that Zayan is a part of it yet. He's this big actor, in case that wasn't clear before. But that leaves a window of two days for us to get things like posters, leaflets and programmes ready. So Zayan's agent suggested a photo shoot, and she's got us a photographer, who signed an agreement to be discreet about the job until we announce Zayan's involvement tomorrow, and here we are.' I finish, sucking in a sharp breath.

Marvin looks between Zayan and me once more, as if trying to work out whether we're genuine. 'Well, that seems . . . logical,' he says distrustfully. 'I'm Marvin. I'm the caretaker of the Limelight Theatre. Been here since its doors first opened. And I make it my personal duty to ensure that everything here runs smoothly.'

There's a vague threat in his voice, one that has Zayan and me nodding like we're bobbleheads. Only once Marvin looks satisfied with his observations does he leave – going back through the stage wings into the darkness and the unknown.

'I bet he scares the ghosts away too,' Zayan muses, breaking the silence first.

I turn to face him again, the two of us at the centre of the stage now. He looks entirely unfazed by this entire interaction, while my face is only just starting to cool down.

'Ghosts?' I ask.

His brows lift, a smile curving his lips. 'You do know that every theatre has a ghost, right?'

'No,' I say uncertainly. 'I did not know that.'

'There's a light that stays on every night in the theatre called the ghost light. It's a way to appease them. And those two seats up there?' Zayan points at two seats in the balcony that have been cordoned off. 'They're kept empty for every show, so, the ghosts have somewhere to sit and watch.'

I look at him again, searching his face for levity, but he looks entirely serious.

'I'm not scared of ghosts,' I say, just in case he's trying to rattle me.

'No thespian can be,' Zayan says solemnly.

I go still, feeling nervous. I think he might actually be serious.

And then he cracks a grin. His laughter is unexpected, but the sheer warmth of it makes me smile in reply.

'You were genuinely terrified, weren't you?' Zayan teases.

'I hate you,' I say, swatting him on the arm. But, inside, I'm not really feeling much animosity towards him. Much less than usual.

We've seen each other only twice this week – aside from today – and that was for media training before we have our debut date tomorrow. Each time we're forced into one another's presence, I brace myself for his cold front, but today he's the most relaxed I've seen. His laughter eventually dies, a smile of amusement still touching his lips. I find myself wanting to hold on to this version of him, the one that is open and amused, not closed off and cold.

'So, are you ready for tomorrow?' I ask. 'Our first date?'

His gaze lifts to mine, his hands lacing behind his head. 'I'm always ready to put on a show. The question is: are you ready?'

'Ye-e-s, I am ready . . .' I say slowly, but then I pause, weighing up whether I want to tell him the truth. When his eyes narrow at me, I decide to spill everything. 'I've just been getting a lot of hate online since our photo went viral.'

I pull out my phone to show him my social-media accounts. Because of the LSDCATS' continued silence and the sense of victory I felt because of it, and after our meeting with The Tragedies at the park, I decided to finally, formally reveal my identity. I did a long Twitter thread on how I wrote the initial Tumblr post, and why I felt it was important to share The Tragedies' stories. That reveal made all my social-media accounts blow up. I'm nearing 10,000 followers on Twitter and 5,000 on Instagram.

Watching those numbers tick upwards, second by second, lit an ember of hope in my chest – a hope that this may actually work – until I saw the responses from some of Zayan's fans. Some of them were downright cruel, calling me every name under the sun, saying I was a mistake for him.

'Are you sure our plan is going to work?' I ask Zayan,

my eyes fixed on my phone as I scroll through the comments. Worry knots itself tightly in my stomach. 'Your fans hate me; I think we should postpone our first date.'

Zayan sighs, still amused, and pulls the phone out of my hand. I make a noise of protest, lunging for it, but he shoves it into the pocket of his dark-grey sweatpants.

'Stop reading those comments; those aren't my fans. They're a small number of individuals who believe they have some sort of ownership over me just because I'm on their TV screens. We're not postponing tomorrow. It's time to start garnering public interest, which means we need to be seen together.'

'Fine! I'll meet you tomorrow. Now, give me back my phone,' I demand, holding my hand out to him.

Zayan grins, leaning forward to hand back my phone, and I try not to shiver at the feeling of his fingertips brushing against my palm. I have got to get these feelings back in order.

I step further away from Zayan when the Limelight's doors swing open and Marvin comes in again – this time with the photography crew and Anushka, David and Nur behind. Less than a handful of people, to ensure Zayan's involvement stays a secret – at least until tomorrow.

'This your lot?' Marvin asks, lifting one very white, very bushy eyebrow.

'Yes,' I reply, still nervous around the cantankerous caretaker. Marvin makes a noise that's a cross between a humph and cough, before shooting one more suspicious look our way and leaving.

'Well, he seems like a peach,' David announces, a grin on his face.

'Like a peach?' Anushka mimics. 'Seriously, are you a hundred years old or something?'

'It's a very common phrase,' David says defensively, and I can see him gearing up for a squabble.

Thankfully, Nur interjects. 'OK, let's agree to disagree and get this photo shoot started.' Her eyes turn to me, a devilish smile on her lips. 'And you, Farah Sheikh – meet me in the dressing room.'

♥

Zayan and I stand on the stage, him dressed in a fitted off-white shalwar kameez and a sage-green waistcoat that sits snugly across his chest, and me in a lavender lehenga that's been embroidered with silver patterns. When I first stepped on to the stage in costume, it felt magical. Nur has outdone herself, considering she's had a week to get this together. Anushka and David were awed by the outfit. Even Zayan's eyes had widened with appreciation.

'OK!' the photographer, Jazz, says loudly. 'I think we have a game plan. I want to have a couple of simple shots of the two of you together. Nothing too complicated. How about we start with Zayan standing behind Farah, looking down at her with a look of love in his eyes, and, Farah, you stare straight ahead at the camera with a coy look in your eyes, OK?'

My first instinct is to say no. The thought of Zayan

standing that close to me, looking down at me with anything other than irritation, makes my chest tighten.

Don't get me wrong. I *don't* want a real relationship with Zayan – he's made it very clear that everything he does with me will be faked, and I have no time for emotionally unavailable men – but it's hard not to instinctively react to how attractive he is. If he had some flaws that would have helped, but everything about him is near perfect. The faint dimples in his cheeks, the way his hair curls just right, the way he fills out everything he wears like it's a second skin . . . does this guy even know what 'baggy' means?

'Farah?' Anushka asks, concern leaking from her voice.

I can feel Zayan's eyes on me, and I imagine his gaze is taunting, his ego inflating with every second of my silence.

I knew you would complicate this. You can't handle being around me.

'Yes,' I say quickly, pressing a smile to my lips. Anushka's eyes narrow, but she doesn't say anything. The crew becomes a chaos of noise, getting into position, and I flutter nervously, trying to work out where I should go.

Zayan has no questions about where to move. He falls into place behind me, his chin ghosting the crook of my neck, his eyes gazing forward at the camera. I find myself slotting into place as well, my hands lacing over my stomach, my expression smoothing into a look of affection. I stare at the camera, at Jazz, at David, at Anushka, at the four-person photography crew. They all look enraptured, delighted, like an audience watching a play.

And that's when it hits me.

This is happening. This is really, *really* happening. We're taking promotional photos for a play that I'm going to star in. Beside an Emmy Award-winning actor. I'm going to be on stage once more. But instead of feeling joy at this thought, I find that from the deepest, darkest depths of my mind a voice unearths itself. Henry. The director from the LSDCATS.

Unsuitable.

My entire body stiffens, like I've turned into stone. Jazz pauses, stops taking pictures. Zayan's gaze lifts to my face, analysing whatever emotion must be displayed so plainly across it.

'Is everything OK?' Jazz asks.

I open my mouth to say that it's nothing. To take a deep breath and let myself treat this like an acting exercise. Except I'm finally realizing what I've agreed to. Before, I was running on adrenaline, on confidence, on the desperate need to get back on stage. But now that I'm here, about to act, I'm filled with bone-deep terror that I've made a mistake.

That I'm not good enough to be doing this.

'Farah?' Zayan murmurs in my ear.

'I can't – this is all too real,' I whisper. White spots from the bright lights dance across my vision. 'We haven't announced your involvement yet – it's not too late to stop –'

'Maybe we could try a different pose?' Zayan interrupts me, turning his attention to Jazz. He's the epitome of calm professionalism. 'We could act out a scene, and you could get some natural shots.'

'Uh, sure,' Jazz says, eyeing me uncertainly, 'if that's OK with you, Farah?'

I don't want to act out a scene. In fact, this might be the only time I want to flee the stage. And I hate that. I never would have felt this way if the LSDCATS audition hadn't happened. But it did happen, and I need to do something to stop Henry's words taunting me on a loop.

'Which scene?' I ask, my voice sounding faraway to my own ears.

'Just follow my lead,' Zayan says, his hands clasping my arms to force me to look at him.

His eyes are shaded by the lights, and his face is drawn with serious lines and something akin to understanding.

'Tell me, Heer, do the stars bewitch you?' The sound of Zayan's voice pulls me into the scene – all deep and angry. When I look at him, I see Ranjha in his place. My forbidden love. Not the irritating, good-looking boy I sometimes want to punch in the throat. The sight of him taking this seriously shifts something in my mind. 'Do they make you believe that my love for you is unreal? Unimaginable? Untouch—'

'Don't patronize me,' I interrupt in a half whisper, as if palace guards could be listening at any moment. 'You have the privilege to feel more. To feel everything so plainly. So blatantly. Duty doesn't weigh on your shoulders. Not like it does on mine. So, yes, I stare at the stars instead of you. Because if I shifted my focus –' I move closer to Zayan, my gaze sliding over his face like I'm trying to commit his every feature to memory – 'I'd never stop looking. I'd spend hour upon hour memorizing the lines of your face.' I reach out like I'm going to trace the sharpness of his cheekbone. The doubts I felt before are faded, belonging to an entirely different girl. Only Heer remains.

Zayan's hand raises to meet mine, before clenching shut in agony because our characters are forbidden from one another. I'm so lost in the scene, but in the distance, I hear the camera shutter going off. I wait for him to say his next line, but he surprises me instead.

'I think it's time for your first lesson,' Zayan says, quiet enough that only I hear.

Confusion pulls me out of Heer and back into Farah. 'What are you talking about?'

'You said you wanted me to teach you, right?'

I want you to teach me everything you know about acting – on film and on stage. I want your knowledge. Train me. Make me better than I am.

I did say that, and now I'm kind of regretting it.

'What's the lesson?' I ask, insecurity creeping into my voice.

Zayan's eyes soften ever so slightly. 'Every time you get a new role, you're going to be afraid.' I flinch, but his gaze pins me in place. 'You're going to doubt. But fear is just another part of acting. It's something you learn to live with, something to use.'

My heart is thrumming in my chest in response to his words.

'I know you thought you couldn't do it, Farah. But what you just did there, the way you embodied the character – that's something raw and dynamic. Something that should be polished and refined. You're meant for the stage.'

The way he's staring at me now makes me believe I can do anything in the world – I can fly up to the moon, cup it between my palms and take it home with me, as long as Zayan keeps looking at me like that. This is the only thing and everything I've ever wanted to hear. And to hear it from him means more than I thought it would.

'The only real question is: how badly do you want to be an actress? Do you still want it, despite the fear?' he whispers, and I think of him at his agent's office. How deeply the rejections have carved into him – and yet, he's still standing here. He's going to extreme lengths to save his career.

His desperation matches my own, because there is nothing I want more than to be on stage. To prove the LSDCATS wrong. To be an actress one day.

I tilt my head closer to his, let a smile play on my lips and gaze up at him like we're madly in love.

And, once again, the camera shutter goes off.

Chapter Eleven

On the first of October, Zayan Amin and I set the timer running on our fake relationship.

We're standing in line at my all-time, hands-down favourite bubble tea store, Bubble-Me-Mine, and usually I'd be thrilled to be here. In fact, I recommended this place *because* of how much joy it usually brings me – it's the place Amal, Maha and I go to whenever we want to celebrate something: a passing grade, a therapy session attended, a milestone reached.

I thought it would be the perfect place for our first date. We'd be photographed walking out of the store carrying a collection of drinks to take to The Tragedies for our meeting ahead of the first rehearsal tomorrow. It would be fun, a little mysterious – the perfect beginning.

But ever since I got here and found Zayan standing in line, we've been encased in this awkward silence. He's had this Joker-like smile plastered on his face, and he keeps looking out of the window for something. He's inattentive, twitchy and just plain weird. So very different from the boy who was calming my nerves on stage yesterday.

'You look like I'm torturing you,' Zayan hisses suddenly, and I jerk my gaze away from the list of drinks Nur has messaged me. The rest of The Tragedies are at the Limelight, waiting for our arrival. He looks fancier today, less laid back in his green turtleneck and tailored jeans. His hair's been tamed too – or as controlled as it can be. 'Smile a little.'

'I think you're doing enough smiling for the two of us,' I murmur, a small frown taking shape instead. 'Also, we don't need to smile yet. We can fake it once we're outside the cafe.'

Zayan throws me a look that screams about how dense I'm being. I shrug helplessly, looking around to see what it is that's got him so agitated. A few people have begun to recognize Zayan, but no one has come up to ask for an autograph. I haven't even heard a shout of 'Hari Fairbanks!' yet.

'We're being watched,' Zayan says finally, and the corner of his fake smile drops to a flat line. 'You do know that, don't you?'

'What?' I ask.

'Paid paparazzi, remember?' he hisses, like it's the most obvious thing in the world. 'Lacey tipped off some reporters to get a couple of good shots of us out today. Expect to be tomorrow's front page. And it would be even better if you could smile, so the world doesn't think I'm holding you hostage.'

'I thought we'd only be photographed *out*side. Not in.' I force a smile on to my lips, despite my cheeks burning in embarrassment. It *is* obvious now that he's said it. There's one guy sitting at a lone table, his camera angled towards us. I don't know how I missed it. Pierre's lesson about paparazzi, and how I needed to control my immediate response to them, surfaces in my mind. Zayan rubs a hand over his face, like he can scrub the negative emotion from it.

He speaks quietly again, trying not to be overheard by anyone as we wait for our turn to be served. 'I'm sorry. I should've told you beforehand, and not just expected you to know.' I look up to meet his eyes, and they're shadowed with sincerity. 'Paparazzi sometimes try to hide in plain sight to get a better shot. My life is very intentional, Farah. From the pictures I post to the coffee cups I'm holding to the brand of every article of clothing I wear . . . Everything about my life is carefully curated, and for that reason I'm aware of my surroundings at all times.'

As Zayan explains his way of life with an unaffected tone, my heart sinks. Not in disappointment, but in pity. He says it so easily, but it sounds hard – to live your life like it's a museum for others to visit. I love acting, but there's a relief in knowing once I'm off the stage I'm allowed to feel what I want to feel.

'But isn't that lonely?' I blurt out, my thoughts loosening my tongue.

Zayan's lips flatline into a frown.

Stop it. Don't ask him. Don't. Ask. Him.

But his silence is starting to become so unbearable that I blurt out the next question. 'How did Laiba handle it?'

As soon as I say it, I wince internally. Maybe even externally. Obviously, right now he won't want to discuss his ex-girlfriend – the one I have a sneaking suspicion he's still in love with, given that he's sworn off relationships.

Zayan's eyes flash with something harsh, a muscle in his jaw jumping from how tight he's got. 'She's in the business as well,' he mutters, sounding robotic as he speaks of his ex-relationship. 'She knows how to handle herself.'

The 'unlike you' sits between us, unsaid. I'm about to apologize for bringing her up when he continues.

'I'd be less concerned about my lifestyle, and more about your appearance from now on,' he says, eyes dropping to my upper body. Had it been any other guy, I'd have called him out on it, but Zayan's not leering – he's analysing. 'What *are* you wearing, actually?'

I look down at my outfit. Per Pierre's request, I'm wearing my bright plum-purple short kurti stitched with gold designs on the borders. I got Maha to do my hair – after deep-conditioning it with my go-to Moroccan hair oil – in an intricate fish-tail plait to finish the outfit off. I left the flat to the sound of wolf-whistles from the girls. I even got The Tragedies' approval – especially after Nur helped me pick out this outfit, since she *is* a first-year fashion student.

'I'm wearing a kurti with a twist – you see, it's short enough to be considered a shirt, but it obviously isn't,' I reply. 'Why?'

'It's just very . . .' He pauses, searching for the right word. 'Pakistani.'

I'm instantly offended at his off-handed tone. 'I *am* British-Pakistani.'

'I know you are. It's just – you wear your culture a lot. Don't you want to fit into *this* country's aesthetic? Don't people stare at you on the street?' Zayan asks, his voice taking on a genuinely curious tone.

I shrug, uncaring. 'Sure. But it's London; people wear wilder things. And I'm comfortable in my kurtis and kameezes – why should I sacrifice that?'

'Because people will always know you're South Asian,' Zayan replies.

'Why is that a problem?' I ask. 'Anyway, unless I'm dressed in Pakistani clothing, no one has ever guessed where I'm from correctly. I've had everything from "Are you from Saudi Arabia?" to "Wow, I've never heard an American accent like that!" But people never guess South Asian.'

Zayan's reply is terse, the line of his broad shoulders tense. 'You've got to be a digestible version of yourself. That means dressing a little more Western instead of Asian, like I do.'

That swell of pity rises inside me again. I wonder if this is why he took the TV-show deal, because he couldn't *see* the harm he was doing to himself.

'You do realize you're giving up your culture for your career, right? You're trying to fit into Hollywood's version of diversity by toning down the very thing that makes you different.'

Clearly, Zayan doesn't see that my response comes from a place of concern, because his next words are intended to hurt.

'If you want to wrap yourself in the Pakistani flag, feel free to do so. But don't expect it to be easy achieving your dreams because you've done so. Lesson number two, Farah: come to terms with the idea of sacrificing something you love for what you want.'

'I want *good* advice. If you don't have any, then maybe you aren't exactly the best actor to be learning from,' I shoot back, wishing the boy from yesterday would make an appearance today.

But my cheeks burn with the searing realization that he's not wrong. Not entirely. He can wield his stardom like a sword, and I have no accolade-shaped weapons for myself.

The silence from before returns with a vengeance. I force a smile on to my lips again. The stretch of it feels unnatural. The paparazzi better get a good shot of us. Zayan's eyes trail over my face; his own is lined with a look of something I can't place.

When it's our turn to order, I quickly request my taro milk tea and The Tragedies' orders too, before letting Zayan do his own. His brow furrows as he looks over the menu. I'd have helped him if he wasn't being so prickly.

'Uh, could I get one mangonada, please?' Zayan asks, with a lilt at the end of his question.

The Bubble-Me-Mine girl nods and goes off to make his drink. We stand in utter silence, and I avoid looking directly at him. A part of me wishes I could time-travel back and stop myself from questioning him, but at the same time I'm glad I did.

Unintentionally, I'm sure, Zayan's unveiled another part of himself. I know he's ambitious, but I never knew how much he was willing to give up to get where he wants to be. I can't see myself doing the same in his situation. I can't imagine giving up my sense of home.

'What the –?' Zayan's bitten-off curse has my attention snapping back towards him in a flash.

He's staring, half horrified and half awed, at the enormous drink being handed to him. The mangonada is sunset-coloured, with a tamarind candy straw and black tapioca pearls at the base. It's much larger than my taro milk tea, which is sitting right beside it, along with the rest of The Tragedies' drinks.

'Would you like a large straw with that, sir?' the Bubble-Me-Mine lady asks, and Zayan levels her with such an incredulous look that I can't help the laughter that escapes my lips.

He shoots me a glare, making me laugh even harder, before gingerly picking up his order. I grab mine too, taking my first sip of sweet, vanilla-like goodness. I love this drink. Almost as much as chai. Almost.

I watch Zayan take a large sip of his own, and it doesn't go well when the slush of his mangonada gets stuck in the straw. The sight of him, cheeks hollowed, angrily staring down at his cup, has me laughing so hard that the tapioca ball I was meant to be swallowing gets half stuck in my throat. The combination of laughter and choking leaves me wheezing breathlessly, clutching Zayan's arm for stability.

'We look like idiots,' Zayan hisses in my direction, not shaking off my arm, eyeing the cameras trained on him. 'Stop choking, I am begging you.'

My eyes are watering, laughter still bubbling in my chest as I recover.

'Thanks for the help,' I gasp sarcastically.

Before Zayan can say anything in return, the Bubble-Me-Mine lady offers him some advice. 'You need to suck less aggressively,' she says, gesturing to his drink.

Zayan catches my eyes. 'If you laugh again, Farah –'

I shake my head, stifling my laughter, face warming as he takes a gentler sip.

'It's good,' he announces, and I roll my eyes.

We finally take our leave then. I help him by taking half the drinks, balancing the paper cup-holder in my hands, my laughter replaced with the silence from our earlier conversation. But before we exit the store, he hesitates.

'What?' I ask softly, trying not to attract any unwanted attention.

His jaw works, as if he wants to say something but isn't sure about it.

'We have a job to do,' I remind him, and his gaze snaps to mine.

He gives me the barest of nods, squares his shoulders and swallows whatever he was trying to articulate from before. As we step out of the store, our harsh exchange turns into October mist, and our expressions transform from armour to the gooey softness of two people in the beginnings of love.

We slip seamlessly into our roles, fake smiles and all.

♥

My cheeks hurt from how hard I fake-smiled all the way to the Limelight. We're let in by a disgruntled Marvin, who I'm starting to believe really does live here. The minute we step through the stage door – marked by a comedy-and-tragedy mask-shaped knocker – I let my smile drop and pull my drink out of the cup holder.

'Well done, Farah,' Zayan comments, but I don't reply. I don't trust myself not to snap at him.

I find The Tragedies all huddled in the middle of the stage, staring down at Nur's phone. Dread balls up in the pit of my stomach, turning the sweetness of the bubble tea into a sharp taste against the roof of my mouth.

'What's happened?' I ask urgently, making my way to the stage, Zayan hot on my heels.

Anushka shoves the phone under my nose, taking the drinks from my hands. I stare down at her screen, the brightness stinging my eyes.

'Uff, your screen is so bright,' Zayan mumbles, and I realize he's standing right behind me, reading over my shoulder. I create some distance between the two of us and the warmth he exudes, still holding on to my irritation as I focus on the Instagram post in front of me.

TheatreSpiller: Well, well, well! Do we have news for you! Turns out the special co-star for The Tragedies' play is none other than Zayan Amin. Need proof? Look at these photos of him and his co-star posing as their characters. And if you want to be even more surprised, the play they're doing is *Heer Ranjha* – a story reminiscent of *Romeo and Juliet*. Now, if you ask us, it sounds like The Tragedies are just a *little* obsessed with the LSDCATS, but then again, that might be their whole MO.

'H-how did they get this information?' I ask, and for one wild, incomprehensible moment, I think the account posting is the LSDCATS. But then I remember their deafening social-media silence, and how sure Lacey was that Zayan's presence would mean their defeat – not a retaliation. 'It's impossible. We haven't even told our picks for the cast that they've been chosen yet.'

Today we were going to be finalizing the cast list, and then we were going to have our first rehearsal tomorrow. If that went as smoothly as we hoped, we'd then announce Zayan's involvement. But now? Now our plans have been completely upended.

'I think it's pretty obvious.' Zayan's scoff steals our collective attention. I whirl round to find his arms crossed over his chest, a hard look in his tea-brown eyes. His glare isn't directed at me, for once, but behind me.

At The Tragedies.

'Zayan,' I warn, already knowing where this conversation is about to go.

But he ignores me, clearly incensed. 'I told you telling them would be a bad idea.'

'You think one of *us* leaked the information?' Nur asks, her tone so offended that it squeaks towards the end.

'Think?' Zayan argues. 'I'd bet every penny earned from *every* movie I've done on it.'

'Not your TV series?' David asks, provoking him.

Zayan's mouth twists with displeasure, and I already know more venom is about to explode out of him.

'Stop it,' I intervene, 'all of you. But especially you, Zayan.'

His jaw slackens, letting out a noise of disbelief from the back of his throat. 'You cannot be serious.'

'Dead serious.'

'Farah –'

'No,' I reply resoundingly. 'You're not going to accuse my friends of leaking information to the press when there's a clear, obvious, logical reason why this went live.'

Zayan raises a brow.

'Look, it was probably one of the assistants from the photography crew. Or anyone who saw you leaving the Limelight. You said it yourself: the paparazzi hide in plain sight. Would it be so hard to connect the dots?'

A contemplative quiet fills the theatre, and while the suspicion doesn't exactly melt away from Zayan's eyes, his arguments are silenced. For now.

I turn back to The Tragedies, expecting their fury, their rage, their offence. But I'm not prepared for the shock painted across their faces – an eyes-widened, mouth-slightly-ajar kind of disbelief that only comes when you've been entirely stumped.

'What?' I ask, confused, as hints of guilt start to bleed into their shock.

No one says anything, and it takes a second for my brain to catch up with all the cues. The realization hits me hard, like a punch to my solar plexus.

They didn't think I was going to defend them. They thought I'd side with Zayan.

'Regardless of the leak –' I soldier on, like I'm not hurt by the idea of The Tragedies thinking I'd so easily discard them – 'we're a team. All of us. This play needs all our involvement in equal measure, because inevitably we're all going to have an impact on how this play runs. So, let's decide how we're going to tackle this.'

Anushka breaks the silence first. 'Whatever we do, it shouldn't reflect badly on you, Farah. You should be protected from any negative press.'

'I agree,' Ben chimes in, and a murmur of matching yeses falls out of David and Nur.

'Let's confirm our selected actors for the cast list now, and then we'll release a counter-statement and the cast list tonight.' Zayan interrupts the moment, sounding entirely unruffled – as if he wasn't practically volcanic before. His arms are still folded, but he's now scrolling through his phone, a small furrow pinching his brows together. 'Lacey already has one drafted and can have it out in an hour. It'll outline how I was incredibly enthused to be a part of this, grateful for the opportunity, highlighting the importance of the play for marginalized voices.'

We all stare at Zayan, and he only notices when he glances away from his phone.

He shrugs and gives us all a pointed look. 'I like to be prepared for all possibilities.'

I let my eyelids shut briefly and shake my head. 'Of course you do.'

♥

@TheLSDCATS: A gentle reminder to all of you out there that theatre was crafted for the underdogs. For those searching for a place in this world. Not necessarily for those who have already made it big, who have reached their own stardom. Today, we call for positivity in the theatre community, for respect between all of us and for support for the underdogs. Always.

The Gossip Queen
Published 8 October 2021

ZAYAN AMIN'S NEW PLAY

AHHH!!

That was my reaction when I heard Zayan Amin is starring in a new play. We're salivating for all the details, but what we do know is: it's a forbidden love story.

CUE: SWOONING

Even better, an inside source told us that Zayan and his rumoured new flame, Farah Sheikh, were seen together recently! If the photo of them outside the Bubble-Me-Mine boba store is any indication of their chemistry, I suggest the front row prepare themselves for the sparks flying on stage.

And I don't know about you, but if I have to pick between plays opening on the same night, I'm going to pick Zayan Amin's play. Especially if those LSDCATS are a bunch of racists!

We'll keep our eyes open for the new couple, and anything/everything that's got to do with our favourite heart-throb. And we promise to keep you, Zay's loyal fans, updated!

Chapter Twelve

Ten minutes before our first rehearsal with the whole cast, my mother calls to scold me.

'Paari!' Ammi's voice is loud on the other end.

'Ammi?' I say, more than a little confused. I'm standing outside the Limelight's doors, watching as cast members come in, waiting for The Tragedies to show up. 'Is everything OK –?'

'I got a call from Safiya Aunty,' Ammi interrupts, her tone anything but amused, 'saying that you have a boyfriend.'

My initial response is to curl up into a ball and bleach from my mind the fact that my mother just said the word 'boyfriend' to me. An extreme response for some, but Ammi and I don't talk about boys. I wasn't allowed to date growing up, and once I turned eighteen I was told that if I felt I was ready to be in a relationship, it would have to be for the long term. It was the only time my parents were truly strict about anything, and it meant that I grew up envisioning love as something that lasted a lifetime. It was a person you wanted to spend forever with. Not a fling or a hook-up or a moment of attraction. I have yet to find that person – which suits me, because I'm still young and, more importantly, my dreams of the stage are my priority.

My second response is to think, *Really, Safiya Aunty?* I thought leaving Karachi meant that I was free from the network of Pakistani mothers who somehow always knew everything and anything that was going on.

'Ammi, I – what? Why would she say that?' I ask, pressing the cold screen of my phone to my cheek.

'She sent me a photo of you with this boy, at some cafe or something,' Ammi replies. In the background, I hear the familiar shrieks of my younger cousins. Every Saturday, back home, my dad's side of the family comes to visit. In my heart I feel pangs of a sudden longing for my life before all of this – for tiny sticky fingers holding my hand, for Ammi's home-made samosas, for Abu's long-winded stories about his day.

'Some actor,' Ammi adds, like we don't both know who Zayan Amin is.

'Zayan Amin,' I offer. 'And we're just friends, Ammi. I promise. Safiya Aunty is exaggerating; that photo she saw was taken out of context. We're working on this play together –'

'Don't fall in love with him,' Ammi interrupts, her voice dropping to a whisper.

Shock reverberates through my body, and my jaw drops. *Did Ammi just talk to me about falling in love?*

'I know he's very handsome, very talented, but he's a star. He will be photographed a great deal. And *his* reputation can survive a scandal. Yours cannot.'

Her words are wrapped in barbed wire, not meant to pierce but to protect. She doesn't let any of her own opinion bleed into what she's saying – it's not about whether she thinks it's right; instead, her explanation is a fact.

'If you go out in public and get pictured doing certain things with a boy, no one will condemn him for it,' she explains. 'Women are held to a different standard. An unfair standard, but it is there nonetheless. Your father and I want to see you succeed, Paari. To buy tickets and watch you in the cinema. Do not squander that for a boy. Do not let him take advantage of you. Boys like this, with fast lives, will spend minutes with a girl – and then, the second they must commit, they turn away. And all anyone will talk about is how it's your fault, Paari. Even though we know it's not.'

A part of me wants to argue back, to say it's not my job to uphold all of Pakistan's values on my shoulders. It's unfair that Pakistani women are held to a higher moral standard than men; it's unfair that men can do what they please but women who exhibit the same behaviour are condemned.

As the argument builds within me, Zayan's words from Bubble-Me-Mine whisper in my thoughts.

Come to terms with the idea of sacrificing something you love for what you want.

As much as I want to rebel against what Ammi has said,

maybe this is my sacrifice. Maybe I have to bear this cultural responsibility if I want my dreams to come true.

'You don't have to worry, Ammi,' I finally say, hoping to calm her nerves. I think of the way Zayan was adamant about not getting into an 'actual relationship' and falling in love again. How his laser focus was on his career and nothing else. 'Nothing will happen between Zayan and me. I want someone who wants to be with me forever, when I'm ready for it.'

'I trust you, Paari. I always have,' she says in the end, before one of my cousins starts demanding her attention. She hangs up after that, with instructions for at least a dozen different things for me to do: be safe, be careful, be wary.

As soon as her voice disappears, I drop my phone from my cheek to breathe in deeply as if it will help calm my racing heart. I can't believe my mother thought Zayan and I were actually a couple. Just how realistic did our photos look?

First, I look at the photo Ammi was most likely sent – the one of us outside the boba cafe. To someone else, we probably look like we're two people getting to know one another and enjoying each other's company. No one could probably tell, but I can see the slight strain to our smiles.

But when I end up scrolling further in my camera roll, I land on the photo-shoot pictures, and it's undeniable. We *do* look good together. Jazz has captured the best moments. In one of them, I'm looking up at Zayan and my expression is shy and yearning – a look I didn't know my face could do – and Zayan has this wide, incredible smile on his lips, like he's besotted.

If this is what he looks like when he's faking being in love, what does he look like when he's actually in love? Is it still these megawatt smiles, or is it softer – more gentle, blushing grins? *Can* he even blush?

'Farah?' Warmth burns across my own cheeks when Zayan comes into view, taking the steps to the stage door. He's bundled up in a long blue Sherlock Holmes-style coat and a comfortable-looking burgundy sweater. His gaze instantly roams across my face in a growingly familiar way. 'You must've been thinking of something pretty great; you didn't hear me call your name before.'

I struggle for a reply – I can hardly tell him I was wondering what he looked like when he was in love – and Zayan smirks at my floundering.

'You're blushing,' he notes, his voice teasing. 'Were you thinking of me?'

Oh my gosh! Can he read minds?

Zayan laughs a little at my reaction. 'I understand the daydreaming then. It must be hard *not* to think about me all the time.'

His teasing snaps me right back into reality, and I'm reminded of his bad attitude yesterday. 'I assure you, I wasn't thinking about you in the slightest. I want to be in a good mood today.'

His smile droops round the edges. 'I deserve that,' he admits, and then he blurts out something unexpected. 'You look lovely, by the way.'

I glance down at my outfit. I've worn another kurti shirt just to spite him, this time a burnt-orange one to match the changing autumn leaves. I thought his face would get all pinched and annoyed, cracking the cold exterior I was sure he was going to wear today. Especially considering how he verbally attacked The Tragedies yesterday.

'I want to apologize,' Zayan continues, and I try not to look too shocked. It doesn't work, and he grimaces at my reaction. 'I was acting like a jerk yesterday. To you. To the group. I've been on edge about all this, and it's because this relationship is my last chance to save my career, and I can't afford for something to go wrong. But that's no excuse for how I treated you, or The Tragedies, and I'm sorry.'

'I've never been in a fake relationship either, you know,' I remind him. 'I'm not here to make your life difficult. I'm here to help. The Tragedies want this play to work.'

He sighs, and his shoulders tighten. 'I know. I'll do better. I'll try harder.'

I think it over for a second before relenting, knowing there's no point in holding a grudge. I need Zayan. We need Zayan. And he needs us. Building animosity between all of us will do no good. I don't trust him, not entirely, but I do know he'll do what's needed to make this play work.

'Thank you for your apology, and I'm sorry if I provoked you yesterday too.' To make it clear that I'm genuine, I add, with a tease to my voice, 'also, you look . . . well, acceptable.'

He feigns being shot in the heart, clutching his chest dramatically. 'You wound me, fair lady.'

A laugh escapes my lips at his theatrics. 'If this is how you plan on acting in the play, then I think we may need a new Ranjha.'

Zayan's smile widens, all self-assured now. 'Please, I'm your Ranjha. No one else. We both know it.'

I know, in the rational part of my mind, that his use of 'your' is in a general sense, but still, an emotion I'm unwilling to decipher flickers deep inside me. It's a quiet feeling, masked by a sudden surge of jealousy. He's so confident, so suffused with sureness about his abilities. No one will question him as Ranjha.

They can question me. Anyone can. They can question why it's me sharing an equal portion of the stage with Zayan, and not someone more talented or more worthy. I wish I could squash this growing feeling of inadequacy; I wish I could go back to that confidence I used to feel so abundantly, before the LSDCATS audition.

'Farah.' Zayan steps closer to me, waving a hand in my face. 'You're spacing out on me again. Everything all right?'

I force my envy to curl up into a ball and nestle between my ribs. I shake my head, pushing a smile on to my lips that doesn't do much to convince Zayan. 'I'm fine. Just nervous about today.'

He pauses for a moment before nodding. 'You've got nothing to worry about. Remember, fear is a part of acting. You're –'

Whatever Zayan is about to say next is cut off by David, Anushka, Nur and Ben's arrival. Nur is standing in between David and Anushka, her gaze flicking between them like she's trying to work something out. Ben, on the other hand, reaches me first, shooting a wide smile my way as he steps in between Zayan and me. Zayan's face becomes slightly pinched in irritation, but at my raised brow, his expression smooths out. As he promised, a pleasant mask slips over his face, locking into place over his sharp cheekbones.

I turn my attention to Ben. 'You ready for this, bodyguard?'

Ben insisted on auditioning for his role – Heer's palace bodyguard – and he got it almost instantly. None of us suspected that Ben – our kind-smiled, twinkly-eyed, leather-jacket-wearing Ben – could play a stoic guard so well, but he did.

'I vow to protect you forever, Princess,' he replies, with a smirk and an exaggerated bow.

I can't help but snort. 'That's an awful nickname.'

'Will you two have nicknames for one another?' Anushka asks Zayan slyly, likely trying to irritate him. 'Most couples do.'

Nur nods sagely. 'It's mandatory.'

Zayan and I glance at one another, and he finally says, 'I'll think of something.'

'I have to approve of it first,' I reply.

'Naturally,' he says, with a small smile.

'Speaking of you guys' fake relationship,' Nur intervenes, 'did you all see the LSDCATS' tweet last night?'

I barely hold back my grimace. 'Yeah, I saw it.'

'It's a little suspicious, isn't it?' Anushka adds, her arms folded over her chest, her body angled away from David.

My brows furrow at the oddness. 'We announce our cast list with Zayan, and the LSDCATS drop a tweet about how "theatre is for the underdogs".'

'As if Zayan being involved in our play is elitist or something,' David scoffs, his eyes darting to Anushka before looking away. Something is definitely up with them. 'Like *they're* the victims.'

Zayan intervenes as the conversation gets more heated. 'Look, if this is the LSDCATS' way of fighting against the backlash, then fine. One tweet is nothing. They've fulfilled their duty by emerging from their silence online, and as long as we don't say anything back, we can put this to rest. And, honestly, I don't expect the LSDCATS want to go up against us anyway. This is their first and final attack.'

'And why's that?' Ben asks. The Tragedies look disgruntled at the thought of not fighting back, and I can't blame them, because a part of me feels the exact same way – filled with the urge to silence the LSDCATS like they tried to silence us.

Zayan smiles and steps closer to me, so that he's back in my orbit. 'Because Farah and I are going to be great at duping everyone. The public is going to fall in love with us, and the LSDCATS can't do anything about it.'

I try to plaster on a matching smile, hoping to showcase the confidence he feels on my face.

The Tragedies look only semi-convinced.

'Are you kids coming in or not?' Marvin's voice startles all of us, and we turn to see him standing with the Limelight doors wide open. His white brows are drawn together, a stern look etched on his face.

Immediately, we start scrambling up the stairs to get inside.

'We're coming in,' Nur says.

'Right away, sir,' David replies eagerly.

'Could you be any more of a suck-up?' Anushka shoots under her breath. But instead of being tinged with humour, her response is sharp. Cutting, even.

I share a look with Nur, who shrugs helplessly. Ben looks disturbed by Anushka's tone, and Zayan's eyebrows are raised at her.

'How about you focus on yourself?' David fires back, equally intense. 'Your obsession with me is becoming a little much.'

Nur stifles a gasp, Ben's jaw tightens and Zayan looks away from the two of them like he's unwilling to watch them argue. I stare, gaping at my two friends who are glaring at one another like they're mortal enemies.

What is going on?

But before any of us can muster up the brain cells to say anything, both David and Anushka stalk through the Limelight's front doors at the same time.

'Does anyone know what happened there?' I ask, vaguely pointing in their direction.

Nur and Ben shake their heads, equal looks of confusion on their faces.

'Well, this will be an interesting first rehearsal,' Nur murmurs, and then gives my arm a squeeze. 'See you in there.'

Following Anushka, David and Nur, Ben gives me a quick nod before slipping through the doors as well. Zayan and I are the last to enter, and just before we set foot into the theatre, his hand catches the edge of my sleeve.

'You OK?' I ask, glancing at him with concern.

His face is a contortion of emotions. Many I can't decipher, many I'd have to spend an age studying to understand.

'We've got this,' Zayan says, holding my stare. 'You're going to be great.'

I let myself smile – and it's not fake in the slightest. '*We're* going to be great.'

♥

Unfortunately, we are not great. No one prepares you for the drama that commences when trying to produce a play. No one tells you about the underlying tension between actors, the multiple mishaps with the tech crew or the fact that it's impossible to stop your real life from bleeding on to the stage.

'They're ruining the scene,' Anushka says through gritted teeth, her entire being blazing as she looks at the group of cast mates on stage. I would put a hand on her arm to calm her down, but her anger will probably throw me from the theatre seats to the stage. 'They can't stop gawking at Zayan. It's terrible. You're the only one who can act beside him. You're the only one who's immune to his face.'

I'm so glad she's not living in my thoughts, then.

'Have you talked to David about it?' I ask, ignoring every

mental image of how good-looking Zayan is by focusing on my friend instead.

David and Anushka decided to *share* the role of stage manager, alongside their respective producer and director roles. Whatever tension they had before entering the Limelight is definitely still present.

On the stage, David is talking to a group of the crew, while Zayan and Ben stand off to one side. Ben's showing Zayan something on his phone, something that makes Zayan's eyes light up in excitement. I stop myself from walking over there and trying to see what it is that can make his mood lift like that.

I was nervous for today, our first rehearsal. I was a little afraid that Zayan *couldn't* act in a play about his culture – that his internal biases would literally ruin his ability. But I've been proven wrong. He's absorbed the script, become the character; the Urdu phrases peppered in the text are rolling off his tongue in an accent that used to lurk quietly in the background of his voice.

Whether he likes it or not, his culture still lies dormant in him. It's clearly not so easy to simply sacrifice that. I bet he unconsciously knows he's held on to bits of his history, his first home, but isn't willing to see it.

But why did he take that TV role if he knew it mocked his culture?

I have to look away from him, the question begging to escape, my resolve to not ask it weakening. I asked him too many intrusive questions at Bubble-Me-Mine. I can't overstep again.

'No,' Anushka says, and the shortness of her tone draws my attention back to her.

'What?' I question, realizing I've spaced out.

'No, I haven't talked to David about the crew,' Anushka replies, answering my earlier question.

The Tragedies and I talk every day on our original group chat – moaning about how terrible the life of a university student is, and our own inside jokes – but we haven't delved beyond the surface. I don't know their innermost desires, their secrets, their fears. We aren't there yet in our friendship, but I want to be.

Anushka sighs, deflating like a balloon losing air. She presses her palms to her eyes and, for a moment, I'm afraid she's about to start crying. Then she inhales deeply, reins herself in and turns to me. 'We had this stupid fight before coming here today. I wanted to meet his parents, who are coming by this weekend, but he didn't want me to.'

'Oh,' I reply simply.

She gives me a small shrug. 'It probably doesn't sound like a big deal, right?'

I shake my head before tentatively broaching the subject. 'Well, it depends how serious you guys are.' I pick Maha's eloquent words. 'If you're in a situationship, and this relationship is going nowhere, then I get why he wouldn't want to introduce you. But if you're both thinking this is for the long term – friendship or more – I can see why you're upset.'

Anushka nods, her mouth morphed into a frown. I reach over to squeeze her forearm. I want to say something cajoling, like 'Forget David; he's awful,' but we both know that's not true.

Instead, I take another avenue. 'You two will work it out,' I say eagerly. But Anushka's melancholy doesn't disappear, and my words fall flat. That ache in my chest heightens, but I persist anyway, wishing that I knew what to say to make it better. A worthy friend would. 'I mean it. You're both friends before anything else, and that can build some of the greatest long-term relationships.'

As if summoned by the words 'long-term relationships', the scent of patchouli – a fragrance I've begun to associate with only one person – invades my senses. I turn to face Zayan, who has the script rolled up in his hands. Most of the other cast members have had their scripts signed by him, an event that's taken up a sizable amount of our rehearsal time today. We probably should've seen it as the first sign of how quickly everything was going to go downhill.

'What can I do for you, Mr Hollywood?' I ask, a brow raised. 'Not enough cast members fawning over you?'

His smile turns rakish, showing off both dimples. 'Well, Dove, it wasn't you showering me with attention, so it's never going to be enough.' I scrunch my nose at the nickname, and Zayan laughs a little. 'No "Dove", then?'

'I hate birds.'

'Duly noted. How do you feel about food items? "Cupcake"?'

'Do I look like a des—'

'Don't finish that sentence,' Anushka interrupts, placing

a hand over my mouth. 'You're practically setting yourself up for a cheesy compliment.'

Zayan makes a mock-groaning noise. 'Really? Did you have to cut in?'

She drops her hand from my face, turning her glare on to him. 'Seriously, what do you want?'

He straightens under her look, replacing the teasing boy with the professional actor in seconds. If I had the time, I'd study Zayan for hours. He can change one thing about himself – so minutely, like the rise of his lips into the barest of smiles, or the narrowing of his eyes – and suddenly he is transformed.

'I wanted to discuss how you planned on getting this show back on track, because from the looks of it we're not getting very far,' he says, and because I've seen it before I can hear the anxiety thrumming under his voice. I'm not sure Anushka can, but it's as loud as a siren to me now. 'And that begs the question of what *I'm* doing here if the cast can't work together. If this play isn't performed well, that doesn't help me either. Doesn't help *us* beat the LSDCATS.'

In unison, my gaze and Anushka's drift back to the cast. The group that isn't being lectured by David about blocking and self-awareness on stage is huddled in the middle of it, giggling and throwing unsubtle glances Zayan's way. There's the costumes team arguing with Nur about their vision, and the tech crew is hunkered over a laptop trying to work out something about sound and lighting.

This cast is decidedly separate – a constellation of unbound stars, floating in the galaxy with no force to bring them together.

'I think I have a way of fixing the atmosphere here,' Anushka suddenly announces, her previous anger dissipating. 'Would you mind helping me with an exercise?'

'How?' Zayan asks.

'Well, the biggest problem we're facing is that no one knows how to act with you,' Anushka explains. 'To fix that, I think we need to humanize you a little bit. Bring you back down to earth.'

'You're saying you want to deflate his ego,' I say.

Anushka nods. 'In a way.'

Zayan grins, his more charming persona leaking past his icy exterior. 'It's an ego made of steel.'

Anushka smirks and gestures for us to make our way to the stage. The cast goes quiet at Zayan's arrival – another thing we don't want.

'Let's go over Act Two, Scene Four. Just a little run-through,' Anushka calls, thumbing the pages of her script. David's gaze flicks between us and Anushka, and I give him the tiniest of nods. He understands immediately and begins to dismount the stage. He joins Anushka, but I notice, sadly, that he keeps some space between them.

'Sure,' Zayan replies, flipping to the right page.

I do the same. There are five acts in the play, and the second one is my favourite. It's the most heartwarming, where Ranjha and Heer's stolen moments are bolder and brighter under their love for one another. They're defying society's rules and not caring, because all that matters is their affection for one another.

'Heer,' Zayan – now Ranjha – whispers. He says the name with such yearning it nestles deep in my heart. My feet – or Heer's feet – begin walking towards him, pulled by his voice. 'Allow me one touch, one brush of my –'

'Stop,' Anushka interrupts, snipping the threads of the scene Zayan was just starting to spool together. 'That was good, Zayan, but I think we can work on your stance a little more. You need to be more liquid. Your voice reacts to your lines instantly, but I can't feel Ranjha's want from your body language. I think it may be because you're used to close-ups, not having your entire body in certain shots, but when you're on stage, every part of you needs to be acting. So when you say that line, lean into Farah's space. Reach for her. The same way Ranjha is.'

There's a beat of stunned silence. The cast share looks with one another, horror etched on their faces. I can practically hear their thoughts.

Did she just critique Zayan Amin?

I glance at the boy in question. Zayan's gaze keeps flicking from his body to Anushka, like he can't quite work out what she's saying. At the sound of my strangled laugh, he shoots me a look that quite clearly says *Shut up*. I bite the insides of both of my cheeks, and Zayan rolls his eyes, but I see a small smile twitching at the corners of his lips. The rest of the cast *doesn't* notice his good humour, and there's a nervous wall of whispers forming around the stage.

He turns his attention to Anushka, slipping back into his professional self. 'Thank you. I'll keep that in mind as we go on.' Anushka's about to say something when he barrels on. 'Actually, would you have some time afterwards? I'd love to go over this scene with you and Farah, really work out the kinks of my character.'

It's a brilliant response, one that makes gratitude erupt in my heart. Zayan could've shouted and stormed off. He could've pulled out all his accolades, throwing them in Anushka's face. But instead he's humbled himself, showing the cast and crew that he is not beyond criticism. From the murmur that simmers through them, I know his answer has had the desired effect, and from Anushka's huge smile, I know her plan has worked. The cast will treat Zayan like he's a little more human now.

We go on after that in chronological order, and the cast is more attuned to the play. We only get through the first scene, as both Anushka and David – who are still not quite working in complete tandem – offer critique upon critique. Zayan and I throw ourselves into our scenes, but also into our ruse. We glance at one another, make sure to stay in one another's orbit, and studiously pretend we're unaware of our fellow castmates' curious looks.

The thought of beating the LSDCATS becomes less of a faraway dream and more of a concrete aspiration. Our talent speaks for itself. That, coupled with Zayan, should be enough to wow our audience and prove to the LSDCATS that we are *all* worthy of being in the theatre.

But while there's a new vigour upon the stage, and the

voice that sounds a lot like Henry in my head is dimming, I can't help but feel that there's still something missing. That nagging feeling stays with me all the way till the end of rehearsal.

'I thought that went pretty well,' Zayan says, sitting comfortably in one of the theatre seats as I pack my bag.

'Yeah,' I say, half enthusiastically. I still can't put my finger on what feels wrong.

'Please, try not to sound too thrilled,' he probes, stretching his legs out and interlacing his fingers over his stomach. 'What's the matter?'

'It's nothing.'

'Farah.'

'Zayan.'

'Come on, tell me,' Zayan wheedles, his voice pitching higher. 'I can help. I *want* to help. Consider it a part of my apology for being a complete and total jerk to you and The Tragedies.'

I sigh, dropping my bag to look at him fully. He's sitting up now, resting his chin against his closed fist, elbow on the armrest, head tilted. A spear of attraction pierces my chest. It's so hard to remember this is all pretend when he's got his lidded brown eyes focused on me, a half smile tugging at his lips.

It's all pretend, I chant in my head. *He doesn't plan on ever falling in love again.*

When I return to my regular thrum of emotions, I struggle to find the words to explain what I'm feeling. 'It's . . . weird. The dynamic in here. I just . . . expected that maybe we'd all gel more. The new cast, The Tragedies. Everyone. I wanted it to be like how my drama club used to feel. Like a family, almost?'

'Well . . .' Zayan says, eyes roving over the people exiting the theatre. Aside from The Tragedies, who are also leaving, most of them glance his way. 'You could start by making *yourself* more available to your cast. Set the tone. Why don't you go talk to that girl over there? The one who's playing your lady-in-waiting – you're going to have loads of scenes with her.'

I look over my shoulder to see the girl he's referring to. She's a dark-brown-skinned girl, with short brown hair that's been pinned up at the front, and she's wearing a patterned top that I recognize to be a kameez. She's also packing up her things, wrangling a laptop and charger into an almost ineffectively small tote bag. My heart lurches with twin feelings of excitement and humiliation at the sight of a Pakistani Society pin on her bag strap.

It's the logo of the Pakistani Society at my university, which means this girl goes there too. Nerves tug at the pit of my stomach as I remember my failed attempts at making friends with people from my classes. I did try in the beginning, when I first arrived in London, but the people I met either wanted to go out for drinks – I don't drink – or they looked at me with a slightly wounded expression in their eyes. They asked questions like *What was it like living, y'know, there? You must've been so happy to leave!*

Not the best way to start a friendship, really.

'Are you going to just stare at her?' Zayan interrupts my swirling worry. I roll my eyes, irritated but motivated by his annoying prodding. I kick his ankles, forcing him to tuck his legs in so I can move out of the row.

My shoulders tense as I approach the girl, my mind working overtime to convince myself that this isn't going to go badly.

'Hi,' I say, my voice faltering at the edges.

The girl straightens from crouching over her bag, hand clasped round a tube of hand cream. Our gazes meet and her eyes betray nothing. No surprise. No warmth. Just a beige sort of neutrality. 'Hi,' she replies.

'We sort of just got thrown into this rehearsal, but I wanted to introduce myself more formally because we're going to be doing so many scenes together,' I continue, watching as she unscrews the cap and places a dollop of pear-scented cream on the back of her hands. 'I'm Farah.'

'Right, I'm Gibitah,' she replies easily. 'I can't wait till we're in costume. I heard Nur Hadi is designing them. I stalk her Instagram all the time – she has the best "outfits of the day".'

'Yeah!' I say enthusiastically. We've already found common ground. 'She's pretty amazing. I always feel underdressed standing next to her.'

Gibitah smiles, and I feel like I've just won a marathon. My heartbeat slows to normal, and I feel myself getting comfortable.

Then a look of mild surprise appears over Gibitah's features, and she sheepishly offers me the tube of hand cream. 'I'm sorry, I completely forgot to ask if you wanted some. I'm just standing here, moisturizing away.'

I laugh and take the proffered tube, squeezing just a little out. 'No worries. Honestly, the weather has been so awful lately. The cold has made my skin even paler; I miss when I had a 24-7 tan from the sun back home.'

My tone is light, jokey, possibly self-deprecating. Or at least I thought it was. Gibitah's silence rattles me, and I turn my attention from rubbing circles over my hands to her. There's a sharpness in her face that wasn't there before. A guardedness that puts me on edge.

It all turns worse when Gibitah lets out a rough, delayed laugh. 'It must be nice to have such problems.'

Warmth travels from my cheeks down my neck and across my chest. 'I'm sorry, I just wanted to commiserate on how cold it is – I wasn't . . . I didn't mean . . .' I stumble on my words, not knowing what to say.

Mercifully, Gibitah cuts me off. 'Look, I'm sure you weren't. But I really don't need another light-skinned Pakistani friend complaining about their *struggles* with being too pale. If you'll excuse me, I've got a bus to catch.'

And with those parting words, Gibitah exits the Limelight – leaving me with a tube of pear-scented hand cream and a cavernous hole of regret growing in my chest.

I walk back to where Zayan is sitting. Just he and I are left in the theatre. And Marvin, who is standing by the stage doors expectantly.

As I approach Zayan, the words leave my lips in a whisper. 'That went terribly.'

Zayan, in response, doesn't look up from his phone. His mouth is pinched in a sharp line, his brows scrunched together in obvious displeasure.

'Aren't you going to ask me why?' I say, my voice turning a little hysterical. But still, he doesn't look up from his phone. Dread pools in my stomach, and my heart starts racing with anticipation.

'What is it?' I demand, holding myself back from snatching the phone out of his hand.

'It's the LSDCATS,' Zayan says, finally looking at me, his tone entirely too grim. 'They just launched their second attack.'

@TheLSDCATS: After many weeks of auditions, we're elated to announce our cast list for this year's rendition of *Romeo and Juliet*. As we're sure you all know, rumours have been flying around about the intentions of this institution, but we're here to say: there's always more going on behind the curtain in theatre, and it's a tragedy that people can't see that. We're sure that you all will be super excited by this brand-new cast, and we can't wait to see you all filling up our seats!
Posted: 9 October 2021

Chapter Thirteen

'Are you really going to stare at the LSDCATS' cast list all night?' Amal asks, from where she's stretched out on my bed, surrounded by scattered books and the *Heer Ranjha* script she's been reading.

'I *was* meant to be working on my essay. It's due tomorrow at 9 a.m., and I don't think the professor is going to give me another extension,' I reply, shutting my laptop with a delicate snap. 'But, honestly, I can't stop thinking about the list.'

Amal turns to lie on her side, her head propped up by her hand. 'Why is it bothering you so much?'

'I don't know,' I moan, irritated at myself for feeling so obsessive about it. 'Ever since I saw the cast names, it's been bugging me.'

'What did Zayan say about it?' she asks, and a smile touches her lips in a way that makes my face heat up. The teasing about Zayan has not let up in my friend group. Just saying his name elicits grins and elbows to my side, like we're all in high school again.

'He told me not to worry about it,' I say, leaning back in my desk chair, keeping my feet propped on the bed.

'See, if the professional actor says the LSDCATS aren't a concern,' Amal offers lightly, 'then they're not a concern.'

I paste a smile on to my face, not wanting Amal to know that my worry hasn't evaporated just yet. I would tell her the truth, but it would mean recounting my every experience with the LSDCATS, and I'm not ready to do that.

'I'm going to be baking chocolate-chip cookies tonight. Owais has a huge quiz on Friday, and I want to give him a box to snack on,' Amal says, while sliding off my bed. 'Then I'm going to go back to writing. If you want, we can watch trashy reality TV until your mind is distracted enough.'

Affection flickers in my heart. *See, best friends like Amal are like lighthouses; they know exactly how to pull you out of the darkness that threatens to swallow you whole.*

'Thanks,' I say, a more genuine smile climbing over my face. 'But I think I'm going to work on my essay first.'

'OK, well, you know where to find me.'

Once Amal leaves, I force myself to spend a couple of hours finishing up my essay and submitting it on Turnitin. I then do my entire night-time skincare routine and I climb into bed with the intention of sleeping.

But, of course, that doesn't happen.

I find myself staring up at the ceiling, uneasy and unable to sleep. Eventually, after more time passes, I sit up in my bed and pull out the script for *Heer Ranjha* to read over one of the more intense scenes of the play. I hear Zayan's voice saying the lines in my head, and I find myself whispering the responding lines under my breath because the rest of the flat is now asleep – as they should be, because it's 3 a.m.

But even reading the script can't lull my mind. I get through one scene before I abandon the script to look at my phone. I stare at the LSDCATS' cast list again. My eyes have surpassed feeling heavy with sleep and have gone straight to sleep-deprivation alertness, a unique kind of awake that only happens when you're pulling an all-nighter. Except mine is an unintentional all-nighter, because I don't want to be reading the LSDCATS' cast list again.

But I can't stop staring at the name.

Kamran Milwala: Tybalt.

Of course the LSDCATS would cast a person of colour after the backlash they got. It's disgustingly performative, and it makes me want to write another essay directed solely at them. But I'm on strict instruction not to by Zayan, who said we should wait to see the public response before making our next move.

The thought of him stopping me from unleashing my wrath at the LSDCATS makes me wonder if he'll have some advice for dealing with the waiting, for having patience. When Zayan offered his guidance at rehearsal, he made it clear he'd be willing to give it if I was willing to take it.

It's that final thought of Zayan as a mentor with the answer to my worries that has me dialling his number at this crazy hour.

'Hello?' Zayan's rough, sleepy tone makes a shiver run down my spine.

I sit up in the bed, putting a pillow behind my back. 'Hi,' I reply, hoping he can't hear how his voice has affected me.

'Farah?' An alertness enters his tone. 'Is everything OK?'

'Yeah – yeah, I'm fine. Were you sleeping?' I ask guiltily. 'Sorry, of course you're sleeping. I shouldn't have called. It's not serious, don't worry.'

I hear rustling on the other end, and I try not to imagine what Zayan looks like in bed – whether his hair is all messed up and rumpled, or if he looks princely and perfect. I bet he has expensive pyjamas on, ones that are tailored to his exact measurements, with a monogrammed Z. A. on the pocket.

'Well, I'm up now, and I've made myself comfortable,' he says, sounding not exactly accusatory. I envision him sitting up in his giant king-sized bed, head resting against his headboard. 'Why'd you call?'

'I . . .' I let out a breath of frustration, unable to articulate what's bothering me about the LSDCATS exactly.

'You're thinking about the cast list, aren't you?' Zayan guesses correctly.

'Yeah,' I reply. 'But I'm not sure why it's bugging me so much.'

'Because it's blatant racism, and waiting to see what the public will say is terrible, because their response should be automatic,' he replies, and then offers a question. 'Want me to tell you exactly what you're feeling right now?'

I laugh a little. 'Sounds like you already are.'

He takes that as a confirmation and launches into a monologue. 'When you first saw the cast list, you were angry. Rageful. Beyond furious. That's an easy first emotion to fall into, and it's not a wrong emotion. You're right to be mad. What the LSDCATS have done, using another person of colour to cover their tracks, is despicable. But once the anger settles, you accept that you can't change the cast list, and that's when your doubt and worry kicks in. Your fear that the LSDCATS have done enough by using a person of colour as their token. That their years and years of prestige will trump your play, and every opportunity you saw for your team will disappear.' Zayan pauses for dramatic effect. 'Did I get it right?'

'Yeah,' I swallow tightly, entirely stunned. This is the second time he's understood me so viscerally. 'Yeah, you got it right.'

Something must have shone from my tone, because his voice softens. 'You're not the only one who felt like that, Farah. I'm sure the rest of The Tragedies did too.'

He's not wrong. While no one's said anything in The Tragedies' group chat yet, other than bashing the LSDCATS, I wonder if they're as worried as I am. They're angry, they want to fight back, but are they afraid and anxious? If they aren't, I don't want them to know I am. I don't want them to feel burdened by my reaction.

And I suppose, in a way, I inherently knew Zayan wouldn't share this worry. I was banking on his confidence, unshakeable as always.

'Tell me what you need from me, Farah. You want my advice, it's yours. You want me to cajole you with my own confidence, I'll do it. But I can only guess what you're *feeling*; you've got to tell me what you *want*.'

Maybe it's because it's 3 a.m., or because Zayan's voice is so smooth, like crushed velvet or chocolate ganache, that I feel like I'm making a deal with a jinni.

'I want your help. I've been struggling with the cast.' My thoughts flit to Gibitah, and the memory strengthens my resolve to fix this. 'I want to help build some chemistry between all of us. I don't want to give the LSDCATS any advantages over us. Their cast will be airtight, no cracks, no conflicts. We need ours to be as good. If not better. I was thinking we could have a more public group date.'

'Two birds, one stone; I think it's a good plan. It'll amp up the speculation about us as well,' Zayan says, instantly catching my drift. A sense of warmth pulses through me. I like that we're on the same wavelength about things now.

'Perfect. The only problem is I have no idea about what we should do. I mean, there are so many things to consider. Everyone has different budgets, drinking habits, sleeping habits, schedules.'

He pauses, and I listen to his breathing on the other end. It's an oddly comforting soundtrack. Outside my window, I can hear the faint sounds of London, the city that rarely sleeps, and it harmonizes with the steadiness of his breathing. In and out. I feel my eyes getting heavy with the urge to fall asleep, with the comfort that Zayan is at the other end of the phone.

'I've got it.'

My eyelids snap open, instantly alert. 'What?'

'How do you feel about confined spaces?'

♥

'I personally don't think MI5 is going to be hiring any of us,' David says, blowing out a breath of frustration as he stares at the quote on the wall.

It's a scramble of letters that we've been collectively staring at for the last ten minutes. Other members of the cast are stationed across the room deciphering clues, trying to open the door that leads into *another* room. Apparently, there are four in total that we need to pass through to finish this escape-room quest.

'Maybe not you,' Anushka replies testily. 'Try not lumping us all in the same category.'

David shoots her a sharp glare. 'All right then, Einstein, what's the quote?'

I share a look with Nur, and we both grimace at the same time. Ben takes a step away from David and Anushka, likely trying to stay out of the blast zone.

'I take it they haven't made up yet,' Zayan says, leaning into my space to whisper. I give him a side glance, only to see him watching the duo with a look of pure amusement rather than worry as their fighting begins to escalate.

'Astute observation, Holmes,' I reply sarcastically.

Zayan's smile broadens, and it's looking just a little less fake than usual. I'm becoming attuned to when his mask slips on. It's always when we're in a group setting, when we're on the streets, when we're in front of anyone we don't know. Really, it's most of the time. But there are moments, glimpses, of when something heart-joltingly real peeks out. That's when I have to remind myself that this is all pretend. That I shouldn't waste my time looking for rare flashes of the real Zayan underneath his veneer, because it would go nowhere. This boy is not for the long haul.

I turn my attention away from Zayan's smiles to Anushka and David once again. They're in each other's faces now, and their insults are becoming more personal, more barbed. I can see other cast members watching them, unease spreading like a virus.

When I proposed an escape-room team-building exercise, I tried to manage my expectations. But once we started our quest, everyone truly got into it. At one end, I can see some people theorizing heavily about the clues. And, sure, there are still some outliers – uncomfortable individuals who haven't quite delved into this new group dynamic. But it's a start.

Unless Anushka and David's fighting ruins it all.

'Guys,' I try to intervene quietly, 'come on. It's just a quote, we can move –'

'It's not *just* a quote.' Anushka's angry gaze slashes into me, and I take a whole step back, colliding with Zayan's shoulder. 'It's a matter of principle.'

'Don't bite Farah's head off because you two can't have a mature conversation.' Zayan's voice reverberates down my spine, just as shock at his defending me floods my system. I imagine he's showing this solidarity because some cast member must be watching us, but I can't help but like the slightly protective edge to his tone.

David flushes a deep red and steps back from Anushka. A flash of hurt flits over her face and she stalks away from him – and the group – to get a moment alone. I'm about to walk over to her when Nur places a hand on my shoulder.

I take her lead, and we all go in different directions. I move to the other end of the room, near a soft brown-leather lounge chair. The room has been set up to look like a bunker, with grey walls and realistic-looking furniture from the 1960s. I flop on to the seat gracelessly, surveying the room.

I see Gibitah laughing in the corner with other cast members. Our eyes meet, and her smile dims.

Great.

I consider going over, but nerves hold me back. It's probably best we don't have that conversation in a locked room. I want to clear up any misconception she might have about me, but I don't want to ambush her with it.

I'm jolted out of my thoughts by Zayan walking over to me; he sits on the cushioned arm of the seat, looking down at me with a grin. 'So, did you enjoy watching Mum and Dad duke it out?'

'Mum and Dad?' I question, with a laugh.

Zayan shrugs, and his arm drapes along the top of the

seat as he nestles in closer. 'Ben and I were talking about how Anushka and David are very much the mum-friend and dad-friend of the group.'

I raise a brow at him. 'You and Ben were talking? Are you two friends now?'

He scoffs and runs a free hand through his hair. 'No. The Tragedies are your friends.'

'I see, and you have too many big Hollywood friends already? Can't you make more?'

Zayan shifts, turning his eyes away from me. I've struck a nerve again. It makes me wonder how many friends he has, how many people he can trust, who abandoned him when his TV series tanked.

'There's nothing wrong with having a couple more people in your corner,' I say softly, just for him to hear, and a muscle in his jaw twitches.

He doesn't respond, but his gaze finally latches on to mine. Usually, when we're in a group setting, he's staring at me with a sort of sickly affection that I know is fake. But right now there's something in his eyes, something soft and warm, that makes my stomach erupt with butterflies.

'Why are you sitting here, again?' I blurt out, suddenly overwhelmed by his presence.

His expression smooths out, every inch of emotion being replaced with neutrality. 'We're being watched. I just saw one of the crew members take a photo of us.'

Automatically, I start to lean forward to look around, but Zayan tugs me back gently with the end of my dupatta. 'Don't make it obvious.'

I look up at him, and his gaze is so warm, lips quirked into a soft smile. Having that look levelled at me turns my bones molten.

It's nothing but physical attraction from you and acting from him. Rein it in.

Steely determination lines my veins, cold against the heat of what I was feeling before. A reminder that none of this is real, and all of it is a means to an end.

'You OK, Farah?' Zayan asks, voice low.

That glint in his eye could've been mistaken for concern, if I didn't know what all of this was. If I still had a celebrity crush on him, living out fantasies that would never be. But I know better. It's more likely that he's doubting me – worried I can't go through with our deal.

To prove him wrong, I plaster on a smile, pretending once again that we're madly in love.

♥

@TheQuestioner: After reading **@TheLSDCATS** cast list, I'm curious to know why everyone is making such a big deal about **@TheTragedies**. It's so clear The Tragedies are trying to make the LSDCATS look like the villains of this story. I know which play I'm buying tickets for.

Chapter Fourteen

The best way to repair major and minor tears in a friendship is by hosting a good old-fashioned get-together. That's why I've invited The Tragedies and Zayan to a meeting of sorts after our classes – it's been two days since the Escape Room, and while the rest of the cast has really begun to gel, The Tragedies themselves are still fractured because Anushka and David can't even be in a room with one another. But today we're fixing that.

I've got all the essentials for a gossip session: a towering stack of pizza boxes, multiple bottles of Coke, and freshly made gulab jamun and vanilla ice cream for dessert. I'm carrying all these things, laden with bags, while walking into the Limelight – the venue for the intervention.

'Need help with those?' Marvin asks, watching my balancing act with an impressed lift of his brows.

'Thanks, if you could just get the door . . .' I reply, giving him a grin.

He opens the stage door for me, but not before doling out a warning. 'Don't forget to clean up after yourselves. I will not have mice running around this theatre.'

'Yes, Marvin. I'll make sure you have no new rodent friends to keep you company,' I call out cheerily behind me. His grumbling has begun to grow on me.

I walk through the doors and find Nur sitting on the stairs leading to the stage, head braced on her knees, crying.

'Nur?' I ask cautiously. I set my bags and precarious stack of pizza boxes on to an empty seat and crouch in front of her, placing my hands gently on her elbows. 'Nur, are you all right?'

Nur lifts her head, and I stare into her bloodshot eyes. She's been crying for a while. I squeeze her elbows before letting go and moving to sit beside her. Her sniffles fill the silence between us, and I weigh up my choices.

When someone is crying, there are only two things to do:

1. Comfort them, let them talk it out, be there for them.
2. Leave the issue alone. Sit with them, but don't pry. Distract them.

From the way Nur glances at me repeatedly, I know which one she wants.

'What happened?' I ask softly. 'If you want to talk about it, I'm here to listen. No judgements from me.'

Nur hiccups, her chest heaving, before the story spills out of her. 'It's so stupid. I have no reason to be upset. But I've been talking to this guy for a while now, and I – I had mentioned that I wanted it to become more serious. I told him if he wanted it to be serious too, then we'd need to do this properly. Like talking to my dad, talking to my family. But he backed out, saying he was l-looking for a fling and n-nothing more.' Her voice breaks on the last word. 'I feel so stupid.'

I wrap my arms round her, pulling her face to the crook of my neck. I've heard this story before – it's one of the reasons my parents were so adamant that I shouldn't dive into a relationship until I felt a hundred per cent ready for a future shared with someone else. My friends have had guys who promise them the world, and the stars, and everything in between, but they can't show up when they need to. The minute they have to legitimize the relationship or actually commit, they disappear in a cloud of, *Woah, this is going too fast* or *I didn't mean it like that! We were just having fun.* And in the end, there's always one person left with a broken heart.

The doors to the Limelight open and Anushka strides in, eyes locked on a file that she's holding in her hands. But the second she notices us, she drops everything. Nur relays the story to her in chopped-up breaths, tears leaking out of her eyes.

'Guys suck,' Anushka says after a beat. 'I'm sorry you had to go through this, Nur.'

I tentatively broach the subject I've been avoiding. 'I take it that things with David aren't great yet either?'

Anushka shakes her head, her eyes becoming glassy too. I take a deep breath, trying another attempt to offer some better advice.

'I know you guys aren't working out as a relationship, but you *are* good friends. You shouldn't throw that away. If you can't see eye to eye on a relationship front, then you need to ask yourself if you still want him in your life in any capacity. You're both hurting yourselves by being in a relationship. Maybe it's time to take a step back into friendship, and to see if it grows organically into what you both want to be.'

Anushka mulls over my advice, and my heart hammers in my chest. Finally she sighs, swiping at her eyes with the back of her palm. 'I know you're right. It's hard sometimes. I feel like if we start speaking again we'll wreck everything. Nothing will be left. Not a relationship and not friendship.'

'I know you feel that way, but David isn't going to just let you go from his life,' I say, determination coating my every word. Hope blossoms in Anushka's eyes, so I go on. 'You two have a great friendship, and you aren't simply going to lose it because you hit one speed bump.'

Nur lifts her head from my shoulder to lean over and grip Anushka's hand. 'We're a pair, aren't we?' she giggles, detangling from me. 'I think Farah's the only put-together one of this entire group.'

'Yeah, and honestly, Farah –' Anushka grabs my hand, looking at me with bright eyes – 'seeing you being happy and joyful and positive all the time, it's such a great reminder of how happy *I* could be as well. Your attitude is amazing.'

My chest warms with pride, knowing I'm a boulder they can lean on; I feel emboldened, and proud of past-Farah for deciding not to burden The Tragedies with my worries about the LSDCATS audition, or what happened with Gibitah. They need a shoulder, a friend, someone solid – I can be that.

'You're delusional.' Ben's voice pulls at our attention. He's walking in, sandwiched between Zayan and David. 'You two think you can beat me at *GTA*?'

Zayan scoffs, arrogance lining his every word. 'Beat you? I could destroy you. I've already beaten David every time we play.'

'Uh,' David breaks in, 'we only started playing two days ago.'

'Excuses, excuses. Just admit I'm better than you.'

David shoves Zayan lightly, and for a moment my heart kicks up in worry that this could lead to a brawl. But Zayan just catches his balance and laughs. A genuine sound. Not smug, or rude, or soft, but loud and free. Eventually, the three of them reach us, and Zayan's gaze lands on me first. His smile drops slightly, and my stomach clenches.

The sight of me is clearly not helping his mood.

'Woah, what happened here?' Ben asks, noticing Nur's tear-streaked face.

'You OK?' David questions, dropping down in front of Nur. 'Please – tell me who to beat up.' Anushka laughs, startling all of us, before clapping her hand over her mouth. I know she's holding back the automatic joke. David looks at her almost pleadingly. 'You got something to say?'

There's hope wound up in his words, and I hear the ceasefire in them. I widen my eyes at Anushka, nodding my head ever so slightly. She lets out a shaky breath and smiles. 'You can't fight anyone, old man.'

It's not the greatest comeback, not even close to what Anushka can do, but it's enough. A smile breaks out on David's face, so wide, so brilliant.

'OK, she's not wrong,' David says with a laugh. He turns on his heels, still crouching, to point at Zayan and Ben. 'But they totally could.'

'And would,' Zayan offers with a shrug. 'I mean, I wouldn't personally punch anyone – it wouldn't be great for my image at the moment – but I could get someone to do it.'

Nur laughs while standing. 'Your kindness is astounding.'

Zayan shrugs bashfully, and Ben elbows his side mockingly. I watch the interaction carefully, confused.

When did they become such good friends?

♥

'I take it we all saw the tweets about the LSDCATS?' Ben asks round a mouthful of pizza.

'You mean the tweets where everyone was calling them saints and us evil villains?' Anushka asks, neatly taking a bite out of her gulab jamun.

Zayan rolls his eyes, leaning back on his elbows, his body stretched out. 'I saw those. It was infuriating. We've got to shift the narrative.'

'That's actually why I wanted us to come here today,' I chime in. 'Other than verbally ripping the LSDCATS apart, I wanted to know if you guys had any ideas for how we could challenge them.'

The Tragedies contemplate my question quietly, taking their time to offer something that's worthwhile.

Minutes later, Ben has a light-bulb moment. 'I've got it.'

'Finally!' Zayan replies, and Ben kicks his outstretched legs with his metal-toed boots.

Zayan hisses in pain, rubbing his leg. 'Violent much?'

'Annoying much?' Ben snarks back, a wide grin on his face.

'I say kick him again,' David offers, and Zayan chucks a crumpled napkin at him – which he narrowly dodges.

Again, I watch them interact, and my heart twists uncomfortably. I thought Zayan said he *wasn't* friends with The Tragedies. This doesn't look like he's not friends with them. What's his angle here?

'What's your idea, Ben?' Nur asks, refocusing the conversation.

'We need to shift the narrative, right? Most of the interest surrounding our play comes from two things: when we called out the LSDCATS, and Farah and Zayan's relationship. We need to really capitalize on Farah and Zayan. We should have TikTok Lives every rehearsal. We can show new things to the public. Behind-the-scenes stuff. Costume design. How the sets are made. The tech behind a major play. And while we're doing that, we'll have Farah and Zayan *conveniently* show up at some point. That way, people will remember that if they come and watch our play, they'll get to see Farah and Zayan – their favourite power couple.'

'Wow,' Zayan says after a beat. 'That's actually a good idea.'

'Your faith in me is great,' Ben teases, before taking a gulab jamun for himself.

'Zayan's right –' I begin, before he cuts me off with an exaggerated gasp. I ignore him and continue. 'That is a really good idea.' And to make sure I'm including everyone in this choice, I ask for their opinions. 'How do the rest of you feel about it? I want us all to agree before we go forward and take any action.'

'I think it's brilliant,' Nur adds. 'I can't wait to show off my costume designs.'

'Yeah, and I think it'll drum up way more support for both of you as well,' David agrees. 'This way, we can engage with our audience, get more public attention and eclipse the LSDCATS without stooping to their level. It's brilliant.'

Anushka, ever practical, sees a possible complication. 'It does mean more acting, though. From both of you. You'll need to look like you're in love with one another all the time. Can you do that?'

I meet Zayan's eyes, and he's got a bright glint in the brown of his irises. I think of how warm I felt sitting beside him in the escape room, of how I'm still attracted to him. Physically, at least. Being on TikTok Lives will mean being around Zayan for longer; it will mean enduring his presence and reminding myself on repeat that this can go nowhere.

The words to refuse are on the tip of my tongue, self-preservation kicking in, but the challenge of it all holds me back. I can't be the one to concede, to let my attraction to him get the better of me. It'll be exactly what he expected.

'You think you can handle it, Gumdrop?' Zayan asks, raising a brow.

I scoff, rolling my shoulders back. 'I can handle it.'

Chapter Fifteen

Even after a whole day of hanging out with The Tragedies, working out the kinks of the TikTok Lives, all I can think about is my LSDCATS audition.

I try to push the LSDCATS out of my mind as much as possible, but they keep rearing up like an unwanted pimple. Now our rivalry with them is growing, becoming so much bigger than I'd like, and for some reason this sends me right back there.

I replay it in my mind like clockwork. I walk on stage, announce myself, give my profile, say my lines, get interrupted, have my dreams shattered. The more I think about it, the louder Henry's voice echoes in my head.

More classically British.

Unsuitable.

Henry's critique sounded so cursory, like he just needed an excuse to get me off the stage and picked the first thing that came to his mind. It didn't feel racist in the blatant way The Tragedies' experiences were. I can't shake the feeling that he really rejected me because I wasn't good enough, and he just wasn't willing to say it.

I turn over in my bed, tucking the blanket up to my chin, staring out of the window. I like sleeping with the curtains open, watching people walk through the streets, the sound of loose laughter in the air, the star-speckled sky winking back at me. It makes me feel less alone to know there's a whole world beyond my doors. Usually, staring out the window would lull me to sleep, but today my head is as noisy as the drunk group of university students stumbling out of the local pub.

I flip over and stare at my ceiling, that aching feeling of rejection crashing through me like waves. Again and again and again, until it's too much.

I scramble for my phone on my bedside table, take it out of sleep mode and dial Zayan's number with nothing but a singular desire pushing my every move: I need to hear him tell me I'm good on stage.

'I don't suppose this 3 a.m. calling is going to become a regular thing, is it?' Zayan's voice is sleep-soaked, rough, like he's been woken up. I look over at my alarm clock and, sure enough, a bright red '3 a.m.' is staring back at me.

The words are on the tip of my tongue to tell him why I need to speak with him. I want to say, *Zayan, say it to me again. Tell me you thought I was good on stage. Good enough to act opposite you. Good enough to rival the LSDCATS. Just tell me.*

But I don't. Why? Because it hits me that I've officially lost my mind. That I've just called my fake partner, desperate for reassurance, all because I can't handle my own anxiety.

Forget the red flag of Zayan's emotional unavailability for falling in love – my impulsive desire to make bad decisions at 3 a.m. is starting to feel like a hazard to the unassuming people in my life.

'Farah?' Zayan questions, becoming more alert.

'I'm sorry,' I whisper, before clearing my throat. 'I'm sorry, I – I butt-dialled you by accident.'

'You butt-dialled me at 3 a.m.,' Zayan echoes doubtfully. I say nothing in response, and silence sits between us like a weight. I'm about to end the call with a sheepish goodbye and make a self-deprecating joke about not calling again when he surprises me with a question.

'Do you want to play a game?'

'That sounds mildly threatening.'

'I mean it innocently.'

'Why do I feel like you're lying?'

'You don't trust me, Farah?' he asks, his voice all soft and teasing. I hear rustling in the background, and I imagine he's adjusting to a more comfortable position.

'Do you trust *me*?' I volley back.

'I suppose this game will tell you if I do.' Zayan's poking at my curiosity now, knowing I'll cave in.

I hold out for all of three seconds.

'Fine,' I say. 'What's the game?'

'You let me ask you one question, any question, and you have to answer it. And in return, I'll offer you the same.'

'And if I really don't want to answer?'

'You owe me a favour,' he says. 'Anything I want.'

'How do you know *you* won't be the one owing *me* a favour?' I ask, affronted.

He laughs. 'Shall we play, then?'

I think it over, trying to predict what he could possibly ask me. He doesn't know much about me, so he could ask something generic. If he thinks he's hitting deep, he could ask about my family, my love life – but those are things I won't mind answering about.

'All right. But I want to go first,' I say, hoping to lay the ground for this.

'Ask away. I'm an open book.'

A laugh escapes me. 'You're more locked up than a thirteen-year-old's secret diary.'

'Just ask the question, Farah,' Zayan replies, but I hear a note of amusement in his voice as well.

I pause for a moment, thinking over my options. I could ask him about his hopes, his dreams, everything in between, but there are really just two things everyone in the world wants to know about Zayan Amin: why did he and Laiba break up, and why did he do that TV series?

They're also the two questions everyone is too afraid to ask him straight to his face. Or, rather, they're the two questions no one is allowed to ask him.

In the end, I pick the one that I think will tell me more about the enigma that is Zayan Amin, leaving the other mystery to be solved at a later date.

'Why did you take that TV-series role?' His shocked intake of breath spurs me on, forcing me to keep talking.

'*The Fairbanks* was such a hit, and after meeting Lacey, I'm sure you pick projects that will clearly benefit your career. It just seems a little strange to me. You're a good actor –'

'Wow, such high praise,' Zayan mumbles lightly.

I sigh. 'OK, you want the truth? You're brilliant. Hari Fairbanks was my childhood favourite. You're probably one of the reasons I wanted to become an actor. So tell me: why'd you sign up for that TV series? What was the thought process?'

'Do you know how many movies I've done over the course of my career?' Zayan questions, his tone edged with something sharp now.

'Uh . . . not off the top of my head,' I lie, because I will *not* inflate his ego and tell him that I've watched all of his films.

'Eleven. I've done eleven movies. I've been acting since I was two years old. And despite doing eleven movies, I'm always known as one specific character.'

'Hari Fairbanks,' I reply quietly.

'Hari Fairbanks,' Zayan echoes. 'And I don't want to sound ungrateful. *The Fairbanks* put me on the map; it made it possible for me to do those movies. But when casting agents and directors would reach out to Lacey, they'd give me roles that resembled Hari. The good kid. The loveable sidekick. It was one role, all the time. So when I learned that *The Fairbanks* was ending, I knew this was my chance to make my mark. To be *more* than just the cute kid on a sitcom, or in a movie. There was so much chaos during that time. Calls with Lacey trying to work out where we'd land my career, what avenue we should go down. Comedy? Drama? How serious an actor was I?' He pauses before sighing deeply. 'And that's when Shawn Jetts approached me.'

'Shawn Jetts – the director?' I clarify.

'The one and only,' he replies, and this time, the bitterness in his voice is unmistakable. 'He took me out for dinners, introduced me to all the big names in Hollywood, proudly boasting that I was ready to make this great big change. That the industry should watch out for me. And he would fill my head with these dreams of being the lead in a new show. He told me I'd get creative licence to finally do what I liked. I didn't need to be in the restraints of Hari Fairbanks any more.' He pauses, and I hear a beat of rustling movement. I imagine Zayan sitting upright in his bed, indignant now. 'When he finally offered the role, I didn't even ask to look at the script. I just signed my name. I didn't give Lacey time to double-check anything. I was so desperate for the chance; I was afraid it would all vanish if I didn't work fast enough. It was only when I'd signed the contract that I got the script. And then I realized why I'd been approached.'

'And why was that?' I ask, curiosity pushing me forward.

His tone is as bitter as a lemon, so sour that my own lips pucker. 'To play a stereotype. They wanted a show about the brown boy who hates every part of himself and desperately wants to be white. It was humiliating to be part of that, and it felt . . .' He pauses, and I wait, heart aching in my chest. 'It felt like I'd betrayed who I am. And my fans saw that. Rightly so. But it hurt more to know that they thought I didn't care. That I was OK with these stereotypes. But I wasn't. I'm not. That's why doing this play is so important. This is my chance to save my reputation, yes, but also to fix my mistakes. You were right when you told me why we should do *Heer Ranjha*. You were right when you said it's sad that I've ignored my culture for so long. I don't want the world thinking I hate who I am. That I've forgotten who I am.'

A freight train of realization slams into my senses. He is a boy who misses home. Even if he won't admit it. A boy who hasn't had a taste of family in a long time. A boy who had to give it all up – and no matter if he says it was his choice, to a degree it wasn't. He did it to survive an industry that stacked the odds against him.

'How long has it been since you've been ho—' I falter and cut myself off, treading the waters of Zayan's past carefully, knowing one wrong move could shut him down. 'How long since you've been back in Karachi?'

He shrugs. 'The last time I was in Karachi, I was thirteen.'

Five years ago?

'I went there to visit my grandparents after winning my first Emmy. Then I went back to the US, and I was lucky to have family living there, so I stayed with them – the only perk of having extended family,' he jokes.

I crack a smile, even as a well of empathy fills up in my heart. 'Your parents didn't follow you?'

'They did, until I hit my teens and it became clear I wasn't going to be living in one place. They asked if I wanted to do this alone. And I did. Plus, I had Lacey and security, and collectively they never let me run wild. Ever. I mean, I've always got two people outside my door or in my car in case a rogue fan slips in.' His tone shifts to something a little softer. 'It was lonely sometimes, but I think it's important to learn how to be happy with your own company.'

In a way, I understand what he means. I've been around my family and friends my whole life, but since coming here, I've become accustomed to dealing with acute loneliness, the kind that occurs when you're still around people. In Zayan's case, he seems to have learned how to deal with that, but I haven't. I find it stifling. I find myself craving friendships to fill the hole I've got gaping in my chest.

Overwhelmed with sudden emotion, I have nothing to add. The silence between us is heavy with memories, with feelings I don't want to have, with questions and answers that are like knives pressing against soft skin.

I hear him swallow roughly. 'I think it's my turn to ask a question.'

I let him change the subject, steadying myself against the headboard I'm now pressed up against. I know it's a long shot, but I desperately, painfully hope he doesn't ask about my LSDCATS audition. I'm not sure I could give him the truth.

'Shoot,' I say, masking the nerves in my voice.

'Why are you doing this?' Zayan asks. 'Why are you so desperate to be on stage? What is it about being on stage that has you agreeing to be in a fake relationship with a guy you don't know?'

The twisted fear and anticipation I had over his potential question dissipates.

This is easy. No matter how bad my impostor syndrome is, I know what my dreams are.

'I like the feeling when I'm on stage,' I start, and I know I should launch into my generic answer – something about enjoying the attention, the production of it all – but I want to reciprocate Zayan's honesty. 'I like the safety of stepping into a character, being someone else on stage. I can't be rejected if I'm not me. I can't be overlooked. I can't be stared at. I can't be judged. I can live out another's story that isn't my own but feels like it. That's why becoming an actress is the dream. I can't see myself doing anything else and being happy.'

We've both answered our questions now, shared more than we probably intended, and naturally the conversation should end here. We should both hang up and go to sleep.

But we don't. I stare out of the window, watching the stars glint in the sky, wondering what I should say.

The sound of Zayan's voice startles me. So does the question.

'Do you want to run lines?'

I press my teeth to my lower lip.

Say no. Go to sleep. Be friendly, nothing more.

'Sure.'

Chapter Sixteen

Desi Night is a fortnightly occurrence among my friends. This October, our flat is hosting it on the fourteenth. It's an all-night event that involves all my London-dwelling friends from back home, even those who I didn't know well when we were at Rocate High.

It's a night that celebrates being brown. A night that makes us remember what home felt like. A night that brings us all together to remind us of where we came from.

'You're making gol gappay, right?' Owais asks, a desperate pleading note in his voice. He stands beside Amal, helping her make garlic naans. 'Last time you made channa chaat, and you promised!'

In response, Amal pulls out the board she prepared this morning; sitting all over it are hollow golden spheres of crispy, thin dough that will soon be filled with imili chutney pani – green in colour – and a mixture of dried chickpeas and fluffy potatoes. Alongside those are an assortment of samosas: fat ones filled with qeema and thin ones filled with cheese. For dessert, we've got your classic mithai: warm gulab jamun to be served with vanilla ice cream, kulfi in the freezer, jalebis soaked in sugar syrup, and this mango concoction Amal has been playing around with.

'All right –' Maha strides into the steaming kitchen, holding her phone in her hands – 'I've got the next episode of *Meray Paas Tum Ho* ready to go. When's everyone showing up?'

'In ten minutes,' I reply, nervously playing with the cuffs of my kameez. I always try to wear a different one for Desi Night – it's why I had Ammi ship me a whole suitcase dedicated solely to winter kameezes. It makes me feel closer to home.

'I'm excited to meet your new friends, Farah,' Owais says, though his attention is on Amal. He's handing her all the right things, orbiting round her like she's the sun, just happy to be there with her. At one point, he simply leans against the stove and watches her with the softest look on his face.

'Seriously, they should just get married now,' Maha says, pulling up a chair to sit beside me. 'I mean, I get that they're waiting till they finish their degrees and are settled and all that, but come on. They're so in love it actually hurts.'

'They are,' I agree, trying to ignore the twinge in my chest by turning my attention to Maha. 'How about you, though?'

She shakes her head and then smirks. 'Nope. No love stories here. But, speaking of love stories, I'm disappointed that a certain someone isn't coming tonight.'

I laugh, albeit uncomfortably. While I did extend an invite to The Tragedies, as a way of continuing to build our patchwork friendship, I didn't invite Zayan. Only because I was sure he'd despise this night in its entirety. A whole event based around Pakistani culture probably wouldn't be something he'd enjoy when he's already so torn up about his identity.

'We're not dating,' I remind Maha. 'I don't date; you know that. I'm a long-term person.'

'Mhm, sure. And who's to say he isn't? Everyone online believes you two are meant to last a lifetime.'

She's not entirely wrong. I turned my Instagram from private to public, and all the comments underneath my photos were about Zayan – asking if I was with him right now. The public *truly* believes something is going on – so do my friends – and the thought of eventually telling them the truth makes my stomach knot with nerves. I really hope they don't kill me.

The sound of the doorbell ringing shoves those worries away for later. I go to get it, knowing it's probably The Tragedies.

'Hey!' Anushka says, throwing her arms round my neck to pull me into a strong hug. 'Wow, I love your flat! It's so cute!'

As Anushka walks in, followed by the rest, a pulse of awkwardness floods me. Whenever Amal or Maha bring home friends from their universities, it's always effortless. They come in, they say hello and we all hang out together. I want it to be the same for me.

I breathe in deeply, press a smile on my lips and lead The Tragedies into the living room, where Maha, Amal and Owais have decided to congregate. They wait, and I realize I'm supposed to lead the introductions.

'Oh, uh, guys, these are The Tragedies. This is David, Ben, Anushka and Nur.'

Nur offers a box in their general direction. 'I brought over some mithai, as a thank-you for inviting us.'

Maha moves fluidly, ever the confident one, taking the box from Nur's hands and introducing herself. 'Hi, I'm Maha, the resident communication and media student.'

A look of intrigue plays on Nur's expression. 'That was my second option, but I ultimately decided to go into fashion.'

'Fashion?' Maha asks, an eager gleam in her eyes. 'I'm always looking for ways to upgrade my wardrobe. Tell me more.'

Nur walks over to the couch to join Maha in a conversation. After that interaction, the tension melts away – and soon David is sitting beside Owais, trading high-school-debate stories, and more of our guests have started to arrive. Music fills the flat, and someone puts on a playlist of TikTok remixes of popular desi songs.

When the last guest shows up, I close the door behind them and stand at the edge of the living room, just taking in the feeling. Everyone's laughing, enjoying themselves, and there's a sense of nostalgia seeping into the space – in the floorboards, in the walls, in the air.

I smile to myself, watching as Ben gets cornered by an

old schoolmate of mine, Nida, and is made to try the gol gappay. His face breaks into a grin, and he catches me staring. He throws me a thumbs up, and I shake my head in amusement.

This feeling is like being on stage, but different. On stage, I'm trying so hard to be anyone but myself. But right now, I don't want to leave.

Still, I decide to escape while everyone is busy to help Amal bring out the dessert. But when I walk into the kitchen, I find Anushka is already there helping her.

'It's just so hard,' Anushka complains, scooping a spoonful of the mango dessert Amal has made. 'The other day, I had someone comment on how I should use this new skin-bleaching cream to survive next summer – like, what? And they said it so casually, as if it wasn't racially motivated in any way.'

My heart drops to my stomach, and I close the doorway of the kitchen so that I'm hidden, but it's open just enough for me to continue listening.

'I get what you mean,' Amal replies, and I'm momentarily confused. Amal has never mentioned anything to me about this. 'I have a similar sort of family dynamic back home. I don't really talk about it much. I'm not sure everyone is going to get it.'

In terms of the skin shades of our group, I'm the lightest, and Owais is the darkest. Amal falls somewhere in the middle, lighter than Maha but darker than me. I've never imagined that the colour of *my* skin may have made it hard for her to share her troubles. I wonder how many times back home I made Amal feel that she couldn't come to me – that I wouldn't understand.

Would I understand?

I know what racism is. I've studied it. I've seen it in videos, and – well, back home I only ever had aunties cooing over the shade of my skin, always clucking at my cousins for going out in the sun, and it never crossed my mind how wrong that was. How messed up it was that I stood by and allowed myself to be fawned over because of my skin tone.

But I really don't need another light-skinned Pakistani friend complaining about their struggles with being too pale.

Gibitah. *Oh*. I close my eyes, a sick sort of nausea climbing up my throat, and rest my head against the wall as Gibitah's words, and her ice-cold demeanour, start to make more sense.

I don't face what The Tragedies endure, I don't battle what Amal has to experience, and it's all because I don't look like them. We share the same country, the same culture, but we clearly don't share the same experience of prejudice.

I can't believe I *missed* it. I think of the conversation I've been avoiding with Gibitah, and I wonder if some unconscious part of me is holding back.

Well, whatever it is, I *refuse* to avoid it. I'll talk to Gibitah. She won't be here for tomorrow's rehearsal – she isn't scheduled in – but on Monday I'll listen to her, I'll learn and I'll change.

Whatever it is I have to do, I'll do it.

As the determination starts to solidify in my veins, I only realize that Amal and Anushka are bringing out the desserts just before the kitchen door swings open.

'Oh!' Anushka exclaims. 'Sorry, Farah, I didn't see you there!'

'No, no problem. I was just wondering if Amal needed help with bringing the desserts.'

Anushka's expression shifts, a sudden worry sparking in her brown eyes. She's balancing a tray in her hands, and she moves from foot to foot. 'I – I wanted to thank you for inviting me. Your friends are so nice, and it's been really fun getting to know everyone.'

My eyebrows draw together at her tentative tone, and then I realize why she's saying that. *Oh gosh. Does she think I'm upset she's hanging out with Amal?*

I squeeze her arm, hoping to convey that I have no possessive claim over Amal. Or anyone. 'Believe me, Anushka, it's a real pleasure to have you here. I've learned you can never have enough friends.'

Anushka must get it, because her shoulders relax. We walk together, Amal following behind us, into the living room.

'Yes! Desserts!' Owais exclaims excitedly. He stands to take the tray from Amal's hands and places it on the table in the centre of the living room. He whispers something to her that makes her blush and shove his chest lightly. I look away, not wanting to intrude on another private moment.

We all settle in to watch the show after that, Owais and Amal occupying the couch, Nur and Maha sitting together on the floor; Ben, David and Anushka sit around me, their large cushions resting against the front of the sofa.

With David's laughter booming in my ears, the fragrance of Anushka's perfume filling my senses and the sound of Ben's disbelief as the main character slaps her love interest with dramatic music playing in the background, my worries settle into the back of my mind.

For now.

Chapter Seventeen

Sunday was meant to be blissful. To a degree, it was. Without any rehearsal, my immediate attention fell to the TikTok Lives and preparing for them with Zayan. The Lives would work two-fold; they'd help with Zayan's publicity, but also with the play's. That was why I reached out to him right after everyone left Desi Night.

> Hey!! Just wanted to know if we could use a portion of tomorrow's practice for planning how we're going to tackle the Lives. 00:00

Zayan (The Actor):

> 00:12 Hey. I won't be able to come to the rehearsal tomorrow. I've got an audition.

> Oh. No worries. Good luck for
> your audition! How about
> Sunday? We could FaceTime
> and just iron out what we're
> going to say and do. Maybe
> we could bring in Pierre too.

00:13

Read: 00:13

Left. On. Read. He left me on read. I didn't message again. That felt desperate, and I was too busy obsessing over why his attitude had changed back to the cold celebrity I first thought he was.

♥

My suspicions about Zayan are confirmed when I see him standing on stage on Monday, holding his script in his hands; the cast and crew's attention momentarily falls to me as I walk in, including Zayan's. When our eyes meet, he doesn't linger. He looks away, going even as far as to turn his body away from my general direction.

I greet Anushka, keeping Zayan and David in my peripheral vision. Zayan has pressed his palm to his cheek, one arm wrapped round his upper body as he listens to David. I will him to look at me, wishing we had some telepathic connection.

I shouldn't care that he's not paying attention to me, but I can't help it. Now that he's *not* looking at me, I feel like I've lost something. Zayan's attention is like a spotlight; it focuses on you entirely. There's no wavering, no gaps – just his undiluted gaze upon you – but when he does switch it off, it leaves you hollowed out. Pushed into the shadows. Unseen.

'I had a great time at Desi Night,' Anushka says loudly, forcing my thoughts towards her. 'All the food, the vibes, it was amazing. I just loved how fun it was to have all of us together.'

I muster up a grin. 'Yeah, it was really great to have you guys. You all have a permanent invitation, by the way. You can come on the twenty-eighth as well, if you want.'

'Well, I have to come. I need to know what happens after that cliffhanger.'

I laugh, remembering how loudly Anushka gasped at the end of the show. Before I can tease her about it, she's called over by another cast member. It gives me a chance to look at Zayan again. His back faces me, and I notice how tight his shoulders are. Zayan breathes nonchalance, ease, but not right now. His body is taut with tension, or agitation.

Something is wrong.

Is this about his audition? It could be, but I don't know why he'd be ignoring *me* if it went badly. Unless . . . unless it's about me – or us? Maybe it's because of how much he shared on our last call; maybe he feels too exposed. Maybe he's afraid I'll use that against him, like how everyone else seems to weaponize knowledge about him to hurt him.

Before I can drag Zayan to a corner of the theatre, away from prying eyes, Ben brings us together himself.

'OK, so we're doing the first TikTok Live today,' Ben says, excitement bright in his smile.

I shoot a look Zayan's way, hoping to convey that he *needs* to speak to me before the Live starts. I know he can feel my stare, but he resolutely, stubbornly looks forward. Aggravation starts building under my skin, my patience thinning.

'I'm going to show the public the tech room first,' Ben goes on to explain. 'And then you guys just need to be in the background together. Maybe for some of the later Lives you can actually talk to the fans together?'

Zayan nods and then walks off. I watch him, my mouth close to hanging open.

'Did something happen between you two?' Ben asks, confused.

'No!' I reply indignantly. 'We were fine when we spoke last. I don't know why he's acting like this. I don't even know how we're going to do our scene today.'

'You aren't doing a scene today,' Ben replies. 'Didn't you see the timetable change?'

I scramble for my phone, looking at the timetable. Apparently, we're going *backwards* and doing a scene we've already done.

'Who made the change?'

Ben shrugs and shiftily refuses to meet my eyes.

'Ben?' I ask warningly.

'Look, why don't you treat today as a break? Just relax and wait for my cue, and everything will be fine.'

♥

I ignore Ben's advice and start searching for something else I can improve in the play. If Zayan doesn't want to work on our chemistry and how that translates on the Live, then that just gives *me* more time to fix another relationship that will help the play succeed.

Gibitah.

I look backstage for her, and I know she's scheduled for today because we're supposed to be doing a scene with one another. When the costume room is also empty, I'm almost ready to give up. Until I remember one more place from my tour with Zayan.

Backstage, in the left wing, there's a trapdoor that leads under the stage. It's essentially a storage place now, with dusty boxes of old costumes, wires and cables. I descend the rickety staircase, sort of hoping Gibitah isn't there, because the room also doubles up pretty well as a murder spot.

'Gibitah?' I call out.

I find a thread hanging from the ceiling, and after I tug on it light illuminates the room. Gibitah's form is the first thing I see, her arms crossed over her chest, her eyes watery, her lips dipped into a frown.

'Uh . . .' I begin awkwardly. If someone stumbled upon me crying, what would I want them to do? 'Would you like me to switch the light back off and leave?'

She turns her head slowly, giving me an appraising look, before turning forward again. Moments of silence stretch between us like taffy, snapping when Gibitah starts to speak.

'I'm thinking of quitting the play,' she says, her tone so solid and sure.

I lurch towards her. 'No, Gibitah, you can't leave. Look, I know I messed up before, but you can't leave because of –'

Her sharp laugh feels like broken glass piercing my skin. 'You cannot be making this about you right now.'

I close my eyes briefly, shaking my head. 'I wasn't trying to. I just meant . . . if I made you feel uncomfortable, and that's why you're thinking of leaving, please don't.'

Gibitah pauses, then fully turns to face me. Her eyes are blazing, her mouth set in a firm line. 'Do you know what my dream is, Farah?'

'No,' I reply uneasily. 'What is it?'

'To be on stage. Not in Hollywood. Just on stage. Theatre. That's where my heart belongs. I don't know if this play is the best chance for me to get there. Professionally. Officially.'

'Well, you're wrong,' I insist, softening my voice. 'Look, I'm going to tell you something that I need you to keep between the two of us.'

'OK . . .' Gibitah says doubtfully.

I choose my words carefully, making sure I don't break any rules by revealing something I shouldn't. But this doesn't need to be a secret. In fact, the whole cast *should* know this, because it would be a great motivator.

'When Zayan signed on to be part of the play, I asked if he could get some talent scouts, casting agents, directors and industry professionals to be in the audience. He – because he's just so *generous* – agreed. Do you know what that means? So many opportunities to be picked up.'

Gibitah's lips remain turned into a frown. Her eyes swing away from me to the walls of the room. I follow them, noticing that there are picture frames all over the surface – aged sepia photos of actors, actresses, plays that have been performed at the Limelight. I move to stand shoulder to shoulder with Gibitah, taking in the years and years of history that this room is steeped in.

The ache in my chest blossoms into a wholehearted desire to have my picture up there. To be among those stars.

'And why,' Gibitah asks, 'do you think any of those talent scouts would pick me over you? Even if we're both on an equal footing for talent, equal footing for skill, equal footing for the roles we play, why would *anyone* pick me over you?'

I know what she's referring to now. Her implication is startlingly clear.

'Gibitah, I understand where you're coming from –'

She rounds on me, angry now. 'No, you don't. You don't understand what it means to be overlooked, ignored. To never be chosen because you're darker-skinned and there's someone else out there who fits the criteria better simply because they *look whiter*. I can't compete with that.'

I struggle to find the right words, not knowing what will sound patronizing or falsely optimistic.

'You're right. I have an unfair advantage. A privilege,' I admit, cheeks burning in humiliation. I rally, not wanting my ignorance to be the thing that takes away Gibitah's opportunity. 'But that's not why this play is here. It's not here to give only me an upper hand. It's here to celebrate all marginalized voices.'

'Do you know what colourism is?' Gibitah asks, after I finish.

The words to snap back at her are on the tip of my tongue. *Of course I know what colourism is; I'm not ignorant.* But the truth is I know what colourism is in the same way I know what photosynthesis is. I know photosynthesis is the process by which plants make their food. I know colourism is a type of prejudice where lighter skin is favoured over darker skin, whether from those of the same race or different races. Both are something I was taught – in a classroom. But I don't think that's what Gibitah's asking me. She doesn't want some *academic* definition of the word. She's asking me if I know how colourism really impacts her every day, and whether I'm aware of how it impacts me.

I lace my hands together and swallow against the ball of shame in my throat before replying. 'I know – I know what it means, but –'

Gibitah's voice is a touch cold, but so raw with anger. 'But not what it *really* is. You haven't ever really thought about what privileges you have because of colourism. Don't you know how insidious it is? How ingrained it is in our culture? It's more than skin-whitening creams, Farah. It's in *every* part of your life. It's in the opportunities that come your way, or don't come. It's growing up being told you'll probably find it hard to get married one day because darker-skinned girls just aren't as pretty. It's having to wear a foundation that doesn't match your real skin tone just in case it makes you *look* lighter, or because there's no foundation available that actually matches your skin shade. It's being overlooked for jobs because it's easier to hire a light-skinned brown girl. And in this system, you win. I lose. Do you *really* get that? Or do you just know what the word means?'

Gibitah's eyes hold mine, and her question makes my stomach turn.

Colourism.

I may not have hated my friends for their skin tone, or treated them differently, but I stood by while they were facing the brunt of it. Unaware. Ignorant. A silent accomplice. I benefited from a system and didn't think about how to help anyone else with the privilege I had.

I reach over and grab Gibitah's hand in my own, holding on tight. 'I'm sorry for how ignorant I was being before. You're right; we live in a society that plays favourites, that is full of biases, that is disgustingly prejudiced, and I'm sorry for not acknowledging my privilege. For not standing up when I should have. But, Gibitah, at the heart of all of this, this play *is* going to give you a chance. To give you an opportunity. It's not a competition, I promise you. If those talent agents wanted Zayan, they'd just go through Lacey, Zayan's agent. If they wanted me, they've had a million ways of reaching out ever since I started being seen with him. Those casting agents who are coming on opening night are hungry for talent. Lacey is making sure of that. It will not be a repeat of the LSDCATS casting. I promise, you are not a token. You are important, integral, just like Zayan, just like me, just like anyone else in this cast. You will not be overlooked.'

Gibitah's hand feels tense in mine, and she slowly pulls out of my grasp. 'Farah, that's a really sweet gesture. But you can't guarantee that casting agents won't come with their own prejudices. You can't make promises like that. Not when I have a situation that is far more complicated than you probably know.'

Embarrassment turns my cheeks hot as I realize how I've made it sound like I can just solve all of Gibitah's problems, and I find it hard to continue meeting her eyes.

'I'm sorry,' I say, keeping my hands to myself this time. 'I realize how unrealistic and over-optimistic my plan is, I just – I want to help. In any way. And I want you to stay, but only if you think it will benefit you.'

'I know you really want things to be different,' Gibitah replies, her tone less guarded than before. A complicated emotion flickers over her face, like she's making a decision, but one that doesn't come lightly. 'I'll stay, for the play. I don't *want* to work for a racist organization like LSDCATS, and I'd rather support someone who's willing to try and help the situation than stand by and let it go on.'

My embarrassment from before doesn't exactly fade away, but it mingles with the relief I feel that Gibitah is staying. I can't fix Gibitah's situation. It was naive of me to think I could. But maybe I can help her in some small way – maybe I can be a shoulder to lean on, or maybe I can help force open a door that wouldn't budge before. All I know is I can't slap a plaster over Gibitah's problems – but I can be there for whatever she needs.

'Give me your number,' I say, quickly pulling out my phone. 'We're at the same university, right? When you're on campus, or when you have a break between classes, hit me up and we'll hang out. We can talk about the play, run lines or discuss anything you want. I'm here to listen. I'm here for you if you need me.'

Gibitah's silence leaves me unmoored, afraid of being rebuked, but then a slow smile touches her lips. I sway a little with relief as she types in her contact details. While I'm adding my details to her phone, there's a knock on the trapdoor above us, and Ben's head popping in has us both craning our necks upwards.

I jolt into my role at the sight of his phone.

'And here we have Farah Sheikh! The star of our show!' he says jovially to the viewers of the TikTok Live. 'Next rehearsal, I'll show you loyal viewers what's actually going on under the stage, but for now let's see what's going on above. Right, Farah?'

Ah, the cue. Subtle as always.

I turn back to Gibitah, and her brows furrow at me.

'What?' she asks, confused.

'Do *you* want to do the TikTok Live?' I ask, thinking of how it would be good exposure for Gibitah. 'Maybe talk about your role? The play?'

Gibitah takes a moment before nodding, and then follows me as I make my way to Ben. We climb out of the trapdoor and back into the left wing, and find ourselves standing right in front of Ben. He's all smiles as we approach, holding the phone with a steady hand.

I wave to the camera. 'Hi, everyone! We're so excited that you guys are watching! I have to dash off to ready myself for a scene, but why don't you talk to Gibitah in the meantime? She's my right-hand woman for all of the play. I don't know where Heer would be without her.'

Smoothly, Gibitah takes my spot, and I watch from behind Ben as she flawlessly answers the questions our Live watchers are asking – inevitably, most are about Zayan, but slowly that changes, and there are questions about the play, about rehearsals and about how *she* got involved in this play.

When she's fully engrossed, I take a moment to rush out of the wings and find Zayan. I know Ben will end the Live with a shot of Zayan and me in the background, to drum up even more support. I need to get to Zayan before the camera does, just so I can bandage over whatever we're struggling with, even if we can't fix it right now.

I'm moving so fast that I don't realize I've collided with someone.

Automatically, David reaches out to steady me by my forearms. 'Woah, woah. Where are you off to?'

I laugh, a little breathlessly, as I step out of his hold. His arms move away, and I steady myself. 'Sorry, I'm just looking for Zayan.'

David smiles, all teeth and glimmering eyes. He points behind me. 'Well, he's right there.'

I do a full one-eighty on my heel, hoping to be greeted with a somewhat thawed Zayan, but instead he's glaring at me. Behind me, David huffs out a laugh at something, but

I ignore him and walk straight towards Zayan – readying myself for the brunt of his cold exterior.

'Hey,' I start, pretending I'm not Farah. I'm on a stage; that means I'm not *allowed* to be me. Instead, I'm a stronger version of Farah. I'm closer to Heer than myself. 'I think we need to talk.' He tilts his head, arms folded over his chest, waiting for me to continue. This is frostier than usual. I'm not even getting a greeting. 'I'm not sure what you're going through, but your attitude is starting to reflect badly on our relationship. Shove a smile on your face, and look like we're having a good, fun, loving conversation, because Ben's coming up with the Live.'

Zayan's face, expressive when he decides it'll be, flashes through several emotions – shock, frustration, anger – before settling as a blank slate. His lips part as if he's about to say something, and I brace myself, but he chooses silence instead.

It hurts in a way I didn't expect.

I haven't deluded myself into believing Zayan and I are friends, not really. But I didn't think we were like this. Impersonal to a new degree. If we were dating, I'd have lashed out at him. Called him out more insistently. But I can be professional.

'You need to look like you're talking, genius,' I say scathingly. 'Otherwise it just looks like we're staring at one another silently.'

Zayan's eyes flash, jaw tightening, before he rearranges his face.

'Were you the one who changed the timetable?' I ask, keeping a smile on my lips. From the corner of my eye, I see Ben videoing us.

'Yes,' he replies, and I'm surprised by his blatant honesty. 'Why?'

'I couldn't be around you today.'

I swallow against the roughness in my throat, thinking of saying something equally harsh when Ben interrupts us.

'All right, guys! We're free!' Ben calls out and waves his phone to show the Live has ended. Zayan wastes no time in walking off, leaving me to bear the weight of our unfinished conversation.

What happened to him?

My anger worsens as I watch Zayan smile and joke with The Tragedies for the rest of the rehearsal. It turns into an inferno as he guides another actress through her scene, completely ignoring me. I barely hold myself together when Zayan rushes out of the Limelight at the end of rehearsals, like being around me has physically driven him away.

It doesn't help my fury that it's raining when I leave – not a smattering of droplets but a full-blown shower – and I'm drenched by the time I get to the flat.

I finally implode when I slip into bed, ready for sleep, and my phone buzzes. I grab it off the side table, hoping it's Zayan with an apology. *He should grovel a little more. I should at least get a phone call.*

But it's not what I expected. It's much worse than a lacklustre apology. It's a nail in the coffin. It's Zayan dehumanizing our deal, turning it into nothing more than a piece of paper with fancy words, saying: *You are a means to an end, nothing more.*

It's a sign of just how recklessly stupid he's being.

From: Zayan Amin

Subject: Relationship contract

Fortune Teller
20 October 2021

TIK TOK VS INSTAGRAM: WHERE ARE YOU?

We were delighted when The Tragedies announced that they were starting a series of TikTok Lives leading up to the opening night of their play! But we were disappointed when the first one happened two days ago – we were hoping to see more Zayan and Farah, but the mere glimpse we got of them didn't really do much for us.

It was nice to get to know some of the other cast members, like Gibitah Siddiqi, who seems so cool. We loved how personable she was, and that she's a cat person! A clear rising star, definitely someone to look out for.

But, overall, the Live sort of fell flat for us.

It's why we were *so* curious when The LSDCATS announced their Instagram Live the following day. It turns out we had nothing to worry about, because the LSDCATS are amazing at showcasing their talent – especially their main actors, Mary Whitter (Juliet) and Rowan Kent (Romeo).

They were too adorable! Especially when studying lines together – the chemistry was palpable. We're sure fans are soon to be obsessed with this new couple!

ARTICLE COMMENTS:

TheatreDreamer: I don't know about you guys, but I'm 100% shipping Rary. They are so CUTE.

ZayanIsMyLove: Rary?

TheatreDreamer: Rowan and Mary.

ZayanIsMyLove: Come on, Zayan and Farah – Zarah – are right there.

TheatreDreamer: IDK . . . on The Tragedies' TikTok Live, they had ZERO interaction.

ZayanIsMyLove: They're private people. They stay away from cameras.

TheatreDreamer: Whatever. All I know is I'm watching the LSDCATS' play and their Instagram Lives. #Rary

Chapter Eighteen

'You two need to make up,' Anushka says, her voice tense. She's decked in a bright-orange boiler suit, her hair in the most stylish messy bun, her winged eyeliner as sharp as her gaze, and in the face of her intensity, Gibitah and I try not to cower.

Gibitah and I were running lines before we were accosted by Anushka and Nur. It was nice; we were getting to know one another, and I even told her that Zayan and I were experiencing some tension. I didn't tell her why – obviously our partnership is still meant to be a secret – but it was nice to have someone to unload on who knew nothing about the inner workings of our deal.

'We only have six weeks left, and we can't afford any setbacks,' Nur continues, her voice more pleading, like I'm the one who's causing this tension with Zayan.

'We're fine,' I reply, refusing to look at Zayan, who is running lines with Ben on the other side of the stage.

We've spent another rehearsal not speaking to one

another, and my side of the silence is all due to my crucial three-step plan for surviving today.

1. Ignore Zayan.
2. Fake my way through rehearsals and don't jeopardize the play by letting my emotions spill over.
3. Throw the signed contract in Zayan's face.

No talking. Not about the contract, which I printed out last night and brought here in a clear plastic folder. Not about anything. If Zayan wants to play this silent game, I'm a more-than-willing participant.

'First off, the LSDCATS literally copied us by doing Instagram Lives, but no one cares about that because you two have inadvertently started a shipping war between you and the LSDCATS leads,' Nur chides, looking as exasperated as Anushka. 'A shipping war that you're losing.'

Nur isn't wrong. The last couple of days have been filled with tweets and comments about how adorable the LSDCATS leads are, and how unlovely and frigid Zayan and I are. Our one bad Live, coupled with our lack of interaction in front of the paparazzi lately, has almost undone all our previous work.

And while it may not be my fault, it is terrifying to know that public opinion really is that fickle.

'The LSDCATS can overshadow us with this new publicity,' Anushka stresses, anxiety present in her voice. 'It's so easy for them to capitalize on our mistakes, on our pitfalls. We need you two to work it out.'

I glance Zayan's way, at the back of his head. In the deepest parts of my heart, I'm worried too. Underneath all that anger, I'm afraid that Zayan might pull out of the play. That whatever happened is so grievous that he won't mind leaving. And that would destroy us.

'I tried,' I say finally, confused about whether I should feel the fear or the anger more intensely. 'He's the one who's acting like I don't exist any more.'

Anushka rubs her forehead wearily. 'Are you sure you can't try talking to him one more time?'

The relationship contract flashes in my mind; embarrassment wraps round my ribs and pushes against my lungs.

'Why should Farah be the one to talk to him?' Gibitah intervenes. 'She's not the one who started this cold-shoulder game they've got going on.'

Anushka stares at us, gaze calculating, lips pursed. 'You're right. It's not your fault, Farah.' She shares a look with Nur and then smiles. 'No worries; I'll deal with it.'

A sense of foreboding prickles under my skin when the two of them walk away, heads bent close together.

'She's up to something. You know that, right?' Gibitah asks with a laugh.

'Yeah,' I sigh, shaking my head. 'I know.'

We go on with the rest of the rehearsal without any hitches. Zayan and I act out our scenes professionally, giving each other blank-eyed stares and nothing more. I get some time towards the end of the act to sit upstage, just reading through my lines, dipping into Heer's world, with Gibitah beside me as we intermittently play intense rounds of snap.

'Farah! Zayan!' I look up from the script at the sound of David's call. He's sitting in the front row, along with the rest of The Tragedies.

As I approach downstage, I catch Anushka's half smirk, and I'm instantly on guard. I share a look with Gibitah, who is leaving to catch her bus. She gives me a sympathetic thumbs up.

I end up at the edge of the stage with Zayan, who's come out of the left wing. I studiously avoid looking at him, sticking to my three-step plan. I'm about to hop down from the stage when Ben stops me.

'Nope.' He annoyingly pops the 'p' with more joy than necessary. 'You're staying up there.'

'Why?' Zayan asks gruffly.

'We're doing our second TikTok Live to counter the backlash we've got from the LSDCATS' Live. You two are going to do a "Cast Q&A",' Nur explains, a sly look in her eyes.

'No,' I immediately say. 'No, we are not. Guys, don't –'

'She's right; we shouldn't –' Zayan begins.

'Too late, I've already started!' Ben interrupts loudly, and Zayan and I snap into place.

'Hi, everyone! Welcome to the second Tragedies Live,' Ben announces, excitedly talking to the camera. David and Anushka come forward, forcing Zayan and I to sit on the edge of the stage, while Ben and Nur entertain the viewers.

'So, today we're going to have a really fun segment. We asked you, our loyal fans, to send in questions you'd like answered about Farah and Zayan,' Nur explains.

I finally share a look with Zayan – both our gazes are asking, *Did you know about this?*

'However, the fun twist is that these are going to be questions about Farah and Zayan that the opposite person has to answer.'

My eyes widen, a protest pressed up against my lips. We can't do this. We aren't *prepared* for this. We haven't had any training on what answers we're supposed to give.

'Just fake it,' Zayan says under his breath, still refusing to look at me. 'I'll agree with whatever answer you give.'

I reply, equally quietly, 'I'm going to say you replace your cereal milk with apple juice because you enjoy the quirkiness of it.'

The genuine horror in his eyes almost makes me laugh, but I harden my heart to stone. He doesn't deserve my forgiveness. His face flashes with something unfamiliar, shadowing his eyes.

'Farah –' Zayan starts.

'All right, let's get started with question number one!' David interrupts, like he's hosting his own talk show. 'Is your co-star a night owl or an early bird?'

The secretive smile on my mouth is so fake it could've been painted on with clown make-up. But I pretend to think my answer over before giving it. 'I'd say an early bird for Zayan.'

'Night owl for Farah,' Zayan replies, keeping his tone just as upbeat as mine.

We go on like that for another five minutes, answering hideously easy questions about one another. Can your co-star drive? (Farah, yes; Zayan, yes.) Does your co-star like animals? (Farah, yes; Zayan, only rabbits.) What's your co-star's go-to hot drink? (Chai for both.)

'All right, final question, does your co-star have any rituals before going on stage?' Anushka asks.

I pause, knowing Zayan doesn't know the answer to this. No one does. I do my ritual before every rehearsal, and I do it by myself. It's not something huge, like Sharpay from *High School Musical* doing her vocal exercises. It's more –

'Farah likes to take a moment before going on stage,' Zayan says, and my head swings to look at him so fast I'm scared I've pulled a muscle in my neck. 'She repeats a mantra to herself, or a prayer. Not exactly sure, because she whispers it to herself. But she does that, and then she comes on stage and kills it.'

How did he even know that? No one knows that. He couldn't, unless he was watching me. But why would Zayan watch *me* so intensely?

My heart bruises my ribs with how hard it's pounding. 'It's a mantra,' I explain to the viewers. 'An affirmation. Telling myself that I've got this, that I'm deserving of this role, that I should be on stage.'

'And Zayan's?' Anushka asks.

I swallow nervously, knowing the answer. I don't know why. It's just unearthed itself from the back of my mind, as if it's unconsciously always been there. As if I've been collecting little pieces of Zayan over the last month and storing them. 'He likes to eat candy before going on stage. A hard candy or a gummy. Something sweet.'

I can feel Zayan's eyes on me, but I don't turn to meet them.

I'm too afraid of what I'll find staring at me.

♥

I take my time packing up and waving off The Tragedies, because I need to think over what happened with Zayan. While stuffing my script into my bag, I find the folder with the contract in it. I pull it out, skimming over the agreement again while making my way out of the rows of theatre seats. It feels heavier than it should for a slim plastic folder and single sheet of paper.

When I finally step out through the doors of the Limelight, the sun has started to set, painting the canvas of the sky in shades of blushing pink and deepening purples. The thick, rainy clouds from before have softened, quieting their tears for the end of the day.

I almost don't notice Zayan sitting on the steps leading to the theatre. He's resting his elbows on his knees, his laced hands tucked under his chin, staring out at the street in front of him.

I should ignore him, walk home. I should stick to the plan and throw the contract I'm holding in his face.

Instead, I find myself sitting down beside him. The silence between us is heavy, weighty with tension. The sunset throws shadows over the elegant edges of Zayan's face. It's fitting. A puzzle with pieces missing. Something I'll probably never be able to solve.

'Are you ever planning on speaking to me again?' he asks, his tone surprisingly aggravated. 'Or is this your new way of dealing with things?' When I don't say anything, he attempts to goad me. 'Seems a bit childish, don't you think? The silent treatment?'

I raise a brow, as if to say, *Seems a bit hypocritical coming from you.*

He sighs, running a hand through his hair, tangling the waves even more. 'You're not supposed to be mad at me. I'm supposed to be mad at you.'

His jaw locks, mask shattered, eyes desperately bright as the light dies around us. 'I'm the one who had to see the photos of you with The Tragedies, Farah. I'm the one who stayed up at night, scrolling through Instagram, shocked to see my *friends* all hanging out with one another and excluding me. Do you know how juvenile I felt? How incredibly stupid it felt to be that hurt by the sight of you all at an event without me?'

As understanding dawns upon me, my silence finally cracks. 'You think I purposefully left you out?'

'Yes.'

'But you don't even like The Tragedies!' I say, incredulous. 'You said they weren't your friends.'

'Oh, come on, when are you going to let that go? I was mad! I didn't even know you,' Zayan replies. 'And when you asked me that question, I wasn't friends with them. But after the escape room, things changed. The rehearsals, hanging out with the guys virtually while playing *GTA* – a lot of conversation happens when you're screaming at one another over a mic. I didn't realize I had to formally announce my friendship. I thought it was obvious. But then I see them all at your flat. What am I supposed to think?'

'It was Desi Night,' I explain, frustration leaking into my voice. 'It's a night to celebrate being brown. You told me before that you find it difficult to connect with your culture. And you know what? If you hadn't been so freaking closed off all the time, and maybe voiced that you wanted to be friends, I'd have invited you. But you're the one who said *Everything I do with you will be part of our arrangement.* You're the one who sent me a relationship contract.' My tone rises in anger at the thought. 'That's not very *friendly*.'

'I sent it because I thought it was what you wanted. You clearly didn't want to be friends with me; why not just cement it with a contract? Make it official.'

I scoff loudly, arms uncrossing. 'I never wanted that! You're the one who didn't want this to be anything more than a partnership.'

'Not true!' he shoots back, his heated tone matching mine. 'OK, partially true. But do you tell all your friends every single thing?'

I open my mouth to say a resounding *yes* before snapping it shut. The audition with the LSDCATS flashes like a bright neon sign in my head.

A smug, satisfied smile touches Zayan's lips before softening. He edges closer towards me, breathing in deeply just as darkness starts to edge into the sunset.

'I want to be your friend, Farah,' Zayan says, his voice soft and firm all at the same time. 'I like The Tragedies. I like the play. You make me like being on stage. I like that you and I know each other's rituals.' He swallows tightly, looking as if what he's about to say next physically pains him. 'I don't have a lot of friends. I have old school friends that I'm out of touch with, one guy I grew up with, but that's about it. I'll be there whenever you need me. I'm dependable. I believe in loyalty above anything else. I'll respect you when you don't want to talk about things. I'll defend you forever. So, if you'll accept my friendship, I can promise you those things.'

My heart stutters, and a yes is on the tip of my tongue. But then I think of what saying yes really means. I'll be around him even more now, this time with added friendship duties. What if my feelings *change*? When this was just a mutually beneficial partnership, I knew there was an expiry date on how long I'd get to be with Zayan. There was no opportunity for my feelings to evolve. But if we're friends, I'm potentially agreeing to have him in my life forever. What if, somewhere in forever, my feelings for him go from attraction to something more? What if I start to want something from him that he can't ever give me?

'No,' I blurt out, horrified at the realization. 'I can't.'

Zayan's face transforms, shattering into hurt so quickly that it pulls at my heart. 'Why not?'

'Because . . .' I trail off.

'Tell me, Farah,' he says, just above a whisper. 'I can handle it.'

There's no self-depreciation in his tone, no condescension either, just genuine curiosity. My chest aches when I realize he actually wants to know. He wants to fix himself, so it won't happen again.

'It's because . . . because . . . Oh, fine, it's because you're attractive,' I eventually say, all the words I held back before tumbling out now. 'I think you're good-looking, all right? And I'm worried that if we become friends it will mean further closeness, which will mean more attraction. I can't promise those feelings won't deepen. I can try to ignore them; I think it would be best if we didn't tempt –'

Zayan's laugh cuts off my rambling. It's a violent laugh, one that judders through him. I watch, amusement coursing through me at the sound, even as my cheeks brighten a little in embarrassment.

His laughter finally fizzles out, and he scoots closer to me, our knees brushing. He leans in, eyes gleaming with delight. 'Do you know how adorable you are?' My blush heightens. 'You don't think it would be hard for *me* to be friends with *you*? You're gorgeous, Farah. Have you seen yourself perform? You're enchanting. You won't be alone in reining your feelings in.' His broad smile pushes a dimple into his cheek.

That abrupt beating of my heart from before has skyrocketed into something that can't be entirely healthy. I need to say something, anything, before I dissolve into a puddle.

'I know you're not looking for a relationship, and that you're focusing solely on your career. I'm doing the same thing, and either way, I want someone who's in it for the long term. Someone who wants to fall in love,' I say, and something in Zayan's eyes dims. Like a spotlight fading. 'I just don't want to make it harder for you to stick to your relationship ban, if we're already, you know, attracted to one another.'

Zayan says nothing for several moments, his gaze locked on mine, and I'd give anything to be in his mind right now.

'I won't let myself step over that line,' Zayan says, his tone serious. But then his lips curve into a half smile. 'Not unless you ask me to.'

My stomach clenches at the challenge in his voice. My fears are still there, but if Zayan is confident nothing is going to change between us, then I suppose I have to trust him not to cross that line – or to let me cross it.

'All right, fine. If you don't think it's going to be a problem for you, then it won't be a problem for me. We can be friends, and just that.'

His grin makes another dimple pop on his other cheek, and in a sudden movement he hoists me up by the arm and propels us so that we're facing one another, our side profiles visible to the street.

'Paparazzi. Lacey kind of told me that we needed to be photographed together today to help get our edge back from the LSDCATS,' he says in the face of my confusion. Of course. That makes sense. No wonder he was sitting outside, waiting for me. However, surprisingly, his smile doesn't melt into his practised one. 'Thought we should give them a little something.'

Thinking of Lacey reminds me of the contract, and I look down to see I'm still holding it. Zayan's gaze follows mine, and he gently takes the folder from my hands. He flips it open and reads the contract, regret shadowing his eyes.

'I was going to sign it today,' I explain, 'and give it to you.'

He doesn't respond to that. Instead, Zayan pulls the contract out of the folder, hands the plastic cover back to me, and rips the paper into big square pieces. He makes a show of letting them fall from his hands, like confetti, before silently meeting my incredulous stare.

'That's littering,' I say finally.

He snorts, a new sound I've never heard from him. It triggers a laugh from me too. And then, the next thing I know, we're in hysterics. About the fact that I didn't want to be his friend because he was *too pretty*. About the fact that he was too emotionally unaware to ask for my friendship. About nothing. About everything.

We laugh until my ribs hurt, and my heart aches, and this moment solidifies as a memory in my mind.

The day Zayan Amin became my friend.

♥

TRENDING INTERNATIONALLY: #Zarah

Theatre Guru
Published 25 October 2021

CHEMISTRY – MORE THAN A SCHOOL SUBJECT?
AN INTERVIEW WITH THE LSDCATS

As you all know, The London School of Dramatic and Creative Arts Theatre Society has years of prestige. They've performed numerous plays, they've entertained hundreds of audiences and we are incredibly excited to share an exclusive quote from the director of this year's play, Henry John Findon.

'In my humble opinion, a play only does well when the people chosen to play the leads have chemistry. That is what makes or breaks a play. Especially when you are performing a romantic tragedy like *Romeo and Juliet*.

'Our actors, Mary Whitter for Juliet and Rowan Kent for Romeo, are incredible. If I didn't know them beyond the stage, I'd think that they truly were in love. That is what makes this rendition of *Romeo and Juliet* so special. Our leads care for one another beyond the roles they're meant to play, and that translates on stage.

'Clearly, we are very lucky that our leads like and respect one another. Not every play can say the same.'

You're absolutely right, Henry, and I'm sure the public is going to be beyond excited to watch your *Romeo and Juliet* – especially with those sparks flying!

Chapter Nineteen

For the last couple of days, we hadn't had to worry about the LSDCATS. Their only retaliation to our TikTok Live Q&A had been a quote from Henry about 'chemistry', which was an obvious attempt to make it seem like Zayan and I still had none. Nur had had the brilliant idea of releasing a clip on The Tragedies TikTok account of Zayan and I acting together – thereby showing just how much chemistry we do have. It had led to a lot more people shipping us together than the LSDCATS' lead actors.

All that success meant we'd needed a celebration. David had had an idea for a group date involving the whole cast and crew. We'd gone to watch *The Mousetrap* by Agatha Christie, a classic play that has been running on stage for thirty-eight years – nothing dissolves the social anxiety of theatre students better than contemplating fake murders.

It had been a fun day – essential for Zayan and me, because it had given us an excuse to hang out and return to our normal tempo, without that awkward post-fight phase.

We also hadn't talked about the whole *I think you're attractive*/*Oh, me too* conversation we'd had outside the Limelight.

But that doesn't mean I've stopped thinking about it.

'Hypothetically, what does it mean when a guy calls you enchanting?' I ask, voicing my thoughts aloud.

Amal, who is sitting opposite me at our very small dining table, shares a look with Maha. Our differing schedules make it hard for Amal, Maha and I to hang out as often as we used to. But then we have times like this, where we stay up till late, just eating a takeaway round our dining table, chatting about the most random things. Nothing is off limits. Global warming, the price of petrol and, in my case, the things Zayan says to me.

'I'd say he was pretty into you,' Amal replies, leaning back in her chair to give me an appraising look. 'I mean, most guys don't go around dropping words like that for any girl. Owais sure doesn't.'

'Please don't tell me all the romantic things my cousin says to you,' Maha interjects, looking queasy. 'I still can't believe you two went from rivals to crushes to rivals again to partners, only to end up as soon-to-be-engaged-and-making-single-people-jealous, all in the span of a year.'

Amal grins, her eyes sparkling with delight. Usually I would tease Maha about her cousin falling in love with her best friend, but right now I still need the answer to a question that won't stop blaring in my mind.

'OK,' I interrupt, pulling their attention back to me.

'But – again – hypothetically, if he followed it up with, let's say, wanting to be friends, what would that mean?'

'Did Zayan say he just wants to be friends with you?' Maha asks, eyes widening. 'Everyone thinks you two are together!'

'No, no!' I rush to fix my mistake, mentally smacking myself for even trying to bring this up with my friends. 'Not him. Anushka. D-David called her "enchanting" but then said he just wanted to be friends.'

Note to self: tell Anushka and David that I have added them to my very, very elaborate lie.

'Oh.' Maha deflates. 'Well, yeah, I mean, he's probably not interested in her, then. He could be attracted to her, sure, but it obviously means he's holding himself back from acting on it. But that doesn't have to be a bad thing – if David knows that he's in a place where he can't give Anushka anything solid, or anything she wants, then it's smart for him to set up that boundary. He's preserving their friendship.'

I turn to Amal, waiting to see if she agrees. When she nods, something akin to disappointment flutters in my chest. I know I should be happy that Zayan is respecting the rules we set up when we started this partnership; I should be relieved that he's so clear about his intentions.

But this conversation now marks the official death of my celebrity crush. Zayan is firmly in friend territory. No more thinking that his looks might mean something more, or that his smiles might have hidden meanings. No crossing lines. Just friends.

'Thanks, guys,' I say, trying to keep my tone upbeat. Amal's eyes narrow on me, and I avoid looking directly at her. 'I'll pass this on to Anushka.'

'Farah –' Amal begins, but her sentence is cut off by the sound of my phone buzzing.

> **Gibitah**
> Did you see?

I quickly try to think of everything that might've been said about my relationship. Last time I checked, *Zarah* was trending on Twitter – a ship name that Ben had way too much fun teasing us about. What possibly could have happened now?

> **Gibitah**
> Are you alive?

I roll my eyes at her dramatics, a smile tugging at my lips regardless. It's strange to think there was a time that we weren't friends, that we never spoke like this.

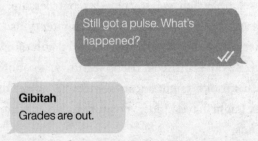

> Still got a pulse. What's happened? ✓✓

> **Gibitah**
> Grades are out.

Relief hits me at the realization that this isn't about Zayan, just as a swell of panic blossoms in my chest.

I stand up from my chair, startling my friends. 'Grades are out for my coursework, aka a deciding factor in my final mark.'

'Go and check them!' Amal says, shooing me out of the room. 'Don't worry – Maha will grab your plate.'

'Why me?' Maha asks, affronted.

'Because I've done your dishes three days in a row now.'

'Yeah, but I did your laundry.'

'I did your laundry too.'

'One time!'

'One time too many. Why do you wear so many outfits in one week, by the way?'

'It's called style.'

I leave them bickering and race into my room, to my laptop.

This year, every module I have is coursework-based. I'll have exams in my second year, but for now every essay holds heavy weight in my final mark. And by no means am I a brilliant student – I'm not like Amal or Owais, who excel at everything they study. I've got my fair share of failed grades (my Year 8 school report was a collection of Cs and Ds). But I've always had a good memory, which is why I chose to study history.

My hands are shaking as I click open the online grading book under my university profile. I squint my eyes, afraid to see the number. Through a sliver of sight and lashes, I find my mark.

Eighty per cent!

Blood rushes to my ears, pounding against my skull as I open my bedroom door and call out the mark to my flatmates. I hear the cheers of celebration right before I collapse on to my bed and start reading through the comments my professor has left. A giddy smile perches on my lips as I read *Good job!* and *I love this!*

I'm so excited I almost miss the final comment.

This was such a surprisingly delightful paper to read, Farah – you are so articulate, and you write so well in English! It's a genuine pleasure to see students from all over the world succeed against the odds.

Bile rises up my throat, and this odd sensation starts to pulse right from the centre of my chest down to my fingertips. I read through the comment again, trying to decipher its hidden meaning, if it even has any. Like, why would she be *surprised* it was a good essay?

No. No. This is my overthinking kicking in. There are compliments in these comments – delight, good writing, pleasure. All good, positive things. I'm trying to see something that's not there.

Unless she thought you weren't going to be good enough to pass her class?

Fear creeps into the ache in my chest, a coldness sweeping through me. I think of the LSDCATS again, and the word 'unsuitable' echoes in my thoughts like a tape recorder that refuses to stop. That feeling of not being good enough, not for the stage, not for my professors, not for my friends, rises in me like a tide.

The sound of my phone ringing is a life jacket I didn't know I needed. I swipe to accept the call with little thought of who it may be.

'I thought I'd change it up a little.' Zayan's voice is warm and scratchy down the line – as if he's woken up earlier than usual. 'Me calling you, instead of you calling me.'

I swallow against the stone that's lodged itself in my throat; my eyes are still trained on the comment.

'Farah?' Zayan asks, and I can vividly see the concerned furrow squished between his brows. 'You OK?'

I imagine reading the comment aloud. Zayan would tell me, with complete and utter honesty, if my worries were right. He wouldn't hold back. He'd see the truth as a way for me to improve, a motivator. But hearing him say it – *They're right. You're good, but you're not enough. Not yet* – would press too sharply against the tenderness of my heart. For now, I'll envision him saying it, and I'll internalize it without his help. I can do it. I can work harder. Prove people wrong. I can be enough.

I clear my throat before responding. 'Yeah, yeah. Everything's fine.' And before the awkward silence solidifies between us, I ask him about his night. 'What were you up to?'

'Up to?'

'Before you called. Were you sleeping?'

The idea of Zayan specifically waking up to call me makes something hot and molten erupt in my chest – the idea that someone would knit me into their life in such an integral way.

'I wasn't, actually.' My chest cools; the momentary lapse passes. 'I was – I was rereading reviews.'

'Reviews?' I question, while nestling into my pillows. I close my laptop, hiding away the results, and focus on Zayan instead of the whirlpool brewing in my head.

'Yeah, reviews from critics.'

I wince. 'That doesn't sound like a good idea.'

Zayan huffs out a laugh, a genuine-sounding one. 'You're right. A lot of them are saying I'm past my prime – that I'm "destined to be a Hari Fairbanks and nothing more".'

His haughty change in tone has me laughing a little, but I can't ignore the undertone of bitterness in his voice.

'You know that's not true, right?'

He pauses before replying. 'Rationally, yes. Irrationally, at 3 a.m., I'll admit I had a bit of a crisis.'

'Zayan, you're a good actor.'

'I know,' he says, and it takes all my strength not to scoff at him. 'This isn't about my talent. If I thought I couldn't act, I wouldn't put you or me through this. I think . . .' He exhales sharply. 'I think I'm more angry than analytical right now.'

'You're angry at yourself?'

'At them.' Zayan's rage becomes more evident as he continues. 'At the public. At the reviewers. I know that TV show was awful, but it was a *mistake*. And no one wants to hear my side of the story – they've chosen a label for me, and I'm supposed to just live with it. It's like they've forgotten how much of myself I've given to this industry.'

I swallow roughly – Zayan doesn't need me to be angry for him; he knows I am. He needs a way to see beyond the rage, the hurt.

'But you're getting auditions now, aren't you?' I ask.

'Yeah, I am. And I like the roles. They're good. The scripts are intelligent. A lot of them are romances, and I owe that to you.' His voice softens. 'I owe anything I'm getting to you, Farah. But I worry that I'm going to do it all over again – the sacrifice, the effort, the emotional bloodshed – but this time . . . this time I can't be sure it'll be worth it.'

'Even if they treat you like that again, you can't justify giving everything up,' I echo. 'You don't want the same regrets.'

'Yeah.'

'Then don't give everything up,' I say suddenly.

'It's not that easy, Farah,' Zayan sighs, worn and weary.

I hate it. I hate that tone. I would do anything to change it.

'Yes, it is. You've given this industry so much. You've given up things to fit in, and you stumbled *one time*, and it was this same industry that turned its back on you. That watched you struggle and did nothing to help. Now, I'm not saying you should throw in the towel and give up acting, but I am saying that maybe it's time you protected yourself. Maybe it's time to be picky, to not sacrifice parts of your identity. Maybe it's time to create your own space in this industry.'

'And if people don't like it?'

'Zayan, if directors, casting agents, producers want you – all of you, every part of you – they won't hesitate. And you'll know they want you for nothing but your talent. And that is worth more than being picked for the girl on your arm.'

'You're more than a girl on my arm,' Zayan insists indignantly. 'And image is important.'

I ignore the first part. 'You're right. It is important. But you've built up your reputation since you were a kid. You're in a fake relationship to salvage what you've worked so hard to craft over the years! I'm just saying, maybe it's time to pick the role that's made *for you*. The movie role that may not have the biggest pay-off, the contract that doesn't include a clause forcing you to become someone you aren't.'

I know Zayan won't make his decision now, that he won't suddenly decide to shed years of trying to fit into Hollywood in exchange for his roots and his culture, but I hope this could be the start – the beginning for him to see that he could have it both ways. I know he could.

'Maybe you're right. Maybe it's time to regain some of that sacrifice I've made,' he concedes gently, and the firmness in his voice says, *This is the end of this conversation.*

I gear up to say goodbye, to give myself back to *my* thoughts, my worries, but Zayan interrupts me with a question.

'What were you doing?'

'Huh?'

'Before I called, what were you doing?'

The little white lie slips too easily past my lips, even as a part of me wishes to tell Zayan the truth. But the truth isn't worth damaging the new friendship we have forming; it isn't worth burdening him. 'I just . . . I was watching this YouTube documentary and got caught up for a second.'

'BuzzFeed Unsolved?'

I smile because my lie was buried in a truth. I do love watching BuzzFeed Unsolved, and I like that Zayan guessed that.

'Yeah, it's an all-time favourite of mine,' I reply, while tucking myself deeper under the blankets.

'Do you have other favourites?'

'What do you mean?'

'Well, we're friends now. Right?'

Before, I wouldn't have heard the vulnerability under the layers of his tone. I do now.

'Yeah, Zayan,' I say, softly but firmly. Not just for him, but for myself too. 'We're friends.'

'So, friends should know things about one another. Tell me more about Farah Sheikh and the things she loves.'

I laugh, and that sharp pain from before weakens. 'Only if the great Zayan Amin shares the same with me.'

'Deal. Favourite colour? Mine's green.'

'Indigo. Favourite musical?'

'Arguably the best musical: *Hadestown*.'

'What? Absolutely not. What about *The Phantom of the Opera*?'

'I've never seen it,' Zayan replies.

'Me neither.' A note of wistfulness enters my voice, and the pain I felt before folds, until it's nothing more than a memory of a feeling. 'But I've always wanted to see it. I've only watched YouTube videos of it.'

'I still think *Hadestown* might be the best.'

'You're delusional.'

He laughs, and that sound is the only thing I focus on for the next hour.

Chapter Twenty

Zayan Amin is standing in my doorway again, but this time he has a box of besan laddu in his hands.

'You didn't actually have to bring a gift, you know,' I say as I let him in.

He toes off his shoes, eyes wandering over the flat as if it's his first time being here. 'Of course I did, Lightning Bug. They're the ones you like, by the way, the pistachio ones. Have people already shown up?'

'Lightning Bug?'

'I'm testing out something new.'

I roll my eyes. 'To answer your question, The Tragedies are here.'

To really show Zayan that I considered him a friend, before ending our call last night, I invited him to a pseudo-Desi Night – a more intimate one with just The Tragedies, Gibitah and my friends – the next day. That way, it wouldn't overwhelm him, or make him feel like he was cornered by fans.

'But your other friends are here too, right?' he asks, and I take in the tension winding through him – the tightness in his shoulders, and the way he's tugging his curls as he rakes his hand through them.

'Are you nervous, Zayan?' I ask, a little incredulous.

He looks at me, eyes darting away from the music-filled room down the hall and back to me. 'Of course I'm nervous. You talk about them all the time – they're like your family. And if they're important to you, then their opinion is important to me.'

Something warm balloons in my chest at his words. Until he hurries on.

'Of course,' he hastily adds, 'I don't want them to hate me. I mean, that would look bad. We still need to convince them something is going on between us.'

Right. How could I forget?

I take too long to respond, and then notice that Zayan is fidgeting with the cuffs of his shirt, rolled up to his forearms.

'Are you –'

'Do you like what I'm wearing?' He cuts me off, and it's the sheer earnestness in his voice that stumps me.

I purposefully allow myself to look over him, the sharp line of his shoulders fitted into his metallic grey shirt and his well-tailored blue jeans. It's nothing out of the –

'Wait, are you wearing a kurta?' I ask, now realizing that the shape of his shirt isn't like a regular shirt. It cinches round his neck and is rounded at the hem, with three buttons going down his chest.

Zayan's smile is blindingly boyish. 'It took me forever to find this. I had to ask my stylist. I used to wear one like this all the time, back in Karachi.'

It's a deceptive outfit – someone could very easily pass it off as a slightly long shirt if they wanted, but I don't see this as Zayan trying to hide. I see this as his attempt to reclaim a little part of himself.

'I love it,' I say genuinely, and the way his eyes light up makes my abdomen tug with affection.

I need to squash this fast.

'We – we should go inside. My friends are dying to meet you.'

I turn on my heel, leading Zayan to the living room, and for a moment before I open the door there is panic sluicing through my blood. I've never introduced anyone to my friends before – especially not someone they think I'm in a relationship with.

'We've got this, Farah,' Zayan murmurs from behind me. Confident as always.

'We've got this,' I echo and lead him in.

Instantly, we're engulfed by sound and conversation. The Tragedies are peppered around the room, but it's my flatmates that I'm looking out for. Amal comes first, followed by Owais, and on her way across the room, Amal tags Maha into their group.

'Incoming,' I mutter.

'I'm ready. Don't worry,' Zayan replies, his previous concerns being folded and tucked away, replaced by a charming smile and forced ease in his shoulders.

'Farah!' Owais booms, unabashedly excited. 'Introduce us, *please*. I have been waiting so long for this.'

A giggle escapes me, a giveaway sign of my nerves. Amal clocks it first and presses the most genuine smile on to her lips. She takes the lead away from Owais, thankfully.

'It's really nice to finally meet you, Zayan,' Amal says, sticking her hand out for him to shake. 'I loved you in *Cloudy Skies*; it's one of my all-time favourite childhood movies.'

I send a glance Zayan's way, surprised to see him smiling gratefully.

'You're Amal, I'm assuming. Farah's said a lot about you,' Zayan replies. 'And you must be Owais. She hails you two as the greatest love story.'

Owais grins, brown eyes glimmering with unrestrained smugness. 'Well, I'd say we're doing OK.'

Maha snorts loudly. 'Please, they're probably going to elope next year. But you and Farah are good competition. You're treating our girl well.'

'Maha, I told you –' I start to hiss, but Zayan cuts me off.

'She's been the best hurricane to enter my life.' My attention snaps to him, and I blush at the intense way he's looking at me. *It's all pretend. It's all pretend. It's all pretend.* 'I'm glad we met at the coffee shop that day.'

Under her breath, I hear Maha let out a breathy 'aww', and even Amal looks softened. We've convinced them. Somehow, we've made them believe that Zayan and I are truly in love with one another.

For the next couple of hours, we talk about anything and

everything – university classes, whether Andrew Garfield, Tobey Maguire or Tom Holland is the best Spider-Man (the right answer is Miles Morales). Eventually – and inevitably, I suppose – we land on the LSDCATS.

'They're being such social-media jerks,' Maha drawls, leaning back in her armchair. 'They keep saying these underhanded things about you and Zayan. As if they're above smack talk and therefore have to say it under their breath.'

'I wish we could put them in front of a camera with both of you,' Anushka adds, sitting cross-legged by the low coffee table. 'I'd like them to deny the chemistry between you two then.'

'We did get an offer for an interview with the LSDCATS,' Zayan says from his place at the other end of the sofa – with a couple of pillows between us.

'We did?' I ask, surprised. 'Was it from The Actors' Guild?'

The Actors' Guild is one of the most prestigious unions for upcoming actors and actresses. Only the greats get interviewed, or the future greats in cases like Zayan's – he'd got his membership and interview at *fourteen*.

Zayan shakes his head, and I deflate a little. 'It wasn't them; it was some entertainment outlet. Lacey got an email today, asking if we'd be interested in doing it. They said the LSDCATS are waiting on what we'll say before giving their response.'

'Cowards,' Gibitah scoffs, while biting into a samosa. She's completely, unabashedly unafraid to talk about how much she hates the LSDCATS. She's always updating me on their latest retaliations and urging us to fight back. She and Nur are practically a tag team now.

'You guys should totally do it,' Nur says excitedly. 'Maybe you'd finally be able to put this LSDCATS rivalry to rest by demolishing them in the interview.'

A round of agreement rings through the group, all of them unaware of the nerves bundling in my stomach. What if Henry was there? Just the thought of seeing him makes me want to curl up under my covers and never see the light of day again.

'Who would we be interviewed with?' I ask, carefully trying to hide the nerves in my voice by eating a handful of crisps at the same time.

'The opposing co-stars,' Zayan says, his gaze like a laser on me, analysing me in a way that I wish he wouldn't. I don't want him to clock my worries. 'And I'd be there the whole time to guide you, of course. You wouldn't be going in alone.'

'As good as that is,' David intervenes, 'this could all still end very badly.'

'How so?' Anushka asks, while taking a long sip of her chai, a brief look of delight painting over her expression.

'Well, what if the LSDCATS have something planned? What if they say something that Farah and Zayan are completely unprepared for?'

'He's not wrong,' Gibitah adds, shooting me a look. 'The LSDCATS have been extremely underhanded lately. Aside from copying the Lives, there's been the tweets and the cast list . . . I'm pretty sure they're the ones filling all these gossip rags with stories about you two, to make you look bad. I read one yesterday about how your and Farah's relationship was actually just a PR stunt – can you believe that?'

I feel my eyes widen as I force out a convincing laugh – The Tragedies don't look at each other, and Zayan wears this bemused expression on his face while the rest of the group laughs around us.

'But think of the great publicity it would drum up,' Nur insists, thankfully, steering the conversation away. 'Do you know how much ticket sales would go up if they did this interview? This could put us over the edge and end this war altogether.'

'But what if David's right, and we're not ready for it?' I ask desperately. 'I don't want to make a fool of myself or jeopardize Zayan's career by messing something up.'

I notice Amal and Maha's expressions turning into twin looks of mush, and I wasn't even trying to convince them of my fake relationship.

'We prep for it,' Zayan says, catching my gaze with his. 'We think of everything the LSDCATS could say, could say, no matter how wild, and we form our own answers for it. That way, we're incredibly prepared for whatever is thrown our way. Like media training, but tailored to the LSDCATS.'

'That sounds like a good idea,' David says, as a thrum of agreement winds through the group. Gibitah nudges me with her socked foot excitedly, Nur's eyes are already glazed with anticipation and the whole room is starting to buzz.

'Farah?' Zayan asks, a note of hope in his voice.

I try to rationalize my decision: if Henry isn't there, then I have nothing to fear. Or at least I have *less* to fear.

'All right,' I say – and then, because Zayan smiles at me, two dimples pressing into his cheeks, I repeat myself with more solid confidence. 'Yeah, let's do it.'

'Good.' Anushka stands up quickly. 'Let's get started, then. Zayan and Farah, you sit on the couch. The rest of us, to the kitchen to make up questions.'

As soon as we're alone, Zayan sidles closer to me on the couch, moving pillows out of the way. 'Thank you for agreeing. I really think doing this interview will be good for me.'

I give him a shaky smile, unable to voice how worried I really am.

'Can I tell you a secret?' Zayan asks. His hand is splayed out next to mine, our pinkies barely brushing.

I give him a sideways glance, not moving my hand away. 'Obviously.'

He grins. 'I'm being cued up to audition for this new movie. It's a heist action-thriller. It's a movie I'm actually interested in doing. No romance arc, but there's great character work in it.'

'Zayan,' I whisper-shout, so as not to alert the group, 'that's amazing. When did you find out?'

'An hour ago,' he says. 'I was on my way here, actually. Which is good, because you were the first person I wanted to tell.'

My stomach somersaults, doing Simone Biles-level

gymnastics. I like it. I like knowing I'm someone Zayan can depend on. It's a position I've been in before, but it feels different. It feels weightier to know he's someone who doesn't trust easily but is willing to open up to me.

'So –' I clear my throat, hoping my cheeks aren't as warm as they feel – 'that's why you want to do the interview?'

'Yeah,' Zayan continues, oblivious to my inner turmoil. 'I want to use the opportunity to reintroduce myself to my fans, this time on my terms. With you there. In fact, it would be a good way to introduce you to the industry too – in a vocal way.'

That causes a spear of fear to pierce straight through me. Again. I look away from Zayan, down to my hands, as if I can hide how I'm feeling from him. Now I'm worried about the LSDCATS and the thought of being introduced to the world.

'We'll be OK,' Zayan says quickly, edging closer to me. Clearly, he can read my nerves.

'I know,' I reply, looking up again. I notice he has a fallen eyelash on his cheekbone, and I resist the urge to reach out and brush it away.

'You don't sound sure.'

'I am.'

'Good,' he replies, giving the kitchen door a brief look before speaking again quietly. 'Because you know I'd never let anything bad happen to you, right? Not on stage, not in the interview, nowhere. You're my partner.'

My throat feels tight, my heart is beating so fast I'm

surprised he can't hear it, and where Zayan's fingertips are barely touching mine they feel like they're burning.

I can't – I don't – What is *happening*?

'Ladies and gentlemen,' Owais' voice booms suddenly, causing both of us to jerk away quickly, the moment fading as fast as it started. 'Welcome to today's practice interview with the esteemed couple of the century, Zayan Amin and Farah Sheikh!'

The Tragedies, along with the rest, stumble out of the kitchen with their phones in their hands, questions poised.

'You ready?' Anushka asks, brow raised.

I glance Zayan's way, and he gives me a short nod.

'The questions are intense,' Ben warns.

'We're ready,' I say emphatically.

'Some of them are stupid,' Nur adds.

'Guys, we're ready,' I repeat.

'OK, but seriously, some of them are downright –' Gibitah begins.

'Just ask the questions!' Zayan loudly interrupts.

'Fine, fine,' David laughs. 'Someone's cranky. So, Zayan Amin, tell us, are you more a boxers or briefs kind of guy?'

'*David.*'

Chapter
Twenty-one

When I first entered the *Entertainment Daily* studio, I'll admit, I was entranced by what I saw. Everyone moved with such speed, with such purpose. I enjoyed watching the chaos while sitting in the make-up chair, being doted upon by the make-up artist. I even liked changing into the outfit Pierre demanded I wear for today – a lavender-crêpe sharara suit with a peplum-flared kurti and capped sleeves, patterned with an array of pastel flowers. I liked pretending that *I* was the star that everyone was orbiting round today.

But now, as I'm being led to the main area, my anxiety is rearing its head again.

I seek out Zayan like a bee finding nectar, and I feel even more relief at the sight of him standing by the craft-service table. He looks blush-inducingly good in his perfectly cut dark-grey suit and light-grey turtleneck.

'I think I might throw up,' I say as a greeting.

Zayan's attention is focused on the iced bun in front of him, and he responds distractedly. 'Try not to aim in my direction, please.'

I swat his arm. 'I'm being serious, Zayan.'

He sighs and looks away from the baked treat, clearly ready to say something, but the words die on his tongue. He just stares at me unabashedly, lips parted, for longer than a couple of seconds.

'I think Pierre might be trying to kill me,' he murmurs.

My face must be redder than a tomato. Friends compliment each other all the time; it's just going to take me some getting used to hearing it from him.

'I think this interview may kill *me*,' I reply, diverting the topic.

Zayan regains his composure. 'You have nothing to be afraid of. Pierre has already briefed the interviewer on what they can and cannot ask. We just have to prove that our chemistry trumps the LSDCATS, as does our play. Which we already know is true. Plus there's nothing, absolutely nothing, the LSDCATS could say that we aren't prepared for after what we endured on Desi Night.'

I bite the inside of my cheek, nodding with everything Zayan says. He's right. We answered so many questions that night, from *Why do you deserve to be here?* to *If you had to save one person from a burning building, your mum or your significant other, who would you pick?*

We're ready for anything.

I survey the studio with an analytical stare to find that

the actor and actress from the LSDCATS are here. No Henry – instant relief hits me.

But it's short-lived when my eyes settle on the LSDCATS leads. The actors look impeccable together. I've already stalked them online – the guy playing Romeo, Rowan Kent, is from Scotland and has reddish curls, a brush of freckles across his nose and a smile that makes you think of jumping off cliffs with him – of the rush of danger, the thrill. Mary Whitter, playing Juliet, is anything but the classic girl next door – she exudes allure with her heart-shaped lips, her soft brown hair piled up into a high ponytail and the little beauty mark on her cheek. They mesh perfectly. They're definitely going to give Zayan and me a run for our money in the chemistry department.

'We've got this,' Zayan says, pulling my attention away from them and back to him. He's confident, easily so. I would do anything to have a fraction of his self-belief.

'Right. We've got this,' I echo back, only half believing it.

♥

'So, let's just break the ice here. You two come from opposing theatre groups. There must be *some* animosity, right?' asks Leona Harris, our interviewer, with a megawatt smile shining our way. Her question sounds like it's for all of us, but her eyes are trained on Zayan.

He is, of course, the star.

I wait for Zayan to speak, because that's the instruction I've been given by Pierre. *Let Zayan take the lead; he'll cue you in when you need to speak.* But before Zayan can say anything, Rowan cuts in.

'I wouldn't say that.' Rowan's voice is like sand between your toes. 'I rarely like to be on the bad side of beautiful women.'

It takes me a second to realize he's talking about me, and I force a laugh past my lips as Leona practically dissolves into hysterics.

'Oh, what a flirt! Perfect for Romeo,' Leona responds, appearing pleased that she doesn't have a dull guest on her roster.

Rowan's smile turns into a half smirk. 'I'd say it was one of the requirements for getting this role.'

'Huh,' Zayan says, and my heart thuds loudly in my chest at the dip in his voice. It's not impolite in any way, but his tone sounds like the serrated edge of a knife – one wrong move, and it will slice into your skin. 'I suppose the LSDCATS have many *requirements* for their roles. It's interesting to finally see who has been cast.'

While Zayan speaks, hinting at the LSDCATS' racist casting, his arm moves from his lap to settle round the back of my chair. We've all been given stools to sit on, and now Zayan's arm rests solidly behind me, his body languid, looking like a king upon his throne. His fingers play with the thread tassels on the sleeves of my outfit. It's comforting to feel him there, like a safety net under a tightrope.

I also realize it probably looks *great* on camera.

Rowan's neck flushes red, but Mary's glossy smile remains

sweet. 'The LSDCATS are known for seeking the best of the best.'

Zayan's smile warms as he looks down at me. I kick into gear, smiling back at him like he's the brightest thing in my life. 'Yes, I only like to work with the best of the best too.'

Leona's face is scrunched up at how cute Zayan and I are. 'Speaking of working together, tell us, Farah, what was it like meeting Zayan for the first time?'

Horrible. I wanted to strangle him. Instead, he kind of choked me with my dupatta. Romantic, no?

'It was the best day of my life,' I say dreamily. Or at least I hope it's dreamy. From the way Zayan's lips twitch at the corners, I know he wants to laugh at me. 'He's been such a delight to work with. He's taught me so much.'

'Ah, you had a lot to learn then?' Rowan asks innocently. So much for the flirty nice-guy act.

Embarrassment threatens to silence me, but with the solidity of Zayan by my side, I bite back. 'Anyone would, if they had the privilege of working with a multi-award-winning actor.'

And you have none, so shut up goes unsaid.

'Of course. And working with Zayan, Farah, has it been fun?' Leona asks, steering the conversation back to us. 'He must have some interesting quirks; all big actors do.'

Zayan laughs, a sound so plastic I almost cringe. But everyone else seems to buy it. 'I'd say I'm pretty normal, right, love?'

Leona's eyes go as wide as saucers, and I play into our game a little more. 'Well, I would say waking up to work out at 6 a.m. every day is a habit I can't get into.' I give Zayan another lovesick glance before smiling sweetly at Leona. 'But this guy, he's just *so* dedicated. When he wants something, he goes for it with a hundred per cent effort.'

'Even a TV series?' Mary asks, her tone equally innocent to Rowan's from before.

I turn to give her a withering glare, but Zayan's foot gently knocks into mine. I force my body to soften, but my mind is still plotting ways of exacting vengeance upon Mary.

'I joke, of course,' Mary continues, unaware of how I wish to skin her alive. 'I think it's admirable when an actor is able to pick themself up after a bump in the road.'

'I agree,' Zayan replies, his tone level. 'I also think the worth of a person – or an institution – stands on their ability to admit that they've stumbled.'

'Rather than simply covering their tracks,' I add, hinting at how hastily the LSDCATS cast a person of colour for Tybalt. 'It takes more strength to admit failure than pretend you never made a mistake in the first place.'

'Yes, well . . .' Rowan blusters – for the first time, he looks genuinely caught out. 'You see, the ethos of the LSDCATS is to preserve the authenticity of literature and playwriting. We just want a cast that accurately represents the past.'

'That sounds like a great way to give only one type of an actor a chance on the stage,' Zayan says, his tone scornful.

'And at the end of the day,' I say, 'Shakespeare's characters are open to interpretation. The character's looks play only one part in the storytelling. Does it really matter if they don't look . . .?'

I pause, the words dying on my tongue. I was going to say *classically British*. But, for the first time, instead of shame, I feel this crackling sense of anger for *myself* when I think of Henry. Not on behalf of The Tragedies. Not for anyone else. I can't help but feel indignant as I realize that Henry's decision to give me feedback that I can't work on – because I can't fundamentally change the colour of my skin, or the shape of my mouth, or the embedded features of my face – is so incredibly unfair. I *deserved* the truth. Henry held so much power in that audition, and he chose to wield it in a way that would cut me down as an aspiring actress, not help me grow.

'Farah?' Leona prompts lightly, pulling me out of my thoughts.

Zayan's looking at me with concern, and a part of my brain is screaming that I'm messing this interview up. The whole thing. But I can't get myself to finish my sentence, because what if I'm *not ready*? What if I tell the world what Henry said, and the LSDCATS do tell me the truth – that they only gave me the critique they did because they didn't want to say, *You're not a good enough actor*. Could I *really* handle that?

Another minute passes, and I force myself to push that question out of my head. This interview isn't the time to answer it – this is still about Zayan and his career.

I press a smile on to my lips as I collect myself, choosing my next words carefully. 'As I was saying, the landscape of theatre is wide and vast. We're delighted both plays can coexist.'

Leona nods sagely, taking in our comments like they're words of pure wisdom. Rowan and Mary look disgruntled, their eyes narrowed on Zayan like he's going to attack.

Leona breaks the tension by asking me another question. 'Is this something you learned from Zayan, Farah? This understanding of the depth of theatre?'

My brows furrow in confusion before I smooth them out, remembering Pierre's instruction to always look pleasant and appealing. Beside me, Zayan's face pinches in annoyance before shuttering into a blank mask. 'I'd say I've learned a lot from Zayan. This is just one of the things.'

Before Leona can get another question in, Zayan continues. 'And I can say, without a shred of doubt, that Farah is one of the best people I've had the luck of working with. She's a star in the making. If you should keep your eye on anyone, it's definitely her.'

Leona laughs and moves the conversation on to another question that allows Zayan to plug the play even more. We share thinly veiled barbs with our rivals, and pretend to be besotted with one another when needed. For the entire interview, I truly feel the sense of partnership with Zayan – that we're on the same team, wanting the same things, wanting this lifestyle.

I want this world, his world, so badly.

I want to have my own publicity manager. An agent.

I want to be able to hear the LSDCATS say *You're not good enough* and not break under the weight of their words. I want to have an interviewer give me their full attention, and I want to dodge questions for myself.

I want to be the star.

@Aamna_Duo: @TheTragedies, answer us, we just watched the interview, PLEASE: ARE FARAH AND ZAYAN DATING???

@Laibastan3: @Aamna_Duo Are you OK? Zayan and Farah are nothing but friends. My babies Zaiba are coming back.

@CallmeZarah: @Laibastan3 Clearly, you're delulu. Did you not SEE Farah and Zayan's interview? The body language? Those smiles? The compliments? They are IN LOVE.

@Laibastan3: @CallmeZarah You can't possibly think they're going to be good together. Farah isn't right for Zayan. They don't even look good together.

@CallmeZarah: @Laibastan3 Uhh, Farah is BEAUTIFUL.

@Laibastan3: @CallmeZarah Eh, she's all right. But Laiba is drop-dead gorgeous. And she actually looks brown.

@TheatreGeek: Yeah, **@CallmeZarah**, not that I'm hating on Farah and Zayan being together, but don't you think it's a little sus that **@TheTragedies** picked a white-passing actress for the lead when they talked about diversity? Is she even talented, or does she just look good next to Zayan?

@CallmeZarah: @TheatreGeek Light-skinned people are still brown . . .

@TheatreGeek: @CallmeZarah I guess . . .

Chapter Twenty-two

'We need the final scene to be really dramatic,' Anushka says. 'Heer's poisoned after taking a bite of the laddu, and I want that moment to be extremely intense. Not only is Ranjha's reaction going to grasp their hearts, but the audience is realizing that this bright, beautiful character is dying. It's a loss for everyone.'

The weight of the scene sits on my shoulders. The pressure feels huge. There are only four weeks left till the curtain goes up, and Anushka's right; the final scene needs to leave a mark on the audience, to resonate in their minds long after they've left. Heer's death is one of the only scenes I have where it's just me on the stage – no ladies-in-waiting, no attendants, no guards.

Just the spotlight and me.

Ever since our interview – my first taste of really being in the entertainment industry – my dream of being a star, of making my theatre debut, has grown wilder and wilder. It's rooted deep into my mind and refuses to let go. Now every scene holds more weight. Every moment on stage feels like one step closer to my dream.

'I can do it,' I reply, injecting my voice with confidence. 'Do you want to do a run-through now?'

The Limelight is peppered with cast members today; Zayan is noticeably absent, because he's got his first audition for another movie. I've kept my phone by my side all day to hear his updates – good or bad.

'Sure,' Anushka says, and we make our way to the stage.

I roll my shoulders back and let the feeling of being on stage wrap round me like a dupatta. I breathe in Heer and exhale her lines like they're my own thoughts. The rest of the world fades away as I get to the monumental death scene – my voice rising as the words slip past my lips, my heart ripping apart at the thought of never seeing Ranjha ever again. When I return to reality, crashing back into my own body, Anushka's clapping.

I smile shyly. 'I did OK?'

'OK? Farah, it was great! I have a few notes, though. I think you could stretch your arms out a little more as you collapse on to the stage, make it seem like Heer is clawing for her life and bring a sense of urgency to the scene.'

We go over her notes and redo the scene again, and again, until exhaustion burrows into the marrow of my bones. I take some time out of the day to work with my understudy – a fellow Pakistani actress – just in case something goes wrong on opening night.

By the time we're done with rehearsal, I'm ready to fall straight into bed. The Tragedies come together – Nur from backstage, David from working with the tech crew, Ben from running lines with the other actors. While they chatter around me, I check my phone and see Zayan hasn't messaged yet.

'Hey,' Ben says, and I look away from my screen to see he's sending a link to our Twitter group chat. 'Did you see this thread bashing the LSDCATS after your and Zayan's interview?'

'Oh, I have to see this,' I reply, quickly pulling out my phone.

But instead of finding that thread, my gaze lands on another one.

@TheatreGeek: Yeah, **@CallmeZarah**, not that I'm hating on Farah and Zayan being together, but don't you think it's a little sus that **@TheTragedies** picked a white-passing actress for the lead when they talked about diversity? Is she even talented, or does she just look good next to Zayan?

My lungs constrict with panic. I take a tentative look at The Tragedies, heart thumping wildly against my ribs.

Did they read the same tweet? Do they feel the same way?

I never did audition for this lead role. Zayan and I all but demanded it. What if The Tragedies secretly feel the same way as this person, but won't say anything about it?

I understand what the person posting is saying. I know how easy it is to choose me over someone who is obviously brown. I know I have privilege. Still, the words *white-passing* brand themselves on to my thoughts.

Two threads intertwine in my head, and both leave me feeling a certain type of sadness. Carving a sense of not belonging anywhere into me. I'm not light-skinned enough to be considered white, and not brown enough to be considered Pakistani – so where do I fit? Will I ever be enough for either side?

Breathlessness tightens my throat, my hands begin to shake and I force myself to turn away from the group – not wanting them to see how this one comment has left me feeling all unsteady and vulnerable.

'Hey, Farah,' David says. 'You want to join us for dinner?'

I'm struggling to get breath into my lungs, so my reply comes out with a slight squeak. 'Thanks, but I, uh, I have this group project to help with for uni. So, rain check?'

I don't wait for his response, making my escape as quickly as I can, but not before I hear Gibitah's wayward question. 'We have a group project? But we have all the same classes . . .'

I rush out of the theatre doors, into the all-encompassing cold of London, and slam directly into someone. Hands grip my forearms, steadying the both of us from crashing on to the ground.

'Woah,' Zayan says. 'Where are you off to?'

From the corner of my eye, I see the camera. We're always being watched. This will be a great article for tomorrow. I place a smile on my lips; the mask has become so easy to put on now.

'Flat,' I reply, hoping that there's no turmoil left on my face for Zayan to see. 'How was the audition?'

My senses buzz with nerves as I wait for his reply, and his silence makes me pause. I search his expression. He's hiding something. He doesn't go entirely analytical or cold, but the corners of his mouth droop ever so slightly. He brightens a second later, shifting closer, so I tip my head back to look up at him. Warmth builds, cloyingly, between the two of us, and I know this is all for show, but I can't help enjoying the feeling.

'It went well,' he says. 'I think I'm going to get the part.'

He says it so simply, but I hear the hope running like an undercurrent in his tone. I, on the other hand, have none of his restraint, and I let an excited noise escape. He shakes his head in amusement, curls waving.

'How was practice?' he asks, finally letting go. 'Did you do your final scene?'

'Yeah, I did, actually. It was pretty good; I think I really nailed that poignancy in Heer's death. Now I've just got to work on emoting all the anguish.' I mask any hitches in my voice, in my expression. I even ignore the smallest, tiniest hint of jealousy I felt when Zayan said he was so sure about getting the role. His dreams are blossoming, and mine still feel like such a *fantasy*.

Zayan's silence forces me to glance at him, and I'm unprepared for the pride in his eyes, glimmering in the brown of his irises.

'What?' I ask.

'It's nothing – it's just amazing to see how much you've grown in terms of confidence with your craft. I mean, you've gone from asking me for my help to feeling confident enough to command the stage on your own. Don't you feel more confident?'

I do feel self-assured on stage, but that's because I, Farah, am *hidden*. How is that confidence? But answering that question, and going down that route, only promises me heartbreak. I don't want to think about why my confidence feels as fake as my relationship with Zayan.

'Farah?' Zayan questions, pausing as we reach the station. 'Is everything all right?'

'Yeah … Yes, everything is all right. I'm just a little stressed,' I reply, knowing that when you throw words like 'stressed' and 'workload' around, people tend to back off.

But Zayan's hand comes up to brush a curl out of my face. For some reason, the thought of him touching my cheek, his fingertips brushing against the curve, feels like it will shatter me entirely.

'Don't,' I choke out, and his hand stills in mid-air, confusion sprawling across his face. 'You don't have to pretend. The camera is gone.'

And, again, it's not a lie. The paparazzi guy that was there has disappeared, likely having got the shots Lacey needed. They never stay for too long – only the amount of time Lacey has signed them up for.

'I wasn't –'

'You did a good job, Zayan,' I continue desperately. 'I'm sure the paparazzi shot is going to look so great tomorrow.'

He drops his hand, jaw tightening, a storm thundering over the crevices of his expression. He sighs, a full-body motion, and shakes his head. 'Let's meet up tomorrow.'

The sudden change in conversation confuses me so much that my only response is a garbled 'Huh?'

'Tomorrow,' Zayan repeats slowly. 'I want to take you somewhere.'

'But we're not scheduled for anything,' I reply tiredly.

I really want nothing more than to go home and sink into a hot bath. I want to wash today off and forget everything that's happened.

'Don't worry about that,' Zayan says dismissively, and then the tone of his voice turns warm, low, *velvety*. 'Come on, Farah. Let me take you out. I promise you'll enjoy it. You deserve it too; you've been working so hard.'

His body is angled towards me, his eyes bright with mischief. I realize, belatedly, that if he looked at me like that all the time, there would be very little I wouldn't agree to.

'Fine,' I concede. Triumph touches Zayan's lips, a dimple popping in his cheek. 'Where are we going?'

'Oh no.' Zayan shakes his head. 'That's a surprise.'

♥

Zayan's text message sends me into a spiral of panic.

> **Zayan (The Actor)**
> I'll pick you up at 5.30. Dress fancy.

I end up in Maha's closet, where I borrow a dress that has these long, romantic sleeves a skirt that tapers round my ankles, and is made of fabric that reminds me of pink starlight. Because I'm so nervous, I finish getting ready a whopping three hours before Zayan is picking me up, but I distract myself by practising Heer's death scene again.

And it's while I'm kneeling on the floor, arms outstretched, echoing a cry, that Zayan rings the bell for the flat.

'Uh . . .' Amal says, poking her head round the door. 'Zayan is here, but if you need a minute –'

I stand up quickly, brushing non-existent lint off my dress. 'Nope, I'm good. Great. Very good.'

Amal smiles knowingly, and I'm reminded of a moment just like this. Except it was Amal getting ready, and me standing in the doorway, back when she and Owais hated one another. And now look at where they are. Something hopeful flutters in my chest as I race out of the flat and into the cool air to greet Zayan.

I find him leaning against his car with his hair swooped to one side, in a black turtleneck and grey trousers. A brown belt is narrowing his waist and accentuating his broad shoulders, which have a stylish indigo-coloured corduroy jacket thrown over them. He looks painfully handsome, and it makes my chest hurt.

'You know, you're making the stars bright with envy, looking like that,' Zayan says, as I approach. The reverence and softness of his words make my body warm, my cheeks heating quickly.

'Where are we going?' I ask, avoiding his compliment and the feelings that come with it.

His grin widens, and he opens the car door for me. 'You'll see soon enough.'

Our ride is filled with conversations about anything and everything, and it's a welcome respite from having to think about the LSDCATS. In fact, it's the exact break I needed.

But that all ends abruptly when I see where we are.

'No way,' I say, clutching Zayan's arm in excitement. 'You got us tickets to *The Phantom of the Opera*?'

'Not just any tickets,' Zayan replies, all smug. 'Royal Circle seats.'

'This is my favourite musical!'

'I know.'

'I will cry when they sing 'All I Ask of You'.'

'I brought a handkerchief. It's embroidered with my initials. Very soft. Good for tears.' His smile turns devilish as he leans over the armrest expectantly. 'I'm ready to hear my "Thank you, Zayan, you're the best" now.'

I take a cursory glance around to see if there are any hidden cameras directed at us. When I deem the area safe, I pretend to lean in closer, like I'm going to press a kiss to his cheek.

Zayan's eyes widen, his lips parting in anticipation, his body tensing. I notice that, surprisingly, he doesn't move away. He stays still and ready. But right before my lips brush his cheek, I stop. His brows furrow in confusion, and I grin smugly because, for once, he's the one who's flustered. He's the one trying to decipher one of *my* moves.

'Thank you, Zayan,' I say innocently, and then I reach out to pluck the handkerchief from his hand. His eyes drop to his now-vacant hand, still confused.

'What?' I ask, when he says nothing. 'Were you expecting something else?'

He rubs a hand on his cheek, and then laughs – a reluctantly proud sound.

'You're very welcome, Farah,' Zayan finally replies, his mouth flicking upwards. His eyes are lit up with a promise.

He's going to get me back for that.

Chapter Twenty-three

From the second the musical starts, my attention is stolen. I lose myself to the world of heartbreak and forbidden love being painted on stage, knowing I'm safe in the darkness of the theatre.

It's only when the trembling opening notes of 'All I Ask of You' start that the memory of a conversation with Zayan plays in my mind. One of our 3 a.m. calls about *The Phantom of the Opera* – how he said it couldn't be his favourite. This song will prove him wrong. I tear my eyes away from the stage to give him a smug smile, preparing my elbow to dig into his side, but I find him already watching me – comfortably, as if he never stopped looking.

His gaze is heated, his smile knowing, and I am unprepared for the combination of it. I tentatively grin back, before getting suddenly shy at the bluntness of his stare.

With Zayan's eyes still locked on me, I turn back to the musical, allowing the song to lull me away. Tears prick in the corners of my eyes, the anguish of the character's emotions cutting like a knife against the sinewy strings holding my heart together.

Slowly, painstakingly, I feel a soft brush against the delicate skin of my inner wrist.

What are you doing?

Zayan's thumb circles the bone of my joint, growing more confident, before dipping back to my wrist. He can probably feel my thundering pulse against his fingertips. I hear his change in breath – the slight hitch in the rise and fall of his chest. I don't shift away from him or make any sort of movement. I've never considered my wrist to be a particularly sensitive place, and yet every nerve in my body has been electrified.

As the song moves into dialogue, as the actors break and resurrect themselves on stage, as the music rises and falls and even when the scene with the chandelier crashing across the theatre passes, Zayan's fingers never leave me. They pause, linger, move in a range of patterns, but they never leave. Not until the theatre lights brighten above us and we're forced to get up from our seats.

'Did you enjoy the show?' Zayan asks as we step through the theatre doors. He speaks normally, like he hasn't had his fingertips on the skin of my wrist for the last two hours.

'It was one of the best I've ever seen,' I reply, unable to hide my giddiness, unsure if we should talk about what happened in there.

'Good. I'm glad.'

'Thank you,' I say earnestly. We're walking out of the lobby now, people chatting all around us.

Zayan's about to say something, probably something smug but sweet, when the sounds of shouting and cameras snapping fill the air. I'm blinded by white lights, stumbling backwards as black spots play across my vision. Zayan catches me, curls one strong arm round my waist, draws me close to his side. His voice is in my ear, fingers pressing into my waist.

'Paparazzi,' he says loudly over the questions being shouted our way.

'Zayan! Farah! Are you two officially dating? Who are you both wearing? Zayan, what about Laiba? Both of you, look here! Pose here! Come on, give us something!'

My heart explodes in my chest, nerves fizzing in my blood. Zayan's hand moves from my waist to the back of my head, and he gently pushes it down. I stare at my feet while he grips me close again.

'We're going through them. Keep your head low, and stay by me.'

Those are his last instructions before we're launched down the steps of Her Majesty's Theatre. The shouting intensifies as we wade through the cameras; my vision is filled with flashes, and my hearing is a cumulation of jeering and shouting. Only when Zayan all but deposits me in the car does everything become muted. He slips into the driver's seat quickly, smoothly driving out of his parking spot. There's a ringing in my ears, and my vision still has black spots dancing across it.

'What was that?' I grind out, disbelief colouring my voice.

'That,' Zayan says, aggravated, 'was what I should've accounted for.'

'What do you mean?' I'm confused, my mind still muddled from the entire ordeal.

'Usually, when we go out for dates, Lacey has a tight leash on the paparazzi. But I didn't consult her for this one. I'm sorry, Farah. I didn't mean for you to face that.'

'Wait, is this what *you* face?'

Zayan nods, jaw locked. 'Yeah, but I'm used to it. You aren't. I should've been more –'

'It's OK,' I interrupt, placing a hand on his arm to stop the protectiveness in its tracks. He throws me a grateful smile, guilt still lingering in his eyes.

'Do you – do you get heckled by them a lot?' I ask, thinking back to how the paparazzi were shouting about my outfit, about Laiba and probably about more that was lost in the chaos.

'Well, I've had them rip apart everything from the clothes I'm wearing to my friendships and my parents,' he offers nonchalantly. At my horrified look, he continues hastily. 'But you become thick-skinned. They're just trying to get a reaction out of you. You handled yourself well for your first time. The first of many, knowing how big you're going to become.'

'I don't know if that's supposed to make me feel good or not,' I say, worried. 'I want to be an actress, but I keep forgetting that all of this comes with the job. The paparazzi, the lack of privacy, the constant worry.'

Zayan hums in agreement, his eyes on the road. 'You're right. But there are things to make it easier.'

'Really?' I ask. 'Like what?'

'Privacy has to look different when you gain fame, but the best thing you can do is build a circle you trust. Find people who have your back, who will book restaurants using a fake name, who don't mind staying in instead of going out. Friends who keep your secrets.' He glances over at me, a slight smile on his face. 'And you've got me in your circle. We're going to survive this industry together, Farah.'

I paste a shaky smile on to my face, my heart still drumming in my chest. Two emotions war inside me – the ambitious, hungry side of me is delighted that Zayan sees a future where I'm in the industry at his level, and the other side of me doesn't feel like I'll ever be good enough and is terrified of letting him down.

Him, The Tragedies, everyone who's rooting for our play. What if I don't live up to their expectations? What if I can't survive?

'Farah?' Zayan's elbow gently touching mine pulls me back into the present.

'Yes, sorry – I was just spacing out,' I reply quickly. 'What were you saying?'

'I was asking if you were hungry.'

My stomach starts to rumble loudly in response. 'I'm

starving. Want to get Chicken Cottage? I'm kind of craving a BBQ burger.'

Zayan throws a grin my way. 'I was hoping you'd say that.'

We end up outside a quiet Chicken Cottage we're way overdressed for. As we walk in a few people recognize us, but it's so late that no one comes up to ask anything. We grab our order and sit in the car park to eat it. It's pretty empty, so we take our boxes and lean against the bonnet of the car. Zayan drapes his jacket over my shoulders.

'So chivalrous,' I tease, and he bumps me with his shoulder, before returning to his burger. I'm about to bite into mine when the memory of his fingertips on my wrist steals into my thoughts once more.

I suddenly feel unbearably shy beside Zayan, unsure whether I should bring it up or not.

He notices my growing silence and gives me an analytical look. 'Is something wrong? Are you still feeling rattled from the photographers?'

'I . . .' I trail off.

In the end, instead of saying anything, I take the coward's way out and turn away from him to take a massive bite out of my burger. I don't anticipate just how much I've bitten off until I feel my cheeks bulge and I'm chewing desperately fast.

Zayan laughs quietly, his eyes dancing with amusement. 'Someone clearly loves a BBQ burger.'

I give him a thumbs up, because my mouth is still full. His gaze softens at the sight of me, and then he's leaning closer. Zayan's hand rises to my face, his thumb sweeping against the corner of my lip to wipe away a stray sesame seed. I swallow, finally, my mouth feeling dry, my body wound tight with tension. His hand drops, but he turns to look at me, and the full brunt of his gaze – the fierce emotion in his eyes – makes my breath catch.

'Did I tell you that you look beautiful tonight?' he asks, his voice barely above a whisper. 'Because if I didn't I'm an idiot.'

'I think you mentioned something about the stars,' I mumble, unsure where this is going.

'You're so stunning, Farah. I'm not sure I even have the right words to tell you how brilliant you are,' Zayan says, like it's a declaration. A fact. And this feels like so much more than a throwaway compliment.

This feels like we're standing on the line, waiting for one of us to cross it.

But one of us also needs to remember why we have the line in the first place. Zayan said it himself; he doesn't want to fall in love again. Whatever could've happened here would've been over in seconds, a fleeting, meaningless relationship – and I want so much more than that for myself.

'Let's take a photo,' I interject, pulling away from his hold. My face is cooling, but my insides are a torrent of warmth. 'We can post on The Tragedies' account. That way, we have some control over tomorrow's narrative in the media.'

He pauses, his body tense even though his words are light. 'It'll be the first picture that we've posted of just the two of us. No people in the background, no Tragedies, nothing.'

I smile uncertainly. 'And? It doesn't *have* to be anything romantic. People will speculate no matter what we post. We're friends, aren't we?'

Zayan shakes his head, his jaw tight. 'Right. Friends.'

'So, a photo of two friends? Not a couple in love?' I say, my tone sounding slightly more desperate than I would've liked. I need him to agree. I need him to remind *me* that his feelings for me are nothing more than attraction.

His eyes latch on to mine, flashing with something that looks close to regret. But that's not the thing that catches my attention – it's the fact that the tips of his ears are turning pink.

Zayan is blushing.

'Yeah,' he replies softly, taking the phone from my hand. 'You look at me like you're not in love, and I'll look at you the way I always do.'

He doesn't wait for my reply, just shifts closer as we pose with our burgers, looking somewhat ridiculous in our fancy outfits and greasy food – both of us standing firmly behind the line.

Celebrity Leaks
Published 11 November 2021

BREAKING NEWS: LOVE CONTRACT REVEALED

We urge all of you to look at this incriminating piece of information we were able to find about Farah Sheikh, alleged girlfriend of award-winning actor Zayan Amin. The image below shows a fragment of a contract between Farah and Lacey Parker, Zayan's agent.

The contract reads: 'I, Farah Sheikh, agree to the terms set by Lacey Parker of Parker's Artists' Agency, with regards to involvement in The Tragedies' play and in the relationship . . .'

While the rest of the contract cannot be found, it is clear what this is. Many have speculated that Farah is with Zayan for economic reasons, and this just confirms our beliefs. Clearly, Farah Sheikh is with Zayan Amin to solidify her own career.

Our source told us that they *needed* to release this snippet of a contract in an attempt to help Zayan see who Farah truly is.

Our final message to Zayan is: RUN WHILE YOU CAN!

ARTICLE COMMENTS:

JadaColon: Wow, totally unexpected! To think she was using him for her own career!

Lopex83: Of course their relationship is fake – she is fake herself! Finally – maybe Zayan can be free from her now.

Anon: Farah had the MOST to benefit from this relationship. No wonder she set it up. Sad that Zayan was forced into it.

Chapter
Twenty-four

Zayan's instructions are exceptionally clear. *Do not, under any circumstances, say anything. I am dealing with it.*

I tried calling him after seeing the article, panicked and terrified, but his line was busy, and when I attempted to get Lacey, I was greeted by her stern voicemail. Then Zayan sent me that twelve-word message, worsening my already gnawing sense of guilt and heightening my fear.

I can't, for some terrible reason, stop my mind from repeating the same question on a loop: did Zayan release the contract for better publicity?

He made a show of ripping it into pieces outside the Limelight, but maybe he released only a snippet of the original copy. He drew that contract up a month ago. He needs the good publicity – everyone is sympathetic towards him now. The victim in all of this is Zayan.

I am the villain.

But I don't want to think he would stoop this low. Not after last night. Not after he declared he was going to be a part of my 'circle of trust'. He wouldn't do that – would he? I have to believe in him.

In the end, I'm saved from my spiralling thoughts by a phone call. Not from Zayan.

'Come out, Farah.' Gibitah's voice is too chirpy on the other end of the line. 'Staying holed up in your flat makes it look like you're hiding.'

'I *am* hiding,' I argue, face pressed into my pillow. Gibitah's ability to understand my garbled words is a talent.

'Well, stop it. Whatever that contract was – and you don't have to tell me what it was – Zayan is dealing with it.'

In this moment, I love Gibitah. I love her for not probing for more, even though she undoubtedly deserves answers. I love her for being there when I need her.

'You're right.'

I don't mention how terrified I am of what he'll say. What if Lacey instructs him to dissociate from me? I didn't ... I didn't get to say goodbye to our fake relationship. I haven't had the chance of imagining my life without Zayan in it.

'Then the best thing you can do is appear unaffected,' Gibitah continues, completely unaware of my inner turmoil. 'Now, come to the library. We'll study, and then we'll gossip about how this contract was most definitely released by the LSDCATS.'

'You don't know that,' I remind her, trying to focus on the mysterious 'inside source' the article mentioned rather than the impending end of my fake relationship.

I know, logically, that this screams LSDCATS, though it's underhanded and cruel in a way I didn't think they were capable of. But my mind won't shut up and stop telling me that it could be Zayan.

Gibitah snorts disbelievingly. 'Whatever you say, Farah. Now, come on. Library, thirty minutes.'

♥

I'm in a mental torture chamber.

I can't focus on what I'm supposed to be studying, so my mind wanders and drifts. I force myself not to think of the article – even as I feel the eyes of all the students around me glaring holes into my skin – but that just means thinking about Zayan.

Why did Zayan touch me like that? What did it mean?

Did he want to cross that line, or did he just get caught up in our attraction?

Was it real or pretend?

The words in my textbook are blurring in front of my eyes from how tired I am. When I look up, I see a couple of people whispering together, eyes darting towards me. A blush warms the back of my neck, worsening my headache.

'You look ready to keel over,' Gibitah murmurs from the seat beside me.

'Your observations are amazing.'

My forced smile causes Gibitah's eyes to narrow in suspicion. Not sleeping has thrown me off my game. But before she can give in to her curiosity, I make a show of turning back to my books and appearing studious. She lets me be, and I spend all of five minutes reading a passage before giving up and searching my bag for my lunch.

While I'm bent over my bag, I hear the first whispers of a conversation, catching the stray sound of my name from someone else's lips. I look up to see two girls on my left. The one who's talking has a smile etched on her face, and her pale skin has a slight pink tinge to it from the cold.

'Did you see that article about Farah Sheikh?' she says, giving a cursory glance around the library. The girl beside her, wearing a sweatshirt that reads ON WEDNESDAYS WE WEAR PINK, perks up, while my heart turns to stone. They haven't noticed me yet, but it's only a matter of time. 'I mean, I'm not surprised. Her people are *so* opportunistic.'

My people?

'Just your average Paki,' the *Mean Girls*-sweatshirted one mutters, loud enough for her friends and me – the eavesdropper – to hear.

I gasp, unwillingly, at her use of the word. I've never heard anyone say it before. I know it exists, but I didn't think someone would ever say it. No one.

Their heads turn to me, and instead of blushing, or paling, or looking even slightly remorseful, they break into quiet giggles. A cold feeling seeps through my body, and as much as I'd like to look away from these girls, I can't. I feel compelled to keep staring. Waiting. Waiting for them to say something. To apologize.

'Maisie,' the first girl whispers, 'I think she just heard you.'

'So? I'm not scared,' Maisie replies, just loud enough for me to hear. 'She's already lost Zayan. She's going to go back to being a nobody.' Then her eyes fall to me once more. 'I'm not afraid of a *Paki*.'

'What did you just say?' Gibitah's voice is loud, and it makes me jump. The three girls startle as well, looking away from me to my friend behind me.

'Gibitah,' I hiss, as other people begin to look our way as well. I can feel them working out who I am, recognition replacing confusion.

'No, Farah! You can't just let that slide.' Gibitah turns to me, all thunderous fury. 'She just called you –'

'Please,' I beg, my heart throbbing in my chest. The whispers around the library are so loud now. The three girls have whipped their phones out, and I just *know* they're twisting this story into something else.

Unsuitable.

White-passing. Paki.

Not. Good. Enough.

Suddenly, all I can hear is their giggles. It pulses in my eardrums, light and mocking.

'Farah,' Gibitah says, urgently grasping the sleeve of my kurti. 'Are you OK?'

'I n-need to go,' I gasp out, pushing myself away from the table. Something clatters on to the floor from the strength of my abrupt movements, and it feels as if every gaze in the library lands on me.

I love the spotlight – intensely, wholly – but at this moment, I want nothing more than to be in shadow. Hidden from everyone. I spare one glance at Gibitah, her expression confused and concerned, before fleeing the library, my fear leading me to the one place I know I belong.

♥

@CelebNews: From a live inside source, we've just got wind of some sort of meltdown from **@FarahSheikh** – she was seen fleeing her university library for some unknown reason. Outlets are speculating the possibility of drugs, a break-up with **@ZayanAmin** or just your general teen melodrama.

Chapter Twenty-five

'Are you sure you're OK, child?' Marvin asks, as the key slips from its slot twice. 'You're looking very pale and clammy. You're not planning on throwing up, are you? I would very much appreciate it if you made it to the bathroom instead.'

'I'm f-fine,' I say, my breath still coming in bursts.

Just get to the stage. Just get to the stage. Just get to the stage.

I would've gone home, I would've gone straight to Amal and Maha, but I can't, because they don't know the truth. So I can't let them see me like this, no matter how lonely and heartbroken I feel. Instead, I'm going to the only other place that feels safe – where I've always felt safe.

'All right, doors are open –'

I sidle past Marvin, making sure the door closes on his

suspicious-looking face. My eyes are burning with tears as I struggle to find the stage in the dark. I haven't spent enough time with the tech crew to work out how to get the lights on.

Just get to the stage.

I eventually stumble on to the stage, my knees hitting the wooden floorboards. Pain explodes down my legs as I brace my arms for the fall. Still cloaked by darkness, I clamp my mouth to stop myself from yelling out. I don't want Marvin coming in and seeing me like this.

I don't want anyone to see me like this.

Why didn't you say anything? Why? Why? Why?

I eventually fall into a sitting position, hugging my jean-clad knees to my body. There will be purple bruises marring my kneecaps tomorrow, but for now the pain has begun to fade into a dull ache. My bag is thrown beside me, with the script for the play in it. I could take it out. Use my phone flashlight to read it again. Say some lines. The feeling of being on stage wants to fall over my shoulders like a warm, comforting overcoat – beckoning me to step out of my skin and into Heer's. I consider it, resting my forehead against my knees, but the memory of what's just happened refuses to leave me alone.

Why did you run away? What if someone took a picture of you? What would they say about you – about Zayan?

On my third cycle of the same thoughts, replaying the same scenario, I feel a warm heat blossoming over my neck and a hand brushing against mine. My head jerks up, my eyes quickly adjusting to the loss of darkness because of the spotlight being switched on. It's bathing both myself and Zayan in a circle of light.

His brown eyes are coloured with concern, there's a crease between his eyebrows and his full lips are turned into a worried line. His thumb brushes against the top of my palm, and something about that simple, comforting, movement releases the dam of tears I was holding back.

'Oh, sweetheart,' he whispers, and before I know it he's wrapped me up in a hug. An odd hug, considering I've still got my knees up to my chest, but I feel a sense of safety nonetheless.

'H-how did you find me here?' I ask eventually, when my sobs have quieted down. I pull away to look at him. 'Zayan?'

He sighs, his arms dropping as he moves to sit cross-legged in front of me. 'There were tweets about your leaving the library, and I had a feeling you'd come here. Marvin all but confirmed it when he let me in.'

A new set of tears wets my lashes, and guilt burns a hole in my chest. 'I'm so sorry. For the pictures, for running out, for everything.'

Zayan's hands grab my own as panic wedges in between my lungs, growing as my mind conjures up scenarios of Lacey telling Zayan to cut off all contact with me.

Then the fear returns, and I can't hold back my questions – no matter how harsh they sound when spoken aloud.

'Did you leak the contract?' I ask, as terror wraps round my heart like a vice.

Please don't be true. Please don't be true. Please don't be true.

His expression goes through stages of emotions: initial disbelief in the furrow of his brow, horror at my question in the slight O-shape of his mouth, anger in his jaw and then understanding, finally, in the light of his eyes.

'Farah,' Zayan says, and it sounds like both a command and a plea. 'I would never, *ever*, do that to you. I'm sorry that I made you believe I would.'

If I went on Zayan's words alone, I wouldn't believe him. Me over his reputation? The thing he's spent two months fixing? Unbelievable. But I know how honesty sounds on Zayan, how desperation looks on him. He isn't lying, and the realization brings a fresh wave of tears to my eyes. Relief forces me to slump in his arms.

'I'm sorry,' I choke out. 'I'm sorry that I thought –'

'You don't have to apologize,' Zayan interrupts, not an ounce of anger in his voice. 'I understand why your mind jumped to that. Especially when I didn't pick up your call. I should've been there, helping you through this. I was caught up doing damage control, and not thinking about how *you'd* be affected by this. I'm sorry. But I'm here now, so tell me what happened in the library.'

At my silence, he squeezes our interlaced hands twice. His hold on me is unwavering, strong in all the ways I feel like I'm not.

'You can trust me, Farah,' Zayan whispers. 'Tell me what happened.'

He waits patiently, and for several long moments we just

breathe. Breathe until I'm sure our hearts must be beating in sync. It's hard for me to justify my silence when I realize that I owe him the truth, in return for how much it must have cost him to trust me. Especially since my public breakdown probably detonated a bomb over our partnership.

'I don't want to burden you,' I confess, and something close to agony shadows his gaze.

'Burden me, Farah,' he replies, his voice tinged with a desperation I've never heard before. 'Please.'

And it's that last word that forces me to speak.

'There was this girl,' I mumble. My eyelids fall shut, like I can't bear to look at him. 'She called me . . . a Paki.' Pure silence sits in the small gap between us. But I keep going, every word hurting as it escapes me. 'And I didn't say anything back. I never would have thought someone would call *me* that. I know that sounds arrogant. I've had a lot of benefits from having fairer skin. I had someone once tell me I was a six out of ten: four points for having a British passport, and two because I looked foreign, despite having Pakistani heritage.' My voice turns into a shameful whisper. 'I didn't know what a privilege that was, not until I came here, and some people started . . . started using my skin as an insult. But then there are people online, since we started our relationship, who think I'm not brown enough. Half of the world sees me as white-passing and opportunistic. The other sees me as too brown and untalented. I don't know how to keep up: am I brown or not?'

'Farah.' The fury with which Zayan says my name causes my eyelids to snap open.

I knew it. He thinks I'm a spoiled brat. I shouldn't have said anything. I try to disentangle our hands, but he tightens his hold, forcing me to stay in place.

'I'm not angry at you,' he says quickly. 'I'm furious at everyone else. For how you've been treated.'

'It's not a big deal,' I whisper, my jaw trembling with sudden nerves.

'It's not an overreaction, Farah,' Zayan says. 'You've just been verbally attacked, and then you're also dealing with this confusion about your own culture and what it means to be brown in a society that says you're anything but. It *is* a big deal.'

Twin feelings of relief and terror pulse through me. 'It's not,' I say. 'Look, I don't even get the worst of it. Anushka and Nur –'

'Don't,' Zayan interrupts urgently. 'Don't start playing Oppression Olympics in your head. What you face is different, but valid. It matters, Farah. You shouldn't have to pretend to be OK when you're so clearly hurting.'

His words sink into my mind slowly, like treacle. A part of me resists; a part of me wants to shout at him and say, *I'm fine*. That everything I'm feeling is just me overreacting, because if it's just that then I have nothing to confront. Nothing to deal with. I can just move on. But I can't. Everything Zayan says shines a new light upon the previous events of my life, and it's impossible to look away.

'I don't know what to do,' I reply. My head feels tangled with so many emotions that I'm too tired to work out right now. 'I don't know where to start dealing with all of this. What . . . How . . . What do I do?'

'You're not going to work this all out in one go,' Zayan says gently. 'But you have to stop running from this, Farah. The only way you're going to really work through it is by talking about it. Maybe we should talk to The Tragedies –'

'No,' I gasp out, attempting to wrench my hand away from his, but he has an iron-clad grip on me. 'I can't – I won't –'

'OK,' he says softly. 'OK. No talking to them. Yet. We'll build up to that, yeah?'

I nod, before hesitantly taking one tiny, miniscule metaphorical step forward. 'Maybe . . . Maybe.'

'Good. I mean, not good, but it's a start,' Zayan replies. 'Acknowledging that you will talk about it one day is a brave thing, Farah.'

I laugh wetly. 'They could hate me.'

'I would physically fight anyone who doesn't immediately see how wonderful you are.' Zayan's voice is so serious I feel a genuine smile press against my lips.

'I'm sure that would be great for your reputation,' I tease, as my heart rate returns to its normal beat, my tears drying.

He smiles too, so softly and sweetly that it makes me hyper-aware of how close we are. Our knees brushing, hands joined, hearts beating like one.

'The damage would be worth it,' he whispers.

My heart threatens to explode in my chest, my mind whirling with questions about what this all means. If it means anything at all. I try to focus on concrete things we need answers for. 'How are we going to recover from this? The play, your reputation? All of it?'

Zayan doesn't look worried. 'Lacey and I talked it over. We're going to say you were signing an NDA. It's common for celebrity relationships, and it will take the brunt off you. You're not going to respond; we won't allow people to misconstrue your words. It's best to ignore the hate and focus on moving forward. As for the play, no one is boycotting it as long as I'm still there. Which I will be. We'll need to do some more promo in the next TikTok Live to recover from this, but we will be fine, Farah.'

'But wouldn't it just be easier if you left?' I say, hating every word coming from my mouth – but it wouldn't be fair not to offer Zayan the chance to escape unscathed. He's an established actor. One of us should get something out of our deal. 'Your audition for the movie –'

'Is fine,' Zayan stresses. 'No one is kicking me out of Hollywood over this, Farah. And even if they were, I wouldn't leave you.'

'Because we're friends?' I ask quietly, though I'm sure he must hear my heart raging once again against my ribcage.

He hesitates. It's a split-second thing. A moment, and then it's over.

'Yeah,' he agrees, and my hope dips in disappointment. 'Because we're friends.'

@ZayanAmin: Any comments made against **@FarahSheikh** are entirely condemned by me, my team and those closest to me. That contract was an NDA that I asked Farah to sign, and she graciously accepted.

@ZayanAmin: Farah is neither your punching bag nor your target. You are not my fan if you insult someone I care deeply about. And Farah is incredibly important to me. So learn to spread kindness, and not to voice your every errant thought – no one wants to hear them.

@TheRelationshipGuru: OK . . . so our questions were answered about what that contract was, but is anyone still feeling off about it? Who makes someone sign an NDA? Is Farah not trustworthy? Is Zayan even into her, or is he afraid of her? IDK, this all just screams SKETCHY to me.

Posted: 12 November 2021

@TheLSDCATS: With all the drama that's been unfolding of late, we feel it's important to remind everyone that 'all the world's a stage, and all the men and women merely **players**.'

Chapter Twenty-six

There is only one dressing room in the Limelight Theatre, and when the entire cast tries to squeeze in there, it can feel like complete chaos enclosed in one space. But tonight, it's just Nur, Anushka, Gibitah, and me – standing on a short stool while Nur adds her finishing touches to my outfit.

'Every single comment on the TikTok Live is about what Zayan tweeted yesterday. People have switched up so fast ever since he showed you support,' Nur whispers as she presses one more pin into my outfit. 'Some people are still a little shady. Talking about things like whether your relationship is real or not. The LSDCATS' tweet didn't help. But, on a positive note, there's less focus on the contract and more excitement about whether you guys will show up at the Soho Gala together tonight.'

'Ouch, Nur,' I complain as she pricks me with a pin near

my hip bone. I'm mostly regretting asking for help with my gala outfit. 'Yeah, I saw those comments. There were only a few, but still – the gala should help. Though Lacey sprang it on us last minute.'

Incredibly last minute. Hysterically breaking down in Zayan's arms led to me crashing into my bed the moment I got home, much to Amal and Maha's concern. They'd seen the video taken at the library and had been worried. But they let me sleep. I was rudely awakened by Zayan's 3 a.m. call, telling me all about this event Lacey wanted us to go to – to help the publicity dip, and because the director of the movie Zayan auditioned for will be there.

In the beginning I was nervous to agree and was going to put off going altogether. I thought lying low was the best thing to do. The play is less than three weeks away now, and I'm already worried that I'm going to let everyone down. The support online is fickle – some people hate me; others love me because of Zayan. I didn't want to draw any more attention to myself by going to the gala, but Zayan convinced me otherwise.

'But what if people –' I began before he cut me off.

'Forget what other people think, Farah. It's the Soho Gala. I don't want to go with anyone else but you.'

I paused. 'It *would* be hard to bring a new date up to speed.'

'That's not . . .' He sighed, cutting himself off this time. 'There'll be free food, the chance to meet industry officials, and I promise you, you won't face any more drama tonight.'

It was probably the combination of his well-thought-out offer and persuasive tone, but by the end of the call I was drafting a text to Nur, asking for fashion advice. Hence today's pinpricking outfit fitting.

'It's sweet that he stood up for you,' Anushka adds, joining the conversation.

'I still think Farah should've said something herself,' Gibitah chimes in quietly before I can say anything.

We share a look in the mirror. Her gaze is innocent, but I know better. Last night, she called repeatedly once I got home, and tried to talk to me about what happened in the library. But I shut it down, telling her I didn't want to talk about it – the same thing I said to Amal, Maha, Owais and The Tragedies. I know Zayan said I should, but I'm not ready for all my friendships to crash and burn in one go.

Gibitah dropped it, but that didn't stop her from hounding me about staying silent, even though that was Lacey's request. She thought I should've said something about the contract, that I should've fought against the narrative the media were trying to create about me.

'Sometimes we have to make sacrifices,' I say, echoing Lacey's explanation when I asked her why I couldn't speak up.

I don't like it – staying quiet, saying nothing – but I've spent this whole relationship like that.

'But they're trying to turn you into something you're not,' Anushka adds, gentler than Gibitah.

I shrug. 'I suppose, but isn't that the price of this industry? We spend all our time pretending to be people we aren't.'

The three of them share a look, and my stomach tightens. I wonder if they can see my secrets written across my face.

'Are you sure you're OK, Farah?' Nur asks. 'You know you can talk to us about anything, right?'

I avoid looking at them directly. I know Zayan didn't react how I expected, but we share an uncanny understanding of one another. I don't want to test the waters and see if it's the same with The Tragedies – if they think I'm overinflating all of this, they'll see me as big-headed, self-absorbed, and I don't want to risk losing their friendship.

'I'm fine,' I lie. 'Just nervous about today's gala.'

Disappointment flashes across their expressions. The laugh that Anushka gives me rings false, and I try not to flinch. 'Sure, Farah,' she jokes, but there's an undercurrent there that I can't place. 'Your lips are locked tighter than a vault, I swear.'

I shrug helplessly, hoping the lopsided smile on my lips doesn't look as fake as it feels. 'I didn't . . . I don't have anything to share. Life is completely ordinary for me.'

All I can hear are the giggles in the library and the edge to Anushka's voice, and my heart almost collapses on itself. I can't stop seeing the chasm between me and them – Anushka, Nur, Gibitah on one side and me on the other. And it's my fault. I created that barrier. But it's necessary. If I burden them with what I've been thinking, they will surely leave.

'All right.' Anushka straightens, and that tense, fragmented moment disintegrates. Her smile becomes so real, I almost feel like I imagined that change before. 'We need to show off Nur's design to the viewers.'

'Look at yourself before we go,' Nur urges, and I angle myself in front of the full-length mirror.

I am suffused with sheer gratefulness for all the prodding and pricks I've endured for the last hour. I haven't worn a sari since my end-of-high-school farewell party, but this – with its ballet-slipper-pink blouse and lace full sleeves – is much prettier than the one I wore then. The dupatta is made of this shimmering silver-and-rose-coloured fabric that is draped over my shoulder. However, the true beauty of this sari is the skirt made of soft, papier-mâché-like roses of varying colours – bruised violet, darkened rouge, pale yellow, aged ivory, sage green.

'Nur,' I breathe out, unable to put into words how much I adore it.

'I know – you're lucky to have me in your life; you want to shower me with gifts,' she teases, a sly smile playing on her lips. 'Now, come on! I want to show the camera.'

As we walk to where Ben is doing a TikTok Live, I find Zayan standing right at the centre of the stage. My gaze locks on to him automatically, taking in the sharp cut of his all-black suit and his gold cuff links. The suit fits him like a glove, moulding over his biceps, tightening across his chest, and my stomach traitorously flips at the sight of him.

I've concluded that I need to put an end to all these tangled feelings I have for Zayan. We will be nothing more than friends – no more confusing moments, no more blushes and bolts of attraction. His friendship is too precious for me to lose, and he's made it so clear that he doesn't want to cross that line. That he isn't looking for someone to be with for the long run.

So I steel my stomach, and walk over with Anushka, Nur and Gibitah.

'Farah, you look . . . Wow,' David says, eyes widening.

'Nur did an amazing job,' Ben replies, and then with a jolt he remembers the TikTok Live. 'Look, everyone! We have our stars standing together, in all their glory.'

I turn my attention to Zayan, waiting to see what he'll say next.

His smile is filled with wicked things he's holding back, his eyes dancing with mirth. I raise a brow expectantly, daring him to say what he's thinking.

'You look beautiful,' he says, reaching over to my sari to press a green petal between his fingers. He looks away from the flower and dead straight into my eyes. 'You're making it hard to breathe around you.'

My stomach somersaults with unbidden chemistry. Does he have to be this attractive? Does he have to say things like this? It makes building an impenetrable wall round my feelings so much harder. And I do have to build this wall, because Zayan and I are getting too close to saying things that can go nowhere.

I have to remind myself: *he's an actor. He's my friend.* Once this fake relationship ends, he's going to go back to his world, and I'll go back to mine, and the only thing keeping us together will be a friendship and a line we did not cross.

'Wow, you could slice the tension here with a knife!' David cuts in, just before Anushka elbows him in the stomach.

Zayan laughs, and I watch him as he interacts with The Tragedies. He jokes with Ben, he listens to Nur ranting about her classes, he can talk for ages with David, he's developed an almost sibling-like relationship with Anushka and Gibitah. He's ingrained in the group.

Guilt clogs my heart, churns in my blood. He's so honest with them. So friendly with them. He's talked about his family with them. He's talked about the industry. They value him as a friend, and I just wonder, *do The Tragedies and Gibitah feel the same about me?*

'All right, we're free,' Ben announces, cutting through my thoughts by ending the Live.

'Wow, they are desperate,' Gibitah says suddenly.

'Who is?' I ask curiously.

'The LSDCATS. Look at their blatant attempt to get *celebrity* involvement.'

We crowd round Gibitah's phone, looking at the screen.

@TheatreGeek: Rumour has it that **@LaibaSiddiqi** is going to be starring in **@TheLSDCATS** play. Everyone who wants this to happen should show their support below!

'They're clearly using a third party to try and strong-arm her into agreeing – it's like emotional blackmail,' Anushka rants.

'Unless it's true . . .' David says, and in unison we all look at Zayan, who stares back at us defensively.

'What?' he asks.

'Seems like you would know,' Ben says leadingly, as I try to school my expression into one of complete nonchalance.

For so long now, I've avoided asking about his past relationship, but now, standing here, I find myself desperate to hear what he has to say about Laiba.

'Why would I know?' Zayan says obtusely.

'Because you dated her,' I finally erupt, tired of going in circles.

The group takes a little step back.

Faint amusement lines Zayan's mouth, and the sight of it irritates me. 'Exactly, *dated*, past tense. I have zero connection to her now.'

'Zero? I find that a little hard to believe. You two were –'

'Were nothing,' he interrupts firmly, all traces of humour now gone. 'I'll give you the very short, very unnecessary rundown: Laiba and I were together for a year. If you can even call it being together. We had extremely different schedules; I saw her a couple of times a month. But then, one day, she just broke up with me.'

I reel slightly; the narrative has always been that their break-up was explosive. Something awful must have happened behind closed doors for them to break up the way they did. Clearly the group has the same thought, because we all wait with bated breath for the rest of Zayan's explanation.

'But why?' David asks tentatively.

Zayan shrugs, clearly uncomfortable but soldiering through it. 'I've never known why. One day she was with me, and then she left.'

'And you never sought her out?' I ask. 'Didn't you want to ask?'

Zayan rubs his forehead tiredly, like this entire conversation exhausts him. 'Of course I did, but it became pretty clear on her end that she didn't want to talk to me. I suppose it has something to do with the fact that my career plummeted thanks to the TV series, and I wasn't getting any new roles.'

Something painful cuts through my feelings at the thought of anybody leaving Zayan because he wasn't successful enough for them.

'Do you still love her?' Gibitah asks, and I love *her* for voicing the question I've been too afraid to ask.

Anticipation beats in my blood like an erratic drum; Zayan's face smooths out as he looks at Gibitah, his mask slipping into place.

Please don't hide. Not now. Please.

'You don't have to answer that,' Ben offers earnestly. 'Seriously, this is getting a little deep –'

Zayan's gaze finds mine, and just like that, he's completely visible to me. No mask. No hiding. Not as he holds my stare with his own. 'I've replayed mine and Laiba's relationship in my mind like a movie and tried to nitpick when it all changed, and all I can think is that she was playing me from the beginning. I let her in, and she left. No reason. Nothing. And believe me, I know I'm vain, but

I can't help but think it's something I did. Why else would she leave?'

I understand his conundrum keenly. The boy with a distant family. The boy with few friends. The boy with a cage round his heart, one of his own creation.

'She left when I was at my lowest,' he continues. His voice is disaffected, but I can see the cracks. He keeps our eyes locked; he wants me to see the honesty in his words. 'And the feelings I once had, they're gone. I'm not still hung up on Laiba. I don't think I *could* be in love with her, not with –'

'Oh my gosh, she tweeted back!' Nur interrupts, and the moment shatters with the excitement of the group.

Zayan's sentence goes unfinished, but it lingers in my mind, like smoke that refuses to dissipate. The rest of the group moves around Nur's phone, but Zayan and I stay locked in place.

@LaibaSiddiqi: I don't speak on rumours, but I would like to say that I am not involved in **@TheLSDCATS** play.

'I know we kind of hate her now for what she did to you,' Anushka says to Zayan, 'but that reply was pretty classy. The LSDCATS' socials are filling up with hate from your fans and her fans. No one is on their side any more.'

Zayan rolls his eyes. 'You know I did the exact same thing with my tweet, right?'

'Yeah, but, you know, girl power,' Gibitah offers.

'Whatever,' Zayan huffs, before turning his attention back to me. 'Not that standing here and sharing all my previous relationship trauma isn't a pure delight, but we do have a gala to get to. You ready?'

There's so much I want to say, want to ask, want to voice.

Why aren't you hung up on Laiba any more – what's stopping you?

But of course I don't say that. I fall back on the silence I've become accustomed to wielding, pasting on a smile and stepping into the comfortable lie of our relationship.

♥

@TheLSDCATS: We would like to formally state that under no circumstances was our institution involved in any negative conversation surrounding the leads of The Tragedies. We look forward to seeing you all on opening night!

@ZarahForever: You guys SUCK. I bet you thought you were super slick, trying to destroy Zarah.

@LaibaLover8: **@ZarahForever** You're so right!! They're so shady. I'm not going to see their play.

@CallMeZarah: 100% you guys are lying, and I'm getting a refund on my ticket.

@ComedyIsTragedy: The only way I'm NOT going to **@TheTragedies** play is if they cancel it. I can't see why anyone would want to watch a play by this shady institution.

Chapter
Twenty-seven

The Soho Gala is essentially a glorified charity event, where directors, screenwriters and actors – aspiring and well-established ones – come together to splurge on drinks and donate money. On the bright side, it's being held at the Underglobe – a venue hidden beneath Shakespeare's Globe.

'This place is stunning,' I say, eyes roaming over the room, arm tucked into Zayan's.

The theme for the night is *The Tempest*, and the details of the décor are meticulous. The staircase has been transformed into glittering makeshift waves that make my head feel dizzy as we descend.

'Careful,' Zayan whispers, leaning into my space, and a shiver runs down my spine. 'I can't have you breaking a leg before our night is over.'

I smile up at him, trying to ease my nerves with the warmth radiating from his look as we continue through the doors. I filled our car ride with nervous chatter, and it could've been my imagination, but judging by the way Zayan let me lead the conversation, I think he was waiting for me to ask him more about Laiba – to complete that unfinished sentence interrupted by Nur.

But I talked about everything and anything else.

I just know whatever he's going to say about it is going to change us. I'm warring inside with the desire to know and the fear of what comes after. But tonight I'm leaning towards not knowing – if for nothing more than to protect our friendship.

The wave-staircase leads us into the main area, and my breath catches in my throat. Right in the centre of the room is a glorious giant oak tree that reaches the ceiling. The lights are a subdued blue, illuminating the room as if we're roaming a clear sea, and each table has an arrangement with a wooden ship on top of a collection of wild blue flowers. The soft sounds of a violin tremble in the air, mixing well with the hum of chatter. I spot Lacey making a beeline for us before Zayan does.

'You two look stunning!' Lacey exclaims, calming my nerves. We haven't been face to face since those photos got released. 'Such a perfect pair.'

I glance at Zayan, trying not to blush at how handsome he looks.

Don't go down that road.

I keep my thoughts from straying towards what Zayan's

touches mean. If I start to think about it, I'll begin obsessing over whether his intentions have changed. I'll play the night we went to watch *The Phantom of the Opera* over and over, again and again, questioning myself about whether I'm imagining something more than simple attraction.

'You need to go and cosy up to that director over there. She's pretty much going to be the last obstacle for your auditions. Once you get her approval, you've got the role. So go – make yourself likeable,' Lacey instructs, her voice firm as her eyes roam the room.

I breathe in deeply, pressing a palm to my abdomen to feel the movement. All around me are industry professionals – those I recognize, those I don't. It feels like they're staring at me, even though I know they likely aren't. I wonder if they have impressions of me that I may or may not live up to.

Zayan must notice my tension, because he brings a hand to my elbow, giving it a squeeze. My heart rate slows, and the panic quiets with the realization that I have a safety net in Zayan – someone who has my back.

'You two ready?' Lacey asks, eyeing me more than Zayan.

'Ready,' I reply, settling comfortably into my role.

Zayan nods, and soon we're weaving past tables like we're on a mission. I tug at him firmly when we get closer to the other end of the room, where the director in question is hosting a conversation, and steer him to the bar instead.

'What are –?' Zayan starts, exasperated.

'You need to calm down before you go there,' I reply, forcing him to a bar stool. I focus on him and not me, on his career and not mine. It gives me a way to escape my own worries.

I smile at the waiter, who is dressed like he belongs on the shipwreck from *The Tempest*. 'Hi, could we get two Cokes, please?'

While he goes to get them, I give Zayan a stern look. 'You can't just barge into that conversation. You need to be smooth.'

He makes a mock-offended noise. 'I'm always smooth.'

'Eh,' I tease, lips pulling into a smile, 'I've seen smoother.'

'Really? Where?' Zayan demands, his eyes narrowing. 'If you say Ben or David, I will have to make a scene.'

I laugh, feeling lighter than I did when we first walked in. 'Fine, fine. You're the smoothest guy I know. But take a minute to recentre yourself. You don't want to come off as desperate for this role. I know you are, you know you are – but the director doesn't need to.'

Zayan absorbs my advice, and we quietly drink our Cokes until we deem enough time to have passed. We make our way to the director slowly, not like before. We're stopped a few times by industry types who know Zayan. I'm introduced as his friend, but everyone levels me with a shrewd look. Like they're trying to work out why I'm *really* here. But, odd looks aside, I do get to meet Rishi Willowy, one of my favourite actresses, and I totally don't lose my cool in front of her.

'You practically threw yourself at her,' Zayan says, laughing, when we're done with our conversation with Rishi. My face is already hot from the excitement of meeting her, so the added warmth of my blush is nothing. Still, he notices it. 'Aw, don't worry. Soon you'll be getting less and less starstruck.'

'And why's that?' I ask, taking a small crab cake from a passing waiter.

'Because soon you'll be among them. They'll probably get starstruck over *you*.'

I feel my cheeks heat even more, and Zayan's eyes soften.

'Farah, I need to tell you –' he begins, but we're cut off by a man – tall, bald, wearing a bow tie – coming up to Zayan. He claps Zayan so hard on the back that I have to swish my skirts out of the way to stop us both from toppling over.

'Zay!' The man booms in a loud, posh English accent. 'I haven't seen you in a long time, boy.'

Zayan's face splits into a strained smile, and I'm instantly on edge. It takes me a second, but I start to recognize the man in front of us. The director of Zayan's failed TV series.

Shawn Jetts.

'It's Zayan,' Zayan replies tersely, a grimace on his face. 'And yes, long time no see.'

'Aw, now, come on! "Zay" is much easier.'

Zayan's jaw clenches, and I see him physically wrestling with the urge to say more.

'It's great to see you,' Shawn Jetts says, unaware of the tension he's caused. His wide forehead is beaded with sweat, his cheeks are bright red, and his eyes are exceptionally bright with excitement. 'But I feel as if I've seen you everywhere for the last month. You're making quite the headlines with your new relationship.'

The last part is said pointedly, and I realize he expects me to be introduced. Zayan clears his throat. 'Shawn, this is Farah Sheikh, my date.'

Shawn gives me a toothy smile, and before I can do anything, he reaches out to take my hand and press a kiss on the back of it. I automatically snatch my hand away, and Zayan's bicep tightens under the palm I've got wrapped round him. Shawn doesn't notice either thing, his smile remaining slick and wide. 'It's a pleasure to meet you.'

'Likewise,' I lie.

Shawn doesn't relinquish Zayan and me from his conversation. He drones on about his latest show, his new home in the Hamptons, his new wife. We stand there for what feels like an eternity, listening to this man tell his grandiose stories. As soon as I think we're about to be freed, another friend of Shawn's lumbers over to our group. Zayan's eyes shut briefly, and I know he's cursing everyone under the sun in his head.

'Jameson!' Shawn says, gulping down another entire flute of champagne. 'Come meet Zayan and his lovely date. She's quite the stunner – Farah, wasn't it? Such an exotic name.'

That same cold feeling from the library seeps through me once more. Before, I would've paid no mind to the word "exotic". I'd have maybe even found it complimentary.

But now all I can hear is the condescension, the fascination with something foreign. Like I'm a prize that can be bought.

My blood thrums, and from the way Zayan's entire body vibrates with anger I know he's upset by the choice of words, and by the blatant misogyny as well. I can see him getting ready to explode, and I take action, steering him away from the conversation. Though we leave abruptly, neither of the soon-to-be-drunk men seem to care.

'Let me go back there,' Zayan grinds out, teeth clenched.

'No,' I reply stubbornly. 'Leave it. You're not causing a scene tonight. *We* can't cause a scene tonight.' I catch sight of the director we've been circling and decide this is the time for Zayan to talk to her. I discreetly bring us closer and then gently shove Zayan in her direction.

'Farah –'

'Go,' I whisper-shout. 'I'm getting another drink.'

I leave Zayan on the outskirts of the group, knowing he must do this conversation on his own. If I'm there, the narrative will just turn to our relationship.

I situate myself at an angle when I reach the bar, pressing my back against the edge so I can survey Zayan. He's been enveloped by the group and is animatedly talking to the director. Any glimmer of worry I had that he would flounder evaporates – of course he's fine.

If I'm being entirely honest with myself, a tiny hint of envy curls in my mind at the effortless way Zayan can slip into his confidence. His dreams take priority every time, and all his other worries, whatever they may be, just fade away. He knows exactly what he wants and how to get it.

I thought I did too. My heart still aches to be an actress, but I'm terrified that I'm just not good enough to be one. Those girls in the library clearly thought I wasn't, so many people online don't and the LSDCATS didn't. If the play fails, and if it fails because of me, I'm not sure I can pick myself back up again. I'm not sure I can keep my dream alive.

'You look like you've sucked on something incredibly sour,' a voice says, startling me out of my self-flagellating thoughts. A man leans against the bar table right in front of me, light-brown hair coiffed into an elaborate style, skin a shade darker than Zayan's and eyes an endless kind of black. His suit is a deep indigo and adds to his aura of mystery.

I point to the lemon wedge on the rim of my glass. 'I wonder why that could be.'

He smiles, and it heightens how handsome he already is. 'Here I was thinking you may be jealous of your beau being deep in conversation with another woman.'

I spare a glance at Zayan, who has his head bent close to the director's. A laugh bubbles past my lips. I already know Zayan is recounting some vivid story from the way his hands are moving. It's not his flirting stance or expression.

'He's not my beau,' I say, because it's true. And maybe because I'm a little tired of only being Zayan's date and not an aspiring actress.

The man's brow lifts, and he leans in just a little closer. 'In that case, allow me to introduce myself: Farouz Latil.'

'Oh!' I exclaim, realizing who he is. 'You were in *Hello Heartbreak*, right?'

Farouz looks pleased by my recognition, preening under the attention. He didn't have a major role in the movie – I think he was a secondary character – but I remember enjoying how cutting and witty he was when surrounded by a lovesick main cast.

'I was,' Farouz replies, an exaggerated tone colouring his voice. 'I take it you enjoyed my performance?'

'You were adequate, I suppose.'

'You wound me.' Farouz's voice dips lower, and he shifts closer so our elbows brush. 'Maybe you could give me some pointers? I wouldn't mind studying lines with you.'

His intention is clear as day, and a blush paints my cheeks. I've had male attention before, but never so blatantly. Before I can reply and ward off Farouz's request with a well-meaning letdown, a figure cuts into our conversation. I look away from Farouz to Zayan, confused by his sudden arrival.

'Hello,' Zayan says, sticking out his hand to be shaken. 'Zayan Amin.'

Farouz's smile never dips; in fact, a hint of amusement flickers in his dark eyes. 'Pleasure to meet you. Farouz Latil.' He turns his attention to me. 'I was just getting to know your lovely friend Farah. We were discussing going over lines together.'

I cringe at the way he's phrased it. 'I wouldn't push it that far. You were asking, and I was about to reject.'

'Allow me to persuade you,' Farouz offers pleasantly. He

gives Zayan a half smile, a dangerous lilt to his voice. 'How about dinner?'

I expected Zayan to laugh Farouz's flirting off, comfortable in his confidence – and, more importantly, I expected him not to care. I'm not actually his significant other.

But Zayan's hand finds mine, our fingers immediately interlace and the cool look in his eyes makes my heart jump straight to my throat. The glass I was raising to my lips pauses; I fear that I may choke on the liquid. Farouz's own humour dims slightly, and now *he* looks like he's swallowed something sour. He exits the conversation swiftly, clearly perturbed by Zayan's blatant show of . . . of . . .

Possessiveness.

When that word whispers in my mind, I attempt to wrench my hand out of Zayan's hold, but he keeps us intertwined. He pulls me, in one fluid movement, to a shadowy corner near the bar – somewhat hidden from prying eyes.

'What was that?' I hiss. 'Were you trying to *mark* me or something? You know I'm not yours to own, right?'

Zayan's jaw tightens, and the cold look he had directed at Farouz has melted into something blazing and heated.

'Of course you're not mine to own,' he says harshly. His cologne fills my lungs, making me feel dizzy. 'You belong to only yourself. But *I'm* mine to give. I belong to you. That guy needed to know that. You need to know that.'

My heart goes into overdrive, its beat pulsing all the way down to my thighs.

Zayan's brown eyes are bright with questions, and hues of blue light from above cut over his face in a mesmerizing way. I know he wants me to push it. To ask him what he means by all this. I can see it in his heavy gaze. But I can't handle asking Zayan if this means something. Not if there is even a miniscule possibility of him disappearing from my life. Not yet.

So I do the only honourable thing I can. I press a palm to Zayan's chest and gently push him away.

'I need to go to the bathroom,' I mumble, and I make my escape.

♥

I place my palms on either side of the porcelain sink and force myself to breathe. My panic is bubbling to the surface, and the feeling isn't helped by the fact that my head simply won't stop thinking. I rapidly replay every single moment I've had with Zayan in my mind, like a movie on fast forward – every 3 a.m. call, every brush of our hands, the breakdown at the Limelight, the times we've shared a stage, a cup of chai, a laugh. He's stitched into every memory I've made over the last two months, and I can't believe I missed it before.

It's so clear, abundantly clear, to me now. I don't know *how* I pretended for so long.

I'm in love with Zayan.

All of him. The small, quiet parts of him. The parts that match my own. The ones that don't. I'm burdened with the realization that I'd like Zayan to meet my mother one day. That I'd like him to come home with me. That I can envision my future with him. A future that goes beyond the next day, or the next week, or even the next month. I can see myself with him forever.

I'm ready for forever.

I love him.

The metronome of my heart beats with these words:

I love him.

I love him.

I love him.

'Enough,' I whisper to myself, wishing I could press the heels of my palms to my eyes, but that would smudge my make-up. I force a breath in against the rising panic and blinding fear. I switch the tap on to its freezing-cold side and push my hands under the stream.

The cold shocks my senses, allowing my terror to recede and a sense of methodical logic – that feels suspiciously like Anushka – to take over.

You could always tell him.

That thought makes every muscle in my body lock up. I'm not oblivious enough to think Zayan's feelings for me haven't changed. That whole *I belong to you* speech clearly means something. But . . . But I'm not sure I'm ready to cross that line. I'm not sure Zayan is either.

What happens when we tell each other how we really feel? What happens next? What if there's even a tiny, minuscule possibility that, after everything, Zayan leaves?

What if we confess our feelings and lose the friendship we've spent so long protecting?

The sound of the bathroom door swinging open cuts through my mental war. I look up to see who's walked in.

And it takes all my strength for my jaw not to drop when my gaze meets Laiba Siddiqi's.

Chapter Twenty-eight

Laiba Siddiqi is as beautiful in the flesh as she is on screen – made up of shades of brown, from the darkness of her eyes to the bronzed glow of her skin, wearing a metallic gold-coloured dress that Serena van der Woodsen would envy. We stare at one another, and I'm surprised to see recognition glinting in her irises. The silence is heavy, weighing down on my neck, forcing me to drop my gaze from our staring match back to the sink. The tap is still running, and I make no movements to stop it.

I hear rustling behind me, and I count slowly to five before looking up, in the hope that this has given her enough time to occupy one of the stalls.

It has.

I breathe in a sharp, silent breath, facing myself in the mirror. I look rattled, like I've seen a phantom. I'm about to leave and find Zayan when his voice flickers in my mind.

She left when I was at my lowest.

Despite my hands shaking, I switch off the tap. Before, I felt like fleeing, as if I was the one who had made some mistake by being here, but now I wait.

The latch to her stall opens, and if she's surprised to see me still there, it doesn't show in her expression. She takes the sink next to mine, bending a little to wash her hands. She's shorter than me (which I already knew, because most of Zayan's fans love to lament his height difference with her), but her presence isn't small. If anything, the atmosphere feels as if we're both on even ground.

'Break up with him,' Laiba says, her voice low and controlled.

Shock hits my system like a punch. *What did she just say?*

'Excuse –' I begin, disbelief colouring my words.

Laiba straightens and faces me. 'You need to break up with him,' she repeats, pointing to the towels behind me. I sidestep, allowing her to dry her hands.

I have so many things I want to say – *Who do you think you are?* is just one of them – but what falls from my mouth is an incredulous but curious 'Why?'

She sighs, rubbing her palms furiously with the towel before turning to face me again. Her lips are painted a glossy nude, her eyelids shimmer in gold and her hair has been slicked back to show off the sharp angles of her face. She's undeniably beautiful, but underneath all that instantaneously captivating allure I see a jagged sharpness, like a shard of broken glass.

'He's a star,' Laiba says, not helping my confusion. 'He shines very brightly. So brightly that sometimes it's impossible to share the sky with him.' Her words are spoken softly, as if to avoid startling me away, but there's an urgency underlying her tone. It pulls my unwilling attention. 'I was with Zayan for only a year, and do you know how many movies I was cast in alone? Not as his co-star? One. In the six months since leaving him, I've been cast in two solo movies and a new TV series, and people know my name.'

'We knew your name before,' I say, confused.

She lets out a sardonic breath. 'No, you didn't. You only knew my name with a condition: Zayan's girlfriend, Laiba Siddiqi. Zayan's partner, Laiba Siddiqi. Zayan's future wife, Laiba Siddiqi. Now I am Laiba Siddiqi. Full stop. No conditions. No additions. I am no longer an afterthought to Zayan's name.'

Understanding filters through my mind like rays of moonlight, but I don't enjoy what it illuminates. I am reminded of the interview we did with the LSDCATS actors – how every question directed to me was about Zayan. How, in every article, I am linked to him. To his prestige. This relationship hasn't set my stage . . . it has allowed me to share the background of his.

I want to crawl back into the shadows and pretend none of this is happening. It's a cowardly urge, a selfish one, but it surges through me nonetheless. And if I was a more indulgent person, maybe I would have walked away. I would've forced myself to forget what Laiba has said. But I don't. A battered, bruised part of me is holding on to that dream of making it big, and it's that fragment that roots me to this conversation.

Laiba continues, a serious expression flitting over her face. 'You should capitalize on your popularity, change the narrative, without Zayan.'

'Why didn't you ever share this with him?' I ask, feeling a loyalty to him and a genuine curiosity.

Her smile flicks downwards, brushed with sadness. 'He wouldn't have understood. He'd have tried to, but I just know he'd never have got it.'

I want to tell her she's underestimating him. I think of his hand intertwining with mine, solid and ever present, but then I think of his one-track mind when it comes to his dreams. I can understand how hard he would've tried to stay with Laiba, both for love and for his reputation.

'I made a mistake by getting into a relationship with him so young,' Laiba continues, her voice desperately sad. 'I wish I had waited. I wish I had thought of myself and not of everyone else for a moment. I would've seen how important it was for me to establish who I wanted to be before I linked myself to someone who was rising through the ranks wildly. Someone who didn't really envision us being together in the long term.' She smiles encouragingly now. 'If you want to be a star, Farah, you have to choose yourself. Break it off now, before you fall in love with him.'

My heart thuds painfully against my ribs at her use of the word 'love'. Zayan was so sure he'd never love me, and I was so adamant I wouldn't fall in love with him.

'I'm going to leave first,' I settle on saying, enjoying the look of surprise on Laiba's face despite the anguish currently coursing through me. 'It'll look less like we've had a massive fight in the bathrooms. I don't want any bad press right now.'

Laiba laughs kindly, in a commiserating way. 'They've trained you pretty well for such a short amount of time.'

I grin, like we're sharing an inside joke, but then my smile dips. Her words are a reminder of my loyalties. 'He deserves to know why you left. He thinks it's because he wasn't enough for you.'

Her smile is wiped off, a guarded look entering her eyes. Maybe she didn't suspect that Zayan and I were truly that close, that he'd bare such a vulnerable part of himself to me, or that he'd have anyone to defend him. Before she can say more, I continue.

'I know you think you can't face him, but that's not fair to him. Not really. He deserves the truth.' My tone turns fierce with how badly I want Zayan to know that this break-up was not because of him.

Hesitation lines her face, but I can see the seedling of urgency I've planted in her mind beginning to blossom. The silence starts to build again, so I make my exit. I see Zayan leaning against one of the marble pillars, facing away from me, head tipped backwards as people walk by.

I belong to you. That guy needed to know that. You need to know that.

My thoughts all scream to leave. Run. To not give into this yet. Not to face change right now. I look to my left to see if I can make an escape. I can. There's a fire exit.

The door to the bathroom opens moments later, and I sidestep to let Laiba pass. She looks confused to see me still standing here, but after a moment her gaze lands on Zayan as well.

I watch as she steels herself, breathes in sharply and fills her bones with determination. She spares me one final glance, and I give her a short, encouraging nod. And then she walks to him.

I stay long enough to see her stand in front of him. Long enough to see him startle and stiffen in shock. Long enough to see Laiba ask to talk somewhere private. Long enough to see him follow her.

Long enough to feel a little forgotten, but also long enough to make my escape into the cool, dark night.

Chapter Twenty-nine

The streets of central London are never quiet, and for once I am grateful. I'm glad I get to focus on not getting trampled as I make my way to the Limelight, leaving behind the Soho Gala, the man I love and the woman who once loved him.

The walk to the Limelight is long, a full thirty minutes longer because of my heels, but the pain is worth it when the familiar comedy-and-tragedy mask knocker on the entrance door comes into sight. Something close to relief yawns through my body, relaxing my muscles and quieting my worries. I'll go and stand on stage and practise my lines, distract my mind from all the confusion and questions.

'Good evening, Marvin,' I say as I push past the front doors, rather than the stage door. Marvin is sitting at the front desk, still decked in his lime-green overalls and looking quite disgruntled. 'I'm starting to think you might be a vampire, you know. Do you ever sleep?'

Marvin lets out an exasperated noise. 'How can you expect me to get a wink of sleep when one of you lot are always knocking on my door? Just an hour ago, another one of you showed up – woke me up, in fact – and now *you're* here.'

'What?' I ask, confused. 'Who was it?'

Marvin shrugs his shoulders. 'How am I supposed to know? There are so many of you kids. A group of you came in, someone from your tech group leading them. Ginger-haired boy.'

'Darren?' I ask, confused. He's an assistant on the tech team – quiet, and not massively a part of the group. I think he only joined the tech team to get course credits, to be honest.

'Yes,' Marvin agrees. 'That one. He came in with a group, and then they left around an hour ago.'

Immediately, I pull out my phone, texting The Tragedies.

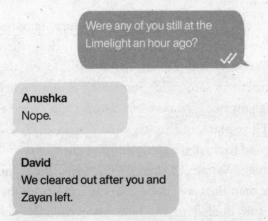

Were any of you still at the
Limelight an hour ago?

Anushka
Nope.

David
We cleared out after you and
Zayan left.

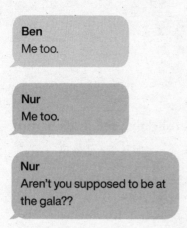

Ben
Me too.

Nur
Me too.

Nur
Aren't you supposed to be at the gala??

I leave Marvin at the front desk, gently pushing open the door leading to the theatre. I see that the lights have been left on, and a furrow of confusion knits my brow.

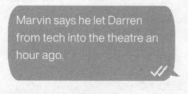

Marvin says he let Darren from tech into the theatre an hour ago.

David
What? Darren texted me an hour ago saying he had to quit the play. Something about obligations and family.

An alarm starts blaring loudly in my head. I step further in, being quiet and careful. Marvin comes away from the desk, hovering behind me with a concerned look on his face.

> **Zayan (The Actor)**
> Do not go inside there alone, Farah.

The door creaks ever-so-slightly, and I creep closer. Marvin follows behind me.

> **Zayan (The Actor)**
> Farah?

> **Anushka**
> She's going inside.

> **Nur**
> Of course she's going inside.

> **Ben**
> This is like a horror movie.

> **David**
> Why would you even say that? I can feel Zayan's heart palpitations all the way from here.

My phone starts buzzing, and I see Zayan's name flash across the screen, but I ignore his call and walk fully into the theatre instead.

A horrified gasp gets stuck in my throat. I stare at the destroyed sets, paint cans left open on the stage and – *no*. Nur's costumes. They're shredded, utterly desecrated in the worst way possible.

I rush to the stage, leaving Marvin in the doorway to gape at the destruction. I bend down to touch the ripped threads of Nur's costumes, the haphazard shards of meticulously painted sets, the scuff marks of shoes against the wooden stage floor. During my investigation of the wreckage, I find a yellow square of notepad paper. Scribbled on it is a message.

CONSIDER THIS A FAVOUR AND GO BACK HOME, FARAH. YOUR SO-CALLED TALENT DOESN'T BELONG ON THIS STAGE.

Bile crawls up my throat, and my hands start to shake – a cocktail of fear and anger burns through me. I tear my eyes away from the paper, surveying the ruined stage again, until my vision begins to blur.

'Those ingrates,' Marvin seethes behind me. 'I can't even call the police – what will I say? "I let them in"?'

I look at Marvin, and whatever emotion is scrawled on my face makes his expression soften. 'I apologize, child. I should've been more vigilant.'

I shake my head. 'This isn't your fault. All you've done is

look after us, after the theatre.' I look back at the wreckage of the stage, and my body suddenly feels incredibly heavy.

Useless.

I feel useless.

My heart squeezes, squeezes so hard I'm afraid it's going to burst. Everything we've worked for. Everything we've done. Gone in one moment. Two months obliterated.

My phone is buzzing again and again. But none of it matters.

My eyes fall back to the note, and just the sight of those words makes my stomach clench with nausea. Whenever the LSDCATS launched an attack before, it always felt like it was us – all of The Tragedies – against them. But this note is personal. It's targeted. It's a message for *me*.

All of this started as a way to bring to light what The Tragedies had gone through. They've risked so much by trusting me, helping me orchestrate this PR relationship with Zayan, allowing me to be the lead. I don't want to ruin this for them. I don't want the LSDCATS to target them because of me. I want them to win. To live their dreams. And maybe there was a time when I could've been a part of that, but it feels like I'm doing more damage than good.

They deserve better.

A chill sweeps through me once more, tears drying on my skin. I know what I have to do.

I fold up the note and tuck it into my purse – there's no need for The Tragedies to see that vitriol. It's a battle for me to handle alone. I take a picture of the destroyed sets, of the ruin in front of me, and text The Tragedies.

Anushka
NO. What happened??

David
This is the LSDCATS. Those cowards. I can't believe they did this.

Ben
I'm literally going to murder them.

Nur
Same here.

Zayan (The Actor)
Farah, you need to leave the Limelight. What if someone comes back? Tell me where you are, I'm picking you up. Or at least stay with Marvin.

I try to breathe against the lump in my throat, my fingers flying as I bring my decision to life.

I'm quitting the play. My understudy knows my part through and through. If I leave, the LSDCATS will leave us alone. They're not going to try and fight Zayan – he's too big a star. I'm bringing too much conflict to something that's supposed to be fun, hopeful, bright. You guys deserve better, and I know you'll find it once I'm gone.

And before any of them can reply, I leave the group chat.

Star-Studded News

Published 15 November 2021

MOVE OVER, FARAH: LAIBA IS HERE

Well, well, well, did anyone expect this?

On Saturday night, Laiba Siddiqi and Zayan Amin were photographed leaving the Soho Gala at the same time. Now, while they did get into separate cars, we have insider photographs of the two of them locked in a deep conversation at the event.

They saw Laiba leading Zayan into a private room.

And the plot thickens when we realize Farah Sheikh was nowhere to be seen. We know that Farah and Zayan showed up together, but they did not leave together.

Surprising? Possibly.

If the online reaction is any indication, the world has been waiting for Laiba and Zayan to reunite. Some are calling it inevitable.

On top of that, *Star-Studded News* is excited to be the first to share that Zayan Amin is going to be gracing our screens again, this time in a brand-new movie. It's an action-thriller that's being shot in Australia, and he's sharing the screen with *another* handsome star – any guesses on who Zayan's new castmate is?

Chapter Thirty

Three days ago, I quit the play. I left The Tragedies. I ended my fake relationship. And if I thought doing all of this would bring me some sort of internal peace, my past self was *seriously* mistaken.

I blocked The Tragedies and Gibitah's numbers because they kept calling, and then I blocked Zayan's because he kept messaging. I didn't leave the flat – I feigned sickness and avoided classes. I've stayed locked up in my room to dodge Maha and Amal, despite their concerned questioning and the abundance of baked goods Amal keeps placing outside my bedroom door.

I've pushed myself into complete, silent solitude and I'm hating every single minute of it.

I didn't realize how ingrained this play has become in my life, how it's burrowed under my skin, a part of my flesh and bone. I miss walking to the Limelight, I miss The Tragedies – playing card games with Nur backstage, poring over notes with Anushka, laughing on Lives with Ben, verbally sparring with David and trying not to break character with Gibitah.

Most of all, I miss Zayan.

I miss him with a fierce ache in my chest and, like a masochist, I can't fully detach myself from him. It's why I'm awake at 5 a.m., sitting on the sofa, scrolling through articles about him. As if reading about him is enough to fill the Zayan-shaped hole in my life.

I zoom into the photos of Zayan and Laiba, the one of them locked in a deep conversation from the gala three days ago. The last photo shows them just looking at one another, staring with these warm expressions on their faces. My heart feels like tissue paper being ripped apart softly. I know I told Laiba to talk to Zayan, I know this could mean absolutely nothing, but I also *know* Zayan.

I know the softness in his stance. The relaxation in his shoulders. His unfinished sentence could've been, *I don't think I could be in love with her, not without knowing the truth*. Now he does, and maybe that conversation with Laiba reminded him that he should love her *more*. Should try and love her wholly – even the parts of her that hurt him.

And the movie role? He's got his dream. He's going to be in front of the camera again. In Australia. A million miles away. Everything he's ever wanted.

I wonder if he's stopped calling now. The itch to unblock him and check is unbearable, so awful that I push myself off the sofa and search for something to do. I can't bake because Maha and Amal are asleep; I can't call home because if my mother asks me *Are you OK, Paari?* I will dissolve into tears. And I don't want to cry. I want to power through. I want to let go. I want to move on and pretend none of this has happened.

In the end, there's only one activity I can do without waking everyone up, one that will make me feel useful: taking out the trash.

With more force than necessary, I tie the black bin bag closed, haul it over my shoulder, slip on my shoes and make my way out of the flat. The street is quiet; faint, indecipherable sounds that belong to the night can be heard in the distance. There are a few cars parked outside, probably belonging to the residents of the building. The sky is an infinite kind of blue, the moon cocooned by wisps of clouds.

I drop the bag on the pavement so I can wheel out the recycling bin, focusing on the way the coolness of the November morning nips at my skin despite the sweatshirt I'm wearing over my pyjamas.

'You know, for a second there, I thought you'd never leave your flat.' The all-too-familiar voice causes me to jump a foot into the air. I barely withhold a scream, clutching at my chest as I whirl round to see Zayan leaning against a car. Right in front of my bins.

I try to breathe to slow my racing heartbeat. He looks painfully handsome and rumpled. His hair is a mess of brown waves, his soft sage-green sweater is creased and, even though there's a faint sense of sleepiness draped over his body, his tea-brown eyes are alert.

'W-what are you doing here?' I ask, my voice shaking with nerves.

His jaw hardens, arms crossing over his chest. 'You blocked my number. You blocked everyone's numbers. You blocked my email. My socials. I was here two days ago, but Amal and Maha turned me away at the door. I came back yesterday and sat on your doorstep, waiting, until Maha threatened to call the police.' I vaguely remember Maha yelling at someone at the door. I'd assumed it was somebody trying to sell us something. 'I'm back here again because you had to come out eventually.'

His expression is livid, softened only by concern, but my mind can focus on nothing other than the memory of how he looked at Laiba.

'Most – most of the articles I've read are happy about you and Laiba,' I offer, trying hard to not think too deeply about the fact that he came back. *He came back*. I breathe in deeply before plastering a smile on to my face. 'And so am I. She's wonderful. We met in the bathroom at the gala, actually –'

He stalks forward, and it takes all my strength not to step back. He comes close enough that I can see the tension in his shoulders, anger lining every muscle in his body.

'You have got to be kidding me,' Zayan interrupts. 'You cannot possibly think I'm in love with Laiba. Or that I care what the media thinks about me right now.'

'Of course you care,' I fire back, annoyed at him now. I don't want him to lie to me; I've always appreciated that he's done what he must for his dreams. Knowing that has been the only thing that's shielded me from entirely sinking into the fantasy of Zayan feeling anything for me beyond friendship.

'This whole thing –' I gesture in the little space between us – 'started because *you* needed your reputation fixed. I've done my part. You're fine now. So I'm fine too.'

And maybe Zayan would've believed it if my voice hadn't cracked over the second "fine".

He scrubs a hand down his face, the tension draining from him. I sink my teeth into my lower lip, trying desperately not to cry. I don't want to cry.

'Can we go inside?' Zayan, asks, more softly than I probably deserve. 'I won't ask you to come back to the play. I just want to clear things up, Farah. And then, if you still want to stay away, I'll respect your decision, knowing you've made it based on *all* the facts.'

'Why can't we just do it here?' I ask, not wanting to get into an enclosed space with Zayan. Being this near to him is already muddling my senses.

'Because the smell of that bin makes me want to gag,' he deadpans.

I sigh, turn on my heel and lead us inside.

♥

We sit in the kitchen, and I automatically start quietly preparing two cups of chai.

Zayan rests his elbows on the kitchen island, hands laced in front of him, eyes determinedly fixed on my every move.

'Why did you leave the play?' he asks finally. 'You said you knew the attack from the LSDCATS was targeting you and me. How?'

My heart feels as crumpled as the note the LSDCATS left in the ruined theatre. I've kept it with me the entire time. I slide it out of my pyjama pocket now, towards him.

He looks up from the note just as I finish pouring the chai into two cups. His anger has returned tenfold; his expression is thunderous. I sit on the seat opposite him, grateful there's a whole slab of marble separating us.

'You know this really isn't your fault, right?' Zayan says.

I shrug, staring at my tea. 'It feels like it.'

'Why?'

There's nothing to lose by being honest with Zayan now – no Tragedies, no fame. And I'm already in love with him.

The words free themselves like a flurry of butterflies escaping a cage. 'To start off, I helped push this play into the spotlight by starting a fake relationship with you. And let's not pretend that my motives weren't selfish –'

'Selfish? Farah, you used the publicity to help –'

'I didn't, though,' I interrupt, with a haggardness in my voice. 'Asking you to bring casting agents and directors to the audience was for *me*. I took the lead role, for *my* dreams. And I should've thought that through. I should've realized I wasn't fit for this industry. I can't be like you. I can't be silent when I need to be; I can't play the role as well as you can.'

Zayan's expression is impossibly soft and sad. 'You don't

have to be like me. No one wants that. I certainly don't. I think I made a mistake by telling you to stay quiet.'

'A mistake?'

'Silence, Farah, I've learned through meeting you, is a great weapon. It's also an awful punishment. To remain silent and be forced to endure. That isn't what I want for you.'

I laugh harshly, an echo of anger pulsing in my voice. 'Isn't that great? Then I should give up being an actor, because there's no place in this industry for my voice.'

'That's not true, Farah. If it were, you wouldn't have fans now. And I know it's so easy to focus on the hate. But there *are* people who love you, who are excited to see you perform this week. Fans of *your* voice. The negativity can overshadow it, but please, please don't let it.'

I want to give in. I want to cave and agree with him. But I can't stop seeing the anger-fuelled comments behind my eyelids, the headlines in my mind. I can't believe that anyone would come and see *me*.

'As for being ambitious, there's nothing wrong with that,' Zayan continues. 'The Tragedies wouldn't and shouldn't judge you for that. Choosing yourself doesn't make you a bad person.'

I shake my head, clenching my teeth to keep the tears at bay. Zayan walks round the table and clutches both of my hands.

'I can't convince you that you're enough, Farah,' he murmurs. 'I wish I could. I wish I could show you what you look like to me. How I see you. Because then there wouldn't be a shadow of a doubt in your mind that you're a star.'

I swallow roughly. 'You shouldn't say these things to me.' *They're unintentionally cruel.* 'Laiba wouldn't like it.'

He presses our foreheads together. 'Laiba's thoughts aren't my problem. I'm not back together with her. We talked that night at the gala; we cleared the air. I got my closure. And then, once we were done, I walked away. I searched for you. I looked all over the gala, and then that text came.' He laughs ruefully, the sound chipping away at my heart. 'I was so scared. Terrified that something had happened to you. Then you disappeared.'

I watch the way his throat swallows, hearing the tremors of insecurity in his voice.

'Leaving you was awful,' I whisper. 'I've been torturing myself by reading things about you. Articles. Tweets, using a secret account I made. Believe me, leaving you was – is – was – never going to be easy.'

'Why?'

I close my eyes, my fingers clutching his sweater like it will somehow stop him from inevitably pulling away.

I'm going to cross the line.

'I'm in love with you.'

He rears back, and I let his sweater go.

'Say it again,' Zayan demands, and I flinch at the disbelief in his voice.

'I know this is going to change everything,' I reply harshly. *I will not cry. I will not cry. I will not cry.* 'But you're the one who started saying things like "I belong to you". So you can't sit here and pretend like this is foreign news to you, OK?'

He smiles, two dimples pressing into his cheeks, and shakes his head. 'You've got it all wrong, Farah. I just – I didn't think you'd ever say anything like this to me. I know we've spoken about attraction. We've put our friendship and our professional partnership above everything.'

'Are you mad at me for crossing the line?' I ask, my voice barely above a whisper.

His smile quietens as seriousness flashes over his expression. 'I'm not mad at you, Farah. I'm more mad at myself that I didn't make my feelings clearer in the beginning.' He breathes in sharply, all his words escaping in a gush. 'That day, outside the Limelight, when I asked for your friendship, I thought that was all I wanted. That I'd be content with companionship. You were looking for someone who was ready for forever, and I still believed I wasn't capable of wanting that again. But, Farah, you star in all my dreams. I want to *jump* over the line. I'm in love with you too.' My breath stumbles at his words, quickening as he slides his palm under my chin, tilting my head. 'You were the first person I wanted to call when I found out I got that movie role. You've seen me at my worst, and you've only ever supported me. As if I couldn't be any more obvious, I changed my entire sleep schedule in anticipation of our 3 a.m. calls, because hearing your voice is a thousand times better than any dream I could've been having.'

Sunlight streams through the flat from our massive lone

window, bathing Zayan in gold and warmth. My heartbeat races alongside his, matching it in pace and intensity.

'You love me?' I ask, now understanding why he wanted me to repeat it earlier. A part of me knew this to be true, but to hear him say it is a feeling unlike anything else.

Zayan's smile widens. 'I love you.'

My heart is running so fast in my chest now it's starting to make me feel faint. And my head, it's full of questions. I want to know what this means. *Where do we go from this? How serious is this?* But, before we can talk about anything, a soft cough forces us apart. Our faces, in unison, snap to Amal and Maha standing in the kitchen doorway.

'What,' Maha asks dangerously, 'is he doing here?'

Amal mirrors this intense anger directed at Zayan. 'No matter what he says, Farah, if he's cheated on you –'

'We were never together!' I blurt, ignoring the wide-eyed expression Zayan is shooting my way.

I don't know what's changed in my head, but the thought of continuing to lie to my friends about Zayan makes my skin crawl.

'What?' Amal cocks her head.

'We were pretending to be in a relationship because everyone thought we were together after that first photo of us. We thought it was best to capitalize on the attention to fix Zayan's reputation, and in exchange he'd bring industry officials to the audience on opening night.' I admit it all in a rush.

Maha collects herself first. 'So you were in a PR relationship?'

'Yes.'

'Why didn't you tell us?' Amal asks, hurt evident in her voice.

I scramble for an explanation before settling on the simple truth. 'I was afraid to tell you guys. I thought if I told you the real reason why I was doing the play, why I needed Zayan, it would upset you.'

'Farah,' Amal says, a touch of reprimand in her voice, 'we wouldn't have judged you. Never. That's not how this friendship works. If we thought you were doing something wrong, we'd have told you, and loved you despite that. You don't give up on people because they make mistakes.'

Zayan's hand intertwines with mine under the table, squeezing when he sees my jaw tremble with the urge to cry again.

'I'm sorry for not telling you,' I reply.

Amal watches me, her face full of soft concern, but Maha still looks hurt, and that makes my chest ache.

'It's OK,' Amal replies, a smile slipping over her lips. 'You were afraid. I get that. But you have to remember that we're your friends. We want to be there for you.'

I nod vigorously. 'I promise to always be honest with you.' I look to Maha, who is still standing there silently. Our eyes meet, and I try to convey how sorry I am for lying to them.

'It – it's going to take me a minute to get over this,' Maha says, and I can't blame her. 'But I will. Get over it. Because we're *best friends*, Farah.'

My eyes prick with tears as I nod.

'But what about now?' Maha continues, trying to ease her tone into something more neutral. 'Not to be rude or anything, but I'm pretty sure you don't need to be standing in a kitchen looking all in love with each other, with no cameras around, to get more publicity.'

I blush furiously, especially when Zayan's mouth lifts into a smirk.

'Well, now –' Zayan meets my eyes and squeezes our hands together again – 'Farah has some things she needs to deal with. Stuff that's larger than our relationship.'

Of course he'd be looking at the bigger picture. I should've known he wouldn't let what happened with The Tragedies go so easily. He wants me to talk to them.

'Zayan . . .' I reply uneasily.

'I'm not going anywhere,' he says firmly.

'What about your new movie role?' I point out, grasping at straws. 'It's being shot in Australia.'

'We can deal with that later,' Zayan argues gently. 'The play is more important. We've covered up your leaving – said you were sick. The public has accepted it for now. The LSDCATS are trying to capitalize on the narrative that's being spun about me and Laiba, and about you and I being over, but Laiba has shut that down.'

'She has?'

'Yes, Farah. You'd have known this,' he says, a little tartly, 'if you hadn't disappeared off the face of the earth.'

I ignore his tone and grab my phone from the table, logging in quickly to the redownloaded Twitter. The first thing I see is Laiba's tweet.

@LaibaSiddiqi: @ZayanAmin and I are not together. We are not getting back together. As for the NDA, that is something I had to sign when I was with Zayan, and it's understandable that Farah did as well. What the public is doing to a budding actress is disgusting. Do not destroy talent before it has the chance to grow, simply because of ill-intentioned rumours and lies.

The next thing I see is a message from Laiba. It's short, and sweet.

> Hit me up when this all blows over. We'll get lunch, or breakfast, or whatever you like. After weathering this storm, you deserve it. Bring a notebook too. I have loads of advice to pass on. XO

Laiba Siddiqi

My heart swells with affection for Laiba – this girl who knows nothing about me and yet has built an invisible connection between us. Another guiding hand through the industry, if I choose to go down this road.

'It's nice to know I've got people on my side,' I say finally.

'You've got lots of people on your side,' Zayan reminds me leadingly. 'The Tragedies, for example.'

Fear flutters like sparrow wings in my lungs, and Zayan must see it in my face.

'No matter what happens, you've got me, Farah,' he says.

'And you've got us,' Maha butts in. Amal jabs her with her elbow. 'What? I wanted her to know she's not alone.'

'How thick can you be? They're clearly having a moment,' Amal hisses back.

I let their bickering wash over me. Zayan moves away, not by much, but just enough to give Amal space to start breakfast.

Our hands remain linked throughout our recounting of how our relationship started, per Maha's demands to start from the beginning. The real beginning.

And as we're stuffing our faces with buttermilk waffles, the weight of our clasped hands anchoring me to this moment, I'm suffused with a feeling of contentment – but it can't cover the discordant twinge in my chest.

Chapter Thirty-one

I'd like to say I had enough willpower to call The Tragedies straight after my breakfast with Zayan and the girls, but I still haven't unblocked them. I'm too afraid to. I know Zayan said that if I shared the truth with The Tragedies and Gibitah, they'd be willing to listen and accept my struggles.

But a part of me still doesn't believe it.

On the upside, I did return to classes. With only nine days left before the play, I haven't been sparing a thought for lectures and seminars. Now that I don't have the play, I'm going to throw myself into studying to occupy myself.

But I'd forgotten how boring some of these lectures were. It's not the content; it's the professor's voice. All slow and monotone. My mind drifts to Zayan and how he dropped me off this morning – we still haven't defined what our future looks like, but it's the conversation I'm least afraid of now.

'Excuse me,' a voice whispers beside me, and I jolt out of the memory. It's a guy behind me, his face apologetic. 'I dropped my pen and it's rolled under your seat; would you be able to pass it, please?'

I give him a quick smile and lean forward to grab it.

And that's when my eyes meet hers.

The girl from the library. Maisie. She's reaching down to get the pen as well. I hadn't realized that we were sitting together. Her lips curl into a smirk, her hand snatching the pen out of my reach. She hands it back, then looks down at me again, mirth in her eyes.

'Just not fast enough,' she murmurs, low enough for me to hear.

She doesn't say the word again. The slur. She's not surrounded by her friends this time. She doesn't have the comfort of a group to keep her safe, to make her bold. But there's a look in her eyes that tells me she's thinking of it – replaying that word in her head, taunting and loud – and I hear it like we share some sick telepathic connection.

At first, I feel that familiar silence wrapping round my tongue like an iron manacle, but then images of The Tragedies flash across my mind, and Zayan's words whisper in my ears.

It's also an awful punishment. To remain silent and be forced to endure.

I have nothing left to lose. Nothing left that I haven't

let others take away from me. The thin thread that was holding me together snaps.

'Say it again,' I demand, keeping my voice level.

Maisie shoots me a confused look, laughing slightly. Everyone else's attention is locked on the professor, though some look my way.

'Go on. Say. *It*. Again,' I dare, my voice dipping dangerously. 'If you have the nerve, say it to my face this time.'

Her mouth twists with a sneer. 'You know what, you're unhinged. No wonder Zayan dumped you.'

I let myself smile, and it's not kind. It's not sweet. Or peaceful. It's victorious. Because this girl *can't* say it again. Won't. Not to me, at least. Not in front of others.

I stand abruptly, causing some students to look at me, disgruntled. The professor goes on with his lecture, completely unaware. I lean close to Maisie, making sure our eyes meet.

'Here's some advice: the next time you insult me, think carefully.' My tone is eerily calm. So different to the war running through my body right now. 'I always have cameras on me. Paparazzi, Zayan's fans . . . and all it will take is one soundbite, one clip of you insulting me with that disgusting slur, and I will have it sent to campus security. I'll post it on every social media site that exists. So think twice before slinging words like that around again.'

Terror is crystallized in her gaze. She can do nothing to me. Can't hit me because campus security will be on her in minutes. Can't shout because she's surrounded by students and a professor. She is the one locked in silence, and it is beyond gratifying.

It is freeing.

I slip my phone back into my pocket, shoulder my bag and walk straight out of the auditorium with one purpose in mind: finding The Tragedies.

I don't want to be here. I don't belong here. I want to be on stage. I want to be with The Tragedies. I want to be with Gibitah in rehearsal right now. I want to talk to them, not hide in silence any more. Zayan was right. Silence can be a punishment. Silence allows *them* – the LSDCATS, the racists, the oppressors – to win.

As soon as I step outside, the cool air hitting my heated skin, I unblock each of the group one by one. My phone is bursting with incoming texts that I've missed. There are too many to wade through, and my phone begins lagging with the onslaught of notifications.

I give up after a minute, deciding I'll just go to the Limelight; hopefully they'll all be there.

But as I'm walking down the campus stairs, I collide with someone. My books spill on to the steps, and I kneel to pick them up before they're trampled.

All the while, apologies slip past my lips. 'I'm so sorry – I wasn't looking where I was going.'

I stand up with all my books haphazardly clasped in my arms, and come face to face with the last people I ever expected to see.

Chapter
Thirty-two

There is a huge chance that one of The Tragedies will murder me today. Right now, from the glower Anushka is levelling my way, my bet's on her.

'How are you guys?' I offer, aiming for pleasant and falling just short of *I'm feeling incredibly awkward, but someone needed to break the silence.*

'How *are* we?' David bursts out angrily. We've walked, silently, to an empty seminar room to have our discussion – all The Tragedies on one side, and me on the other. 'Are you kidding me right now, Farah?'

I squeeze my eyes shut, trying to grasp the confidence I'd felt when confronting Maisie only twenty minutes ago.

'I'm sorry,' I say immediately. 'I know you're angry that I quit the play –'

'Forget the play,' Nur interrupts, and defensiveness walls

up round me. 'None of us care about the play. We care about *you*. We care about how you just left, out of the blue, without talking to any of us first.'

My heart aches in my chest; exhaustion tugs at my every cell. I'm so tired of all of this. Of the anger. Of the sadness. Of the secrets.

'I thought it was for the best,' I whisper, the familiar burn of tears irritating my eyelids.

'Nur,' Ben admonishes quietly. 'Attacking her isn't going to fix anything.'

'No,' Nur argues back. 'We can't go on like this. It's not healthy.' She trains an unblinking stare on me. 'Farah, you have been such a rock during all of this. We know you care about the play – I mean, the fact that you trained the understudy just in case something went wrong says enough. But quitting our friendship? Refusing to speak to us? That was wrong.'

My jaw trembles, like a chill has settled into my bones. Nur's breathing heavily, but her gaze refuses to leave mine.

My voice feels stuck in my throat. The words are formed on my tongue, but saying them feels wrong. I consider retreating again, but the memory that I've spent so long trying to forget dances across my mind, tauntingly, mockingly.

Unsuitable.

The audition. The library. The little comments, needling away at me.

The Tragedies watch me with a mixture of confusion and encouragement – their plain desire for me to tell them what's going on is easy to read.

'You don't owe us your secrets,' Anushka says finally. She's been silent for most of this, blank-faced as well. Now her gaze is filled with understanding, with more compassion than I think I deserve. 'You have your boundaries, you have things you want to keep to yourself, as is your right. But we want you to know that we will listen to whatever you want to share with us. We are here for you. Sometimes I worry that you don't know, or don't believe that.'

Tears burn in the corners of my eyes. 'I do. I just – I'm afraid that you guys . . . that you won't like me after I tell you the truth of what happened. That you'll hate me for not being a strong shoulder to rely on.'

'Did you murder someone?' David asks, blunt as ever.

'No.'

'Then we won't hate you. Will we disagree with you? Maybe. Will we talk about that? Yeah. And you know what? We may never be friends again. Or we may be friends forever. But we can never know the future, Farah. We can only promise you the present. Right now, we are here for you. We've been vulnerable with you because that's how friendships grow. We hope that you feel safe enough to do the same with us.'

I understand what he's saying. Trusting them will be like taking a leap of faith in our friendship. Like Anushka said, I don't owe them my secrets, not unless I want to give them. And if I don't, I have to accept, to a degree, that I will never be as close as I want to be with The Tragedies.

In the end, it's my choice to make.

'OK,' I say in a small voice. 'It all started with the LSDCATS audition.' My heart beats wildly in my chest. This is it. The biggest secret I've kept. 'The director, Henry, said that I didn't look "classically British".' Frustration forms an undertone in my voice. 'And when he said that – I . . . was just baffled.'

'Why?' Anushka asks, her eyes wide. 'Weren't you angry at him for using your skin shade against you?'

'Because I didn't think he was being racist towards me.' The Tragedies look at me in complete disbelief, so I hurry on with my explanation. 'I rarely get acknowledged for being brown, and I don't always feel brown. So when Henry said I didn't look "classically British" I felt like I was overreacting by feeling angry. I thought Henry had picked some random reason to reject me because, in truth, he thought I just wasn't good enough for the stage.'

The silence that blankets our little circle is so deafening it rings in my ears.

Anushka breaks it first. 'My skin is darker than a light-skinned person, and I get all the hate of an Asian person. But I don't feel like one sometimes.' Her confession confuses me. I've never considered Anushka's complexities. I've always boxed her in the opposite category to me – she is darker-skinned, and I am lighter. In that, we face different things. I've never thought about how we may cross over. 'I haven't been to India in years now. I know more about British customs than Indian ones. Often, I feel like I'm doing a disservice to my culture, my country, my great grandparents, by not being browner.'

'You're enough,' I blurt out.

Anushka gives a smile, sad and sweet. 'I know I am, and it took me a long time to accept that. And I don't need you to say it to me. I've learned to hold that phrase in my heart for myself.'

'Anushka's right,' Nur adds. 'I've always been clocked as brown, but I've not always felt it. I've got cousins that are darker-skinned than me, and they face such blatant racism. Mine is more subtle at times.'

My mind flashes with all the little moments I've ignored – every Instagram comment that judged me solely on my skin tone, the professor who was awed at my writing ability solely because of where I'd come from, Henry's words gleaming under a new light.

I open my mouth to voice this before closing it. I don't want to take away from Nur's confession with my own problems.

'Go on,' Nur says, interrupting my overthinking. 'You were going to say something.'

'I've been feeling like I'm going crazy,' I say desperately. 'I couldn't tell if what I was facing was – was prejudice or not. I still can't tell if what Henry said to me was really rooted in hate or if I'm just deluding myself into believing that.'

'What you faced, Farah, was most definitely prejudice. That's why microaggressions are so insidious; they make you feel inadequate without actually appearing blatantly racist,' Ben says gently.

'But I don't want to pretend that my skin tone doesn't give me privileges,' I explain softly.

'Then don't,' David replies, like it's the easiest thing in the world. 'Farah, our group was created for every story, for every struggle, and that's going to look different with every person. We all endure microaggressions to varying degrees. Sometimes, racism against me is blatant – like when I get made fun of for my eye shape. Other times, it's subtle. It's when people slow their speech down because they think that my accent means I can't understand English. That's a microaggression I deal with all the time.'

'It's so wrong,' I say, my throat aching with the urge to cry. 'You shouldn't have had to go through that.'

David shakes his head. 'None of us should have to experience this. Don't exclude yourself. You're just as much a part of this. The existence of your suffering won't erase or demean or lessen the existence of ours.'

'And it is wrong that you're made to feel like you're not brown enough to be a part of your very own culture,' Anushka says fiercely. 'Look, we can't make you believe you're enough. None of us can. That's something you're going to have to work on. But I can say that if you felt what you were facing was not racist enough to matter, simply because you don't face exactly what we do, then you're wrong. Racism, colourism, cultural erasure aren't straightforward. They're messy and complex. But one of the ways to detangle the impact is if we talk about it all. If we're open about it.'

Ben leans forward, elbows on his knees. 'My racism is never quiet. Never subtle. It always feels blatant. But that doesn't mean I think yours is any less valid than mine.

I think all prejudice is emotionally eroding. It does get easier when I know I have people to turn to. People who won't compare their experiences with mine. It doesn't matter how it happens; it matters that it *is* happening, when it shouldn't.'

That ball in my throat tightens again, but this time it's not with sadness but regret. 'I'm sorry,' I choke out. 'I'm sorry that I never said anything.'

Nur loops her arm in mine, pressing her head against my shoulder. 'It's OK.'

'It's important that you know this is a safe space for you as well,' Anushka says.

'And you're allowed to be angry for yourself too,' Ben adds. 'You were so enraged for us, so furious, but you're allowed to be angry for yourself. For your play. Are you angry?'

I look around at the emotional ruin encasing us, and that bitterness returns. 'I'm angry.'

'Good,' David says. 'I was starting to think that just because you were named after the word "joy" you were incapable of feeling anything else.'

Once he says it, it becomes blindingly clear how much I've lived by that statement – that belief that I'm not allowed to be hurt, or sad, or angry. That I am undeserving of such emotions.

'I'm so . . . so frustrated,' I say, everything projecting out of me. 'I'm tired. I'm sick of seeing comments about my skin, about being told I'm not enough, about not feeling like I'm good enough for this role, because I'm afraid of being perceived as not brown enough. I'm mad at myself for being so silent and afraid of saying what I feel. I'm tired of doubting my talent. I want to be confident.'

'Hating yourself won't change anything,' Anushka says. 'The only thing you can do now is change how you live life. No more being afraid. No more worrying about things you can't control. I know it's not going to be an easy change, not when thinking a certain way has become a habit, but I think things are going to be different for you now, Farah.'

'And from now on, no more holding yourself back from our friendship,' Nur demands, waiting for my agreement.

'I promise,' I vow, meeting all their gazes one by one. 'You guys are stuck with me forever.'

'Or at least until David gives in to his old age,' Anushka adds.

Before David can retort, the seminar-room door swings open again. Zayan rushes in, taking long strides to reach us.

'You're having a group meeting without me?' he asks. 'Not one person replied to my messages. I thought you were all dead. You're lucky I had David's location.'

'That seems a little dramatic,' Ben says with a shrug.

Zayan's mouth drops open at Ben's nonchalance, and I know he's gearing up to say more when his eyes land on me – taking in my likely-red eyes and puffy face. I don't hide it. He's seen it before. Before he can ask what's happened, forcing me to rehash it all, I give him a small smile.

'If one of you *had* responded to me, you'd have seen the link I sent,' Zayan continues.

We all check our phones at the same time. I find myself staring at an Instagram post from the LSDCATS.

> **@TheLSDCATS:** We're not ones to believe in rumours, but after hearing some speculation about plays ending abruptly, we would like to invite any unfettered castmates to last-minute auditions for our play. We're sure we can find you a role!

'What does this even mean?' I question, completely confused. 'Who would leave our cast?'

Silence sits in the room, heavy and weighted. The longer it goes on, the more nervous I get.

'Hello?' I probe. 'What aren't you telling me?'

'They stole Gibitah from us,' David blurts out.

'Excuse me?!' I shout.

'Yeah, she texted on the whole-cast group that she auditioned and was leaving. The rest of them got immediately nervous, and now – now they're also thinking about leaving.'

I can't believe Gibitah would leave. It sounds hypocritical, because I left, but my reasoning was misguided. I can't imagine why Gibitah would ever want to join the LSDCATS.

'We need to find a way to make sure that no one else leaves.' Anushka's tone is urgent. 'We need a way to make it clear to the LSDCATS that they can never attack us like this again.'

We fall into a quiet silence once more, each of us contemplating what we should do next.

'What's the one thing that would bring the LSDCATS down?' Zayan asks. 'What's the one thing they fear?'

The answer hits me at once. It becomes so startlingly clear.

'The truth,' I say, heart hammering in my chest. 'They're afraid of the truth.'

Chapter Thirty-three

Outside the stage door of the Limelight, I am greeted by a star-bright sky, a full, cloudy moon and Gibitah. She stands with her chin tucked into her turtleneck, her arms crossed over her chest and a spiky sort of frustration draped over her weary shoulders. She looks up when she hears the door open.

I make my way towards her until we're standing a few steps away from one another. Neither of us speak.

When I texted Gibitah, I didn't think I'd get a reply. I'd asked her to meet up, and I'd been left on read. I also didn't tell The Tragedies or Zayan that I was coming here today. Not because I didn't trust them, but because this conversation was for Gibitah and me. This was our friendship – one that wasn't a part of The Tragedies. One that was made up of sharing a stage together, spending rehearsal breaks together. A friendship that stemmed from a troubled beginning.

'I'm not accusing you; I'm asking you,' I begin quietly. 'Did you help Darren get the LSDCATS into the theatre?'

Gibitah's eyes flash with anger, and I already know the answer. 'No, I didn't. I actually *care* about this play.'

Her words are pointed and sharp, aimed directly at me. 'What's that supposed to mean?'

She scoffs loudly. 'I know you left the play. That article came out about Zayan and Laiba, and Anushka and David changed our rehearsals to focus on background scenes that weren't featuring you. But you blocked me. So instead of asking about me, how about I ask why you left?'

I fight against the defensiveness crawling up my veins, trying to think of the best reply.

'You abandoned us. Even though your understudy is great and whatever, you still left,' Gibitah continues. 'You promised that the play would support voices of colour. Would be there to give us opportunities. And then you left. You let . . . you let me down.'

Shame slams into me, almost forcing me to buckle at the knees. I muster up the courage to continue the conversation. 'I thought it would be better if I left. I thought the play, you, the cast would be better off with a different lead. I've been struggling, Gibitah, with my self-image. I didn't know where I fitted in this world, in this industry. I thought my insecurity, my doubts, made me a bad lead. A bad person. I didn't want to burden you with that or poison the play. But I've learned that to fit in this world, I must be OK with who I am. I must make a space for myself first, and then for others.' I infuse my voice with an apology and an earnestness. 'I promise, Gibitah, I won't give up like that again. I've learned better. Come back to the play; let me explain everything – the whole truth. And then, if you still want to leave, I'll understand.'

'I can't let my one opportunity be squandered,' Gibitah replies. 'You leaving showed me that the LSDCATS are secure. Yes, they're conniving, but their white privilege keeps them secure in this industry. I've been a part of their cast for three days, and I already know that. They're *unashamed*, Farah. They don't mind gloating about their underhanded tactics.' She confirms all my theories with a harsh, pained laugh. 'They're the ones who released that snippet of your contract, they're the ones who broke into the Limelight, but – despite all of that – people will inevitably fill up their theatre seats. Your play is a risk. Being a part of it is a risk.'

'And being part of the LSDCATS' play is allowing yourself to be used. It's tokenism,' I shoot back, giving her a dose of sheer honesty. 'You're going to be their pawn, their weapon, and you're not going to be valued for what you bring to the table beyond your skin tone. That's how they're going to treat you.' I soften my voice at the sight of the glossy sheen in her eyes. I know she's in an impossible situation and, like all of us, she's just trying to make her dreams come true.

'I can't promise that everything is going to be perfect with our play, Gibitah. I can't promise that it will unlock every one of your dreams. But I can promise you that you will be respected by your castmates, that you'll be treated as a *person*.'

Gibitah watches me with uncertainty, her gaze flicking to the half-open stage door behind me, and the empty street she can walk down.

'What do you say?' I prod softly. 'Will you trust me one more time?'

Chapter Thirty-four

Sneaking into the LSDCATS' theatre was far easier than one would think. Since they were hosting last-minute open auditions for their play, the doors to the theatre were swung wide open for the general public. Eager actors and actresses were made to occupy the theatre seats while waiting for their turn to audition.

That's how The Tragedies got in – by pretending to abandon their own play.

Zayan and I couldn't exactly just waltz in here, open audition or not. So we called in Lacey. I'm not sure how she did it, but when we arrived in front of the university gate, we were greeted by a tall security guard. He then took Zayan and I through a series of staircases and back doors before we were deposited at our seats in the balcony. We're sitting here now, masked by shadows, watching Henry and Lisa host the last-minute auditions.

I lean forward in my seat, making sure not to draw attention to myself, to see the back of Henry's dark-haired head. He's sitting beside Lisa, her blonde plait running down the length of her back. Behind the two of them, the theatre is full of people murmuring quietly to one another in anticipation.

Henry and Lisa have gone through an hour of auditions already, and the effort on their part is minimal. They're only casting these actors and actresses of colour in background roles – trees, marble statues, people in crowds. Lisa gives the critiques, the yeses and nos, while Henry sits there, his minimal replies sounding bored and unimpressed. I glare daggers at the back of his head – why host auditions you don't even care about? Why give young actors and actresses false hope, only to know you're going to put zero effort into helping them?

Henry only sits up at full attention once during the auditions, and that's when The Tragedies take the stage.

'Well, well. How the tables have turned,' he says, and just the sound of his voice makes my entire body clench with displeasure. 'Where are your fearless leaders?'

Anushka's tone is hard, made of steel. She doesn't let her eyes flick towards me, doesn't betray any part of our plan. 'That's not why we're here.'

Henry's laugh echoes around the theatre. 'Of course not. Well, it's unsurprising that they both decided to jump ship.

Just as it's unsurprising that you have all come to be part of our play.'

'And we're *so* happy to have you here,' Lisa adds, her tone a touch too sweet. 'In complete honesty, we've hosted these auditions for your cast.'

'How generous of you,' David deadpans, and Zayan has to hide a smile with his hand.

But I can't find any humour in this. Not when it's time to deliver our first blow.

'You broke into our theatre,' Nur says, and the energy in the room shifts. The other people in the audience begin to glance at one another, whispers filling the air. My heart races with every second that passes.

'That's a weighty accusation to make when you have zero proof,' Henry scoffs. Lisa nods vigorously.

'Who said we didn't have proof?' David spits out, and from the bag slung across his body he pulls out a folder.

From it, he takes out the note the LSDCATS left on the ruined Limelight stage, along with a thick journal.

'That's *my* property,' Henry snarls, standing abruptly. There's an undercurrent of violence to his stance that makes me glad that we have protection and safety from the security guards Lacey has planted around the theatre, just in case anything goes wrong.

'Actually, they're both your property,' Anushka says casually. 'The handwriting on the note matches the writing in your diary.'

'We had to do a fairly in-depth search to make sure,' Ben

says. 'But I'll admit, reading your almost Freudian thoughts was pretty funny.'

Henry's hands clench and unclench. Lisa looks up at him, her eyes wide with alarm. 'How – how –?' he splutters, before finally unleashing his question. 'How did you get that?'

Without waiting for a reply, Gibitah and the LSDCATS' only other desi cast member, Kamran Milwala, walk out from the left wing. They wear matching expressions of contempt, but I can see the fear under their layers of armour.

They're taking an enormous leap, revealing themselves like this. Gibitah's trust in us was so solid – she didn't waver as she stole Henry's journal – and Kamran's unexpected allegiance was secured when he met with The Tragedies and asked to be involved. They are so strong, and the sight of them makes me emotional. I want to be down there with them, but I know that I need to let them – all of them – make these moves on their own.

'This is criminal!' Lisa grasps at straws, standing beside Henry now.

'So is breaking and entering. Along with destruction of private property,' David counters calmly.

Lisa and Henry fall silent. A nervous energy buzzes through the theatre. Beside me, Zayan shifts, leaning closer to the edge. We know what's coming next, and as if we're watching our favourite play, we can't help but be captivated by the performance.

'But we won't press charges,' Ben offers, and my stomach

somersaults. The people in the seats below us move imperceptibly, tension twining around person after person as they watch this story unfold.

'What's the catch?' Lisa asks, her tone suspicious.

'We want you to listen to the pain you've inflicted,' Nur says, her voice growing louder. 'I want you to look me in the eyes when I tell you that you rejected me because of my hijab.'

Henry snorts, unimpressed. 'You want to tell me how I ruined your life? Is that it? Fine. Go ahead.'

The smile that curves Anushka's lips is sharp. 'As you wish.'

The first story comes from the back row. A woman stands, her skin matching Anushka's, her smile as blood-red as roses, as sharp as thorns. Henry and Lisa whip round in their seats, horror painted across their expressions as they realize that their open auditions are actually an ambush.

'My name is Nadia, and I was seventeen years old when I auditioned for a role at the LSDCATS. I was rejected for being dark-skinned and bold enough to try for a white role.'

'Wait – wait – you're all here to audition, not . . .' Lisa stumbles.

Nadia's announcement is a trigger, a signal, a sign – the initial tremor of an earthquake. It shakes the LSDCATS' theatre, fills the air with a rumble of fury and dissent.

One by one, a person stands and shares their story.

'My name is Dennis Walters,' a man from the fourth row

says, interrupting Lisa's spluttering. 'And I was twenty years old when the LSDCATS used me as an example of someone who couldn't play the role of a white man.'

'My name is Abigail Huang, and I was nineteen years old when the LSDCATS told me that my accent was too hard to decipher, and that I'd have to Westernize to survive in this industry or move on to something else.'

'My name is Anushka Menon,' Anushka says, her voice trembling. My heart balloons in my chest at the sight of her speaking up for herself. 'And you thought my skin tone made me unqualified to be a director. You made me believe that the colour of my skin had some influence on my ability. You tried to break me, but you didn't succeed.'

Untold stories, whispered cautionary tales, paint themselves in front of us. My heart thuds sharply, but my body is filled with sheer pride. Watching The Tragedies start this has emboldened me. Strengthened me. It's made me feel powerful.

Henry is wearing a bored mask over his face as he listens. Lisa's gone pale beside him, her hands anxiously fluttering by her side.

'Fine, fine. I've heard your pieces,' Henry says when the last person finishes, his expression full of displeasure. 'And now I would like you to leave my theatre, *quietly* –'

'We're not done.'

As I stand, my declaration echoing around the silent theatre, Zayan remains seated. But I feel his gaze on me. I feel The Tragedies watching me take the baton from them. Surrounded by their bravery, I feel my own begin to grow.

'My name is Farah Sheikh, and you called me unsuitable for your stage. And you were right. I would never fit in here.' My eyes are locked on Henry, on the sheer anger in his gaze. 'You didn't allow me to. You didn't allow any of us to. You believe that theatre doesn't have space for people of colour, but it's people of colour who have revolutionized this industry, brought to it a thousand new stories and ideas. Theatre doesn't belong to you. It's a stage for everyone.'

Henry looks like he's been slapped across the face, and I soak in the satisfaction of saying what I've been wanting to say for the last two months. I draw on the strength of The Tragedies, of every person in here.

'And you have spent far too long trying to silence us,' I say, my throat working with sudden emotion. 'I always believed that we needed one story to spark a flame. One person to bear the brunt of everything. But I was wrong. This is just the beginning. Together our stories will make change. Our collective voices will start the necessary conversation that you have spent too long avoiding. It is time for you to face your audience.'

'Oh, please!' Henry crows, genuine amusement replacing his disbelief. Next to him, Lisa places a hand on his arm and hisses something at him. Henry's expression darkens. He tries to shake off her hand, but she clutches on anyway.

'Henry, please,' Lisa says, louder, more insistent. 'Don't say anything. You're just going to incriminate yourself.'

I scoff loudly, their attention snapping to me again, but my eyes are on Lisa. 'So, you're aware that his rhetoric is wrong?' I ask her. 'You're OK with that?' Lisa's expression is stony, her mouth turned into a flat line. I remember how she tried to stop Henry during my audition, and I wonder how much she censors him. How she dulls his words so they're still awful, but more subtly so.

'We hosted these new auditions to give you all a fair chance,' Lisa replies finally. 'We have open hearts –'

'Liar,' Anushka snaps, fury making her eyes bright. 'You're trying to make the claims that you're a bunch of racists disappear. It's performative and fake.'

Henry's expression is one of pure anger. He's reaching his breaking point, and Lisa sees that – she tries to placate him once more, but this time there's no use. 'You – you – you have no *right* to be standing on our stage spitting in our faces as we try to do a good thing. I didn't even *want* to host these auditions. I told Lisa this was a bad idea–'

'Henry –' Lisa begins, but he's on a roll now.

'And the truth is I want my play to be authentic. I want it to represent what Shakespeare was. I want it to be classically British –'

'White,' I interrupt him. His eyes meet mine, and a part of me still curls away in fear, but a larger, louder part of me stands strong. 'Don't pretend. Say what you mean.'

The challenge in my voice makes his lips curdle into a sneer. 'Fine! You're right. I wanted an all-white cast. Because they represent true Shakespeare, true *theatre*. And you people *don't*.'

A collective gasp fills the theatre, followed by silence. The Tragedies look stunned on the stage, Gibitah's face grim, Zayan's made of granite and tension. But me? I feel vindicated. I'm not shocked that Henry finally said it, and there's a kind of relief at being proven right. At knowing that the whisper in my head, so quiet compared to the loud echo of my imposter syndrome, was right.

Henry's critique was racist. It was racist during my audition. It's racist now. And it is *not* a reflection on my acting. Or anyone else's. He said things like 'classically British' and 'authentic' because it allowed him to get away with being racist in an unsubtle, insidious way. In the kind of way that allows everyone to look away. But no more.

'You do realize that to be historically accurate to Shakespeare, you would have all the female roles played by men, right?' Anushka breaks the silence first, her voice bordering on a laugh. 'Your desire to "represent true Shakespeare" is just an excuse to be racist.'

'No, it's not,' Henry replies stubbornly, his face flushing an angry red.

Anushka looks ready to sling another point his way – probably something about how people of colour existed in Britain during Shakespeare's time, and that Henry can't just erase that fact from history – but I shake my head at her, stopping her short.

I've realized it's not worth arguing with him. He will not change his mind, and it's not our job to teach him.

'I know you believe that the world will agree with you,' I begin, more softly now, as Lisa flutters around to shush Henry, the people in the theatre watch with anticipation and my friends look on with excitement. 'And I'm all for testing that out. Let's see, Henry Findon: whose side will the world be on – yours or ours?'

Zayan stands, and with that signal the people who've been filling the audience seats clamour towards Henry and Lisa. Some of them are genuinely actors and actresses slighted by the LSDCATS, here to share their story, but the rest are reporters, social media influencers and everyone and anyone with a platform and a voice.

They'd been promised a story that would shake the world. A story that was the truth and nothing less. We just needed Henry to show his true colours, to show the LSDCATS' values in the plainest way possible.

The sound of cameras clicking fills the air, along with flashes of light, jeers and questions. The crowd engulfs Henry and Lisa, probing them to say more, having witnessed everything that happened in the last ten minutes. Zayan wears a look of satisfaction on his face, and The Tragedies stand on the LSDCATS' stage wearing expressions of shock, because they *actually did it*.

Henry has turned as white as a ghost; Lisa looks close to fainting. Their terror brings me no real joy, but I am suffused with the feeling of unadulterated justice being served.

♥

@TheTragedies: We would like to confirm that our play, *Heer Ranjha*, will still be going ahead. Doors open at 7.00 p.m. sharp. We hope to see you all there!

Chapter Thirty-five

Backstage is a whirlwind of chaos – cast members shove past one another, tech people are whisper-shouting instructions, Nur is doing last-minute costume adjustments, Anushka and David are preparing the opening scene, Ben is somewhere helping with the sets and Zayan is in his dressing room, getting ready. I peek through the stage curtain and see that the Limelight is full.

Earlier this evening, the LSDCATS were trending on Twitter, for having an empty house and for their "I didn't know I was racist" sobbing apology video, which went viral on TikTok. They were being decimated online, and it felt like a victory. But now panic wraps itself round my lungs as I spot the industry officials Lacey promised in the front row, and my mind explodes with doubts.

I can't do this. I thought I could do this, but I can't. The opening scene features Heer entirely alone. Zayan won't be out there; he won't be by my side. Everyone is here to see us, but when the show starts, it will just be *me*. Who am I on stage without Zayan?

'Miss Sheikh?' A voice interrupts my lurking, and I whip round to see a young girl with a green hijab standing in front of me. She isn't from the cast or crew; she's too young – maybe sixteen.

'How did you get back here?' I ask, steel lining my tone. This could be a Zaiba fan hoping to ruin everything. 'I'm going to have to call security.'

The girl doesn't blanch, and that's when I notice the camera hanging round her neck.

'My name is Jamilah,' she says, sticking out her hand for me to shake. 'Jamilah Mansoor.'

'I'm sorry,' I say, kindly but cautiously. 'I'm not sure who –'

'I'm an aspiring journalist,' she says. 'I write for my school newspaper. I bought tickets today just to see you.'

'Me?' I ask. 'Not – not Zayan? Because if so, I can take you to him.'

Jamilah ignores the offer. 'I wanted to thank *you*.'

'What for?'

'For being the lead in this play,' Jamilah replies, tone soft and reverent. 'For not being the secondary character. For holding your own narrative. You've already done so much for young Pakistani girls like me, and I think you're going to change the face of this industry.'

My throat aches with emotion, tears prick behind my

eyelids and I just know that if I cry, Nur will kill me for ruining my make-up. Jamilah takes a pencil from behind her ear and a notepad from her bag, looking at me eagerly.

'Before I go back to my seat, I was hoping I could get a quick quote . . .?' she asks hopefully.

I motion for her to continue.

'When people leave here tonight, what would you like them to be thinking?'

Immediately I want to tell Jamilah that I hope people leave with a sense of joy in their hearts, and heartbreak from the ending of the play. I want them to leave the Limelight thinking about what they've just watched, replaying their favourite moments in their minds and remembering our names. But that's the surface-level answer.

'I hope . . .' I begin, scouring deep in my heart for the truth. 'I hope people leave with an understanding of how multilayered this story is. It's a play of forbidden love, of heartbreak, but also of identity. It's about two people struggling to work out who they are, both alone and when with one another.'

'And,' Jamilah continues, 'why do you think a play like this is needed?'

My lungs expand with the deep breath I take, fear crawling through my bloodstream, but I bite my tongue to temper it. I've spent too long ignoring this – weighed down by guilt, by terror, by worry – but I know the answer now. And I want to give an answer I believe, not some line I've been fed or some watered-down version of what I mean.

'Because this play celebrates the colour of your skin, the roll of your accent, the country you come from, the religion you follow, the friends you have, the people you choose to love. It's a play that will – hopefully – open doors for others.'

Jamilah's pencil moves rapidly. I'm excited to see that printed online tomorrow. And scared – my truth will be laid bare for everyone to see. And not everyone will like it. But I can't worry about that. Not any more.

I refuse to measure myself by anyone else's standards. I think of Jamilah's hopeful eyes, her soft words, her pride in me. I may not represent every Pakistani – and I physically cannot – but there's a group out there that looks like me, speaks like me, has stories like my own.

I'll go out on stage for them.

For me.

And that will be enough.

Chapter
Thirty-six

We have a celebratory party at the end of our first show. Anushka and David have rented out the pub opposite the Limelight, and soon it's filled with cast and crew members, friends, people from the audience and anyone else who wants to come and revel in our success.

'You were stunning,' Anushka shouts over the music. 'Amazing. Fantastic. That final monologue? You killed it. Killed it!'

David is behind her, his face bright red with excitement. 'Stunning. Brilliant. A star!'

'And now we just have to do it again,' Nur says, with a mock cheer.

'You think you can make the audience cry with that final monologue to Zayan again?' Ben asks.

I grin. 'I can try.'

'Where *is* he, by the way?' Anushka asks, changing the topic.

'Getting ready,' I reply, while taking a sip of my coke.

'I swear, you'd think he was coming to a fashion show and not an afterparty.'

I snort at her tone – no matter how derisive it may be, I know Anushka likes Zayan.

'Farah!'

The Tragedies and I turn in unison to the sound of Lacey calling out for me. I excuse myself and meet her halfway, allowing her to grip my arm and lead me to a lone table on the other side of the pub.

'I've been looking all over for you,' Lacey says, and I have to bend closer to hear her properly. Her cheeks are flushed red with excitement, and there's a hungry look in her eyes. 'I have so much to tell you. Everyone's buzzing about you and Zayan. And, look, I've seen how you two look at one another. This has to be real. And even if it isn't, it *is* a goldmine. We've got to keep it going. You two could do movies as a couple; you could follow Zayan's lead in this industry. I want to offer you representation.'

My heart soars, shock forcing my jaw to drop slightly. Lacey chuckles lightly, taking a long sip of her drink, waiting for my reply. The words *Yes, let me sign the contract right now* are on the tip of my tongue, but surprisingly I find a sense of hesitancy holding me back.

'Could . . . I need a minute to breathe,' I tell Lacey, and her excitement dims by a fraction.

'Yes, of course. Of course. I'm sure this is all so overwhelming for you,' she says finally, giving me a warm smile. I return it, unable to shake the tentativeness that's growing through my body.

I leave Lacey, making my way out of the pub, soaking in the cool night air. I'm decked in the kameez and jeans I had on before the play started; my make-up is still Heer's, but I've wiped off the tear-tracks I had sliding down from the final scene. The sky is empty, starless for once, with only greyish-blue clouds slicing through.

Rather than standing and analysing my thoughts about the offer, I allow myself to sink into a small temptation. I slide out my phone to read what people have been saying about the play.

@CriticCentral: Just finished watching *Heer Ranjha* by **@TheTragedies**. It was total trash.

Not pulling their punches, I see.

@Mack86: *Heer Ranjha* was so amazing! Cried my eyes out.

@BismaQasim: Farah Sheikh delivers a stunning performance as Heer, stealing our hearts with every line and proving to every Pakistani girl out there that we can be the leads of our own destinies. And that final scene! I was mesmerized.

I close my phone and think of that final scene. The memory of it erupting in my mind through fragmented feelings. The swish of my midnight-blue lehenga against my ankles, the warmth of the spotlight skittering across my skin, the emotion vibrating through the silence of the theatre. My favourite moments on stage tonight were when I was entirely encased in Heer – when it was just me and her intertwined as one.

Voices cut through my memory, pulling me back to this reality.

'She was great.' I turn to see Bashir Junaid, a renowned theatre critic, leaning against the brick wall of the pub, talking to a companion whose face is shadowed by darkness.

Shock pulses through my arteries. I thought most of the industry officials had left after the play – Zayan told me they'd probably reach out through Lacey if they had anything they wanted to say.

Neither of the two men know I'm standing there. Maybe they can't recognize me now that I'm shrouded by the night.

'I loved her as Heer. She's got talent,' Bashir Junaid says.

My heart swells up to three times its size.

'I was a bit surprised,' his companion says.

'Surprised?'

'Well, I guess I'd always thought of her as "Zayan Amin's latest love". But she stole the show. He felt like an afterthought, truly.'

The two men talk for a few more moments about something before leaving. I stay outside, facing the Limelight Theatre. I feel this odd sense of disappointment and delight: joy because my performance was recognized by a renowned critic; disappointment about the critique of

Zayan's performance, and because before this play debuted I was nothing more than the girl on Zayan Amin's arm.

And I suppose the question that keeps pulsing in my head is: can I have both – my own fame and my love?

'Farah?'

Zayan's presence is hard to ignore, and I'm forced to turn round. I'm not ready for the smile curling at the corners of his lips, the fond look in his eyes or his outfit. The light-sage-coloured sherwani, embroidered in gold, fits him like a glove. I notice, at the end of my slow perusal of how good he looks, that he's holding a medium-sized rectangular box in his hands.

'You like?' he asks, and I step closer to him.

'I do. You look very Pakistani,' I say, avoiding his eyes. My head is still wrestling with that question. *Can I have both – my own fame and my love?*

'I'm relearning how to be proud of who I am. I've decided that I no longer want to be Hollywood's version of Pakistani; I want to be my own version. No more muting myself for someone else,' he says softly, ducking his head so our gazes clash. 'I have to tell you something.'

'Famous last words.'

He smiles, but I see hints of worry round the corners of his mouth.

'Zayan?'

'I got the call this morning, and they're starting filming in Australia straight away.'

'Oh my gosh, that's amazing –'

'I'm not taking the part.'

I step away from him, staring like he's grown an extra head. 'What? Why?'

'Because –' Zayan's tone is soft, his eyes wide – 'this just became real. We just became real. And I want to do this right. I want to meet your parents; I want us to be forever. You mean more to me than this role, Farah.'

I say nothing. I feel like I've been robbed of words. No one, *no one*, has ever loved me like this. So uncontestably. So wholly. The idea that Zayan would sacrifice one of his dreams for me, for us, makes my heart ache with an affection I didn't know I could feel until now.

'Here,' Zayan continues when my silence persists. 'I got you something.'

I reluctantly look away from his face to see the box in his hands. He passes it to me, and when I open it I'm faced with a crinkle of white paper. I pull it away to see a beautiful pale-butter-yellow dupatta, neatly folded. My teeth sink into my lower lip as I take it out of the box and fully open it, entranced by the slight shimmer to the fabric.

'Zayan,' I whisper, overcome with memories of how this all began.

'I realized that I never got you a new one,' Zayan says, his voice both teasing and nervous. He takes the dupatta from my hands and gently drapes it over my shoulders – just like how I was wearing it all those weeks ago. 'I want you to know, Farah, I'm all in for this. For our relationship. I know we said we loved one another, but I want to make it clear: I want to be with you forever.'

The question whispers in my mind once more. *Can I*

have both – my own fame and my love? But this time I have an answer.

'You need to take the role, Zayan,' I say, and when he looks like he's about to protest, I place the box on the ground beside us and step closer to him once more – not touching him, because he needs to *hear* me. 'Before you came out here, I overheard these two critics talking about me. One of them was amazed by my ability on the stage, and the other was amazed by my ability because they'd only ever thought of me as your "latest love".'

'Well, whoever it was is an –' Zayan begins, but I cut him off with a look.

'Don't make me use the dupatta to shut you up,' I warn, and the tips of his ears turn a pink that's starting to become my favourite shade. 'It got me thinking,' I continue lightly, 'about whether I could have both things. Whether I could be an actress in my own right and have you in my life.'

I feel his intake of breath, sharp and worried. I can see him gearing up for rejection, the walls rebuilding round his heart one brick at a time. 'And?'

'And,' I say slowly, 'I realized that I love you, Zayan Amin. I love you, and I love being on stage, and I refuse to believe that those two things can't coexist. It'll be harder, I know, to make a name for myself when attached to another celebrity. Laiba laid out the arguments. But you and I, we aren't you and Laiba. We're forever. And if what you're saying is true, then I want to do it right as well. I want to meet your parents. I want to visit Pakistan with you. I want forever – not a fake could-be-something. Forever.'

Zayan's throat bobs with emotion, his eyes reflecting the glow of the moon hanging in the sky. His hands find my waist, pulling me in closer.

'That's why you need to take the job, Zayan,' I say, and this time my tone is heavy with emotion. 'Even though spending six months away from you will be awful, it's also going to be our new reality. If we're in it for the long haul, who's to say I won't land a job in another country, with a crazy schedule that keeps me away for a few months? We'll have to learn to love through that. I will not let you give up on your career. I will not give up on mine. We can have our dreams.'

'My dreams include loving you for eternity,' Zayan says, his forehead pressing against mine. 'I want to see your name right beside mine. I want it to glow in glittering lights. I want to watch your movies, your plays, your shows. I want you to come to mine. I want to cross every single line with you, when we're ready.' His expression turns fierce, like a candle bursting into flame. 'We're going to have it all, Farah. Promise me: you're going to live your dreams, I'm going to live mine and we're going to keep coming back to each other.'

Under the moon, with our theatre in front of us, Zayan Amin and I make another vow to one another. Another contract. Another promise.

But this time, it's forever.

Epilogue

TWELVE MONTHS LATER

There are moments in your life that you will remember forever. Memories so special, so traumatic, so violent, so wonderful, so beautiful that they're stitched into your consciousness for eternity.

This is one of those moments. This will be one of those memories.

Me, Farah Sheikh, being interviewed by The Actors' Guild.

The Actors' Guild.

Just saying that title makes a flurry of nerves erupt from my heart to the tips of my fingers. I give myself a final once-over in the mirror, studying the hours of work my team have put in to get me to this point, smoothing out imaginary crinkles from my butter-yellow shalwar kameez. I lightly trace the embroidery on the dupatta, feeling both anchored by it and reminded of everything about the boy who gifted it to me.

I force myself to step away from the mirror, and the

memories. I walk to the door instead, standing a few steps away in preparation. The Actors' Guild wanted to host the interview in my flat, the new one I'm renting out – it's closer to the theatre where my latest play is showing. Leaving my old flat was hard but necessary. It was like starting afresh, standing on my own two feet for once. And it's not like I lost any of my friends. Maha and Amal come over all the time, and The Tragedies spend ninety per cent of the day blowing up my phone.

Anushka
Farah!! Send us pictures!!
I want to see what you're
wearing for the interview.

David
Yes, Farah, please give
Anushka another excuse to
procrastinate.

Anushka
Don't get me started on the
unfair treatment of second-
year students, David. They're
overworking us and stressing
us out with exams.

David
Maybe if you slept less in class, you'd be less afraid of exams.

Anushka
Maybe stop staring at me in class while I sleep, weirdo??

Ben
Yeah, David. That's very Edward Cullen of you.

Nur
New theory: David's a vampire.

Anushka
So, he really is an old man in a young guy's body.

David
I hate every single one of you.

Hey, I didn't even say anything.

Nur
Farah!! You're here!! Are you excited?

Beyond excited. But also scared? What if I say something stupid?

Anushka
You won't say anything stupid. Relax. Haven't you gone through a million hours of media training by now?

I sigh, knowing she's right. I have gone through all that's needed. It doesn't lessen my stress, though.

David
What's Zayan saying? He could probably help.

The early screening of Zayan's new movie happened last week, and, as expected, movie critics and reviewers loved it. Originally, his plan had been to be in Australia for six months, and then come back to London for the rest of the year while the movie was in post-production. After that, he'd leave again to promote the movie, but for six months we'd be back in the same time zone.

But he ended up having to spend the *whole* year in Australia due to scheduling conflicts and reshoots, and because it was easier to have the star of the movie available at all times. Then, of course, the promotional tour took priority and I'd mentally prepared myself for another month without seeing Zayan. Another month of FaceTime calls at random hours.

> **Nur**
> Yeah, doesn't he have some advice?

The last twelve months have been strange. We agreed not to say anything to the public. We wanted to survive these six-months-turned-twelve-months first, and then we'd come together again. It meant getting used to long-distance Zoom calls and lots of tabloids romantically pinning us with different people just to get a story.

'My advice would be to be as honest as you can,' Zayan says, and I look over my shoulder at him. He's leaning in the kitchen doorway, his eyes jet-lagged and sleepy.

'You can go back to sleep, you know,' I say, my gaze tracing his mussed hair. Turns out Zayan Amin just wears a regular old shirt and bottoms to bed. I'll need to buy him that monogrammed set.

He yawns but shakes his head persistently. 'I've got a call with Lacey in an hour anyway. We need to discuss the play.' His eyes turn worried once more. 'You sure you're OK with this, right?'

When Zayan had come back from Australia last night, I'd been overjoyed and confused. I wasn't expecting him until after the promotional tour. But then, he'd showed up outside my door, saying he'd got permission to come to London early to support me with The Actors' Guild, and I couldn't have loved him more for it.

But he also came back with secrets.

'Are you still happy about your decision?' I counter, brow raised. 'You're going to go from big blockbusters to small theatre shows? It'll be less recognition, quieter fame . . . Are you sure you're OK with that?'

His expression turns serious, like he's mulling everything over for the millionth time. But then his eyes clear, and this contentment makes his entire body soften. A smile curls at his lips.

'I'm more than OK with it,' Zayan replies. 'Before, my whole life was my career. My entire childhood has been "lights, camera, action", but I'm tired of that. I want to rediscover what home means to me. I want to think about you, and us, and my friendships. I want to be waiting for you to come home from work to hear about your day *in person* and not behind a computer screen. And I want to visit Pakistan and rediscover the culture I feel like I've lost.'

A zip of energy runs down my spine at his words. I would never ask him to give up any part of his life for me. Twelve months ago, when he was talking about giving up the movie role after *Heer Ranjha*, that felt like a sacrifice. But now Zayan's gone and lived the dream he used to have, and he's returned with something new in mind. This isn't a sacrifice. This is Zayan at his fullest. Striving for what he wants. Seeking it out.

'If this brings you happiness, then there's nothing more I want for you,' I say softly, and a look of relief passes over his face.

A thought sparks in my mind, and then my own lips curve into a grin. 'And it's a good thing that we both have the next month free, right? That trip to Pakistan is going to be great. I can't wait for you to meet my parents.'

It's wrong. I know it's wrong. But watching Zayan's expression flash from his usual confidence to endearing nervousness makes my heart ache with affection. We planned the trip to Pakistan last night, after he told me all about his shifting dreams. Then, when he'd fallen asleep on the couch and I was moving his bags into the hallway, I found the second secret he was keeping from me. The one he has yet to confess.

A small square-shaped black box. I didn't open it. I didn't need to open it. I knew what it was – it was more than a piece of jewellery or a ceremony in the future; it was reassurance for when things got too intense, a vow to keep coming back to one another, the promise of forever. It was part of the reason why he wanted to go back to see our families so badly.

Zayan's eyes narrow on me, and I know he wants to ask if I know what he's planning, but the risk is too big.

He's saved from having to make a choice by a knock on the door.

'It's happening.' My stomach drops straight to my feet. Zayan pushes himself off the door frame and towards me. 'This – this is happening. This is really happening. I'm going to be interviewed by The Actors' Guild.'

Zayan's hand finds mine, our fingers intertwining like puzzle pieces that have finally been matched. 'And you're going to be stunning, Farah Sheikh. You're a star.'

I meet his eyes, soaking up his unwavering confidence. He's my anchor when every other emotion feels like it's going to drown me.

'Thank you,' I say, because I mean it, and because I want him to know how much he means to me.

He smiles, and even though it feels much harder than it should, I eventually have to let go of Zayan's hand – knowing he'll be here when it's all over.

I hear him move upstairs as I turn to face the door. Another knock, and my hand clasps the doorknob. My fear is still there, as I know it always will be, but there's also excitement and joy to overshadow it.

Behind this door is another dream of mine waiting to be lived, and there is *nothing* holding me back.

THE ACTORS' GUILD INTERVIEW: FARAH SHEIKH

We're sitting on a balcony overlooking the bustling London streets, an assortment of pastries piled up on the table between us. It was raining earlier today, but now, in perfect British fashion, the weather has decided to turn up the brightness. Large magnolia and cherry-blossom trees are hanging close to the railing, giving Farah Sheikh an unintentional backdrop of spring and new beginnings.

A year has passed since her debut in *Heer Ranjha* – a year that has been filled with her rise to fame. When I voice this, that she's famous now, Farah has an air of humility about her, smiling abashedly as if she can't believe she's reached this position in her life.

Sitting here today, giving this interview, is just one example of how her life has changed.

You seem a little tense. Let's start off easy, shall we? I'll throw you a softball with this first question: how did you find your agent, Sofiya Hadi?

Is it that obvious that I'm a little nervous? I've been telling myself not to be, but I'm glad you're going easy. I didn't really find my agent; she found me. I was doing a community theatre production of *Antony and Cleopatra*, about a month after *Heer Ranjha*, and Sofiya Hadi was in the audience. She showed up outside my tiny dressing room asking for a meeting, simply because she said she saw some magic and wanted to refine it. I knew I had to take that leap.

That's inspiring, but I'll admit, we all thought you'd sign with Lacey Parker. Was that ever an option?

So you give me one soft question and then go straight in for the kill?

Sorry about that.

No, no, don't apologize. To answer your question, it was an option. Lacey did approach me, but I wanted an agent that was passionate solely about me. Lacey has an incredible amount of talent, but her attention belongs to her bigger stars. Sofiya and I were on an even field, both of us trying to make it big.

A camaraderie formed between you two, then.

Yeah, kind of. More like an understanding of how far we'd need to go to make our dreams come true. I think that's important in a relationship – communicating your goals. It lets the other person know where you stand.

Tell me, Farah, since you mentioned *Heer Ranjha*, are you still friends with the cast?

Oh, I don't think I could get rid of The Tragedies if I tried; they're blowing up my phone right now, actually. Anushka's telling us about her latest class, and they're teasing me for dropping out of my second year of university. It's an ongoing thing.

Did you drop out?

No, I'm taking a gap year. I realized I couldn't give both things – acting and studying – equal time and effort. I'm privileged to have supportive parents, who are always rooting for me. And amazing friends. The Tragedies plan to come to every show I'm in. Front row. And I will to go to theirs. In fact, for any of you reading this, Anushka Menon is directing a new production this winter – it's Shakespeare's *Othello*. Tickets go on sale soon!

Speaking of new shows, let's talk about your new projects. I've heard you're up for a movie role – an adaptation of *Heer Ranjha*.

Rumours, rumours. I'm not sure how much I can share. I have heard of the project. I have been contacted. Where that all goes, who knows?

You're playing coy.

I'm pretty sure it's your job to get these answers out of me.

All right, the gloves are coming off now, Sheikh. Ready for the hard stuff?

Hit me.

You've spoken up about the racism you've faced in this industry. How has it affected your journey as an aspiring actress?

Yeah, let's talk about it. I've been denied auditions because of the colour of my skin, because of my ethnicity, and it's unfair. It's rooted in years of prejudice and hatred. At the same time, I've been privileged because of my skin tone. From the way your eyebrows just quirked, I'm guessing you don't understand how that's possible. I have a lighter skin tone, which, in this industry, makes me more acceptable to some. It's messed up. It gives racists the perfect excuse to hire me when they want to tick the diversity quota for their productions.

How do you counter that?

It can be emotionally draining to know that casting decisions are tokenistic. But moving up this ladder means you're allowed to make change for those that come after you. I now look at casts, crew members and staff when I join a new production, and I see what percentage is made up of people of colour. I demand the equality we all deserve. My contracts stipulate the same wages as my co-stars. I've participated in a couple of mentorship programmes for other actors and actresses. Sometimes people just need a helping hand. I was lucky to get one a month after *Heer Ranjha*. But most of all, for all the success I gain, I must hold myself accountable. Give back. Help those around me. It means being self-aware.

Oh, and talking. Conversations. Speaking up about the privilege I have, and the racism I face, spreads awareness. But even that isn't easy – it's not always an option for a person of colour. This issue in the industry won't simply disappear, but I hope, with time, that the conversations broaden – to include everyone.

You said you had a helping hand with launching your career. Is it safe to say that it was Zayan Amin?

[Smiling] I knew he was going to come up today.

We don't have to talk about him; this interview is ultimately about you. If I wanted to interview Zayan Amin, I'd have reached out to his agent. I'm here for you today.

I think you just became my favourite interviewer. But no, I want to talk about Zayan. He changed my life, left a mark on my career that I can't ignore. He came into my life just when I was starting out, and he provided me with the opportunity to be a part of this industry.

His new movie just came out. After your play together, there were rumours that you two had broken up. But neither of you commented on it officially.

[Laughing] I saw his new movie! He was so good. Everyone should go watch him. Right now. Buy your tickets this second. I'll also give you a little more than I give other interviewers, just because I like you so much.

You're making my day.

He's my best friend. When we went our separate ways after *Heer Ranjha*, it was hard. It's difficult going from seeing someone every single day, talking to them all the time, to adjusting to new time zones. I know the online world loves to obsessively speculate about whether we're really together or not.

The media _is_ a little obsessed with the two of you.

[Laughing again, eyes darting to the space behind me] I take it as a compliment. We're good together. Dynamite on stage, if I'm allowed to be a little arrogant.

I'd say it's allowed. I came to your production of *Heer Ranjha*. There were literal sparks flying.

[Laughing again] I'm sorry to interrupt, but he won't stop goofing around behind you.

[To provide a little context, I turn around to find **Zayan Amin** standing behind the balcony doors, making silly faces at Farah. He's dressed comfortably – sweatpants, loose long-sleeved T-shirt, hair mussed – as if he's perfectly at home. He wasn't here when I walked into Farah's flat, but then again, I never got a house tour.]

Is it all right if we don't invite him in?
[Looking surprised at my suggestion] Why not?

Well, I meant it. This is an interview for you. I only have one question for you both, regardless of whether he's here or not.
Which is?

Are you two together – officially this time?
[Farah looks past me, meeting Zayan's gaze through the glass door. Her expression softens, a blush on her cheeks.]
Yeah. We're going to be official. Print that in bold letters, would you?

That answers my question, then. You seem happy.
I am. I'm not always happy. That's OK too. You can't be happy all the time, even if everything you dreamed of is coming true. But right now, at this exact moment, I am happy.

I know we have more to talk about – I want to ask you about this new play you're doing – but I have one quick question before we move on.
I'm on the edge of my seat.

Let me say it with the right dramatic tone. Farah Sheikh, for all those kids out there who want to be a star, how did you get here?

I'll tell you how it all started.

I fell in love at eighteen. With a feeling, a buzz of nerves, a jumble of butterfly wings, the warmth of a blush and a person with brown eyes, a sharp tongue and a smile unlike another.

But at nineteen, I fell in love with myself – wholly, entirely. I put the time in to untangle the confused parts of myself, to decide what it was I wanted my future to look like, and I learned to forgive myself when I couldn't always reach it.

And it's only then, when you've loved a passion, a person and yourself, that you can be a star and share your light.

Acknowledgements

I'm a chronic daydreamer, which means I thought about writing these acknowledgements back when this book was nothing more than a blank document and a title (one that ended up being changed three times). But to actually be sitting here typing this out feels surreal. It is my wildest dream come true, and so for every person who has helped me get here, I could not be more grateful.

To start, I want to thank my agent, Alex Rice, who quite literally changed my life with her offer of representation. Thank you for loving Farah's story as wholly as I did, for having an unwavering faith in my writing, and for always answering my endless double-emails and questions with the utmost thoughtfulness and care – I could not have gotten here without you, and I cannot wait for all the future stories we're going to work on together.

To Charlotte Moore, thank you for making so many of my dreams come true. Your kindness and thoughtfulness have made this experience a delight, and I could not be happier to have gotten the opportunity to work with you. To Awo Ibrahim, thank you for seeing potential in this story, stepping up to guide me to the next stage of my writing journey, and for always advocating for Farah's dramatics – it has been the best experience to work with someone who understands and loves these characters the way I do.

To Jo Stimfield, thank you for being an amazing copy-editor, and for dealing with my excessive use of commas. To Shreeta Shah, thank you for managing the editorial process so wonderfully – you made this part of the journey so smooth. To Katie Sinfield, thank you for your fantastic notes that helped shape TGA into the book it is today – going through your edits were always a delight. To Dr Aisha Phoenix, thank you for your thoughtful and kind authenticity reader notes; your vision for Farah and Gibitah were incredibly appreciated. To Aaliyah Jaleel, thank you so much for the beautiful cover – every element was better than I could ever have dreamed up. To the entire Penguin UK team, I have an endless gratitude for the way you have supported my story; from the cover design to the marketing plans, you've made this journey everything I could have wished for.

To my best friend, Abbey Francis Williams, who has read every single version of this book – each draft with a new title – thank you for being there to love this book when I couldn't, and for continually fighting my imposter syndrome with voice notes, Kirby-memes and endless love. To Ananya Devarajan, thank you for giving me the confidence to publish a book with two unabashedly brown characters, and for being the best ride-or-die friend a girl could have. To Kalie Holford, thank you for being my mentor, and for sharing your editorial eye for my words – your love for Amal is what got me here.

The Girlfriend Act could not exist without the thoughtful feedback of the betas who read it: Kamilah Cole, Brittney Arena, Famke Halma and Camille Simkin, thank you for your time and your love. Thank you to the online writing community, who always made me feel like I had a place where my joy for words and books was seen and reciprocated, and to every single person who has shown support for a snippet, an aesthetic or more.

I would not be a writer without my family. To my mother, who gave me my love for books, writing, theatre and so much more; to my father, for believing in me every step of the way; to my sister, Iman, for being there whenever I got bad or good news, and being my partner-in-crime; to my brother, Ibrahim, for always keeping me humble.

And, finally, to every reader who picks up this book, who relates to Farah, to Zayan, to The Tragedies, and sees themselves on these pages – thank you for loving this story, for supporting me and for giving me a space on your shelf.

About the Author

Safa Ahmed is a British-Pakistani content marketer who lives in London. Ever since she scribbled down her first story – a mystery featuring stolen cookies and an incriminating teddy bear – it's been her dream to be a writer and publish books that celebrate joy, heartbreak, swoony love interests, fierce female characters and everything in between.

When she's not writing, she is usually rereading her favourite fantasy novels, wreaking havoc in the kitchen or expanding her ever-growing TBR pile.

You can find her on X, Instagram and TikTok as: @safaswritings.

HOME IS WHERE THE BOOKS LIVE

Discover your next read
on our TikTok channel @houseofya